In the dark stable, Jamie's white teeth flashed in a smile shadowed by the night and by the brim of his leather hat . . .

"Going out for a ride, are you?" he asked.

He reached out and rested his hands on Bliss's waist. In the next instant, he pulled her close and bent his head to brush her lips with his own.

The sensation was tantalizing, delicious, and completely frightening. Bliss felt her breasts, hidden beneath her coat and dress, meet the hard contours of Jamie's chest. "I—I was going to America," Bliss said lamely, her mouth still touching Jamie's. His laugh was gruff and gentle.

"It really would be simpler if you just let me go," she told him, as the tip of his tongue played at the corners of her mouth and promised other mysterious pleasures. Jamie lifted Bliss slightly and pulled her forward, so that she was pressed against him. She made a soft whimpering sound as he kissed her at last, thoroughly and with all the passion of a husband about to claim his rights. A trembling began in Bliss's thighs and spread to her knees, which would barely support her. Jamie caught her as she sagged toward the floor, whisking her deftly up into his arms.

"It would serve you right if I made love to you right here," he vowed huskily . . .

Books by Linda Lael Miller

Angelfire
Banner O'Brien
Corbin's Fancy
Desire and Destiny
Emma and the Outlaw
Fletcher's Woman
Lauralee
Lily and the Major
Memory's Embrace
Moonfire
My Darling Melissa
Wanton Angel
Willow

Published by POCKET BOOKS

ANGEL-FIRE

LINDA LAEL MILLER

POCKET BOOKS

New York   London   Toronto   Sydney   Tokyo   Singapore

For Sisters-in-love:
Susan Burgess
Donna Mahar
Karen Miller
Karon Lael
and
Maureen "Mo" Hamilton

This book is a work of historical fiction. Names, characters, places
and incidents relating to non-historical figures are either the product
of the author's imagination or are used fictitiously. Any resemblance
of such non-historical incidents, places or figures to actual events or
locales or persons, living or dead, is entirely coincidental.

An *Original* Publication of POCKET BOOKS

POCKET BOOKS, a division of Simon & Schuster Inc.
1230 Avenue of the Americas, New York, NY 10020

ISBN: 0-671-73765-1

First Pocket Books printing June 1989

10 9 8 7 6 5 4 3

POCKET and colophon are registered trademarks of
Simon & Schuster Inc.

Printed in the U.S.A.

Prologue

Near Brisbane, Australia—December 1872

THE BARK OF THE ACACIA TREE FELT ROUGH AGAINST THE INSIDES of Jamie McKenna's wrists and the midday sun burned hot, scalding his bare back. Resting his forehead against the tree trunk to which he was bound, he closed his eyes and fought back the panic that threatened to engulf him. And he waited. That was the worst part, the waiting.

"Jamie?" The feminine voice came from behind him. "I brought you some water."

Jamie opened his eyes, and his jawline hardened. "You shouldn't 'ave come, lass," he said. His voice sounded hoarse, hurting as it emerged from his dry throat.

Peony came to stand boldly beside him, her enormous green eyes filled with sadness. "I have a knife," she whispered. "I'll cut that rope and we'll escape, the two of us together."

In view of what was to come, the idea was not without appeal, but Jamie knew that the master would find them if they tried running away. The punishment for such flagrant rebellion would be that much worse, and it would include Peony. "No," he said.

Tears welling in her eyes, Peony opened a canteen and

lifted it to Jamie's parched lips. She was a beautiful woman, with her emerald eyes and golden hair. At twenty-five, she was eight years older than Jamie, and she belonged to Increase Pipher as surely as his favorite horse and the gold-handled walking cane he carried.

"I can't bear this," she choked out.

The water was sweet in Jamie's mouth and it soothed his throat as he swallowed. "You've got to get out of 'ere before someone sees you," he muttered.

"At least let me set you free," Peony pleaded, clutching at Jamie's arm with one hand. Although she was agitated, her touch was cool, soothing.

"Do you know what Pipher'd do if he caught you?" he countered, in a whisper gruff with fear. "I'll tell you, Peony: he'd do just what he's going to do to me now—tie you to a tree and 'ave you whipped."

Peony squeezed her eyes shut. Her slender alabaster throat worked, but no sound came out of her mouth.

"Go," Jamie said. "Please."

The rumble of male voices rolled on the muggy summer air like thunder preceding a storm. They were coming, the wait was over.

Jamie steeled himself for the ordeal he would face, determined to get through it without giving Pipher the satisfaction of breaking him. "Run, Peony," he rasped, and after a moment's hesitation, she disappeared into the trees that surrounded the small clearing.

Pipher and his men arrived seconds after the woman had gone. Jamie refused to turn his head to look back at the man who had enslaved him; the old man was forced to come and stand at his side.

Pipher smiled, showing his enormous yellow teeth— horse's teeth, Peony called them—and the sun glinted in his snow-white hair and muttonchop whiskers. "Hello, lad," he said, in a voice that could only have been described as cordial.

Jamie glared at his tormenter, knowing that Pipher

wanted him to beg, telling him by his expression and his bearing that he'd die first.

The plantation owner threw back his head and laughed, and Jamie felt a fine mist of saliva settle on his skin.

"God, but you're a stubborn little mick!" the old man marveled.

Increase looked back at his henchmen, who twittered halfheartedly at his subtle cue. Jamie knew some of those men pitied him, but instead of feeling any kinship with them, he hated the lot.

Pipher lifted his cane, with its handle of beautifully molded gold, and tapped Jamie's shoulder with it. "Where's that quick tongue of yours now, Mr. McKenna?" he asked, his foul breath fanning over Jamie's face and causing bile to rise in his throat.

Jamie swallowed and said nothing, and his gaze remained steady, defiant. His message was clear enough, he knew. It said: *Go to hell.* And Pipher understood.

"The whip," the planter grated out, infuriated, extending one hand.

Someone came forward with the coil of black leather, and Pipher made a point of unfurling it with a sharp crack. He was skillful with the lash; even when there was no punishment to be meted out, he often practiced for hours at a time.

The rich man stepped back, out of sight, and again Jamie heard the whip crack. His stomach muscles tensed; he forced himself to let them go slack. The others had told him that it would hurt less that way.

The first lash weakened Jamie's knees; the pain was like fire raging across his sunburned back. He made himself think of his brother, Reeve, and of the old days in Ireland as he listened to the whip being drawn back with a *whoosh* and then heard it slicing through the thick air again.

Sweat beaded on his forehead and upper lip as the strip of leather lacerated his flesh a second time, but he did not cry out. Not one lash or a thousand could make him do that.

He counted ten more biting slashes before the summer air went dark and his legs refused to support him any longer.

The sun was low on the horizon when Jamie regained consciousness. He was still bound to the tree, though he'd slipped to his knees, and Peony was sawing frantically at his bonds with a kitchen knife.

Jamie's back was ablaze with pain, and the tree bark had scraped one side of his face raw. His throat was all but swollen shut and the smell and taste of blood made his stomach churn. "Go—away—" he managed to croak.

Tears were streaming down Peony's cheeks. "Just shut up, Jamie McKenna," she said, still slicing at the thick rope. "We've no time to argue—I don't know if the blaze caught properly or not."

When his bonds gave way, Jamie rolled to the ground, unable to hold himself upright. He was disoriented; the earth felt spongy beneath him and the sky seemed to have fallen in, thick and smothering.

"Left you here to die, he did," Peony prattled to herself. "Boar's bait, that's what he called you. The devil's waiting for that old man in hell's front parlor, I'll tell you that." Jamie heard the knife thump against the ground, felt her efforts to lift him to his feet. "I've got a place to hide you," she said, breathing hard from the struggle, "if you'll—just —get—up!"

Nausea roiled in Jamie's stomach, so ferocious was the pain. At great cost, he turned his head away from Peony and vomited.

She stroked the back of his head until the violent spasms of sickness had ceased, then began pulling at him again and yammering, "Jamie, please—you've got to get up—you've just got to—"

"I—can't—" he rasped, willing himself to die.

As broken as he was, Jamie felt the fury surge through Peony's body just as though the two of them were linked somehow, sharing the same emotions. "I thought you had more courage than that!" she cried. "Maybe that old beg-

4

gar's right about you—maybe you're not worth that odd bit of brass you wear round your neck!"

The challenge gave Jamie the strength to thrust himself to his knees. He touched the beggar's badge, given to him so long ago in Dublin, and thought of Reeve and his poor lost mother. Because he knew they'd ask it of him, he battled the dizziness that swelled around him like a dark mist and then, with Peony's help, rose to his feet.

His friend supported him and, at the same time, led him. He could barely see, but the sound of crackling underbrush met his ears and he caught the scent of burnt sugar on the wind. "Where . . . ?"

"Never you mind where, Jamie McKenna," Peony replied, and there were tears in her voice. "Just never you mind. You and I are going to do what we should have done long ago—we're going to put this place behind us."

Jamie hadn't the stamina to argue that any attempt at escaping would not only be futile but perhaps fatal as well, so he leaned on Peony and allowed her to lead him away through the acacia trees and the specterlike gums.

Just when he was sure that he couldn't take another step, they reached a lean-to of some sort and Jamie sank facedown onto a bed of sweet straw. Peony bustled about, making noise, but he didn't bother to look and see what she was doing. His body and his spirit screamed for sleep.

"This is going to burn like the fires of Hades," Peony announced reluctantly, "but I've got to clean those wounds or you'll surely die of the infection."

A cry of agony exploded in Jamie's throat when she poured what felt like liquid brimstone over his lacerated back, and then, perhaps mercifully, he blacked out.

He dreamed that he was at home in Ireland, where December brought cold winds that dampened the very marrow of a man's bones. He was in the cottage off that Dublin alley, and his mother was there, stoking up the fire that guttered in the grate.

"You're a good lad," she said, over one shoulder. "Aye.

No matter what Father McDougal says, you're a good lad, Jamie me boy."

In the dream, Jamie asked where Reeve was, and that was when his mother turned. Her face was a blank expanse of skin, with no features to be seen.

"You're a good lad, Jamie me boy," she said again. "Aye. No matter what—"

"Reeve!" the young Jamie screamed, terrified. "Reeve!"

"Hush now," scolded a gentle voice from somewhere above, in the waking world. "It's no use calling out for him. There's just you and me now, Jamie. Just you and me."

Chapter 1 🌿

New Zealand—*August 1888*

THE SHINY STEEL TINES OF THE PITCHFORK PLUNGED THROUGH the mixture of hay and straw in which Bliss Stafford had spent the night, missing her face by mere inches. Her eyes widened and a startled scream escaped her before she could stop it. She sat bolt upright in the haystack, spiky bits sticking in her cinnamon-colored hair and clinging to her coat. "Just what do you think you're doing, you bloody fool!"

A tall, solidly built man with light hair and eyes the color of a summer sea was staring at her, obviously confounded. He was wearing a heavy coat of dark navy woolen, along with gloves and a floppy leather hat, and his breath made a plume in the frigid winter air.

"You nearly skewered me!" Bliss protested, struggling to her feet and dusting bits of straw from her shoulders. It is virtually impossible, she reflected to herself, to maintain a dignified manner when one has just slept in a pile of hay.

Hugging herself, she began stomping both feet in an effort to get warm. She hadn't eaten since the morning before, when the last of the food she'd stolen from the refreshment table at Alexander's party had run out, and her stomach rumbled loudly.

7

The farmer grinned, showing pearly-white teeth. "You've got some gall, lass. This happens to be my barn you're trespassing in."

Bliss thought she heard a faint lilt of the Irish in his voice, but she considered this only briefly. There were too many other matters that needed thinking about. Such as extracting herself from this unsettling situation. She thrust out her chin and challenged, "I haven't hurt your stupid barn, now have I?"

This time, the man laughed outright. With a shake of his handsome head, he flung the pitchfork deftly into the hay. Bliss shuddered, thinking how easily she could have been pinioned to the floor of this isolated stable.

"Name's McKenna," the farmer said, turning to walk away even as he made this announcement. It was plain that he expected Bliss to follow meekly after him. Because she was hungry and cold, she could not have done otherwise, but it was irritating to comply with an order so offhand that it hadn't even been uttered aloud.

"Stafford," Bliss answered in kind, bracing herself for the winter cold as they left the relative shelter of the barn. She hadn't gotten a good look at the farm the night before, having taken shelter at a very late hour, but now she saw that it was a substantial place with a house built of white stone and sheep dotting the deep green of the hillsides. The whisper of the sea and a certain salty scent to the air told her that the water was not far away.

Mr. McKenna's boots made a crisp sound on the board steps leading up to the porch of his house. Bliss decided that with a place this size, there must surely be a Mrs. McKenna and a covey of children. The thought filled her with a vague sense of regret.

Reaching the front door, which was made of some heavy, unplaned wood, McKenna opened it and stepped back, for all the world like a gentleman might do, to let her pass ahead of him.

With a queenly lift of her chin, Bliss proceeded into the

house. The scent of meat and eggs being fried teased her nostrils and her stomach grumbled again, spoiling her attempt at nonchalance.

"Is that all the name you have, then?" Mr. McKenna asked, hanging his hat on one of several pegs beside the door. "Just Stafford?" His pale blue eyes twinkled as he shrugged out of his coat.

"Bliss," she admitted, though grudgingly. Since her flight from Alexander's party several days before, she'd been secretive about her name. Not that any great number of people had asked.

He chuckled and shook his head, in the throes of some private wonder, and then ran one hand through his hair. "Come along then, Bliss Stafford, and we'll see about quieting that stomach of yours."

She followed him, still wearing her shabby plaid coat, peering into this room and that as they passed down a wide hallway toward the back of the house. The place had a certain spartan prosperity about it; there would be few luxuries here, but nothing needful would be lacking, either.

The kitchen was spacious and filled with wintry light, and the glare dazzled Bliss so that she had to blink several times in order to see again. A lovely Maori woman was standing at the stove, cooking, and again Bliss felt a peculiar stirring of sadness.

"Found her in the barn," Mr. McKenna said, and that was his only comment. He went to the washstand in a far corner of the huge kitchen and poured water from a crockery pitcher into a basin.

Bliss felt a blush moving beneath her freckles. She smiled lamely at the cook, who responded with a pleasant look but said nothing, and Mr. McKenna made a tremendous splashing as he washed.

Feeling very self-conscious, Bliss intertwined her fingers in front of her and rocked once or twice on the worn heels of her high-button shoes. "I suppose you're wondering what I was doing sleeping in your barn," she piped, though Mr.

McKenna had not actually inquired about that peculiar occurrence. "Well, I'll be happy to tell you."

The handsome farmer rolled up the sleeves of his blue cambric workshirt and grinned. "That's good of you," he remarked as the cook added another place to the table, which had been set for one, then discreetly left the kitchen. "Won't you sit down?"

Bliss was stung by the mocking formality of the question, as well as by the courtly bow her host executed. With a sniff, she settled herself at the table, still wearing her coat. The smell of the fried meat and eggs made her light-headed, she was so hungry.

"It just so happens that I'm on my way to America," she announced, scooping food onto her plate with as much dignity as she could manage.

The ice-blue eyes were twinkling again. "An ambitious jaunt, that. What's in the States?" Mr. McKenna took what remained of the eggs and mutton, politely failing to notice that Bliss had left him relatively less to eat than one might have expected.

Bliss swallowed before answering, for even though she had spent the night in a stranger's barn and been forced by circumstances to accept what amounted to charity, her manners had not deserted her. She thought of all the glowing letters she'd received from her mother over the years, and she could hardly wait to get to the place.

"Everything," she said, in a musing, dreamy voice that would surely have brought desultory comment from Alexander—had Alexander been there, that is. She peered across the table at her benefactor, squinting a little because her eyes were tired. "Have you ever been to America?"

"Do you need spectacles?" Mr. McKenna countered, chewing.

Bliss was mildly insulted. "No, I don't," she snapped, "and it was rude of you to change the subject that way!"

He looked amused; it was obvious that he didn't care in

the slightest whether other people perceived him as mannerly or not. "Sorry," he said, with an utter lack of sincerity.

If Bliss hadn't been so ravenous and the food hadn't been so good, she would have gotten up from her chair and walked out of Mr. McKenna's house at that moment. As it was, she refrained from comment and continued to eat.

"I know a Yank," remarked the man across the table from Bliss.

She stopped eating and leaned forward in her chair. She didn't mention her mother, for if she did, she'd surely be asked to explain the whys and wherefores of the woman's departure. "Really?"

A brisk nod was the only reply; Bliss's obvious interest seemed to be lost on McKenna.

She narrowed her eyes. "Well, who is this person?" she demanded.

The farmer gave her a look of feigned surprise, mingled with amusement, and shrugged his powerful shoulders. "My sister-in-law, Maggie."

Bliss scooted forward on her chair. Her mother had told her a great deal about America, but there were still so many questions that sometimes Bliss thought she wouldn't be able to contain them. "Does she live near here? Might I meet her?"

McKenna rolled his remarkable blue eyes, as though Bliss's request had been totally untoward. "No to both questions, love—she lives in Australia."

Bliss allowed the inappropriate endearment her host had used to pass unchallenged. She was very curious about this Maggie woman. "Why did she leave America, do you know?"

"I don't believe I ever asked her," he replied, with a pensive frown that furrowed his forehead. "Things have a way of getting hectic when a bloke's around Maggie McKenna."

An odd sensation of jealousy rippled through Bliss's

spirit, and she sat up a little straighter in her chair, her food forgotten even though her hunger had not been assuaged. "You know my first name," she said stiffly. "In all fairness, I should be given yours."

Another grin creased the sun-browned face. "It's Jamie," he complied, with a near-elegant nod of his head. Then, before Bliss could say anything else at all, he added, "It's a very long way to America, you know. Exactly how were you planning to get there?"

He spoke as though all her plans had been canceled, and Bliss bridled with annoyance. "Why, I was planning to swim, of course," she answered tartly.

Jamie favored her with an unfriendly look that brought a strange warmth to her blood. "Whoever named you Bliss was a fanciful sort," he said. A moment later, he was waving his fork at her accusingly. "You've run away from a husband or a father, haven't you?"

He'd struck very close to the truth—so close that Bliss's face heated and she had to avert her eyes for a moment. When she had recovered her aplomb, she met Jamie's snapping gaze squarely and replied, "Not a husband, actually. I was only betrothed to Alexander—we never married."

Jamie scowled at her, as though she'd caused him great trial and turmoil by sleeping one night in his barn and eating some of his food. "I've got better things to do," he informed her, "than take you back to wherever you came from, lass."

Bliss pushed away her plate and slid back her chair. No one was taking her back to Wellington and that grasping, drooling old man her father wanted her to marry, ever. "I've imposed upon you quite long enough, Mr. McKenna," she said, in a cold voice. "I'll be on my way now."

"You're not going anywhere," Jamie responded flatly, finishing his breakfast. "It's winter out there and you're obviously a bit down on your luck. You'll have a bath and get yourself into bed."

Bliss felt her throat close painfully. Her ink-blue eyes

went round and she managed to squeeze out one squeaky word. "Bed?"

Mr. McKenna's laughter came suddenly, uproariously. "And now she thinks I want me way with 'er," he marveled aloud, once his mirth had subsided a little. His voice was thick with the brogue that had only been hinted at before.

Her face bright red behind its sprinkling of freckles, Bliss was too insulted to be relieved that her virtue was in no immediate danger. "I just thought—well, a man living all alone, so far from civilization—"

"I don't live alone," Jamie reminded her, "and Auckland's near enough."

Bliss would have been pleased to learn that Auckland, her destination, was close by, if she hadn't felt so bothered by the idea of that lovely Maori woman living there in that sturdy, no-nonsense house. She sniffed haughtily to hide her uncertainties and said, "If I can truly be sure that you won't molest me, Mr. McKenna, I would very much appreciate that bath you offered."

A spark danced in his eyes. "I'm not sure I can bathe you, Duchess, and still stay within the bounds of civilized behavior."

Rich color throbbed in Bliss's face. "I wasn't speaking literally, of course," she told him in tones of cold rigidity, "and you are a rascal for implying that I was."

The laughter lingered in Jamie McKenna's gaze even though the rest of his face showed a most serious composure. "Have you had quite enough to eat," he asked quietly, glancing pointedly at Bliss's empty plate, "or should I have another sheep slaughtered?"

Before Bliss could think of a suitably scathing response, the Maori woman returned. Her skin was a warm sandalwood color and her rich black hair flowed down her back in glistening ebony waves. Her figure was at once slender and womanly, and she wore a skirt and an off-the-shoulder blouse. The scent of some mysterious spice floated around

13

her as she cleared the table, her dark eyes meeting neither Jamie's gaze nor Bliss's.

Bliss was dying to know the woman's name, but she was damned if she'd ask. The relationship between Mr. McKenna and his cook was none of her affair, after all.

Oh, but the low, companionable note in his voice as he addressed the lady made Bliss ache in an inexplicable way. "Carra, Miss Stafford is in need of a bath, a fire, and a feather bed, in roughly that order," he said. "Will you see to it?"

Even though the two hadn't touched, it was almost as though Jamie had reached out and squeezed Carra's slender brown hand. Carra nodded before turning to carry the plates and flatware away to the cast-iron sink.

Bliss put her feeling of bereftness down to her hasty flight from Wellington and the rigors involved. She lowered her eyes, and when she looked up again, Jamie was gone and Carra was standing beside the table, waiting politely for Bliss to notice her.

There was a stairway at the back of the kitchen, and Carra led the way up it. The second floor of the house was as practical and austere as the rooms Bliss had glimpsed downstairs. A certain sadness possessed her; she sensed that Mr. McKenna didn't truly live here—this was only a place where he sometimes stopped.

"Mr. McKenna travels a great deal, doesn't he?" she asked, in a quiet voice, as Carra pushed open the door of a room at the far end of the hallway.

The Maori woman looked back at Bliss over one smooth brown shoulder and nodded, a flicker of surprise appearing, just briefly, in her eyes. "Yes."

There were a lot of other questions Bliss wanted to ask, and all of them were patently improper. She was going to have to learn to curb her curiosity before it got her into serious trouble.

With the utmost courtesy, Carra waited to one side of the doorway until Bliss had entered. The room was spacious, or perhaps it only appeared so because the narrow bed, wash-stand, and chest took up so little space. There was a small stone fireplace on one wall, and Mr. McKenna's attractive housekeeper crossed the room to kneel on the hearth and wrestle with the damper.

The chill of winter was upon Bliss's soul, as well as her body. Hugging herself and speaking in a very bright voice, she tried to make conversation. "Did you know that it's summer in America at this very moment?"

Carra showed her true feelings for the first time: a look of indulgent disdain moved across her face and then was gone. "I'll bring up the tub and some hot water soon," she said. Her tones were melodic, her accent no different from Bliss's own. "Have you a bag?"

Bliss remembered the satchel she'd left behind in Mr. McKenna's barn and clapped one hand to her mouth. Lord knew she had little enough in the way of worldly goods now that she'd left Wellington in such a hurry. She was going to have to be more careful or her best dress, her leatherbound diary, and the ribbon-bound letters her mother had sent from San Francisco would be lost as well. "I've left it in the hay," she said, starting toward the door.

In the hallway, she collided with Mr. McKenna, who was wearing his heavy coat again and carrying her bedraggled old carpetbag.

"Looking for this, then?" he asked, with that touch of the Irish making a soft, lilting music in his voice.

Greedily, Bliss reached out for her bag and clutched it close. After a moment, though, she relaxed. "I can be most forgetful," she confessed.

Jamie said nothing in response; he simply looked at Bliss in an odd way for several seconds and only when Carra cleared her throat did he turn and walk away.

"I'll be back with the tub in a few minutes," Carra said, her eyes never quite meeting Bliss's as she lingered in the hallway. "The water will take a while to heat, of course."

"Of course," Bliss responded, wanting nothing so much

as to be alone with her thoughts. It was a pity, she reflected, that Alexander had never engendered the feeling of angry sweetness in her that Jamie McKenna did. Had that been the case, she wouldn't have run away.

She gave the door a push and it closed with a click. Biting her lower lip, she carried her bag to the chest and set it down. After a few moments of struggle with the catch, she opened the satchel and took out her journal. In her haste, she had left Wellington without her pen and ink.

After tucking the journal back inside her bag, Bliss went to the door and opened it decisively. She would further trouble the long-suffering Carra for a bottle of ink and a nibbed pen.

She was down the rear stairs and partway through the kitchen—enormous kettles of water had already been set on the stove to heat—when she heard the conversation drifting toward her from the hallway that led to the front of the house.

"Just let her go on to Auckland and catch a ship to the States," Carra was saying, her voice low but full of anger.

"They'd chew her up and spit her out, those Yanks," Jamie muttered. He was clearly annoyed, though his hostility seemed to be directed toward the entire population of the United States instead of Carra.

"What concern is that of yours?" his housekeeper demanded.

There was a chilly pause and then Jamie responded, with a cutting lightness, "I found her in me barn, love. I guess I 'ave a proprietary interest."

Instinct told Bliss that she was about to be discovered; she whirled and dashed back across the kitchen, pretending to arrive as Carra stormed in, glaring.

It didn't seem like a good time to ask for a pen and ink. "I came to see if you needed any help," Bliss lied.

Carra's wide brown eyes burned with a pagan fire. "I've gotten along remarkably well without your help until now," she replied.

Bliss retreated a step, at a loss for words.

Carra muttered something, crossing the room and wrenching open the door of a huge and well-stocked pantry. She disappeared inside and then came out, moments later, carrying an enormous copper washtub. "You can bathe here," she said, letting the tub clatter to the floor. "I'm not about to carry water upstairs for you."

So much for the ignorant native, cowed by the conquerors, Bliss thought to herself. With a lift of her chin, she countered, "I'll carry the water myself. I don't make a habit of bathing in strange men's kitchens."

"That," retorted Carra sourly, "is a big relief."

Bliss had tried hard to refrain from asking impertinent questions, but one slipped past her resolve. "Do you?"

"Do I what?"

"Do you bathe right here, in Mr. McKenna's kitchen?"

Carra stared at her for a moment and then laughed, and there was a begrudging warmth in her face. "You are an odd little creature. Tell me, do you always ask such outrageous questions?"

Bliss sighed and began unbuttoning her coat. "Yes, most times I do."

Carra's expression had turned solemn again, in the wink of an eye. She regarded Bliss in silence for an instant, then took the patched, hay-flecked coat from her arms and carried it outside.

Bliss bent to pick up the copper tub—it was lighter than it looked, but still cumbersome—and lugged it upstairs and into her room. To her discomfort, Jamie McKenna was kneeling on the hearth, lighting the fire he'd laid. When the blaze caught, he rose, turning to face Bliss.

There was a deadly kind of grace in the way he moved; Bliss sensed that Jamie McKenna was a man who could look after himself, even in the most desperate situations.

She let the tub fall to the floor with a clanging *ker-thump*, feeling stricken in a way that defied explanation.

"Carra's refused to haul up your bathwater, has she?"

The question was mundane enough to bring Bliss back to her senses. "Yes, but that's quite all right. I can carry my own water."

Jamie's gaze was fixed on Bliss's bodice, and she remembered that she was wearing the black silk gown she'd had on when she'd raced out of Alexander's house in Wellington. Pearl and jet beads trimmed the hemline and the plunging neckline.

"What happened?" Jamie asked quietly, moving his eyes to Bliss's blushing face with obvious effort. "Exactly what— or who—are you running away from?"

Bliss felt the strangest urge to pour out her heart to this impudent stranger, to tell him all about her father's determination to marry her off to Alexander Zate, but in the end she held her peace. The less Mr. McKenna knew, the better.

She drew a deep and rather shaky breath. "I've already told you," she said. "I plan to travel to America."

Jamie arched one eyebrow and ran a hand through his rumpled, wheat-colored hair. "Where the streets are paved with gold," he gibed.

Bliss squared her shoulders. "I don't believe that nonsense."

"Good," he responded, and that strange irritation was back in his voice again. "Because that's exactly what it is. Nonsense, claptrap, drivel."

He blurred a little, and Bliss squinted to bring him back into focus.

"You are very prejudiced, Mr. McKenna."

Jamie looked insulted. "What?"

"You dislike Americans, and I can't think why. Your own sister-in-law is one, after all." Bliss jutted out her chin a little way, to show that she didn't approve of his narrow viewpoint. "But, then, you referred to her as a 'Yank,' didn't you?"

Jamie's handsome face was mottled with annoyance, and the brogue was back, thicker than before. "I'll not be defendin' me opinions to the likes of you, miss, and it so 'appens that I love me brother's wife very much! They don't come any finer than 'is Maggie!"

I love me brother's wife. The words lodged in Bliss's mind like a fishbone in the throat, scratching painfully and making it hard for her to breathe. She couldn't think why an insight into a stranger's innermost feelings should hurt her so.

She turned away, baffled by the effect this man had on her, and whispered inanely, "Have you a pen and ink that I might borrow?"

There was no reply, but for the rhythmic sound of Jamie's bootheels as he crossed the bare hardwood floor. The door closed behind him with a click that, for all its quietness, made Bliss start slightly.

She caught a glimpse of herself in the mirror over the chest of drawers. Dressed for a formal ball, yet with straw in her rumpled and dirty hair, she was indeed a sight. It was no wonder that Carra disliked and mistrusted her.

Bliss began to pace the small, immaculately clean room, planning, waiting, wondering.

She would have her bath, and a much-needed rest, and then, when night came, she would escape again. No one was taking her back to Alexander.

No, Bliss meant to be in Auckland before more than another day or two passed. Now that she was so close, she could afford to spend some of her scant supply of money on coach fare. When she reached Auckland, she would make her way to the harbor, find out which ships were bound for America, and go from one to another until she found someone looking to hire a governess or companion.

Despite her earlier insistence that she would do nothing of the sort, Carra brought hot water upstairs for Bliss's bath. Although her expression was grim, she also provided the unwanted guest with a warm flannel nightgown, a pot of tea, and a plate of sweet cakes, along with more wood for the fire.

The bath and the tea made Bliss languid, lowering her defenses. The weariness she'd been fighting overwhelmed her, and she crawled into the narrow bed, with its clean, crisp sheets, and fell into a sound sleep.

When she awakened, the room was dark, except for the silver light of an icy winter moon. The tub had been taken away, as had the tea tray, and the fire had shrunk to a few flickering embers in the grate.

Bliss crawled out of bed, stretched, and carefully dressed herself in the black silk gown, wanting to save her good tweed skirt and linen shirtwaist to wear when seeking a post in Auckland. She took great care to be quiet in packing her few belongings and crossing the room.

Holding her breath, she reached out for the doorknob—and found that it wouldn't turn.

The door between Bliss Stafford and her glorious future in America had been soundly locked.

Chapter 2 ❧

JAMIE LAY ALONE IN BED, HIS HANDS CUPPED BEHIND HIS HEAD, HIS mouth curved into a grin as he listened to Bliss Stafford's futile struggles with the door of her room. She was determined, he'd give her that.

With a chuckle and a shake of his head, he sat up. Not bothering to light the lamp first, he reached out for the tin packet of cheroots on his bedside stand. A flame rasped in the darkness, smelling of sulfur, as he struck a match. Next door, Bliss was still grappling hopelessly with the knob.

Jamie drew deeply of the smoke from his cheroot and listened in amused silence. The misnamed little chit was trying to kick down the door now, from the sounds of things.

"You're a scoundrel and a bastard!" she shrieked suddenly, her shrill voice carrying. "Do you hear me, Mr. McKenna?"

Jamie sighed. A man would have to be deaf not to hear her, he thought, wondering why he didn't just let her go and be done with the whole mess. The fact was that he couldn't bear the thought of Bliss all alone in the world, making her bumbling way to far-off America. She needed a man, be he father or husband, to look out for her.

21

"Let—me—out!" The words were screamed, punctuated by wrenching rattles of the doorknob and furious kicks at the panel itself.

In another minute, Jamie reflected, she'd be knotting sheets together to climb out the window. He smiled and then snuffed out his cheroot and clambered out of bed, both in the same motion. Saints in heaven, it would be like her to try that—she hadn't a brain in that beautiful little head of hers.

Hastily, he struggled into his pants and a woolen shirt. The silence from the room next door to his was unnerving. "Bliss?" he called out, in question, at the same time wrenching open his bedroom window.

The night wind was brisk and icy, taking away Jamie's breath. Still, he managed to rasp a curse, for a twisted bit of sheet was just slithering out of Bliss's window, like a fat white snake.

"You'll break your fool neck!" he shouted, before slamming the window shut and whirling around. He wrenched his boots onto his bare feet and dashed down the rear stairway, stumbling once and nearly falling down the steps.

He didn't bother with a coat, and the cold stung his face and hands and seeped through his clothes. Swearing under his breath, he rounded the large stone house to stand directly beneath Bliss's window.

Sure enough, the little fool was halfway down the side of the house, nimble as a spider. And herself dressed in that evening gown, with no coat to cover her bare shoulders.

Jamie couldn't remember being angrier—or more frightened. He stood perfectly still, watching as Bliss descended the makeshift rope, praying that she wouldn't fall. The moment she was within reach, he grasped her by the waist. The motion sent them both toppling backward onto the frosted ground.

Bliss fought for her freedom, kicking and clawing and making a furious, incoherent sound in her throat, while

Jamie used every ounce of strength he possessed to subdue her.

Finally, she lay gasping on her back, Jamie kneeling astride her hips and pressing her wrists to the ground with his hands. The moonlight gave her skin an opalescent glow; the evening gown barely covered her full breasts, which were moving rhythmically with every breath she drew.

The hint of a pink nipple taunted him, and though it was nothing he hadn't seen before, a thousand times, he was stirred by the sight. After a moment, he thrust himself to his feet, breathing hard, as though he'd run a far distance.

"Are you out of your mind?" he demanded, extending one hand to the woman raising herself from the ground.

She glared at the offered hand, and for a moment Jamie fully expected her to spit upon it. In the end, however, she took it and allowed herself to be hauled upright.

Jamie was furious, his mind full of the injuries Bliss could have suffered had she fallen. She might even have been killed. "I asked you a question!" he bellowed.

Bliss squared her moon-kissed shoulders and then bent to take up her satchel from the ground. "So you did," she answered coolly. "But it just so happens that I don't choose to answer."

The visions of this redheaded snippet lying broken and bleeding on the frozen ground were instantly displaced. In fact, Jamie considered carrying Bliss back upstairs and *throwing* her out the damned window. He grabbed her by one elbow and flung her toward the back of the house.

She bristled, drawing her dignity around her as she would a shawl or a cloak, and marched ahead of him. She put a man in mind of a martyr, on the way to the gallows or the stake.

Inside the kitchen, glass clinked as Jamie angrily lit a lamp. "Sit down," he bit out, and to his utter amazement, Bliss obeyed him, taking a seat at the table. Her eyes, blue as wet ink, were full of pride and challenge, and her red hair tumbled down her back in a coppery cascade.

She smoothed the skirts of her black satin evening gown, and her manner said that climbing out a second-story window in the middle of the night was behavior a normal person wouldn't presume to question.

"I'm cold," she announced, with frosty stateliness, "and I would like a cup of tea."

"A cup of tea, is it?" Jamie muttered, but nevertheless he ladled water into the pot and slammed it down on the stove. Since the fire had been banked for the night, he had to add kindling and stir the embers. "A cup of tea, she wants, after climbin' down the side of me 'ouse like a thief—"

Bliss's nervous but glad giggle startled him. He whirled to face her, glaring.

She pursed her lips and sat up very straight in her chair. "You left me no choice but to escape by any means available to me," she said loftily.

Jamie shook his head, marveling, and reached out for the tin of tea leaves Carra kept on a shelf above the stove. He slammed it down on the counter with a crash that made Bliss give a satisfying little start of surprise.

"Men," Bliss observed, extending her bare, chapped hands and assessing them as though she were wearing a fine and immaculate pair of gloves. "They are always so upset to discover that a woman has thoughts of her own and the gumption to carry them out. Gumption is highly admired in America, you know."

"How the 'ell do you know what's admired in America?" Jamie demanded, furious beyond all good sense and grateful that he didn't have to explain why. He couldn't have done that, even to himself.

He hurled spoonfuls of tea into a crockery pot as heat began to surge through the kettle on the stove.

Bliss wet her lips with the tip of her tongue—Jamie found the gesture patently disconcerting—and kept her eyes averted. "One couldn't possibly expect a man of your insensitivity and social awkwardness to understand," she sniffed.

Jamie drew a deep breath and let it out slowly. "Keep your 'ead, man," he muttered to himself. Then, in a louder voice, he added, "Thank you very much, Miss Stafford. I 'old you in the fondest regard, too."

She blushed beneath a soft, golden spattering of freckles. Jamie found himself wondering whether or not the rest of Bliss Stafford's lush little body was so decorated.

"We seem to be at sixes and sevens, you and I," she said, in that haughty way of hers.

Jamie fought conflicting urges to carry her off to his bed and to turn her across his knee, right then and there. The little bird on the spout of the teakettle, the one frivolity he'd permitted in his house, began to whistle. Leaving Bliss's observation to dangle unanswered in the air between them, he turned to take the kettle from the stove and promptly burned his fingers on the handle.

"Good heavens." Bliss sighed, standing up and dipping water from the bucket beside the sink. "Put your hand in here," she ordered briskly, holding out the ladle.

Jamie did so; the numbing cold soothed his burn. Utterly baffled by the new emotions he was feeling, he could only stare down at Bliss Stafford and wonder what capricious fate had sent her to hide out in his barn, irritate Carra, and then scare him out of his hide by shinnying down the outside wall of his house. Saints in heaven, he'd hardly lapsed into the brogue in years, and now he was thinking in it!

Bliss was examining his fingers. "Better now?" she asked, as though speaking to an injured little boy.

Jamie remembered himself and jerked his hand from hers. "Never mind that. If you 'ave to 'elp, make the tea."

A small and rather annoying smile touched Bliss's mouth as she obligingly reached for a potholder, took up the kettle, and poured scalding hot water over the tea leaves. Jamie sank into a chair with a despondent sigh.

Bliss found mugs and carried them to the table, along with the pot of freshly brewed tea. Anyone would have thought, Jamie observed miserably to himself, that she belonged in this house. Was its mistress.

She sat down across from him and poured tea for him and then herself. Every move was one of dignity, until she took a noisy sip from her cup.

In spite of his confusion and his anger, Jamie laughed, and Bliss glared at him, insulted.

"It's hot," she explained.

He inclined his head slightly. "Yes, Duchess," he replied, fighting to keep a straight face.

In the next instant, without any warning at all, there were tears brimming in her indigo eyes. "You needn't make fun of me," she said, sniffling. "It isn't as though the past few days have been easy for me, you know. I've had hardly anything to eat the whole time, and I've slept in the most dreadful places." She stopped and drew a deep and very moist breath. "I have been in terrible danger, too. I might have encountered bushrangers, after all."

Jamie took a leisurely sip of his tea, then quipped, "Or broken your neck climbing out an upstairs window."

A single tear streaked down Bliss's cheek, and Jamie found himself thinking soft, silly thoughts.

"You have no right to hold me prisoner, Mr. McKenna," she pointed out. "I'm a subject of the Crown, after all—"

"Strange talk, coming from a future Yank," Jamie interrupted lightly. "They bend their knees to nobody—nary a king or a queen among 'em."

Bliss blushed, and again Jamie was possessed of a longing to see her without her clothes.

"Sometimes," she confessed softly, "I wonder if I'm ever going to get away from New Zealand." She lifted her beautiful eyes to Jamie's face. "You're going to take me back to Wellington, aren't you?" she asked.

Jamie only nodded. For some reason, he couldn't speak.

"I know you believe that's the honorable, upright thing to do—"

He waited, willing to listen even though his mind was made up. And Jamie McKenna rarely retreated from a decision, once he'd made it.

"You can't possibly know what a mistake you're making, of course," Bliss went on distractedly. She was a little pale, and he suspected that her hands were knotted in her lap.

He'd seen such female theatrics before.

"Alexander will force me to address him circumspectly, as 'Mr. Zate,' from the day we're married," she said.

"I've 'eard of worse things," Jamie remarked, after taking another swallow of tea.

All of a sudden, Bliss's small, cold hands were out of her lap and reaching across the tabletop, gripping Jamie's. "I'll have to share his bed," she whispered, "and I don't love him."

Jamie thrust himself out of his chair, turning his back. He didn't want to hear what privileges her husband would have; he didn't want to think about them. "You're not my problem, Duchess," he said, after a lengthy silence. "Not after I leave you off in Wellington, anyway."

Bliss rarely wept; she'd found it such a fruitless occupation in the past. Now, however, faced with the prospect of a lifetime spent curtsying and crawling to a man she didn't love, she gave free rein to her emotions. A heartsick, snuffling wail escaped her, and she covered her face with both hands.

Jamie McKenna's voice was surprisingly gentle. "Don't cry, please," he pleaded hoarsely, crouching in front of her chair. "It can't be as bad as all that, now can it?"

"It's every bit as bad, and worse!" Bliss sobbed. She fought for the dignity to blurt out, "Rest assured—you shall have me on your conscience, Mr. McKenna, for the rest of your life!"

He gave a rueful chuckle and straightened, taking one of Bliss's hands in his and pulling her easily to her feet. His next motion should have incensed and terrified Bliss, but instead she found it comforting. Jamie McKenna lifted her into his arms, seemingly expending no more effort than if she'd been a child.

"There, now," he said, his voice coming rough and soft from the depths of his throat. "I doubt if this bloke is as bad as all that. What you want is a good night's sleep, Duchess."

Bliss stared at him, blinking away her tears. Her arms had automatically wound themselves around his neck. Perhaps there was still hope of escape, if she remembered to keep her wits about her. "I don't want to be alone," she heard herself say.

Jamie laughed softly. "Don't worry—I wouldn't think of turnin' me back on you. You might be out the window again."

He paused to quench the flame in the lamp, then carried Bliss through the darkness, up invisible stairs, along a hallway glowing faintly with stray shafts of moonlight.

Bliss marveled at herself. She'd always been independent and strong-minded. Now, just because Jamie McKenna had lifted her into his arms, she had all the resistance of an unstarched petticoat. "Put me down," she said, but she didn't mean a word of it and Jamie obviously knew that.

He carried her into a darkened room with a rumpled, unmade bed and tossed her onto the mattress. "Reminds me of another night," he muttered, sitting down on the edge of the bed to wrestle off his boots. "In Melbourne, it was."

Albeit at a rather late date, Bliss had recovered her strength of character. "Now, just a minute!" she sputtered, inching toward the side of the bed. "You can't possibly think that I'm going to spend the night—"

In a deft motion of one hand, Jamie reached out, caught her wrist in a grasp as steely as a manacle, and effectively pinned her in place. "That's exactly what I think. I'm not about to let you out of me sight, Duchess."

Bliss's heart was thumping in her throat. If she screamed, would Carra come to her aid? "What are you going to do?"

"Dived out of a carriage, she did," Jamie went on, as

though Bliss hadn't spoken. He stretched out on the bed, fully clothed, and she had no choice but to do the same, since he was still holding on to her wrist. "Came rolling toward me like a Texas tumbleweed."

If he thought Bliss was going to be swayed by a chummy reference to something American, he was dead wrong. "Let me up! I'll be spoiled for Alexander, or any other man!"

"Isn't that what you wanted?" he asked, pretending befuddlement.

Oddly enough, a part of Bliss wanted to be besmirched. By this man, at least. It was exciting, in an uncomfortable sort of way, to be lying beside him in the darkness. "Yes—no!"

He laughed. "Make up your mind, Duchess."

"Stop calling me that!"

"Never. It suits you too well."

"I hate you, Jamie McKenna!"

He sighed companionably. The man had a gift for overlooking the incongruities of a situation. "Tell me about yourself, Bliss. Did you grow up in Wellington?"

His grasp on her wrist had loosened, if not relaxed entirely, and Bliss realized that she wasn't afraid, though by all accounts she should have been. "No. My father keeps a lighthouse down the coast from Wellington, and I spent my childhood there."

Subtly, Jamie's fingers had shifted; he was holding Bliss's hand. His thumb stroked the tender flesh of her wrist in a way that produced feelings of sweet discomfort.

"Have you any brothers and sisters, then?" he asked, and the meter of his voice was such that they might have been at a very proper lawn party, instead of lying, alone and unchaperoned, in a dark bedroom.

An old sadness filled Bliss. "I had a brother, but he died when I was small. I hardly remember him." It was a lie that she didn't remember Colin; her father had never allowed her to forget that the lad might have lived if he hadn't gone out to search for her that stormy night.

Jamie was silent for a few moments, seeming to sense Bliss's reluctance to speak of her childhood. His thumb continued its disconcerting work along the inside of her wrist.

"I have a brother," he told her, at length.

"I know," Bliss responded, possessed with sweet misery. "You're in love with his wife."

Jamie let go of her wrist and sat straight up in bed. "What!" he demanded.

"You told me so yourself." She started to leave the bed, but Jamie pulled her back.

"I said I loved her," he admitted. "But I didn't mean it the way you're thinkin'," he said, with that Irish lilt in his voice. "She's a sister to me, is Maggie, and nothin' more."

The importance Jamie attached to convincing her of this secretly pleased Bliss. "I see," she said coolly.

"Why am I explainin' to you, anyway?" he muttered, folding his arms across his chest with such force that the whole bed shook.

Even though Jamie was no longer holding her hand, Bliss made no move to climb off the mattress. "How should I know why you're explaining, Jamie McKenna? As far as I can tell, you're a maniac. Why, if my papa knew that you were forcing me to share your bed, like a common strumpet—"

Jamie laughed and turned onto his side, facing Bliss. The light of the moon caught in his fair hair and glistened on his white teeth, and the odd, achy sensation in the depths of her, at once pleasant and frightening, grew worse.

Or better. It did depend on how one chose to look at the situation.

Ever so gently, Jamie McKenna touched Bliss's lips with his own. A delicious tremor went through her; she used the only defense she had.

"Is this what you do with your Maori woman when no one is around?" she asked ingenuously.

His chuckle was a wholly masculine sound, rumbling up from deep inside his broad chest, vibrating against Bliss's lips. Instead of answering, he kissed her.

Bliss was deeply shaken by this gentle conquering. For the first time in her life, she felt utterly powerless. She trembled as the tip of his tongue touched her lips, prodding them, shaping them, demanding of them something Bliss couldn't begin to anticipate.

Her mouth opened of its own accord, trained by Jamie's lips and tongue, and then he was exploring her. The sensation was uniquely pleasurable, and she wrapped her arms around his neck, absorbed in the kiss.

It was Jamie who drew back. He was gasping, as though he'd had his head held underwater, and he spat a curse.

Bliss was roundly insulted. "I didn't start this, you will remember," she said primly.

Jamie sat up, turning his back to her, running one hand through his rumpled hair. "Shut up, Duchess, before you get us both into trouble."

"Where are you going?" Bliss wanted to know. She should have been relieved that Jamie had stopped holding her or kissing her, but she wasn't.

"Not far enough that you can hope to get away," he replied, reaching for his boots. "Do us both a favor and go to sleep, will you? We'll be off to Wellington first thing in the morning."

"Doesn't it matter to you that I don't *want* to go to Wellington?" Bliss cried, in a panic. Now that she knew how a kiss could make her feel, she was even less eager to marry Alexander Zate than before.

"No," came the clipped answer. He clumped over to a rocking chair in the corner of the moonlit room, wearing one boot and carrying the other. He was beyond a doubt the most cussed man Bliss had ever encountered, and he was certainly the first one she'd shared a bed with.

"You're wasting your time, traveling all the way to Wellington," Bliss pointed out, sitting up and, after smoothing her hopelessly crumpled skirts, folding her arms. "I'll only run away again, you know."

"Then that will be your husband's problem, won't it?" Jamie reasoned wearily, settling back into the chair after pulling on his other boot. Apparently, if he had to give chase, he meant to be ready.

Bliss was frustrated to the point of tears. "All men are in league with each other," she complained.

"Don't you ever shut up?" Jamie sighed.

"No!"

The rocking chair made a squeaky sound as he rocked back and forth. "Go to sleep, Duchess. It'll be a long day tomorrow."

"You have no idea how long, Mr. McKenna."

He sounded stern. "Don't be threatenin' me, lass," he warned, lapsing into the brogue again. He indicated an infinitesimal space between his thumb and forefinger. "It's this far I am from takin' you over me knee!"

Bliss hoped that the shadows slashing through the moonlight would hide her heated face. "That was a perfectly reprehensible remark," she protested.

"Aye, but it's true," Jamie replied. He let his head fall back and Bliss was sure that his eyes were closed.

She settled back on her pillows, sighing and giving a great yawn. And then she waited, with infinite patience, for the sound of snoring.

It never came, although, after a while, Jamie's breathing was deep and rhythmic. Still, Bliss waited.

Finally, when at least an hour had passed, she sat up. "Jamie?" she whispered. "Are you awake?"

There was no answer.

She tried again. "Jamie?"

Silence.

Cautiously, Bliss slipped off the bed. Her coat and satchel were downstairs, in the kitchen. If she could just get past this one man, asleep in his rocking chair, she would get away. By sunset, at the latest, she would be in Auckland.

She walked as silently as a ghost, afraid to breathe, and finally reached the door. Her hand was just curving around the knob when she felt two arms close around her middle.

Jamie's voice was a hoarse rush of warmth moving past her ear. "Duchess, for shame. What am I going to do with you?"

It was not being caught in the act of escaping that made Bliss's heart catch in her throat, but the way that Jamie was holding her. Her face ached with burning embarrassment.

She drew a deep breath, entangled in her lie and determined to extricate herself gracefully. "I assure you that my errand was entirely innocent," she lied. "As you are well aware, nature makes certain demands—"

"I've thought of nothing else for most of the night," Jamie pointed out, but he released her.

Bliss's knees had weakened, so that it was almost more than she could do to stand on her own. Her cheeks flamed. "I suppose you're going to escort me to the outhouse," she said stiffly, turning, with a regal tilt of her chin, to face her captor.

He gestured grandly with one hand. "If you'd rather use the chamber pot, be my guest," he said.

Bliss was outraged. She moved to kick Mr. McKenna soundly in the shin, but he anticipated the attack and stepped aside. His body was as fluid as molten gold; Bliss had never seen anyone move so quickly and yet with such grace.

"I'll repay you for your—kindness, Mr. McKenna," she promised him evenly, "if it takes the rest of my days."

He laughed. "You're a feisty little thing. I'm going to miss you after I drop you off in Wellington. I am indeed."

Again, Bliss's fury overtook her good sense. She stepped back, believing herself to be out of his reach, and lifted her foot to kick him. This time, she wasn't aiming for his shin.

Before her delicate little shoe could make lethal contact, however, Jamie had grasped her by the inside of her upraised knee, holding her off balance for an instant and then, in another of his lightning movements, thrusting her close to him. Not even their kiss had been as intimate as the way they were touching now.

He bent his head and claimed her mouth again, at the same time releasing his hold on the inside of her knee. Bliss's leg slid helplessly along the hard length of his until her foot reached the floor.

Chapter 3 🌿

THE AUGUST AIR WAS BITING COLD ON THAT EARLY MORNING, AND Bliss paced in front of the barn door, rubbing her hands together and stomping her feet in an effort to keep warm. Her breath made wisps of fog as she huffed, "It would be simpler, it seems to me, if you just put me on a coach in Auckland and washed your hands of the whole matter."

Jamie, who was hitching a team of horses, one sorrel and one bay, to a wagon, looked back over his right shoulder and grinned. "That's very tempting—the part about washing my hands of you, I mean—but I'm smarter than I look, Duchess. You'd be off that coach and on your way to the waterfront the moment I turned my back."

What Jamie had said was quite true, but Bliss was insulted, nonetheless, at having her character questioned. "Of course you're smarter than you look, Mr. McKenna," she observed, with a lift of her chin. "If you weren't, you wouldn't be able to feed yourself."

Jamie gave a hoarse shout of laughter, causing the horses to snuffle nervously and toss their heads. At the same time, the front door of the house opened and closed again with a smart slam.

35

Carra was standing on the porch, her beautiful black hair flowing in the brisk wind, her dark gaze fixed on Jamie. She set a large picnic hamper down at her feet, and there was something rebellious in the gesture, as ordinary as it was.

Jamie grinned and shook his head. "So that's the way it's to be, is it?" he said, speaking more to himself than to anyone else, as was evidently his habit. Then, after only the merest hesitation, he strode off toward the house, leaving Bliss alone beside the wagon.

She felt a twinge of jealousy as she climbed aboard the creaky vehicle and settled herself in the seat. Although Bliss did her best not to stare, her gaze did drift off in Jamie's direction now and again.

Toward the end, Carra was gesturing wildly with her arms and periodically stomping one foot while Jamie tore his ancient, battered leather hat from his head and slapped it hard against one thigh. Even though Bliss couldn't hear the words they were exchanging, it was obvious that Jamie and his woman were not parting on amicable terms.

Finally, Jamie shouted something that was unintelligible to Bliss and Carra whirled away, her hair flying like an ebony cloak behind her, and stormed into the house. Jamie gave the door a good hard kick, then, eyes blazing, turned and nearly stumbled over the picnic hamper.

Bliss clapped one hand over her mouth to stifle a laugh.

Apparently sensing that she'd found the near disaster amusing, Jamie glared at Bliss as he hoisted the large lidded basket into his arms and started toward her.

"If you'd bothered to wait," he remarked, hurling the basket into the back of the wagon with a total disregard for the delicacy of anything that might be inside it, "I'd have helped you into the wagon—just as if you were a lady."

Bliss's cheeks flamed. It was bad enough that he'd kept her a virtual prisoner throughout the night; now he was implying that her manners were less than admirable. If they were, it was certainly none of his affair.

He climbed up into the wagon box, sat down heavily, and

took the reins into his gloved hands. His sea-blue eyes were snapping as he inclined his head formally and asked, "Did I strike too close to the truth, Duchess?"

Bliss chose to ignore his question and present one of her own. If she was expected to be unladylike, then so be it. She would behave accordingly. "Was your lady love angry because you're going away with me?"

Jamie brought the reins down on the horses' backs with a little more force than necessary, and the team bolted forward. Caught off guard, Bliss nearly lost her balance and tumbled backward into the wagon bed. Only her desperate grasp on the sleeve of Jamie's rough woolen coat saved her.

"You were saying?" he prompted, attempting to hide a smile, as Bliss struggled for composure. She drew a deep breath, smoothing her frightfully tangled hair with her hands and willing her heartbeat to slow to its normal pace.

The wagon was moving, rolling and bumping over the rutted lane beyond Jamie's gate, before he broke the thick silence. "Not that it's any of your business, Duchess, but Carra cleans my house and cooks my meals—she does not share my bed."

"But—"

Jamie cut Bliss off by saying, in a tone that did not encourage challenge, "Carra is young, and she has a few romantic ideas about me, but that's as far as it goes. Her father is a powerful man among the Maori—if I dishonored Carra, I would also dishonor him, and that's asking for more trouble than I care to have."

Subdued, Bliss lowered her eyes to her lap. She was relieved that he and Carra weren't lovers, but she wasn't about to let this hardheaded sheepherder know that straight out.

"It's a very long way to Wellington," she said, fixing her eyes on the familiar hillsides, green even in the dead of winter, with their neat hedgerows.

Jamie said nothing in response, and a surreptitious glance in his direction revealed that his jawline was clamped down tight. Probably, he resented taking time away from his work to run a fool's errand like this.

The lane dipped and then rose again, at an almost vertical angle, and Bliss grasped the wagon seat hard in both hands, fearing that she would go tumbling backward. She could hear the contents of the picnic hamper rattling dangerously.

In the next moment, however, they had crested the hill, and there, a stunning surprise in shades ranging from deep blue to pale green, was the sea, quietly muttering an ancient promise to the shore. Although Bliss had seen the ocean a million times, having grown up in a lighthouse, she had never lost the feeling of wondrous awe it inspired in her.

She drew in a deep breath of frigid salt air and smiled contentedly.

It was immediately apparent that the sea had no such soothing affect on Jamie. He scowled at her and encouraged the horses to travel a bit faster now that the road was level.

Disappointed in Jamie's blunt lack of appreciation for a truly splendid sight, Bliss returned his glower tit for tat.

He struggled to look sober and solemn but finally laughed. "That," he said, "is a hate-filled mug if I've ever seen one."

Bliss was relieved at the chance to strike up a conversation—any kind of conversation. "I've never hated anyone in all my life," she said magnanimously. "Not even Alexander, though I expect I'll come to truly despise him once we're wedded."

The mirth dancing in Jamie's eyes was instantly gone. Somehow, it comforted Bliss to know that he didn't like being reminded of her impending marriage to the man her father had chosen.

Jamie fixed his gaze straight ahead, but his jawline was tight. "What kind of no-gooder is your father, anyway?" he demanded after several moments had passed.

Bliss knew a sensation of gentle triumph, though she carefully hid the fact from Jamie. "Papa's not a bad man, all things considered," she replied with a tender and rather theatrical sigh. "He's just tired of having me underfoot all the time, that's all. And then, of course, there's the money."

She had Mr. McKenna's full attention, at long last. "Money?" he asked. "What money?"

Bliss gazed out at the sea. Above the waves, a foggy mist shifted eerily in the icy daylight. "Alexander—Mr. Zate—plans to settle a rather large sum on my father after the wedding."

The silence from the man beside her was ominous. When Bliss dared glance at Jamie, she saw that his face had hardened with rage, and she knew a certain satisfaction. Perhaps she had finally made him understand her plight.

"He's sellin' you, then," he said, in a deceptively soft voice, after several moments had passed.

Bliss bit her lower lip, hesitating for what she hoped was exactly the right length of time. Then she willed her eyes to brim with tears and answered in a small, quavering voice, "Yes."

Even though the horses were clearly doing the very best they could, Jamie brought the reins down hard on their backs, urging them to an even faster pace. It was a measure of his annoyance. "Blighter," he muttered.

Bliss sniffled delicately and dabbed at her eyes.

"How do you do that?" Jamie asked, out of the blue, and Bliss was so surprised that she fell to stammering.

"D-do what?" she hedged.

Jamie reached out, with one of his gloved hands, and smoothed a tear from her cheek with an agile motion of his thumb. "Cry that way," he replied, frowning. "You made up your mind to do it, and then you did. And don't bother denyin' it, lass."

If it hadn't been for the fact that she was headed toward Wellington and Mr. Alexander Zate instead of an outgoing ship and an exciting new life in America, where her mother awaited her most eagerly, Bliss would have been amused. It was rare to meet a man so perceptive.

Still, being able to cry on order was a skill that came in handy on occasion, and Bliss, like a magician with his tricks, was quite jealous of the secret. She gazed at Jamie in stubborn silence and, to her utter amazement, he burst out laughing.

She did wonder what it was about her that amused this man so thoroughly. Quite miffed, she stiffened on the hard wagon seat and hugged herself with both arms to keep from assaulting Mr. McKenna in the purest rage.

Still grinning, he touched the tip of her nose with an index finger covered in soft, worn leather. "What a fiery little 'ellcat you are, Duchess. A man could spend all 'is life just learnin' 'ow to read you."

Bliss felt a strange, warm shiver at his touch, and a series of forbidden pictures rose in her mind. Memories of the night before, when she'd lain beside Jamie McKenna in a dark bedroom, caused a tender and throbbing ache in the very depths of her femininity.

I'm never going to feel this way about Alexander, she thought to herself, and she was filled with utter despair. If only her father were forcing her to marry Jamie—a girl could live with an ultimatum like that.

They traveled in silence, beside the misty sea, for a considerable distance, and then Jamie drew the wagon to the side of the road in order to let the horses rest. Bliss, longing to stretch her cramped legs, scrambled down from the wagon seat before her companion could help her.

She rubbed her hands together in an effort to warm them; though it was near noon, the weather was still inordinately cold. Jamie, meanwhile, spoke quietly to both the horses, pausing to rub their soft muzzles and offer them lumps of sugar from the palm of his hand.

Remembering the picnic basket Carra had so grudgingly provided at the farm that morning, Bliss felt a sudden and keen hunger. She found the wicker box and lifted it out of the wagon.

"By all means, Duchess," Jamie said, watching her with a laughing tenderness in his eyes, "help yourself."

Bliss felt her cheeks grow hot. It seemed to her that Mr. McKenna was forever pointing out some lapse in her deportment. She made no apologies—it was too late for that, after all—before opening the basket's wicker lid and taking out a thick sandwich wrapped in a plain cloth napkin.

"This Zate fellow—does he have any idea how much it's going to cost to feed you?"

Bliss did not appreciate this observation. She ignored it and took a bite from her sandwich, which contained cheese, butter, and sliced chicken.

Jamie left the horses to join her at a little distance from the road, bending to lift a sandwich of his own from the basket. His eyes sparkled with quiet humor as he unwrapped the food. "A man's got to take his food when he has the chance," he observed companionably. "How you can eat like a prize bull and stay so skinny is beyond me."

Bliss nearly choked. "Skinny!" she cried, choosing to overlook the fact that she'd just been compared to a farm animal. "I am not skinny!"

The azure eyes slid lingeringly down the front of Bliss's ragged old coat and back to her throbbing face. "You're not fat, either," he returned, in a strange, husky voice that had a distracted sound to it. Having made this observation, he finished eating and shuffled Bliss toward the wagon just as she was unwrapping her second sandwich.

Without so much as a by-your-leave, he lifted Bliss off her feet, fairly flinging her back into the wagon seat.

"It's time we were moving along," he said, quite unnecessarily, as he climbed up beside her and took the reins into his hands.

Bliss was just catching her breath, and embarrassed color mottled her cheeks. "It is," she began, "most distracting the way you keep grabbing me up like a sack of beans and putting me wherever strikes your fancy!"

He made a startling sound meant to spur the horses on and chuckled grimly at Bliss's leap of surprise. "You'd be amazed at what strikes my fancy, Duchess," he said.

Bliss could think of no proper response to that, so she kept her peace and quietly consumed her sandwich.

A pale sun was just setting over the sea when the inn came into sight. Bliss had been riding on that hard wagon seat for hours, cold to the very marrow of her bones, and she had a wild, soaring hope that Jamie would stop for the night.

She closed her eyes for a moment, in sheer relief, when her escort guided the horses through the inn's wide gateway.

Two grinning stableboys appeared immediately to attend to the tired horses, greeting Jamie with simultaneous cries of, "Good evenin', Mr. McKenna!"

Ignoring Bliss for the moment, Jamie climbed down from the wagon bed and handed each of the grubby boys a coin. Even though he had to be almost as stiff and sore as Bliss was, he moved with his usual subtle ease.

Presently, after a chat with the lads, he came to Bliss's side of the wagon and extended his strong arms to her. She moved into them without hesitation, too weary to rebel.

In the warm, well-lighted interior of the inn, other travelers, mostly men, sat at long tables, drinking ale and consuming succulent venison pies for supper.

Bliss's stomach grumbled, and she lifted her chin at the sound of Jamie's chuckle. The man missed nothing.

Once Jamie had guided her to a smaller table, not far from the huge fireplace, Bliss moved to take off her coat. Remembering the low-cut evening dress beneath, however, she hesitated.

A heavy, lumbering man with coarse lips and a bulbous nose approached the table. He wore a stained apron over his broad middle, but his eyes were friendly as he glanced at Bliss and then greeted Jamie. "'Ello, mate, and welcome. Tea for the lady?"

Jamie nodded, ordering a mug of ale for himself and two venison pies as well.

Even though Bliss was ravenously hungry by that time, she resented Jamie's blithe presumption in choosing her supper fare for her. "What if I'd wanted something different to eat?" she asked in a whisper, bending toward him.

He smiled in the flickering light of the fire and the kerosene lamps. "Then you would've been out of luck, Duchess, because venison pie is all they serve here."

"Oh," Bliss said, settling back as best she could. The truth was that the bench she was sitting upon was every bit as hard as the seat of Jamie's wagon. It was a mercy, though, that it didn't roll and pitch about; she couldn't have borne much more of that.

The tea was brought by a young woman with a lush figure and heavy brown hair that threatened to fall from its pins. Her full lips formed a pout as she inspected Bliss.

"This your missus, then, Jamie boy?" she fussed.

Bliss was about to interject a comment of her own when Jamie answered smoothly, "Aye, lass, this is me lovely wife. See we 'ave a good soft bed and a warm fire for the night, won't you?"

The "lass" was fuming as she walked away, but she was no angrier than Bliss.

"How dare you introduce me as your wife and ask for a soft bed?" she hissed, her hand trembling as she reached out to pour herself a much-needed cup of tea.

Jamie was unruffled. His ale had arrived with Bliss's pot of tea, and he took a leisurely draft of the potion before replying, "These blokes aren't the gentlemanly sort, sweetness. If they get the idea that you're fair game, you and I are both going to have to fight for our honor."

Bliss felt a shudder move up her back as she risked a glance around the inn's crowded main room. Now that she thought about it, it was odd that there were so many men about, considering how isolated the place was. "These men are—criminals?" she whispered.

Jamie nodded solemnly. "Stay close to me, Duchess, and you'll be safe enough."

43

Bliss was taking no chances. She didn't look away from Jamie's face as she lifted her teacup to her lips. "I'm not sharing a room with you," she swore tremulously.

Jamie grinned. The petulant serving girl, who said her name was Dorrie, had brought the meat pies, and their metal tins made a clanking sound as she slammed them down onto the table. She gave a little squeal and flinched, and Jamie's grin grew wider as the cheap trollop giggled and scampered away.

Despite the fact that Bliss had led a relatively sheltered life, she well understood what had happened, and she was furious. "You pinched her!" she accused, struggling to keep her voice low.

Jamie only nodded, watching her in an insolent way that challenged her to protest.

Bliss plunged her fork into the meat pie in front of her with a ferocious motion of her hand. "Libertine," she muttered.

Jamie shrugged and began eating his supper with zest. Too soon, the meal was finished and the simpering Dorrie was showing the way to their room. It was on the ground floor, toward the back of the inn; though small and cramped, and close to the kitchen in the bargain, it looked clean enough.

Bliss eyed the one bed ruefully.

"The bed's real soft, gov'nor," Dorrie was telling Jamie flirtatiously. "I've tested it meself."

"I'll just bet you have," Bliss interceded icily. "That will be all, and thank you very much."

Jamie handed the creature a coin and, after seeing her out, he leaned against the door and assessed Bliss with a flicker of mischief in his eyes. "Tired, Duchess?" he asked sympathetically.

Bliss was exhausted, and every part of her body ached. "Yes. If you'll just turn away, I'd like to get into bed."

After only a second's deliberation, Jamie turned his broad back to Bliss and folded his arms. "Where am I supposed to sleep?" he asked reasonably.

"In that chair, by the fire," Bliss suggested, proceeding to tear off her coat and struggle out of the black silk evening dress beneath it. She was wearing only drawers and her petticoat, which she'd pulled up to cover her breasts, when she slipped into bed.

She snuggled down beneath the covers and appeared to be sound asleep before her traveling companion could offer a reply of any sort.

"God's eyeballs," Jamie muttered, looking grimly at the ladderback chair facing the fireplace. He was worn out, having spent much of the night before sitting straight up and all day traveling, and he'd been looking forward to stretching out on a mattress.

Bliss shifted restlessly and made a crooning sound in her sleep, and Jamie went to the bedside and looked down at her. He felt tenderness, followed by a familiar, grinding ache in his groin, and he moved resolutely away. If he made love to the Duchess, he'd be no better than any of those bleeders out front, swilling ale and lying to each other.

He considered visiting Dorrie—she'd taken pains to let him know where she slept and when she'd be through waiting tables—but immediately decided against it. Much as he might have wanted things to be different, he desired only one woman.

One small, trusting, stubborn woman, misnamed Bliss.

With a grin and a slight shrug, Jamie decided that one last mug of ale would serve to bring on a sound sleep. After glancing out the single window and taking one more look at Bliss, he left the room, closing the door and turning the key in the lock.

Bliss was out of the bed and grasping for her clothes the moment she heard the click of Jamie's key. The fact that she was locked in did not daunt her in the least.

After buttoning her coat and snatching up her satchel, which Dorrie had brought in earlier, she hurried across the room. The window squeaked loudly as she raised it and climbed through the opening.

Darkness greeted her as she leaped the short distance to the ground, and the smell of manure filled her nostrils. Making a face, Bliss crept around the corner of the inn and made for the road.

Full of ale and ready to sleep standing up if he had to, Jamie hummed softly as he unlocked the door of the room he'd hired. The chill draft that struck him the moment he stepped inside told him everything he needed to know.

Muttering a curse, he strode through the darkness to the window and slammed it closed. He knew the bed was empty without looking.

Truth to tell, Jamie McKenna was tempted to let Bliss deal with her fate as it came to her. Whatever happened, it would serve her right.

He was thinking these thoughts even as he checked to make sure his blade was still strapped to his side and snatched up his coat and hat. When he found Bliss Stafford, he vowed, he'd give her a talking-to she wasn't likely to forget.

If he found her.

Not wanting to draw attention to himself and thus to Bliss's disappearance, he left the inn through the kitchen, which was empty except for the two stableboys who'd greeted him on arrival. Neither of them dared question him.

In the stable, he collected the fastest of his two horses, the sorrel, and helped himself to a saddle and bridle. He'd settle up with the innkeeper later, when Bliss was back at his side, safe and warm.

For the first time since he'd left Ireland, Jamie McKenna permitted himself a silent prayer: *Watch over her. Please, watch over her.*

It was cold and dark and the moon was a frigid sliver, high in the sky. Bliss looked back toward the inn with a certain longing, though only the faintest glow of its lights was visible now.

With a sigh, she set herself toward Auckland and trudged on. She had only to think of America and the grand future she would have there; that would keep her going. For what seemed like hours, she put one foot in front of the other.

In America, she promised herself, she would be happy. With her mother's help, she would find a nice husband—a man she truly loved—and have children. Lots of children.

Jamie McKenna's handsome face loomed in her mind. By now he probably knew that she was gone; maybe, at that very moment, he was setting out to look for her.

Bliss sighed. It wasn't likely that Jamie would give chase. She'd been a trial to him from the very first, and he was almost certain to be glad that she was gone. He'd be happy enough to wash his hands of her, that he would indeed.

A single tear, utterly unexpected, slipped down Bliss's cheek, leaving a chilly trail. The wind was rising, and it nipped at her through her clothes.

When she heard the horses in the distance, Bliss was relieved. Jamie had been worried about her after all. He'd organized a search party.

The fact that the riders were coming from the wrong direction didn't strike Bliss until she found herself face-to-face with a half-dozen bearded strangers. Their leader wore a hat low over his eyes and a sheepskin coat.

Too late, Bliss realized what a terrible mistake she'd made by leaving the safety of Jamie McKenna's side. She retreated a step, meaning to turn and run, but the man at the front of the pack had snatched her off the ground before she'd even completed the thought.

She landed in the saddle in front of him with a painful thump, and her precious satchel toppled to the ground, forgotten.

"You'd better let me go," she warned, operating on sheer bravado. "My—my husband will come looking for me."

"Will he now?" the ringleader taunted, the smell of him

47

filling Bliss with sickness and fear. "When he does, love, he'll find you some the worse for wear."

Bliss knew it was hopeless to struggle. The stranger was holding her in an inescapable grasp, and he'd spurred his mount to a brisk gallop. Even if she managed somehow to free herself and jump, she would almost certainly be trampled to death by the horses following behind.

Chapter 4 🌿

THE MAN WHO HELD BLISS CAPTIVE SMELLED INCREDIBLY BAD. OF course, she reflected, the blighter's personal hygiene was the least of her worries: she was being carried off into the night by a band of no-gooders, after all. She was cold, and she was weary.

And she was scared—oh, so very scared. Even a lifetime of marriage to Alexander Zate would have been preferable to the experiences that probably lay ahead of her now.

Unless she could escape.

Too soon, the riders reached a camp, hidden away in what appeared to be a canyon. There was a fire burning, and shadowy forms encircled it. Gruff greetings were called out and the man who'd taken Bliss prisoner released her so suddenly that she slipped from the horse's back to the ground.

One of the murky shapes huddled near the fire solidified into a man. "What's this? A lass?" He cupped a hand under Bliss's chin and she twisted away from him.

"Leave me alone!" she warned.

All the wastrels laughed. "Spirited little bit o' baggage, ain't she?" queried the man who'd carried Bliss in front of

49

him in the saddle. He reached out to rest a hand on her tumbledown, tangled hair, and she sidestepped him, angry as a hissing cat.

"Don't you touch me!"

Again, the dark camp seemed to rock with harsh laughter, and Bliss felt a choking terror as the full scope of the situation came home to her. The only weapon she had left was bravado, and she wielded it with the last shreds of her strength.

"Jamie McKenna will cut your livers out for this!" she cried in a loud and tremulous voice.

There was an unexpected silence, broken at last by the head cutthroat, the smelly giant in the sheepskin coat. "Who?" he asked, almost politely.

"My husband," Bliss answered, her chin high. "Mr. Jamie McKenna." All right, maybe Jamie wasn't her husband, she reasoned to herself, but this was no time to be splitting hairs. The situation was desperate.

"Shit," said the man who'd come forward from the fire to look Bliss over so insolently. "I don't believe this." He strode over to the giant and gave him a push. "Out of all the women in New Zealand, you've got to pick *McKenna's* to carry off?"

All of the sudden, the camp was in a flurry of activity. Men were gathering belongings, saddling horses, riding away. Incredibly, within the space of a few minutes, Bliss found herself standing beside the fire, abandoned. Forgotten.

Had circumstances been different, she would have considered it an affront. After pacing restlessly back and forth for a few minutes, Bliss finally sat down on a log and held out her hands to the campfire.

Jamie's arrival was hardly dramatic. He simply appeared out of the darkness, rounding the log and sitting beside Bliss.

"Some help you were," she said, with an offended sniff.

"If it had been up to you to save me, I'd be in a sorry state by now, wouldn't I?"

"I've been around for a while," he answered evenly. Bliss sensed that a struggle was going on inside him, but she didn't care to explore the matter.

She wondered if he'd heard her claim him as a husband, but didn't voice the question. Instead, she sighed and said, "Well, I guess we'd better be getting back to the inn."

Jamie made no move to rise from the log, and his voice was frighteningly quiet. "Do you 'ave any idea what those men were plannin' to do to you?"

Bliss gulped a mouthful of air. "Yes. But I'm safe now, aren't I? No thanks to you, I might add. At the very least, Jamie McKenna, you might have rescued me."

Jamie spread his hands wide, and even though Bliss had at last found the courage to look directly at him, she could not read his expression in the flickering light of the dying campfire. "There were a dozen of them. Do you think I'm stupid?"

Roundly annoyed, Bliss flew to her feet. The rapid motion made her dizzy, but even as she swayed, Jamie caught her by the hand and wrenched her downward, so that she was sprawled across his lap. For an instant, she was too stunned to react.

She felt the cold through her petticoat and drawers as he flung her coat and the skirt of her dress up, and in that moment the awful truth struck her. She was enraged, and began to twist and squirm, making a furious sound in the depths of her throat.

"I should 'ave speared you with that pitchfork when I 'ad the chance," Jamie rasped, subduing her with discouraging ease.

Bliss squeezed her eyes shut, bracing herself for the first stinging blow to her upended posterior.

It never arrived. Instead, with an exclamation of disgust, Jamie hurled her aside, so that she landed with an undignified thump on the ground. As her skirts were only inches from the fire, she snatched them out of harm's way before glaring up at the man who sat regarding her with infuriating calmness.

"How dare you!" she cried, disobliged beyond all bearing.

"The question is," Jamie inquired, rubbing his chin and frowning pensively, "what stopped me?"

The paralysis that had held Bliss in check was gone in that moment. She lunged at Jamie, not bothering to rise from her knees, both fists doubled up to hammer at his chest.

He caught her wrists in his hands and stayed the attack with a dismaying lack of effort. Gently, he drew Bliss forward, until she was trapped between his knees and her mouth was only inches from his, suspended there, waiting.

After muttering a curse, he kissed her, angrily at first, as a punishment, and then with an unrestrained hunger that set Bliss to aching for his possession. She would have given herself to him, then and there, if he'd pressed her, but he didn't.

In a sudden change of attitude, he shot to his feet, hauling a dazed Bliss roughly along with him. "Blisterin' you would 'ave been a better idea," he grumbled, half wrenching and half hurling her away from the fire and into the chilly darkness that surrounded its wavering glow.

Bliss had been through a great deal in recent days, and especially in the last few hours, and she was overwhelmed. Tears of unadulterated self-pity filled her eyes, and she made a small, despairing sound.

The sun was just rising over the sea, which glimmered in the distance, and Bliss could see the sorrel standing patiently in the brisk morning breeze, steam puffing from its nostrils as it snuffled a greeting to its master.

"H-how did you find me?" Bliss dared to ask.

"It was an accident," Jamie retorted, scowling at her from beneath the brim of his disreputable leather hat.

Her satchel was hooked over the saddle by its handle, and Bliss was as glad to see it as she would have been to encounter an old and sympathetic friend. She sniffed as Jamie continued to ignore her and began untying the sorrel's reins from a low tree branch.

"You might at least have the decency to ask if I'm all right," she pointed out.

Jamie didn't look at her. "I might, but I'm not going to," he responded crisply. "Consider yourself lucky, Duchess. If I'm inclined toward anything right now, it's plain, old-fashioned murder."

The dawn air was cool, and Bliss hugged herself, trying to keep warm. She could feel her tears drying on her face. "Jamie, I—" The words froze in her throat, nearly choking her. After an internal struggle, she tried again. "I—I'm sorry."

Without answering her, or meeting her eyes, Jamie helped her into the saddle and mounted behind her. She felt a delicious and entirely inappropriate sense of pleasure at his nearness.

They were making their slow and weary way back toward the inn before Jamie condescended to speak.

"What the hell did you say to those bleeders to send them packing like that?"

Bliss smiled, despite her exhaustion and the strange pain that Jamie's anger stirred within her. "I told them that my husband would cut out their livers," she replied.

Jamie was silent for a long moment, then, grudgingly, he gave a grunt of amusement. "May God have infinite pity on *that* poor bastard, wherever and whoever he may be."

Stung anew, Bliss sat up straighter and held more tightly to her satchel, which Jamie had no doubt found in the road when he'd gone out looking for her the night before. "As far as those rascals are concerned, that 'poor bastard' is none other than your own self, Mr. Jamie McKenna. They were either scared to death of you or understandably repelled by the mere mention of your name!"

The strong, gloved hands drew back on the reins and the sorrel came to a brisk stop. Jamie's voice rumbled past

Bliss's ear. "Maybe you'd prefer to walk back to the inn, Duchess, rather than suffer me company."

Bliss's chin jutted out. She was dizzy with weariness but far too proud to beg Jamie's indulgence. "The choice is yours, Mr. McKenna," she said with quiet dignity.

At a subtle, silent command, the horse bolted forward, moving at a trot, then a lope, then a gallop. Bliss held on as best she could, and by the time the inn came into sight, she was half sick with fatigue.

Jamie dismounted in the busy dooryard, ignoring the frank stares of those travelers standing outside, smoking and exchanging flasks. With a tenderness Bliss would not have dared to hope for only minutes before, he lifted her down and carried her toward the door. One of the stable-boys followed with Bliss's satchel, his eyes wide in his grubby face.

"Found 'er, did you?" was Dorrie's desultory comment as Jamie crossed the near-empty dining room where she was clearing tables, Bliss still cradled in his arms.

"Bring food and hot water for a bath," Jamie responded brusquely, proceeding toward the room at the rear of the building, beside the kitchen.

Bliss had never expected to see that particular chamber again. She uttered a sound of protest when Jamie dropped her unceremoniously onto the bed, then snuggled down to go to sleep.

"Oh, no you don't," Jamie protested, taking one of her hands and hauling her back to an upright position. "You're staying awake until you've had a bath and something to eat."

Having made this pronouncement, he began unbuttoning Bliss's now-grimy woolen coat. When he'd tossed that aside, he flipped her over like a pancake and began working at the fastenings of the evening dress she'd run away from Alexander in.

It seemed she was forever and always running away from someone or something. She yawned into the soft covers.

54

"I'd really rather sleep, if you don't mind."

Jamie gave her a smart slap on the rump. "And sleep you will, after you've had some food and a bath."

Bliss rolled over and sat up, indulging in another yawn. "I don't know why you're being irksome about this. I'm so very tired—"

"So am I," Jamie broke in resolutely. "And I'm not sharing a bed with a grubby little chit like you. You're a mess, Duchess."

Bliss's mouth dropped open and her eyes went wide.

Jamie grinned at her disgruntlement and stood to help Dorrie as she struggled into the room with a massive copper bathtub.

"She could 'ave used Mistress O'Malley's water," the servant grumbled. "But no-o-o-o. That ain't good enough for Miss Tall Snout, is it?"

Bliss shuddered and made a face. By then, Dorrie was distracted—she was admiring Jamie from behind as he positioned the bathtub near the fire and then began shedding his coat, hat, and gloves.

It was clear enough, from Dorrie's expression, that she'd learned to enjoy watching Jamie take off more than coats and gloves. Bliss knew a flash of bitter jealousy, and she glared at Jamie as he looked up and smiled at her.

He shrugged in reply to a question she hadn't asked and then said, "Dorrie will see you have all the hot water you need, won't you, love?" He started to give the serving woman an affectionate slap on the derriere, stopping just in time to prevent Bliss from scrambling off the bed and scratching his eyeballs right out of his head.

"I hate you!" she sputtered, the moment Dorrie had left the room.

"How do I get myself involved in these things?" Jamie asked, of no one Bliss could discern, and went out, closing the door quietly behind him.

It would have served him right if Bliss had gone to sleep right then, flouting his edict that she must have a bath if she was going to share a bed with him—as if she wanted to snuggle up with that insufferable lout! But the truth of the matter was that she was wide-awake, desperately hungry and longing for the soothing luxury of sinking into a tub of hot water.

Presently, Dorrie reentered the room, carrying a tray that contained the inevitable wedge of venison pie, a pot of strong, fragrant tea, and a jagged hunk of bread.

Bliss was so hungry that she fairly jerked the tray from the woman's hands.

The servant left without comment, returning sometime later with two huge buckets of steaming water. Jamie was directly behind her with two more.

They made a great ceremony of filling the bathtub, then Dorrie went out. Jamie lingered.

Bliss remembered that she was wearing only her underclothes and covered herself with a blanket snatched from the foot of the bed.

"Get out," she said clearly.

Jamie grinned and remained exactly where he was. He folded his arms across his chest. "If you're going to go around claiming me as a husband," he remarked, "the least you can do—the very least, Duchess—is let me help with your bath."

"My water is getting cold!" Bliss wailed.

One of Jamie's shoulders lifted in a halfhearted shrug. "Don't think I'm not sympathetic," he said.

It was quite clear that he wasn't.

Bliss's annoyance was unbounded. She scrambled off the bed, dragging her blanket along, stomped over to the bathtub, and summarily climbed in, underclothes and all.

With a great, furious splash, she sat down, sending water surging over both sides of the tub to pool on the floor. Some of it poured onto the hearth and sizzled as it was consumed by the fire blazing there.

Jamie stared at her in wonder for a moment, then strode

toward her, taking the blanket from her, flinging it aside. He took her hand and drew her to her feet, and Bliss didn't resist him.

Her camisole was drenched, and she knew it revealed her high, full breasts, but she did not cover herself. The hungry look in Jamie's eyes met some elemental need within her, and she was powerless against the primitive things she was feeling.

One of his hands strayed out to touch her breast, the thumb caressing a thinly veiled nipple. Bliss stood motionless, knowing that she should resist but unable to do so. She whispered Jamie's name and suddenly, cruelly, the spell was broken.

He withdrew as though her flesh had burned him and stormed out of the room, slamming the door as he went. Stricken and confused, weary to the point of exhaustion, Bliss wept as she peeled away her sodden underthings and tossed them aside.

She made short work of her bath and then, still feeling wounded but unable to cry anymore, she crept into bed like a wounded creature seeking refuge, snuggled down deep, and drew the covers up over her head. She was sound asleep in an instant.

Hours later, when the room was filled with the shadows of early evening, Bliss awakened, raising herself on one elbow. Jamie lay beside her, sprawled out on his stomach, the covers reaching only as high as his waist.

Bliss drew in her breath at the sight of the scars crisscrossing his back and then reached out, with a trembling finger, to trace the path of a mark that reached from his right shoulder blade to his left hip. Feeling sick all the way to the core of her soul, she counted.

The disfigurement could only have been caused by the lash. Twelve times Jamie had felt it slicing into his flesh . . .

Bliss squeezed her eyes shut and raised one hand to her mouth to suppress a moan of horror and of shared pain, and at that moment, Jamie awakened and rolled over onto his back. His blue eyes read her expression accurately and a wall seemed to rise up between them, invisible but real.

"Jamie," Bliss whispered brokenly, and all her feelings were contained in that single utterance.

He shifted his gaze to the ceiling and Bliss, realizing that her breasts were bare, lifted the covers to her throat. She couldn't help noticing the medallion he wore around his neck, affixed to a strip of weathered, discolored rawhide.

Tentatively, she reached out to touch it, just as she had touched his mutilated back. "What's this?"

Jamie closed his eyes, and there was a stubborn set to his jaw. Even before the silence lengthened, Bliss knew he didn't mean to answer.

She bent to squint at the words imprinted on the round piece of brass, now almost worn away. " 'Blessed—is he— who considereth—the poor.' " Bliss frowned. "The poor?"

"It's a beggar's badge," Jamie conceded, though he still wouldn't look at Bliss. "Are you satisfied?"

"No, I'm not," Bliss responded. "What in heaven's name is a beggar's badge?"

At last, Jamie opened his eyes, and in their depths Bliss saw remembered misery. "Back in Dublin, a priest—Father McDougal—gave it to me," he said, in a soft, faraway voice. "It gave me leave to beg."

Though she was an imaginative person, Bliss could not envision Jamie McKenna begging for anything. "Did you?" she asked, in a stricken, barely audible voice.

He chuckled, low in his throat, but both the sound and the expression on his face were totally devoid of humor. "Never 'ad to," he replied, gazing up at the ceiling again. "I was transported for stealin' before it came to that."

Bliss bit her lower lip. Transported. That explained the scarred flesh on his back.

She said nothing because nothing came to mind.

Jamie sat up, reaching out to take Bliss's chin very gently in his hand. "Don't," he said hoarsely.

Bliss was still gnawing at her lip, and he stopped her by caressing her mouth with his thumb. A shiver of need went through her, and at last she realized that she was naked, as was Jamie, and that they'd been sharing a bed for hours.

Jamie's eyes danced as he watched hot color climb up over her cheekbones; obviously, he knew precisely what she was thinking. "Nothing happened, Duchess," he pointed out. There were cheroots on the bedside table, and Jamie lit one with a wooden match.

Bliss was hardly reassured. She squirmed to the edge of the bed and then sat there, miserable with embarrassment, wondering how she could dress without exposing herself. The heated abandon she'd felt earlier, when she'd stood in the bathtub and Jamie had caressed her, was a thing of the past.

After considerable wriggling and wrenching, she managed to wrap another blanket around herself and stand up. Without once looking back at Jamie—indeed, she was trying to pretend that he didn't exist—she found her satchel, opened it, and took out the tweed skirt and shirt-waist she'd been saving to wear while seeking a position in Auckland, along with clean underclothes. Hastily, she dressed, all the while trying to shield herself behind the blanket.

When she turned around to face Jamie, he was sitting on the edge of the bed, wearing his trousers and buttoning up his shirt. He winked at her. "Everything's all right, Duchess," he assured her, with gruff tenderness. "I promise."

Bliss looked at the tumbled bed and swallowed painfully. Nothing had happened between her and Jamie, but it might as well have. If word of the time she'd spent with this man ever got back to any of the people she knew, she'd be ruined.

"Don't take me back, Jamie," she pleaded, without thinking first. "Please—I couldn't bear being married to Alexander—"

Jamie regarded her in thoughtful silence for a long time.

Then he said, unwillingly, as though the words were torn from him, "You are so beautiful."

No one had ever said that to Bliss before. With her fiery red hair and her freckles, she'd felt conspicuous, but never beautiful. She stood motionless, unable to speak, until Jamie held out his hand to her.

Like a sleepwalker, she went to him, and he drew her down to sit on his lap. Bending his head slightly, he nipped at the peak of one of her breasts with his teeth, and Bliss moaned. The sensation was exquisitely pleasurable, even though she was fully dressed.

A sharp rap at the door sent Bliss scrambling off Jamie's lap. Flushing with embarrassment, she found her brush in the depths of the battered satchel and began grooming her hair.

Jamie crossed the room and opened the door, and Dorrie came in, carrying yet another tray. "I've brought your supper, gov'nor," she said, simpering and batting her eyelashes at him. "Just like I said I would."

"There's a love," Jamie replied easily, taking the tray and sort of herding Dorrie back toward the door.

Dorrie wasn't about to be shepherded out—not, at least, before she'd said her piece. "There's some men out front," she confided, lowering her voice to a loud whisper, "askin' after you and 'er majesty 'ere."

Jamie's face went solemn, and Bliss stopped brushing her hair.

"What do they look like?" Bliss demanded to know. "And how many of them are there?"

Clearly, Dorrie preferred to deal directly with Jamie and ignore Bliss. "There's two of them," she told him earnestly. "One's tall, with 'air as red as this one's." She gestured distractedly toward Bliss before going on. "The other's a little bit of a man, with a paunch and bulgin' eyes and 'ardly no 'air at all."

Bliss's brush clattered to the floor as Jamie turned to give her a quizzical look. Before she could utter any kind of a warning, her father stepped into the room, followed by Alexander, who was as short and fat and old as ever.

"So," boomed the tall, redheaded lighthouse keeper. "It's true what I'm hearin'!"

Bliss's heart was thudding against the inside of her rib cage. She didn't dare look at Jamie, though her every instinct told her that he was braced for a fight. She lifted her chin, sent a silent prayer winging toward heaven, and asked, "How did you find me, Papa?"

Nils Stafford stared at his daughter with mingled grief and contempt in his eyes. Bliss had long since accepted the fact that he didn't love her, but that didn't stop the knowledge from hurting. "Never mind how I found you. What are you doin', sharin' a room with this blighter?" He gestured toward Jamie, who stood completely still and kept his peace.

Bliss swallowed hard. This was her chance to escape Alexander, once and for all, and she meant to grab it. With her right hand painfully clasping her left, she lied, "I thought Jamie loved me, Papa. I gave myself to him and now—now he won't do right by me."

Nils made a sound reminiscent of an enraged bull, while Jamie muttered a curse and followed that with a hoarse, "Now, just one damned minute—"

Bliss began to weep, copiously and with suitable drama. Wringing her hands, she paced and wailed, paced and wailed. Alexander sputtered ineffectually, Jamie cursed, and Nils drew a pistol from the inside pocket of his bulky coat.

Everyone fell silent at the sight of the weapon, except for Dorrie, who gave a little squeal of dismay and cried, "Don't shoot 'im, now, gov. 'E ain't a bad man, really—"

Bliss would have laughed out loud if she hadn't been holding her breath.

"Get a preacher," Nils said, and Dorrie scurried to obey.

Jamie swallowed visibly. "A preacher?" he echoed.

Nils looked as though he might be weakening, so Bliss let

out another agonized lament, and Alexander pulled out his handkerchief and dabbed at his forehead, muttering, "Oh dear, oh dear—"

Jamie, meanwhile, looked at Bliss with utter contempt. "Tell him, Duchess."

Bliss moved a step closer to her father. "We've been together for two nights now, Papa," she confessed, with proper pathos. "We've shared the same bed."

With the barrel of his pistol, Nils gestured toward the front of the inn. "The blokes out in the dinin' room, mate—they say you're a man of property. That true?"

Jamie sighed and gave Bliss a look fit to singe leather. "It's true," he admitted.

Nils smiled broadly. "Good," he said, and then he took out his pocket watch and frowned at it. "What do you suppose is keepin' that preacher?"

Chapter 5 🌿

"TRY AND UNDERSTAND," BLISS PLEADED IN AN URGENT WHISPER. "I'm desperate!"

A muscle in Jamie's cheek twitched, and he kept his eyes fixed on Nils Stafford, who was still waving the pistol. "That makes all the difference, Duchess," he said derisively. "Why didn't you say so before?"

Alexander dabbed at his nose with a lace-trimmed handkerchief and gave Bliss a wounded look. "I will, of course, expect to be reimbursed for all my expenditures."

Nils was glaring at Jamie. "Mr. McKenna will see to that—won't you, mate?"

Jamie rolled his eyes, but he made no move to escape the small room or to disarm Nils. It occurred to Bliss that he was being remarkably compliant, given the situation. "I'll double the amount," he said evenly, addressing Alexander now, "if you'll go ahead and marry her."

Bliss felt all the color drain from her face. Oh, she knew well enough that Jamie wasn't in love with her, but she'd thought he had more consideration for her feelings than this!

Alexander made a snuffling sound and shook his head. "It's too late for bargaining, Mr. McKenna," he said primly. "I never deal in used merchandise."

Several seconds passed before Bliss absorbed Alexander's meaning. When she did, she gave a cry of outrage and stormed toward him. "Used merchandise? How dare you

63

talk about me as though I were a pickle jar or a piece of furniture? I'm a *person,* with thoughts and feelings!"

Jamie reached out unexpectedly, caught Bliss by the cloth of her skirt, and wrenched her backward to his side. "Shrill little bugger, isn't she?" he asked companionably, assuming an expression of long suffering.

Her face hot and probably red, Bliss whirled on Jamie, one hand raised to administer the sound slap he deserved. Instead of submitting, however, he grasped her wrist before she could strike him and hauled her against his torso. It was like hitting a rock wall at a dead run; Bliss was rendered breathless.

"Time you learned who'll be wearin' the pants in this family, little lady," Jamie informed her, in a deliberately obnoxious drawl. "Time and past, in fact."

Bliss was dizzy with fury. Who the devil did this rounder think he was, anyway? "Let me go," she hissed, for Jamie's benefit alone, "or I swear I'll sew your left knee to your chin!"

His mouth moved suspiciously; Bliss caught the hint of a grin before his lips descended to hers and appropriated a fierce kiss. At once humiliated and consumed with her own inexplicable passion for this man, Bliss struggled at first and then submitted, having no choice in the matter.

She was still gasping for breath when Dorrie arrived with a dour-looking clergyman in tow. He was a skinny fellow with a cold-reddened nose, and his spectacles were steamed over.

Jamie looked skyward. "At any other time," he muttered, the brogue upon him, "there wouldn't 'ave been a preacher within screamin' distance."

The minister glanced suspiciously from Jamie to Bliss, his mouth drawn into a tight, hard line. It was clear that he suspected them of the grossest wrongdoing.

"If you please," he said, in crisp, no-nonsense tones, shooing the small congregation toward the front room of the inn.

Jamie and Bliss were positioned before the fireplace, where a homey blaze was crackling, and the sacred words were spoken. Only Dorrie, the housemaid, seemed profoundly moved by the ceremony; she twisted her apron into a handkerchief of sorts and sobbed with loud sentiment throughout.

The moment the wedding was over, Bliss turned to Jamie and whispered, "I'm sorry."

He gave her a look chilly as a winter wind at midnight and turned away as if to leave. Instead, he all but collided with Nils.

"I'll just have a word with you, if I might," Nils said, his tone laced with the kind of friendliness that lacerates. He was trying to maneuver his son-in-law aside, out of Bliss's hearing. "You don't mind, do you, mate—since we're family and all?"

Jamie's gaze sliced to Bliss and then returned disdainfully to her father's face. "Anything you have to say to me can be said in front of my—dear wife."

Bliss felt color rise in her face. Jamie had spoken with a cruel sort of gentleness, and his words had left her wounded. She was anxious to be alone with her "husband" and explain to him that his life didn't need to change and neither did hers. Since there was no question of consummating the marriage, they could obtain an annulment in Auckland and then go their separate ways.

"There's the little matter of Mr. Zate's expenses, and my own," Nils said, not even having the decency to be embarrassed. Not for the first time, Bliss reflected that it was little wonder her mother had run off to America with a man who wrote poetry and played the mouth harp.

Jamie's look was level and steady, never wavering from Nils's face. "If you think I'm going to reward you for doing this to me, you're dead wrong," he said flatly.

Though he was big and strong, with little reason to fear any other man, Nils retreated a step. He didn't seem so sure himself now, and his normally ruddy complexion paled. "I don't see any need to be unreasonable," he complained, in a near whine.

Clearly, Jamie was a man to press an advantage when he had one. He inclined his head slightly in Nils's direction and once again prevailed. "You 'aven't yet learned the meanin' of the word *unreasonable*, me friend," he said.

Intimidated by Jamie, Nils turned his ire on Bliss. She was afraid of her father, with good reason, and her heart surged into her throat at the look in his eyes.

In a lightning-swift movement of his hand, Nils entangled his fingers in Bliss's hair and pulled hard. "You were never anything but trouble—" he began. "You're no better than that slut of a mother of yours!"

Jamie's intervention was as much a surprise to Bliss as it was to her father. A knife materialized in his hand, so quickly that it seemed to appear out of nowhere, and the point of the blade made a nasty-looking indentation at the base of Nils's throat.

"Unless you fancy comin' up short a few pints of blood, mate," he warned, in that dangerous undertone that was rapidly becoming familiar to Bliss, "don't ever do that again."

Nils released Bliss, with a spasmodic motion of his hand, and the wicked-looking blade was withdrawn from his throat.

"Now, see here," protested Alexander, albeit belatedly. "This is a public inn and you, Mr. McKenna, have no right—"

Jamie's knife made a whistling sound that chilled Bliss to the bone as it flew through the air and landed, with a reverberating thump, squarely between Alexander's expensively shod feet. Bliss's knees felt weak, and she sagged onto a bench beside a nearby trestle table, one hand rising briefly to her forehead. Merciful heavens, she'd gone and married a ticket-of-leave man, a criminal.

It did appear that she might have gotten herself into more trouble than she had the wits to deal with.

"Get out," Jamie said coldly, and no one in the huge and drafty room had the slightest question in their mind who he was talking to.

Nils was clearly enraged, but he gestured to Alexander and, together, they left. It was now completely dark outside, and Bliss knew a moment's trepidation. Nobody was more aware than she was of how many perils could befall those foolish—or desperate—enough to go abroad at night.

She shifted uneasily on the bench, afraid to speak.

"You was a bit 'ard on 'em, Jamie boy," protested Dorrie, and there was an intimacy in the remark that distracted Bliss, however momentarily, from the immediacy of her situation. "It's cold out there, and it's dark."

"So it is," Jamie conceded. "Be a love, Dorrie, and fetch them back." For the first time, he seemed aware of the travelers seated at the tables around the dining hall. "Ale for everybody," he added as a generous afterthought.

A coarse cheer rose and, before Bliss could decide what to do next, Jamie's fingers closed inescapably around the nape of her neck. He drew her to her feet as easily as a fiddler draws music from a violin, and even though he caused her no pain at all, she couldn't remember being more uncomfortable.

"You and I, my love," he said, "are going to have a word or two—in private." With that, Jamie propelled Bliss across the dining room, lewd cries of encouragement rising on every side, since the crowd entirely misread the bridegroom's intentions.

At least, Bliss hoped they did.

They proceeded down the hall and into their room, and Jamie kicked the door closed behind them with the heel of one boot.

"I've been waiting for a chance to explain," Bliss was quick to say. Jamie had at last released his hold on her, and she retreated a few steps, only to feel the foot of the bed come up hard against the back of her legs.

"Oh, I'll just bet you have," Jamie said, with an unnerving

tone of indulgence in his voice. Bliss hadn't missed the fact that his jawline had gone tight again and his eyes were glittering, and she was careful to keep her distance.

She swallowed hard, remembering Jamie's shady past and his deftness with a blade, and eased to one side so that the bed no longer barred her retreat. "I beg you, just take me to Auckland—o-or Wellington. An annulment should be easy to get, given the fact that we're not—we won't—" Bliss paused to swallow again, miserably embarrassed. "In any case, I can still travel to America and you can go on about your business."

Jamie held up both hands, palms out. "Wait a minute. It seems to me, Duchess, that you're assumin' a great deal. After all, as your 'usband, I've got me rights."

Bliss bit down on her lower lip. She'd known Jamie McKenna for only a very short time, but she already knew that, when he fell into the brogue, his mood was generally uncharitable. "Rights?" she whispered, fairly choking on the word.

He folded his muscular arms. "Aye, Duchess," he replied. "Rights."

"I don't know what you mean," Bliss lied valiantly.

Jamie smiled a slow, obnoxious smile. "I think you do," he replied. He shifted, placing his hands on his hips, and looked pensive for a few moments. "I'm going out and celebrate me weddin' with a mug or two," he announced presently. "When I come back, I'll be expectin' you to be in bed and ready."

Bliss's throat tightened painfully. Granted, she'd felt longing for this man hardly more than an hour before, but that had passed. Now, she was cornered, and more than a little afraid. If she didn't submit to this stranger who was her husband, would he force her?

Jamie gave Bliss a lingering look and then went out. She was reminded of a fairy tale she'd loved as a child: Rumplestiltskin. She'd been left, in a manner of speaking, to spin straw into gold, but no temperamental elf was going to come along and help her. She was on her own.

A sudden rap at the door made her start. She was almost expecting that elf when she turned the knob and pulled.

Dorrie was standing on the threshold, her eyes puffy and red from crying, a stack of clean sheets in her arms. "I've come to make the bed ready," she said, quite unnecessarily.

Bliss thought quickly as she stepped aside to admit the maid. Dorrie began stripping the blankets and sheets from the mattress, sniffling loudly as she worked.

"I never thought I'd be makin' up a marriage bed for me own sweet Jamie boy," the servant lamented. "Never."

Cautiously, Bliss approached. A flicker of jealousy moved in her heart, but she quelled it with her considerable will. This was no time to be worrying about Jamie's romantic history. He'd probably tumbled many a serving girl in his time, and if Bliss were to start fretting over the number, she'd get nothing done for counting.

"You've known my—my husband for a time?" she asked.

After making a truly disgusting sound to clear her clogged nose, Dorrie nodded. "Aye—I knew Jamie long before 'e became a man o' property, I did. Things was better, I swear, when 'e wasn't above pickin' a pocket now and again. It's ruined 'im, bein' rich."

Bliss suppressed a smile. In a little while, Jamie was going to come through that door planning to deflower her, in this very bed. She certainly had nothing to smile about. "Jamie was a pickpocket?" she asked, wondering at her own surprise. After all, he'd told her that he'd been transported for stealing.

"That he was, mum," Dorrie answered, without pausing in her work. "And worse."

Bliss couldn't help remembering how those thugs had flown in every direction at the mere mention of Jamie's name, abandoning her in their camp the night before. "What changed him?" she asked in a soft voice.

Dorrie gave a moist sigh. "Well, missus, it 'appened when 'E went to Australia, two, maybe three years ago. Somebody bested 'im in a fight, I think—'e 'as a nasty scar on 'is arm, you know. I wasn't none too clear'eaded when Jamie was about, though, so I couldn't tell you exactly what 'appened. 'E ain't one for explainin' such things, neither."

Bliss drew a deep breath. Dorrie's sympathies surely lay with Jamie, though she might be a sort of hostile ally, considering the circumstances. "I have to escape, Dorrie," she confided, "and I need your help."

The pillow Dorrie had been fluffing fell from her arms, and she looked at Bliss with enormous eyes and a mouth rounded into a horrified *O*.

Bliss glanced back over one shoulder at the door, all too aware that Jamie might return at any moment. A part of her yearned for that, and for the conquering that would inevitably follow, but Bliss took her emotions firmly in hand and pressed, "If you could just—just invite him to your room or something. That would give me time to take one of the horses and get away."

Dorrie's mouth finally closed, but she looked pale and her eyes were still big as saucers. "You want me to bed Jamie—your own 'usband—and this your weddin' night?"

The very thought caused Bliss incomprehensible pain, but she refused to give in to her baser instincts. For the moment, however, she could not speak.

Dorrie looked appalled. "Didn't you learn nothin', mum, by what 'appened last night?"

Bliss shivered with remembered terror, but quickly recovered her self-control. Given Jamie's anger over being forced into a marriage he hadn't wanted, the two situations weren't so different. It was a matter of numbers, that was all: she was about to be thoroughly used by one man instead of a dozen.

"Do you want to help me or not?" she countered.

A certain mischievous lechery was shining in Dorrie's swollen eyes. "Well, it ain't a 'alf nasty job, pleasin' that man," she mused.

Bliss's cheeks burned hot. Even though she had only the vaguest knowledge of what it meant to "please" a man, she hated the idea of someone else rendering the service to Jamie. "What's your answer?" she demanded. "May I count on you or not?"

Dorrie extended one chafed and callused hand to seal the unholy bargain. "Aye, Mistress McKenna. When Jamie's proper into 'is cups, I'll lead 'im upstairs."

Bliss gathered the few belongings she'd taken from her satchel earlier and repacked them, feeling the need to make preparations even though it might be a long time before it was safe to leave. "How will I know when you've—when you and Jamie are t-together?"

Dorrie paused in the doorway. "My room is right above this one, love," she said, with a sort of coy smugness in her voice and in her face. "You'll know when you 'ear a ruckus."

Bliss fought down an urge to cross the rough wooden floor and box Dorrie's ears. She'd made her choice and she must abide by it. After all, she could not both go to America and stay in New Zealand with Jamie McKenna.

Still, she felt tears gathering in her throat as she proudly turned her back, waiting for Dorrie to go on about the business of seducing the one man Bliss had ever truly wanted.

A full hour passed before Bliss heard the promised hubbub upstairs. With tears stinging her eyes, she took her satchel into her hand and, for the second time in twenty-four hours, opened the window and climbed outside.

This night was darker than the one before had been, and it was only her proficient memory that guided Bliss around the side of the inn, along the splintery fence of the paddock, and into the stables.

There were lanterns burning there, and the two lads who had been so eager to look after Jamie's horses were sitting in one flickering cone of light, playing a game of cards. Bliss caught her breath and receded into the shadows near the rear door.

71

Not once, for all her hysterical planning, had she considered the possibility that the stables might be occupied by anyone with fewer than four legs. For the next minute or so, not a single useful thought entered her head.

It didn't help that the stableboys seemed to be talking about Jamie. "I've seen 'im use the blade before. The big man and the fop—they was wise not to vex 'im more'n they did."

The other lad agreed, and then luck turned in Bliss's favor. Someone in the distance began beating on the bottom of a kettle or pot, and both boys leaped up eagerly at the sound. Clearly, the inn's cook was summoning them to their evening meal.

Bliss remained in the darkness, careful not to breathe until the boys had passed her by and rounded the corner of the building. Then, moving as quickly and quietly as she could, she set down her satchel and took up the lantern the boys had been using, creeping past each stall in the stable in a frustrating effort to recognize the sorrel and the bay that belonged to Jamie McKenna.

Presently, she found the sorrel, though it was hard to be absolutely certain. After all, she could see nothing more than the tail and haunches. She had just set down the lantern and was fumbling to open the stubborn catch on the stall when the voice sounded, startling her so that her heart nearly stopped beating.

"Goin' out for a ride, are you, Duchess?" Jamie asked.

Bliss whirled, one hand rising to her throat. She felt both terror at being caught and wild relief that Jamie was not in that room above their own, making a "ruckus" with Dorrie. She tried to speak and failed.

To her utter surprise, Jamie's white teeth flashed in a smile shadowed by the night and by the brim of his leather hat, and his hands came out to rest lightly on her waist. In the next instant, he pulled her close and bent his head to brush her lips with his own.

The sensation was tantalizing, delicious, and completely

frightening. Bliss felt her breasts, hidden away beneath her coat and dress and underthings, fill with some warm nectar as they met with the hard contours of Jamie's chest.

"I—I was going to America," Bliss said lamely, her mouth still touching Jamie's.

His laugh was gruff and gentle. "Where else?" he muttered.

A sort of grinding ache had begun in the secret place where Bliss's femininity was hidden. "It really would be simpler if you'd just let me go," she told him as the tip of his tongue played at the corners of her mouth and promised other mysterious pleasures.

Jamie lifted Bliss slightly and thrust her forward, so that she was pressed against him. She made a soft whimpering sound as he kissed her at last, thoroughly and with all the passion of a husband about to lay claim to his rights. A trembling began in Bliss's thighs and spread to her knees, which would barely support her. Jamie caught her as she sagged toward the floor, whisking her deftly up into his arms.

"It would serve you right, Duchess, if I made love to you right 'ere," he vowed hoarsely.

Bliss was well beyond the point where she could protest. Wherever Jamie chose to take her, she knew she would submit. Gladly. "I th-thought you were in Dorrie's room," she said inanely as Jamie put out the lantern and then shifted her weight in his arms and started toward the door of the stables.

She saw his smile in the darkness and read a confidence there that would have annoyed her completely at any other time.

"That's what I wanted you to think," he replied. "Dorrie's been me friend for a long time, love."

Bliss felt a fleeting, hopeless sort of rage. "She told you everything!" she exclaimed.

Jamie nodded as they approached the front door of the inn, and Bliss, hitherto floating in a sea of physical and emotional sensation, suddenly came surging to the surface of rational thought. In another moment or so, Jamie would carry her through the public dining room, like pirate's loot, and everyone would know what he meant to do.

"Stop!" she cried, kicking her feet.

Jamie didn't so much as hesitate. He took the steps as though they were nothing and crossed the crude wooden porch. One of the boys from the stable accommodatingly opened the door from the inside and light spilled over the brigand and his captured bride.

Bliss buried her face in Jamie's neck, humiliated beyond all bearing, when the diners laughed and called out the odd suggestion. She would have sworn she'd heard one or two of those voices in the robbers' camp the night before, but even that disturbing thought could not distract Bliss from the mortification of what was happening.

It seemed to Bliss that an eternity passed before they'd reached their room again. Once the door was closed, Jamie released his bride, at the same time flinging her satchel onto the bed. Without taking his eyes from Bliss's burning face, he took off his hat and tossed it aside, then shed his coat and gloves.

Bliss turned away before he could advance to his shirt or his trousers, and Jamie's response was a gruff chuckle.

"Tell me, Duchess," he asked, in a near whisper, his hands closing gently on Bliss's rigid shoulders. "Were you so anxious to get away from me that you'd chance meetin' your admirers again?"

Bliss thought of the men who'd captured her when she'd made her last bid for freedom and shuddered to think what they might have done to her if it hadn't been for this man and the remarkable terror he inspired. "I don't think anyone could be that unlucky," she answered in a small voice. "Not even me."

Gently, Jamie turned Bliss around to face him. He was unbuttoning her coat—and avoiding her eyes—when he said, "I was only teasin' earlier, love, when I told you to be

74

in bed and ready. I'd never take you unless you were willin'."

Bliss was touched. She was also tired and overwhelmed. Her eyes brimmed with unaccustomed tears—she was not one to cry easily or often. "The trouble is," she whispered, "you can so easily make me willing, Mr. McKenna."

Jamie smiled sadly and planted a soft kiss on her forehead. "How you flatter me, Duchess," he scolded, sliding her coat back off her shoulders and down her arms. It fell, forgotten, to the floor. "You've never been with a man, have you?"

He made the words sound almost like a reprimand and, however foolishly, Bliss wished for a moment that she could lay claim to at least one scandalous assignation. Since she couldn't, she simply shook her head.

"Saints be praised," Jamie said under his breath, and then he began unfastening the buttons of Bliss's prim shirtwaist. She stood powerless, speechless, as he pulled the blouse free of her skirt. Only a moment later, she was standing before him in her thin camisole.

He paused to caress her breasts, first one and then the other, his touch making Bliss's blood surge hotly through her veins and causing her nipples to harden and turn dark.

"A-are you going to h-have me?" she whispered as he removed her good tweed skirt, which was closely followed by her petticoat.

Jamie bent his head to taste the tender skin at the place where Bliss's neck and shoulder met, chuckling at the shiver and soft moan she could not suppress. "I mean to teach you pleasure," he said in a low, hoarse voice. "As to the other, Duchess—that decision belongs to you."

Bliss's heart beat faster when she felt the worn ribbons at the front of her camisole give way to Jamie's fingers, and heat washed over her in crushing waves as she was bared to him for the first time.

Chapter 6

Bliss had no memory of walking or being carried to the bed; instead, she felt as though she had been hurled there by a hurricane wind. There was no breath in her lungs, and her eyes and ears perceived only dimly, so dazed was she by the power this man had over her.

A delighted whimper broke from Bliss as Jamie stretched out beside her and continued to caress her breast. A strange, compelling heat was building within her, gathering strength with every pass of Jamie's skillful fingers. She was certain that the loving could get no better than this, certain that she would explode at any moment.

It was just then that he bent his head and encircled one taut, puckered nipple with the tip of his tongue, surprising Bliss with a new joy. She gasped, entangling her fingers in his tarnished-gold hair, and arched her back.

A throaty chuckle penetrated the fog of enchantment sheltering Bliss from the realities of the world. Somehow, Jamie knew what she'd been thinking, and he proved it by whispering, "This is only the beginning, Duchess. Only the beginning."

Bliss murmured something senseless, still holding Jamie close, but when he suckled, she couldn't help moaning like a person racked with fever. The sense of thrumming suspense within her grew in magnitude until it was nearly unbearable, but Jamie would not be lenient; instead, he traveled a path of soft kisses to the breast he had not yet won and submitted that tender softness to the same excruciating pleasure its twin had known.

Fairly delirious by that time, Bliss began to toss and writhe on the bed, even though the last thing she wanted was to escape this man's persistent attentions. When he added a new element to her sweet torment by deftly working her drawers down to midthigh and then touching her in that place where no one had ever touched her before, the exultation was so great that Bliss's reason fled. She tilted her head far back in utter abandon, while her heels dug into the mattress with the ferocity of her effort to raise herself to Jamie in proud acquiescence. Her hands left his hair to tear wildly at her drawers, which prevented the absolute vulnerability she craved.

Jamie was still absorbed in the breast he was enjoying, but with a husky, fevered cry of his own, he grasped the skimpy muslin bloomers in one hand and freed Bliss of their bondage with a single, swift motion of his hand. She heard them rip and did not care. Cool air washed over her bare skin, but instead of soothing her, it only increased her frenzy.

Round and round Jamie's fingers moved in the moist warmth of her femininity, each pass causing Bliss's hips to soar higher. Presently, he released her nipple from the pleasant teasing of his tongue and lips and began kissing her belly. The strokes of his hand grew slower and slower until she sank, quivering, to lie still on the mattress, terrified that he would abandon her before the mysterious pinnacle she'd been climbing toward had been reached.

"Oh, Jamie, please," Bliss whispered, unsure of what she

was pleading for, but so desperate to obtain it that begging was no longer beneath her.

His fingers shifted, so that he was holding her open, like a flower, exposing the bud hidden away beneath. When his mouth suddenly closed over her, the pleasure was so savage that Bliss flung her arms back over her head to grasp the iron rails of the bedstead in frantic fingers and gave a hoarse, lusty groan. Of their own accord, her hips began rising and falling, writhing and twisting from side to side, but Jamie followed, unshakable, drawing Bliss over the edge of a great precipice. Shuddering wildly, she soared on wings of ecstasy for long, breathless moments, then began to drift softly toward earth, where Jamie awaited her.

She was weeping when she reached him, and her arms went out to pull at his shirt, wanting to strip it from him. Instinctively, she knew that Jamie's own desire would tear at him like the talons of some great, fierce bird until he had been gratified.

The swiftness of his withdrawal had the impact of a slap across the face. Muttering curses, Jamie bounded off the bed and turned away, his broad shoulders moving as he drew in rapid, gasping breaths.

Bliss sat up slowly, conscious of her nakedness now that Jamie had left her. She groped until she caught hold of a fold in the blanket and used the thick, woolly cloth to cover herself. "What is it?" she whispered.

Jamie rasped another curse and thrust the splayed fingers of one hand through his rumpled hair.

"Jamie?" Bliss pressed, feeling more bereft than she had at any time since her mother's death.

He was unable—or unwilling—to look at her, and his voice, when he spoke, was hoarse. "If we go on," he said, after a silence so long that it was agonizing to suffer through, "there'll be no annulment."

Few things Jamie might have said could have wounded Bliss more. In the heat of their loving, her desire to be anywhere but at this man's side had been seared away like dry grass in the path of a raging fire. Now, he was telling her that this wonderful, ferocious intimacy they'd shared had changed nothing.

She drew a deep breath in an effort to steady herself. "Oh," was all she could manage to say, and the word sounded hollow. Weak.

Again, Jamie shoved a hand distractedly through his hair. "I need a drink," he said, and then, without once looking back at Bliss, who still cowered on the bed, he left the room.

The tears Bliss had been struggling to hold back broke free, sliding down her cheeks and dripping ingloriously off her chin. Something terrible had happened. Somewhere, in the tangled confusion of all her plans and intentions, she had made a tragic mistake.

She had fallen in love with Jamie McKenna.

Jamie did not return to his bride that night, though she awaited him, listening for his footsteps between bouts of crying. At dawn, Bliss was finally desperate enough to go in search.

Hastily, she gathered up her rumpled shirtwaist, petticoat, and tweed skirt, which had been tossed aside the night before, and put them on. Since her drawers were hopelessly torn, Bliss took another pair from her satchel and shimmied into them, and although she gave her hair a quick brushing, she was too hurried to pin it up. She crept into the hallway, just in time to see Dorrie come out of the kitchen, carrying a tray and humming happily as she headed toward the dining room. There was a certain sway to the woman's sumptuous hips that, coupled with an obviously cheery mood, caused Bliss to approach the stairway and look up.

Dorrie's room was directly above hers; the serving girl had said so herself.

Full of despair and desperate hope that her suspicions were wrong, Bliss started tentatively up the stairs. She had progressed only a step or two when Jamie suddenly appeared on the upper floor, tucking his shirttails into his trousers as he started down.

He stopped cold, a look of wary puzzlement in his eyes, while Bliss stared up at him, too horrified to speak. The most she could do was pray silently that she wouldn't humiliate herself by bursting into tears.

"Duchess—" Jamie began, in a low, grating voice.

Bliss could not bear to hear him lie to her. The blunt and terrible truth was that he had turned to Dorrie for what he'd refused to take from his own wife.

With a lift of her chin, Bliss took her skirt in one hand and retreated back down the stairs. "You needn't explain," she said, longing to tear her gaze from Jamie's but unable to manage the feat.

He hesitated, looking worried, and then shrugged and spread his hands slightly. "Aye, love—as always, you're right. I'll not be explainin'."

"Very well," Bliss agreed stiffly, and at last she was able to turn and walk away. It was a good thing that Jamie didn't follow, for her eyes were very moist.

"Blast and damnation," Bliss muttered to herself, dashing away tears with the heels of her palms as she took refuge in the room where she'd been brought so near to full womanhood and then abandoned on the brink. All her father's neglect and cruelty hadn't been enough to reduce her to tears, yet Jamie McKenna had managed to do it several times in the short course of their acquaintance.

Bliss slammed the door hard and leaned back against it, as if to keep out all the contradictory feelings Jamie had stirred to life within her. Of course, it was too late for protective measures. She was bonded, perhaps for all eternity, to a man who had no use for her.

There was a tap at the door, startling Bliss so that she leaped away and then asked in a tremulous voice, "Who's there?"

"It's me, Mistress McKenna," sang Dorrie's voice. She

sounded so happy that Bliss wanted to slap her. "Open up now, for I 'ave your breakfast."

Rare was the trauma that could sour Bliss's appetite. Slender though she was, she was almost continuously hungry—like a shark, her father had been fond of saying. She wrenched open the door, scowling hatefully, and Dorrie came swishing and swaying through the opening, face glowing, eyes alight.

She set the tray down on the bedside table and chirped, "Can't think why you'd want to eat in 'ere, all alonelike and everything."

Bliss only glared at her.

"Be about it," Dorrie ordered, making a shooing motion at Bliss with her apron. "Jamie boy, 'e's wantin' to be on the road while the sun's shinin'."

Bliss turned her head, gazing blindly at the spectacular view of the inn's barnyard. "I imagine you know all about what Jamie wants, don't you?" she reflected, only realizing that she'd spoken aloud when it was too late.

"That I do, mistress," Dorrie replied, and that smug note was back in her voice. "That I do indeed."

Bliss took a slice of bacon from her plate and shoved it into her mouth, mostly to keep from answering. Heaven knew, she'd made enough of a fool of herself as it was, writhing and moaning for Jamie McKenna like a wanton, then as much as admitting defeat to the woman he'd preferred over her.

Dorrie slipped out, leaving the new Mrs. McKenna to her singular miseries and her breakfast.

Jamie was hungry, and he knew the day ahead would be long and difficult, but he could not bring himself to eat. His throat closed whenever he so much as looked at the food lying untouched on his plate.

Images of Bliss spun in his mind, shifting and changing like the bits of colored glass in a kaleidoscope. Just remembering the way she'd entrusted herself to him the night before made him ache all over. He lifted his mug of coffee to his mouth and then set it down again, with a resounding thump, knowing that he would never be able to swallow the stuff.

His jaw clenched tight as he relived—for perhaps the dozenth time—his encounter with Bliss, on the stairs, earlier that morning. He knew that she believed he'd spent the night with Dorrie, and it took all the forbearance he possessed not to go to her and correct the misconception.

It would be better for Bliss, and much easier in the long run, if she went on thinking that he'd betrayed her. Jamie let out a long sigh and ran a hand through his hair. That hissing, spitting little hellcat probably wouldn't appreciate the sacrifices he'd made over the past eight or ten hours, even if she knew about them.

On the far side of the dining room, Dorrie was flirting with Nils Stafford. Jamie smiled. He'd wondered what—or who—accounted for the girl's bright mood that morning. Now he knew.

His smile faded to a scowl. It galled Jamie to know that Stafford had probably been in ecstasy all night while he'd tossed and turned in an agony of wanting. Lost in his various sufferings, he was unprepared for the sudden appearance of Alexander Zate on the bench opposite his own.

Zate looked haggard and rumpled, and there were deep shadows under his bulbous eyes. It was clear enough that he'd had no more sleep than Jamie, and probably for much the same reason.

A stubborn, hot-tempered, redheaded reason.

"I've often thought," Zate began philosophically, "that whoever named that woman ought to have been shot for falsehood in the first degree."

In spite of himself, and the hellish night he'd just passed, Jamie had to smile, though he said nothing.

Zate was clearly reading the signs of sleeplessness in Jamie's face. "Perhaps, given the distinct pleasures of the marriage bed," he said sadly, "the name 'Bliss' is more suited to the lady than one might think."

Jamie had been beginning to like Alexander Zate, at least a little. The presumptuous nature of the man's remark forestalled that worthy emotion. "Is there a point to this conversation," he asked coldly, "or are you just tired of livin'?"

With a bleak smile, Zate held up one pasty hand in a bid for peace. "Contrary to what you—and probably the young lady herself—might believe, I would have been a very good husband to Bliss. I am a wealthy man, and not disposed to the same unkindnesses as her father."

Jamie's interest was caught. Since his throat had opened again, he took a sip from his coffee, found it cold, and frowned in distaste. "What unkindnesses?" he demanded.

Zate shrugged, but there was compassion in his face. Jamie assessed him to be a weak man, but not a cruel one. "She hasn't told you?"

Jamie shook his head and, for just a fraction of a second, his gaze strayed to the lighthouse keeper, who was laughing with Dorrie on the other side of the room. "We 'aven't 'ad much time for talkin'," he muttered.

The pain in Zate's face made it clear that he'd misunderstood the remark, and Jamie did not correct him. There came a point when such mercies only made matters worse.

"Stafford's long been anxious to be rid of the girl," Zate confided, for God only knew what reason. "He's made no bones about it, and I suspect that he's beaten her on occasion."

Jamie felt a surging, choking rage rise in his throat like bile. Not since he'd been forced to stand still for Increase Pipher's lash had he known such hatred. He was possessed by it. "That's not a charge that should be made lightly," he said as Dorrie came swishing toward him to replace his cold coffee with a hot, fresh mugful.

His mood softened slightly. God bless her, Dorrie did know what a man liked.

Zate sighed as Jamie watched the serving girl walk away with a sort of weary appreciation in his eyes. "At least," Bliss's would-be husband pointed out, "I would have been faithful."

Jamie was instantly angry. It was bad enough that he'd had to let Bliss believe she'd married a man without honor. He would not endure even the implication from anyone else.

He knotted his right hand into a fist and slammed it down onto the tabletop, causing cups, plates, and utensils to rattle. But before he could give voice to his ire, Bliss herself appeared at his side, carrying her satchel and groomed for traveling.

"I'm ready to leave now," she said, in a clear voice.

Jamie was embarrassed at the interest displayed by everyone else in the dining room, as well as annoyed that Alexander Zate had remembered to stand up in the presence of a lady while he hadn't. Belatedly, he rose to his feet.

"Sit down," he told his wife, in a somewhat strangled undertone.

There was a defiant snap in Bliss's blue, blue eyes, and a bright pink flush glowing behind her freckles. "Yes, Mr. McKenna," she replied, making no effort to moderate her tone.

Jamie was painfully aware of the attention focused on this domestic tidbit. He supposed everyone in the place knew that he hadn't spent the night with his bride, and that awareness galled him almost as much as Bliss's scathing obedience.

He glared at her, and she sank to the bench, setting her satchel on the floor with a plunk.

"Did you sleep well, pet?" Alexander asked cordially, his bulging gaze fixed on Bliss.

She gave Jamie a sidelong look that could only have been described as hateful as he sat down again. "Yes," she answered, in a voice designed to carry. "I slept very well, thank you."

This statement elicited a variety of muttered comments from the populace of the dining room.

Jamie, who had just lifted his coffee mug, set it down again with a crash. Above all things, he hated to have his privacy breached and, after giving Bliss a look of undiluted fury, he stood, collected his coat and hat from the row of pegs on the wall behind him, and strode out of the inn to hitch up the team.

It was time he and his new wife started home.

"Do you love him?" Alexander asked gently.

Bliss had been watching Jamie's abrupt exit with her soul in her eyes, but she turned her attention back to the man her father had wanted her to marry, surprised by his question. "Yes," she answered miserably.

"He's only getting the wagon ready, you know," Mr. Zate assured her. Amazingly, he'd discerned her fear that Jamie was planning to leave the inn without her.

Bliss sighed. Out of the corner of her eye, she saw her father approaching, and that made her eager to be away. She moved to stand up, but she was too late.

Nils Stafford put one of his huge, heavy hands on her shoulder and forced her back down. "Not so fast," he said.

Alexander was flushed with indignation. "Now, see here—" he sputtered.

Nils's fingers now held Bliss's chin in a painful grasp. He paid no attention at all to his friend's protests. "You be good to that husband of yours, lass," he warned. "And you see that he's good to your old papa."

Bliss swallowed hard, longing to twist free of Nils's grip but afraid to try. It was a sin to hate her own father, she knew, but she couldn't seem to help it. "Jamie's a stubborn man," she said evenly. "And he's not very fond of you."

"If you're smart," Nils replied with a cold smile, "you'll make sure he knows what a fine, generous father I was."

"I must insist that you release this woman!" Alexander

cried, shooting to his full and thoroughly unimpressive height.

To everyone's surprise, Nils obeyed, though it was surely through no fear of his traveling companion. Perhaps he felt that he'd made his point.

Bliss hastened to her feet, took up her satchel, and fled the inn, hoping that she'd never see that place, or her father, again.

Yes, she assured herself as she hurried toward the stableyard, where Jamie was harnessing the team in the cool morning light, her life would be different from now on. She'd get this unfortunate marriage annulled as soon as she could get to Auckland—her Aunt Calandra would help her.

And once she was legally free again, she'd get that position she'd been dreaming of and work her way to America. She smiled to herself as she approached the man who had inadvertently become her husband.

Her mother was waiting in San Francisco, California. Come hell or high water, Bliss meant to join her there.

Jamie's eyes were watchful, and he made no effort at conversation until they'd traveled a considerable distance along the road that curved by the edge of the sea. The knife he was so adept at using was lying on the wagon seat instead of in its scabbard.

Bliss felt a shiver of fear roll down her spine. "A-are we in danger?" she dared to ask.

His lips curved into a smile, but his gaze was solemn. "Anything can happen, Duchess," he said quietly. And then Jamie bent his head to look a little closer at her chin. "Is that a bruise?" he demanded.

A bruise was a bruise and Bliss didn't see how she could deny what was plain for him to see. She sighed. "Papa thinks pain improves my hearing," she answered, avoiding Jamie's eyes.

He drew back hard on the reins, at the same time calling out to the horses, and the cumbersome wagon rattled to a stop beside the road. The salty scent of the sea was on the crisp morning wind, along with a gentle mist.

"Your father did that?" Jamie asked, and Bliss could no longer avoid his gaze, which was far colder than the wintry sea.

Bliss was stubbornly silent. She wanted no more trouble. Jamie's voice was a volcanic rumble. "Answer me!"

Bliss nodded, her own temper rising, and Jamie urged the team into a broad turn in the middle of the road. Laying one hand on his arm, Bliss cried out, "No!"

The word was not a plea, but a warning, and to Bliss's unending surprise, Jamie heeded it. He let the reins go slack in his hands and gazed at her in undisguised bewilderment.

"Maybe Papa did hurt me," Bliss said, now that she had her husband's attention, "but it wasn't half so bad as the pain you caused, Jamie McKenna. If you go back to that inn and take vengeance on my father, you'll be the worst kind of hypocrite!"

Shame moved in Jamie's handsome face. "Bliss, about last night—"

"Please," Bliss interrupted, almost desperately, unable to bear being reminded of that particular humiliation. "I think we should just forget that."

Jamie gazed at her in silence for a few moments, then turned the team and wagon around again. They'd rattled and jostled along for some time before he politely requested, "Tell me what your life was like before you woke up in my barn, Duchess."

Bliss sighed. "It was uneventful, for the most part. I helped Papa with his duties, and I walked and read and dreamed."

Jamie favored her with a soft grin. "Is that why you wanted to go to America? Because you read about it?"

A tentative happiness straightened Bliss's shoulders and hoisted her chin a degree or two higher as she smiled. She wasn't sure whether it was the mention of America or Jamie's company that had cheered her, and in point of fact, it didn't matter. She was full of joyous enthusiasm. "It was partly the reading. My mother lives there, and she's written such wonderful letters—"

Jamie's frown made her fall silent.

"Did I say something wrong?" she asked presently.

"Mother or no mother, Duchess, America's a world away," Jamie countered. "What makes you think I'm going to let you go traipsing off to some other country?"

Bliss's backbone went stiff, and her smile faded completely away. "I don't need your permission to do anything, Jamie McKenna," she pointed out in very formal tones. "You're not my husband—not in the true sense of the word." Color throbbed in her face, for they both knew what that "true sense" was.

"You aren't goin' anywhere," Jamie said flatly. "I'd never get another decent night's sleep as long as I lived for wonderin' what mischief you'd gotten yourself into when me back was turned."

The resurgence of the brogue did not intimidate Bliss, not this time. "I'm quite certain that your nights won't be a problem to you, Mr. McKenna," she told him primly. "There's sure to be a woman handy."

"So we're back to that, are we?" Jamie shouted. It was interesting to watch him; his eyes turned a shade darker and his nostrils flared slightly. "Dammit, Bliss, I've 'ad that thrown in me face one too many times! I slept alone last night! Do you 'ear me?" His voice had risen to a bellow now, and the horses were nickering and tossing their heads nervously. "Alone!"

Bliss was pleased, for she knew somehow that Jamie was telling the truth, but she was careful not to let this conviction show. "You're scaring the horses," she pointed out.

All the little muscles at the base of Jamie's ear bunched together in a single knot. "I don't care!" he hissed.

Bliss could no longer hide her amusement, and she burst out laughing. Jamie glared at her for a moment, and then, grudgingly, he grinned and shook his head.

It was in that unguarded moment that disaster struck. The band of men on horseback rode calmly out from behind an outcropping of rock to block the way.

Jamie's jawline was like iron as he drew back on the reins and called out an easy command to the team, bringing the wagon to an unhurried stop.

Bliss's heart sank. As far as she knew, none of these men were members of the band she'd encountered when she ran away from the inn, but they were up to no good all the same. The rifle the leader carried was proof enough of that.

Chapter 7 🐟

BLISS STOOD IN THE BOX OF THE WAGON AND SHOOK AN IMPERIOUS finger at the group of men barring the road, certain that she knew how to deal with a crisis of this nature.

"Do you realize," she inquired, in a ringing voice, "that you are dealing with Jamie McKenna?" Dimly, she heard her husband mutter a curse.

The brigands remained where they were, some of them grinning.

"It's not working, Jamie," Bliss complained in a whisper. "They're not running away—"

Jamie caught hold of the back of her skirt and wrenched her down onto the seat, hard. There was an easy smile on his face as he regarded the men, though Bliss could sense his wire-tight alertness. Inwardly, he was making ready for a fight.

The bushrangers parted as one man rode forward. He was dark-haired and handsome, in a smarmy sort of way, and the leisurely inspection he gave Bliss made her skin creep. Finally, he shifted his gaze to Jamie's face.

"I'm not sure," he said, addressing the seven men behind him. "It's been a long time."

The side of Jamie's leg, touching Bliss's, was rigid, though that same unruffled smile still curved his lips. His fingers were already caressing the handle of the knife he'd kept close at hand, and he didn't speak.

The insolent ringleader's eyes had strayed back to Bliss. "That's a fine-lookin' woman, mate," he observed. He rode nearer, and that was when Bliss noticed that the man's nose was grossly misshapen, as though he'd fallen upon it from a great height. "You are Jamie McKenna, aren't you?" he asked, squinting. "Like the little lady said?"

Jamie didn't reply, and Bliss wondered why he wasn't speaking up for himself, telling these rounders to be on about their business. Although he was tense, it was apparent that Jamie wasn't afraid.

He handed the reins to Bliss without looking at her and climbed down from the wagon to stand facing the villains square in the middle of the roadway. Bliss's heart began slamming against her rib cage, and even though the morning was bitterly cold, perspiration moistened her skin.

The leader and several of his companions dismounted.

"I asked you if you be Jamie McKenna, mate," the dark-haired man said. He was clearly losing his patience. "It'd be best if you answered."

"Maybe he ain't McKenna," reasoned one of the men still on horseback.

At that moment Bliss felt something cold against the side of her hand and looked down. Unbelievably, Jamie had left his knife behind on the wagon seat—he was facing those men with no other weapons than his wits and his own two hands.

"I know how to find out," the kingpin said, and again his gaze traveled over Bliss.

Suppressing a shudder, she closed her hand around the hilt of Jamie's knife and readied herself for battle.

"Fetch that pretty thing down from the wagon," ordered the leader, after a sly glance at Jamie. "We'll have a little fun with her, whether this bloke's the one we want or not."

For the first time, Jamie spoke. "You'll be disappointed," he said coolly. "She doesn't know the first thing about pleasin' a man."

The calm amusement in Jamie's voice was, for Bliss, as lethal as a blow. She felt the color drain from her face as his disdainful words echoed in her mind. Two men came at her, lust in their eyes, their breath making white plumes in the cold air.

Bliss raised the knife, prepared to defend herself, and there were curses and blood as she drove the scoundrels back. At the same time, a fight began on the ground.

"Get his shirt open," one man called. "We'll know soon enough if this be McKenna."

Bliss was too busy wielding the blade to watch Jamie, but she knew there was no way he could prevail against so many men. Pure fear burned in her throat as she repeatedly brandished the knife.

When Jamie was, at last, overcome, the two thugs Bliss had been carving at lost interest in her. She jumped down from the wagon, without thinking, and hurried around to the front.

Jamie had been forced to his knees. His face was bruised and bleeding, and one of his eyes looked to be swollen shut, but there was a stubborn pride in his bearing that said he'd never be truly defeated, no matter what was done to him.

With a knife of his own, the ringleader sliced away the buttons of Jamie's heavy woolen coat, then tore open the shirt beneath. The medallion—a beggar's badge, Jamie had called it—appeared to be what the man was looking for.

He threw back his head and gave a gruff shout of triumphant laughter. "By God, it's him!" he shouted. "It's him!"

The men on either side of Jamie wrenched him to his feet. Bliss caught his eye once, but he looked through her, as though she'd never mattered to him at all.

"Take the woman," he said evenly, "and leave me alone."

There was a murmur of agreement all around; the evildoers obviously liked this idea.

Only the man facing off with Jamie shook his head. "Our business ain't with her," he said. Then, after a slow, hateful look at Jamie, he asked, "You remember me, don't you, McKenna? Bert Dunnigan?"

Jamie nodded. "I remember."

The sounds of bleating sheep and barking dogs mingled in the brisk, blood-scented air, but Bliss was too furious and too scared to place any importance on that. She and Jamie were in dire straits, and he'd offered her to these monsters in an effort to save himself!

Dunnigan drew back his fist and planted a sudden, hard blow in Jamie's midsection, and Bliss heard the air rush from his lungs. He was powerless to defend himself, since his arms were being held, and he was nearly unrecognizable for the blood on his face, but he spat in defiance all the same.

"I've had this to remember you by all these years, mate," Dunnigan said, pointing to his own disfigured nose. "Now, I'll have me revenge. You'll live to tell the story of the day Bert Dunnigan fixed you, but you won't be so pretty, Jamie boy. I mean to crush that muzzle of yours just like you done to me in Queensland."

Recalling how Jamie had tossed her to these lions like a piece of raw meat, Bliss elbowed her way forward to stand at Dunnigan's side. "Let me do it," she said, glaring at her husband and knotting one hand into a fist.

Incredibly, she thought she saw the merest hint of laughter in Jamie's one good eye. In that instant, she knew she had to defend the man she loved, even though he had betrayed her, and hoping for the element of surprise, she lunged at Dunnigan with her knife raised high.

A hard slap across the mouth sent her flying backward. There was an anguished grunt as Jamie's foot wreaked vengeance on Dunnigan for the blow, and then Bliss's head struck the hard, frost-laced road and the world receded into a darkness shot through with silver sparks.

As her vision cleared, she saw a dog hurl itself at Dunnigan, snarling like a wolf from hell. The brigands scattered as their leader struggled against the furious beast, screaming for help.

The bleating sound was all around Bliss. She sat up, dazed, and looked about her in bewilderment. She was surrounded by woolly, fretful sheep. And dear lord, how her head ached—

A white-haired man with a coarse, bushy beard was crouched amid the sea of confused animals, a shepherd's staff in his hand. If he'd been wearing a velvet cloak, he would have looked rather a lot like Father Christmas. "Dog!" he commanded sharply. "That's enough!"

The animal stepped back, allowing Dunnigan to scramble to his horse and escape.

"Jamie?" the old man was saying. "Jamie boy, can you hear me, lad? It's Cutter."

Bliss scrambled to her feet and waded through the sheep. "Is he—is he dead?" she choked out.

The elderly shepherd shook his head. "No, but he's hurt bad. Help me get him into the wagon, lass—we've got to take him someplace warm and see to him proper."

Jamie was lying still on the ground, and despite the fact that he'd virtually thrown her to the wolves, Bliss was moved to true despair by the sight. She sank to her knees beside him, heedless of the sheep and the man who called himself Cutter.

The beggar's badge lay in the bloody hair that matted Jamie's chest, catching the wintry glint of the sun, and he stirred when Bliss touched his battered face. "Oh, Jamie," she whispered in an anguish as great, in some ways, as his. "Why? Why would anyone want to do this to you?"

Jamie opened his eyes then, tried to speak, and failed. Gently, his fingers caressed Bliss's swollen cheek.

"You're going to have to walk if you can, boy," Cutter told him with a stern sort of affection. "You're too big for me and the lass to carry."

The hint of a rueful smile touched Jamie's mouth. "Aye," he croaked out. "Just 'elp me up, me friend. I can make it as far as the wagon."

"And that's all I'm asking of you, mate," Cutter assured him. With Bliss's help, he hoisted Jamie to his feet.

The strangled cry Jamie gave at the resultant pain made tears sting Bliss's eyes, but she fought them back. This was no time for sniveling; Jamie needed her.

Getting their moaning, half-conscious burden into the back of the wagon was a hellish task for both Cutter and Bliss, seeming to take forever. By the time he was settled, Bliss was wet with perspiration and breathing in short, desperate gasps.

"There's an inn back that way," she said, crawling up beside Jamie and looking about for something to cover him with. She was trying to pull his shirt and coat closed when another shepherd joined them.

"The cottage is closer," Cutter answered shortly, before turning to explain the situation to his companion.

When he'd done that, the tall white-haired man set his staff in the wagon bed and climbed up into the box without so much as a look or a word for Bliss. Dog jumped in beside her and laid his muzzle on Jamie's chest, making a sympathetic whining sound in his throat.

Bliss held Jamie's head in her lap as they traveled over steep, rutted roads, despairing at every groan her wounded husband uttered, struggling against tears of confusion, fear, and pure agony of the heart. She would love Jamie McKenna all her life, she was certain, but she would never, never forgive him for offering her to those men. . . .

After an inordinately long distance, the rig lumbered to a stop in front of a small, isolated stone cottage. Cutter climbed over the box into the bed of the wagon and caught Jamie's chin in his callused hand, giving him a gentle shake.

"Wake up, lad. We're here now."

Jamie's eyes rolled open. "Aye," he said, and the word

was a ragged sigh. "I suppose I 'ave to walk somewhere again."

Cutter's chuckle sounded almost like a sob. "That's right, mate. You ain't lost any weight since we picked you up down there on the road."

Her eyes stinging, Bliss turned her head for a moment, in an effort to recover her composure. Far down on the main road, the sheep were moving in a shifting, bleating mass of grayish white, driven by a second shepherd and several barking dogs.

After taking a deep breath, Bliss again helped Cutter with the laborious task of moving Jamie from the wagon to a bed in the corner of the little cottage's main room.

"This is—me wife," Jamie said, in an anguished attempt at cordiality, as Bliss and Cutter placed him carefully on the mattress. Bliss knew that he was talking to distract himself from the pain, and the familiar scalding sensation seared her eyes and branded the back of her throat.

"Charmed." The shepherd spared barely a glance for Bliss; his manner was so stiff that it almost seemed he blamed her for Jamie's condition.

Jamie laughed, but the sound was half groan. "They fixed me up right and proper," he said, as if that weren't perfectly obvious from the bloody state of his flesh and his clothes. "But 'e didn't get to break me nose, Cutter."

"Aye," Cutter teased, with gruff fondness. "You're as bonny as you ever were, Jamie me boy."

"I'll need hot water and clean cloths," Bliss announced, feeling forgotten.

Cutter gave her an unreadable look, then nodded his bushy head and went off to fetch the things she'd asked for. It was then that Jamie raised one scraped, unsteady hand to caress her face.

"They didn't 'urt you, did they Duchess?" he rasped, and there was an expression of such tenderness in his eyes that Bliss's breath caught in her lungs.

Unable to speak, she shook her head.

"God be thanked," Jamie whispered raggedly, and then he was unconscious.

Bliss was gentle as she cleaned and dressed his wounds, flinching every time Jamie moaned in his sleep.

"What happened, lass?" Cutter demanded, the moment she'd finished the arduous task, covered Jamie with a warm quilt, and turned away. The shepherd still sounded and looked as though he believed her to be responsible for the whole tragedy.

Stubbornly, Bliss put off answering until she'd wrung out the cloth and tossed the last basin of water away in the dooryard. She was washing her hands when she finally said wearily, "We were set upon." She remembered how the men had torn open Jamie's coat and shirt for a look at the medallion he wore. "It seemed that they'd known him a long time ago in—in another place; Queensland, I think."

Cutter was sitting at the table nursing a generous shot of the Scotch whisky he'd said he planned to pour down Jamie's throat later, if the pain was bad. He let out a long, low whistle. "Queensland, is it?" he muttered, speaking wholly to himself. "Saints in heaven, could they be part of that lot old Increase kept about?"

Jamie had begun to shift and writhe on the bed. "No," he cried out hoarsely before Bliss could reach his side to lend reassurance and comfort, "don't 'urt 'er—in the name of God, don't 'urt 'er—"

Cutter, it turned out, was even quicker than Bliss. He got to Jamie first and laid a huge, gentle hand on his bare shoulder. "Nobody's hurting anybody, lad," he vowed, raw emotion grating in his voice. "You're safe now, and so is the lass."

Jamie, who had never really come awake, settled back into the depths of a healing sleep. Bliss turned away, to stand staring blindly into the little fire on the hearth, her arms folded.

"Be you his wife?" Cutter asked suspiciously, coming to stand at her side. The old man smelled none too good, but

Bliss didn't care. She faced him with fire snapping in her eyes.

"I am," she answered coldly. "Do you disapprove?"

Cutter shrugged. "I'm just surprised, that's all. I never thought the lad'd marry."

"Why not?" Bliss wanted to know. She was beginning to feel weak, and she yearned for something to eat, a hot cup of tea, and a long, uninterrupted sleep.

The shepherd glanced toward the bed where Jamie lay, then shrugged his great shoulders again and said, "I guess there's no harm in telling it true. He loved a woman, did Jamie, and she did him wrong. Near broke him to pieces, that Eleanor."

Bliss lowered her head, as cruelly struck by the mention of the mysterious Eleanor as she had been by Jamie's blithe willingness to abandon her to the mercies of a band of rakehells. It was wounding to know that he had ever loved another woman.

A single tear streaked down the side of her face and, as luck would have it, Cutter noticed.

It softened him somehow. "Oh, lass—I'm sorry," he said. "If you be Jamie's wife, it's sure that you've given him your heart, and here I am telling you things to cause you pain."

With a brave sniffle, Bliss wiped her cheek dry with the back of her hand. She lifted her chin and straightened her shoulders. "There's no love lost between Mr. McKenna and me," she said. "We had our own reasons for marrying—purely practical reasons."

There was a gentle twinkle in Cutter's eyes, which were a soft green in color. "Aye, lass," he agreed. "Whatever you say. Now, be you hungry or in need of tea, the way ladies sometimes is?"

Bliss couldn't help smiling a little. Jamie's friend had a certain crude charm, now that she thought about it. "I'd like a cup of tea very much, if you have it," she responded, casting a doubtful look toward the shelves beside the stove, where Cutter's meager store of foodstuffs seemed to be kept. "And I am just a bit hungry, thank you."

Pleased that there was something he could do to make up for his earlier gaffe, Cutter shooed Bliss toward the table, and when she was seated, he filled a kettle with water dipped from a bucket and set it on to boil. Then, he brought out cheese and bread and Bliss ate generous helpings of both, being careful not to look at the food too closely.

While tea usually made her feel wide-awake, that cupful set her to yawning and sent her stumbling toward the bed where Jamie lay. Seeing there was room, she lay down carefully, not wanting to cause him discomfort, and closed her eyes.

She was only dimly aware that Cutter had spread Jamie's blanket so that it covered her, too.

Jamie was awake when Bliss opened her eyes, hours later, at first uncertain where she was. When she saw his swollen, bruised, and lacerated face, she remembered everything and sat bolt upright.

She was full of sleepy exultation to see that Jamie was well enough to grin at her, and that gave her license to be angry with him. "May God curse the day you were born, Jamie McKenna!" she hissed, flinging back the blanket and moving to scramble off the bed.

Jamie restrained her with surprising strength, considering what he'd been through. Cutter cleared his throat and made some excuse about seeing to the horses, then hurried out of the cottage.

"Oh, no, Duchess," her husband said evenly. "You're not goin' to make a remark like that and then flit off like a butterfly. What's the matter?"

"What's the matter?" Bliss mimicked furiously, trying in vain to pull free of his grasp on her wrist. "What's the matter indeed!"

Light dawned in Jamie's pitiably distorted face. "Oh," he said, remembering, and his fingers went slack against Bliss's flesh. "It's got to be that business about my tellin' Dunnigan to take you."

Just the memory stung in Bliss's blood like snake venom. She got herself a good distance from the bed, then fitfully smoothed her skirts and hair. "If you think I give a damn whether you want me or not—"

"I do think you give a damn," Jamie interrupted gently, and even though Bliss was trying hard to ignore him, she could see out of the corner of one eye that he was holding out a hand to her. And she wanted so desperately, for all of it, to go to him.

"Go hang yourself," she blustered.

Jamie laughed and then made a strangled sound at the pain the indulgence had cost him. A long time passed before he spoke, and when he did, his voice was soft and serious. "Bliss, look at me."

She didn't want to obey, but something inside her decreed that she must. Bliss turned wounded eyes to her husband. "I hate you," she informed him, out of self-defense.

He sighed. "I think we've established that, 'aven't we?" he replied. He patted the mattress with one hand, and Bliss's determined heart softened a little because she could see that the knuckles were all but stripped of skin.

If her heart had softened, she reflected, her head hadn't. She took a chair from Cutter's crude table, set it at a safe distance from the bed, and sat down, her arms folded across her chest. Everything in her manner was meant to tell Jamie that she'd listen, but what he said had better be worth hearing.

He smiled again, at her ire, and then sighed heavily. "What do you think would 'ave 'appened, Bliss, if Dunnigan 'ad guessed that you're more important to me than the breath in me lungs?"

For a moment, Bliss was too stunned to speak. Then she remembered how crafty men could be when they were trying to get themselves out a fix. She set her jaw and refused to answer.

100

"Very well, then," Jamie conceded magnanimously. The brogue, so much in evidence moments before, faded away. "He'd have had his way with you, love, and then given you over to his men. Chances are, you and I'd have been shaking hands in heaven by now."

Bliss looked down at her lap. "That's a convenient excuse, Jamie McKenna. How do I know you weren't just trying to save your own hide?"

Jamie settled back against his pillows. "Look inside your heart," he replied wearily, and then he fell silent.

Bliss slid forward in her chair, peering at him in the shadowy light from Cutter's kerosene lamps. "Are you asleep?" she demanded.

There was no answer, so Bliss went to stand in front of the fire, with her back to Jamie and all the complicated questions he raised. As Cutter made a great to-do outside and then came in, she shook her head in despondent wonder.

If only she hadn't picked Jamie McKenna's barn to sleep in that night.

Cutter made a dramatic business of suppressing a yawn. "I guess I'll just go on up to the loft and rest me eyes," he said pointedly. And when Bliss looked away from the fire, he was halfway up a ladder affixed to the far wall of the cottage.

"Cutter?" she ventured shyly.

"Aye, lass," the old man replied, hoisting himself into the loft with a lusty grunt of fatigue. "What is it?"

"Thank you," Bliss responded. "Thank you for everything."

Cutter uttered a gruff disclaimer and crawled off into the shadows of the loft. Within minutes, he was snoring fit to shake the floorboards.

Smiling, Bliss banked the fire, blew out the lanterns, slipped off her soiled shirtwaist and skirt, and crawled into bed beside Jamie. He stirred as she settled beneath the blanket, but didn't awaken.

For the next little while, Bliss lay looking up at the darkness, silently thanking God that Cutter and Dog had come along when they had. If it hadn't been so, she had to confess, she and Jamie might truly have been "shaking hands in heaven" at that very moment.

There was a shifting on the mattress beside her, along with a muffled groan. "Duchess?"

Bliss laid her hand on Jamie's arm. "Yes, my love," she said softly, "I'm here."

At her touch and words of quiet reassurance, Jamie went back to his rest.

Much later, in the depths of the night, Bliss opened her eyes, uncertain as to whether she'd been roused by a sound or a feeling. Fear possessed her, and she groped in the darkness with frantic hands. Finding the bed empty, except for herself, she whispered, "Jamie?"

"Here I am, darlin'," he told her. She heard the door close and the draft that had chilled her began to dissolve.

"What are you doing out of bed?" she asked angrily as she felt the mattress give under his weight.

He stretched out beside her. "No gentleman over the age of two stays in bed to do what I just did," he said.

"Oh," came the meek response. "Well, good night, then."

There was a mischievous silence. "I need something for the pain," Jamie said.

Bliss sighed. "There's Scotch on the table. Shall I get it for you?"

Beneath the blankets, his fingers began unfastening her camisole. "It isn't Scotch I want," he replied in a low and husky voice, cupping her bare breast in his hand and training the nipple to the shape he wanted with the pad of his thumb.

Now it was Bliss who groaned, and not from pain. She decided to address him formally; perhaps that would serve to remind him of the proprieties. "We are not alone, Mr. McKenna," she said.

He chuckled in the darkness, his hand still doing its devilish work. Soon enough he'd be up to real mischief. "Cutter sleeps like the dead," he told her. "I could have you on the ladder to the loft and he'd never know the difference."

The very idea made heat throb in Bliss's face and caused a moist ache between her legs. "You forget yourself, sir," she insisted, at once desperate and angry. "Furthermore, you're in no condition for such goings on as—"

His hand left her breast to sweep down over her silken belly and dally dangerously close to the nest of curls where her womanhood was concealed. "As this, for instance?"

Bliss trembled and bit down on her lower lip to stifle a delighted cry as he found what he sought. She could see his grin in the darkness.

"You forget yourself, Mrs. McKenna," he said.

Bliss's legs moved apart as he thrust his fingers inside her. The sensation was new and delicious and it was all she could do not to blurt out a lot of silly words of surrender.

Gingerly, Jamie turned so that he could enjoy the breasts he'd bared, while subjecting Bliss to the sweetest torment she could have imagined.

"Oooooh," she whispered in desperation as he intensified his efforts, driving his fingers deeper and, at the same time, using his thumb to caress her. "Jamie, Jamie—"

He circled one straining nipple with his tongue, made a sound that was half amusement and half misery far down in his throat, and drew from Bliss a comfort that the Scotch whisky waiting on the tabletop could not have given him.

Chapter 8 🌿

EVERY PART OF JAMIE'S BODY ACHED, AND NOW THE WANTING OF A woman had been added to the general malaise.

Beside him, Bliss slept soundly, well satisfied. Jamie allowed himself a moment or two of stark envy before letting out a long, ragged sigh. Even if he'd been able to forget the legal and moral requirements for an annulment, there was the little matter of the beating he'd taken. It would be a day or two, at least, before he'd be nimble enough for making love.

In the meanwhile, it was a sweet sort of torture to lie beside Bliss in a warm bed, well aware of the lush contours and silky feel of her flesh. Involuntarily, he recalled her wholehearted surrender to the small pleasures he'd offered her, and he swallowed a groan of need.

She stirred beside him, then lifted her head and asked, through a yawn, "Jamie?"

He closed his eyes for a moment, concentrating all his efforts on speaking normally. "Aye, Duchess." The words sounded gravelly and harsh. "What's wrong?"

Bliss yawned again. "I was going to ask you the same question."

104

Jamie moistened his dry lips with his tongue. "Go back to sleep," he said brusquely. "It's nothing you can do anything about."

Bliss immediately bristled; inadvertently, Jamie had stepped on her formidable pride. "I'm not so naïve as you think, Jamie McKenna," she told him stiffly. "You're suffering from more than bruises and cuts."

Jamie was annoyed. "Is that so? And exactly what malady would I be sufferin' with, Duchess?"

Beneath the blanket and sheet, her hand touched his bare abdomen lightly, then progressed to the heart of matters. He gasped hoarsely and closed his eyes, and Bliss's gentle amusement was all around him, like the scent of her and the feel of her skin against his.

"Oh God," he whispered as she began a rhythmic stroking that must have come to her by instinct.

"Tell me how to please you, Jamie," she pleaded quietly.

He gave a ragged chuckle. "You're doing just fine, lass," he responded. He knew he should push her hand away, but he couldn't bring himself to do that. The sensations she was creating were too powerful, too exquisite, too compelling to be set aside.

Encouraged, Bliss became more confident—and more aggressive. All of a sudden, the blankets seemed to be crushing Jamie, holding in more heat than he could bear, and he tossed them back. The cool night air played over his sore body, making his desire all the more urgent. On and on the pleasuring went, stripping Jamie of all pretense and, for the moment, all pain.

He rasped Bliss's name, over and over, when the joy grew almost beyond his tolerance. Then she lowered her head to taste him, and he lost his reason entirely. With a strangled shout, he arched his back in full surrender, and Bliss received him without hesitation or shyness, seeming to revel in his fulfillment, to share it.

"There, now," she said, when the glorious storm of satisfaction had passed, leaving Jamie's mind clear, "wasn't that what you needed?" At some point before his thoughts had become coherent again, she'd fetched warm water and a cloth, and for a time she bathed his raw flesh, soothing him more with each caressing motion of her hand.

The washing was a kind of lovemaking in and of itself, and the tenderness he found in Bliss's touch made Jamie want to weep. It wasn't going to be easy, once they'd seen a magistrate in Auckland, to turn his back on Bliss and walk away. He had never known a woman quite like her.

Presently, she dispensed with the basin and cloth and cuddled close against Jamie's shoulder, at the same time drawing the blankets up to cover them. Within seconds, Jamie slipped into the sweet, cosseting darkness that was sleep.

Jamie was up and fully dressed when Bliss opened her eyes early the next morning. Recollections of the night just past made her blush and slide beneath the covers to hide.

She heard Jamie's bootheels striking the stone floor of the cottage as he came toward the bed at a pace only slightly slower than his normal gait. In another moment, he pulled back the blankets, just as far as Bliss's shoulders, and smiled down at her.

"Hello, Duchess," he drawled. "Having second thoughts, are you?"

Bliss glared at him, for she despised being teased, especially when she'd just woken up. Her cheeks burned as hot as the embers in the grate. A quick glance around Jamie's right thigh revealed that they were alone.

"Where's Cutter?" she asked, ignoring Jamie's question.

"He and Dog have sheep to look after, love. They've been gone for hours."

Bliss wasn't sure whether being alone with Jamie McKenna was a plus or a minus, and she didn't try to decide. Careful to keep herself covered, she sat up, yawning, and ran the fingers of both hands through her tangled russet hair. She started with pleased surprise when Jamie handed her a mug of fragrant coffee.

Milk and sugar had been added, and Bliss wondered idly how Jamie had known how she liked her coffee. He sat down, wincing a little, on the edge of the bed, while Bliss avoided his eyes and took a cautious sip of the hot brew.

"We need to talk," Jamie said gently.

Bliss still could not look at Jamie; the things they'd done in that very bed the night before were too fresh in her mind. "About what?" she asked, and though she attempted to sound blithe, the effort was fruitless.

Jamie curled an index finger under her chin and lifted, so that Bliss had to choose between meeting his gaze and closing her eyes. She came very near to doing the latter, but in the end, her natural fortitude won out.

"About last night," he replied. When he smiled, his handsome face all askew from the battering he'd endured, Bliss's heart clenched painfully in response. Trembling a little, she took a sip of her coffee in an attempt to steady herself.

"Oh," she said, and again she felt wildly embarrassed. If it hadn't been for the mug of coffee, she would have burrowed back under the covers.

Jamie spoke with typical bluntness, but with sensitivity, too. "I've never known a woman to take hell and single-handedly turn it into heaven," he said quietly. "Not before you, that is."

Bliss swallowed. Jamie's words were high praise, but it wasn't as if he'd said he loved her, or that he would refuse an annulment. And she was still not sure herself.

"Tell me how you met Cutter," she said, when the silence lengthened to the point where she could no longer bear the strain.

Jamie grinned to let her know that she hadn't fooled him, but his expression turned sober as he set himself to remembering. "When I came to New Zealand, those scars on my back were fresh. I was young and bitter, and though I had a friend who tried to help me, I went back to stealin'. Cutter took me in and taught me everything I'd yet to learn about the trade."

Bliss closed her gaping mouth. "Cutter is a thief?"

Jamie gave a short, rueful chuckle. "Not anymore. He's too old for the life. The—uncertainties of it were getting to him."

"What about you, Jamie McKenna?" Bliss dared to ask, the half-filled mug grasped tight in both her hands. Dorrie's words about Jamie's mysterious transformation following a trip to Australia were clear in her mind, and her gaze dropped to the sleeve of his borrowed shirt. Beneath the fabric, she knew, was the scar he bore as a reminder of that journey across the Tasman Sea. "What brought about the change in you?"

A haunted look came into Jamie's eyes, and even before he spoke, Bliss knew he was going to hedge. The brogue was further proof of his agitation. "We'll be leavin' this place while the sun's 'igh, lass, so tend to what needs tendin' and let's be gone from 'ere."

Bliss reached out and caught his hand in her own when he would have risen off the bed and walked away. "Jamie," she insisted.

"I was in a fight," he confessed, his tone grudging. "I tried to rob a man, and 'e got me knife away and near sliced off me arm." Jamie paused, lowering his head for a moment. "'Twas an equal match, it was, but when I saw the beggar's badge 'angin' round 'is neck, the strength went out of me."

Bliss touched the medallion Jamie wore. "The man was wearing one of these?"

Jamie nodded, his gaze still fixed on something long ago and far away. "Aye, Duchess—I'd jumped me own brother, Reeve."

There was a short silence, then Bliss said gently, "I'm sure he's forgiven you."

"Aye," Jamie said doubtfully, taking Bliss's mug from her

and rising from the bed. Even though he turned his back to her, he could not hide the depths of his emotions.

Bliss got up quickly and looked around for her satchel. Her shirtwaist and skirt were ruined, thanks to the bloody battle she'd fought the day before with Jamie's knife, so she started to put on the only other garment she possessed—her black evening gown.

"The first thing we're going to do in Auckland, Duchess," Jamie said as he helped her with the fastenings at the back of the dress, "is get you some decent clothes to wear."

Bliss felt her throat tighten. "Will that be before or after we have our marriage annulled, Mr. McKenna?"

His fingers hesitated in their husbandly work of hooking buttons. "Before," he said, in a voice that revealed nothing of his feelings.

"I'll send money to repay you as soon as I'm settled in America," Bliss ventured, testing the emotional waters.

Jamie fastened the last button rather more forcibly than he needed to, giving Bliss an eloquent shake in the process. "I've told you 'ow I feel about that idea, Duchess. I don't want to 'ear so much as the mention of that place again."

Bliss whirled, raising angry eyes to meet Jamie's. Blast that man, he didn't want her for his wife, but he expected to dictate her every move all the same. "What place?" she challenged furiously. "America?"

His jawline hardened, but Jamie was too stubborn to rise to the bait. He turned his back on Bliss, struggled awkwardly into his buttonless coat, and stormed out of the cottage, slamming the door behind him.

Bliss muttered a few colorful words herself as she brushed her hair and went looking for something to eat. She was devouring a piece of bread when Cutter came in, nose red with the cold. His mild green eyes widened at the sight of her low-cut evening gown, and before he could stop himself, he'd given a low whistle. Dog, always at Cutter's side, perked up his ears at the sound.

"No wonder the lad's half out of his head," the old man commented when he'd partially recovered from the shock.

Bliss had no idea what to say, given the fact that she didn't know whether she was being complimented or criticized, so she simply dropped her eyes for a moment. Now that Jamie had told her about Cutter's teaching him the finer aspects of thievery, she wasn't sure how she felt toward the shepherd, but she did know that she was grateful to him. He and Dog had saved Jamie's life the day before, and probably hers as well.

In the next moment, it became evident that Cutter was annoyed, though not with Bliss. "That hardheaded mick," he muttered. "I tried to tell him he ain't ready to do any traveling, but he just says to me, 'Don't tell me what to do on me own property, old man,' he says."

"His property?" Bliss echoed, surprised.

Cutter spread his big, hoary hands and arched one snow-white eyebrow in puzzlement. "He didn't tell you?"

Bliss shook her head, more aware than ever of how very much she didn't know about her husband.

"It's all his, lass—the cottage, the land, the sheep. Me and Dog, here, we just work for Jamie."

Bliss's eyes widened. At the inn, she'd heard Jamie referred to as a man of property, but she hadn't realized he had holdings beyond the place near Auckland. "He's come by a great deal," she mused, talking as much to herself as to Cutter. "For a man who was picking pockets a few years ago."

Cutter grew red in the face in his desire to defend his friend. "Got it all honestlike, he did," he declared angrily. "Jamie's a smart lad and all he ever needed was a leg up."

Before Bliss could respond to that, Jamie walked into the cottage, gave Cutter a quelling look, and said, "It's time to leave, Duchess."

Bliss rose from her chair and donned her coat, while Jamie took up her satchel. She went to Cutter and took both his hands in hers. "Thank you," she said softly. "For everything."

Cutter was clearly embarrassed. " 'Twas no trouble, lass." His gaze sliced to Jamie. "It's nice to know some people is grateful when they gets a hand from a friend," he added pointedly.

Jamie offered no reply.

"When you get to Auckland," Cutter forged on, "give my regards to Miss Peony."

First Eleanor, and now this Peony. Bliss's curiosity was more than piqued, and she risked a glance at Jamie, who was glaring coldly at the man who had prevented his murder not twenty-four hours before.

"I'll tell her you're as windy as you ever were, old man."

A charge of anger seemed to pass between the two men.

"The truth always comes out, Jamie boy," Cutter returned, giving as good as he got. "I'd remember that if I were you."

At this, Jamie turned without another word and opened the door. Cold air rushed into the cottage and made Bliss shiver. She had no choice but to follow Jamie outside; if she didn't, she knew he would leave her behind.

"What was that all about?" she demanded when she and Jamie were both settled in the wagon seat and the rig was moving toward the main road. Bliss had already noted, with mingled uneasiness and relief, that there was a rifle lying on the floorboard, within easy reach.

Jamie shrugged, his jaw set in a stubborn line that brought out the same obstinacy in Bliss. "I've told you all you need to know about Cutter," he said, after long moments of silence had passed.

Bliss folded her arms across her chest. "I'll tell you what I think, Jamie McKenna—"

"Oh, I'm sure you will," Jamie interrupted.

Bliss had been holding her breath, and a stream of words rushed out when she released it. "I think you didn't want him to tell me any more about this Peony person, whoever she is."

Jamie's ice-blue eyes chilled Bliss more deeply than the cold ever could have when he looked at her. "You're wrong there, Duchess," he said tightly. "Peony is the best friend I 'ave in all the world. She's closer to me than Cutter or even Reeve. Without 'er, I'd 'ave nothin', for 'twas Peony that staked me to a new start."

Bliss swallowed hard, so hurt by the tone and meaning of Jamie's words that she didn't trust herself to speak. She averted her eyes, and when she dared to look at him again, he spoke gruffly.

"That's the way of it, Duchess."

The brusque words were of no comfort to Bliss. She knew that she had been wrong. After all, she really had no right to question Jamie about his personal business. Her voice came out sounding strangled and hoarse. "Do you think we'll be safe on the road?" she asked.

"Safe as ever," he replied, shifting uncomfortably on the seat. It was obvious that Jamie was in severe pain, though he was doing his utmost to hide the fact, and Bliss wondered what had made him so anxious to leave the safety of Cutter's cottage.

She had no more than completed this thought when the answer occurred to her: Jamie was eager to get to Auckland and rid himself of one unwanted wife.

"You look like your best friend just died," Jamie commented, his voice so low that Bliss could barely hear it over the clatter of the horses hooves on the hard-frozen road. "Tell me what's troublin' you, Duchess."

Bliss's temper, always a dependable defense against emotional pain, flared to life. "Why should I, Jamie McKenna?" she fired back at him. "You won't tell me any of the things that I want to know about you!"

Jamie's gaze was level, and once again Bliss thought she saw a glimmer of amusement deep in his eyes. "Fair enough," he said solemnly.

But Bliss hardly heard him. Spreading her hands, she cried, "I know you're angry because my father made you marry me, but I notice you didn't fight! You must be tough, or those men who kidnapped me wouldn't have run off just because I mentioned your name, so I'm sure you could have handled my father. And Alexander—well, Alexander would have been no trouble at all—I think I could have trounced him myself!" She paused to draw a deep breath, then rushed on. "As for those rounders on the road yesterday, well, you wouldn't have had any difficulty with them, either, I'll wager, if you hadn't left your knife with me!"

Jamie was watching her in astonishment. "You wouldn't 'ave needed me knife, Duchess," he remarked. "You could 'ave *talked* those bleeders to death."

Bliss was not going to be distracted from her point. "If you didn't want to marry me, Jamie McKenna, why didn't you refuse to be bullied into taking the vows? And if you don't care about me, kindly explain why you left your knife behind in the wagon seat yesterday."

Jamie shrugged, evidently expecting that gesture to pass as an answer. Bliss noticed that he was very careful not to look at her.

They traveled in complete silence for a great distance, and then Jamie drew the wagon to the side of the road. He wound the reins around the brake lever after setting it in place with an awkward movement of one foot. His face was pale beneath the cuts and bruises.

"Cutter sent along some food," he said, getting down from the wagon and then walking away from Bliss and disappearing into the trees lining the road.

Bliss, having had nothing to eat since the crust of bread at breakfast, was ravenous. She opened the bundle the old man had packed to find cheese, dried meat, and two slightly withered apples. When Jamie returned, she offered him a share, but he shook his head and turned his attention to scanning the road stretching ahead.

113

Bliss, concerned, started to protest that he needed food to keep up his strength.

Jamie gave her a bleak look and then said distantly, "Enough, Duchess. I don't need you telling me when to eat."

Bliss's own appetite, usually insatiable, faded away at the lack of warmth in his voice. She wrapped what remained of their meal, tucked the bundle back under the seat, and barely trusting Jamie not to drive away without her, made her way into the woods to attend to some business of her own.

When she returned, Jamie was seated in the wagon, his face set grimly against the pain.

"I'm sure I could drive," Bliss offered brightly, without thinking before she spoke. "That way, you could lie in the back of the wagon and rest."

Jamie's response was a glower and a harsh, "I told you, woman—I don't want you mollycoddlin' me. Now back off."

Bliss's eyes burned with tears, but she was quick to turn her head away, in the hope that Jamie wouldn't see. What had happened to the passionate, vulnerable man who had loved and been loved so willingly the night before? And what of the words he'd said just that morning, that Bliss had turned hell to heaven for him?

For all her efforts to preserve her pride, a sob escaped Bliss and Jamie heard her, for he immediately stopped the wagon and, taking her shoulders in his raw-knuckled hands, turned her to face him.

With his thumbs, he brushed the tears from her face. "Try to understand," he said, his voice no more than a husky whisper. "No one, anywhere, 'as ever scared me the way you do, Duchess."

It was probably the worst thing Bliss could have said, but the words were out before she was able to stop them. "Not even Eleanor? Or Peony?"

Jamie's hands, warming and caressing her icy, wind-stung cheeks only a fraction of a moment before, fell away.

By then, there seemed no point in turning back, since the grave mistake had already been made. Bliss compounded it. "Cutter told me that you loved Eleanor," she said.

Jamie had taken up the reins again, and he brought them down on the horses' backs with a near-cruel force. "I ought to pull that old gossip's beard out!" he bellowed over the clomping of hooves and the frightened nickers of the team.

Even though she knew it was highly inadvisable, Bliss couldn't help laughing at the image that sprang up in her mind. She covered her mouth with one hand and held on to the seat with the other as Jamie drove the team to a near run.

"What's so funny!" he roared at Bliss, who should have been intimidated but was not.

She laughed until tears were streaking down her face, scalding her cold-reddened skin, and Jamie grudgingly slowed the wagon to a more judicious pace.

"I could do without all this interference!" he fussed, and he sounded so ridiculous that Bliss squealed with amusement and was carried away all over again.

Presently, her mirth subsided, but Jamie's high dudgeon did not. They had reached their destination and were pulling to a stop in the gathering dusk before he said another word.

"Go and tell Carra to warm some brandy," he told Bliss abruptly, easing down from the box and moving with obvious stiffness to begin unhitching the exhausted team.

Bliss knew he was hurting and, for that reason, she was willing to forgive an attitude that would normally have been insufferable. "I think," she said, bunching her skirts in her hands and climbing down from the wagon seat with care, "that I can manage to heat brandy without Carra's help, Mr. McKenna."

Jamie made a rude, grumbling sound and went on about his work. After allowing herself a notion of putting her tongue out at him—Bliss doubted that he'd even noticed the gesture—she turned and started across the barnyard toward the sturdy house. A light burned in the parlor window, and Bliss quickened her pace at the promise of warmth and food and maybe a taste of brandy for herself.

Carra met her at the front door with a face turned to stone. "You came back," she said.

Bliss knew the time was wrong to announce that she and Jamie were married. She wasn't without sympathy for Carra, after all, because she knew what it was to love Jamie McKenna and have no hope of ever being loved in return. "Yes," she answered simply. "But I doubt that I'll be here for long. Carra, Mr. McKenna was—injured—on the journey. I'm going to warm some brandy for him, and I wonder if you'd mind making a nice fire in his room so that he can rest in comfort."

Carra's determined dislike seemed to be giving way, at least briefly. She nodded, an expression resembling politeness visible in her eyes before she turned toward the stairway.

Bliss found the brandy Jamie had asked for toward the back of the house, in an austere-looking room that seemed to be a study. There were account books stacked on the neat surface of the desk and, on impulse, mostly because she'd never seen Jamie's handwriting, she opened the cover of one.

Columns of neat and very impressive numbers filled the pages. Jamie's penmanship was as practical-looking as the manner in which he'd furnished his house, and Bliss was smiling when the voice sounded unexpectedly and startled her.

"Thinking like your dear father, are you?" Jamie asked.

Bliss's smile faded as she realized what the man was implying. He actually thought she was examining his books to see how she could profit by the marriage. "If you weren't already beaten to a pulp," she said stiffly, "I'd kick you in the shin."

He ran a hand through his hair and then approached, taking the brandy bottle from Bliss in a peremptory grab. "Good night—Mrs. McKenna," he said, and every word had the lethal sharpness of the knife he was rarely without. He'd turned his back and was leaving the room when Bliss stopped him quite effectively.

"You needn't say good night to me yet," she said, her tone deliberately coy. "There'll be time for that when we've put out the lamp and snuggled down into our lovely warm bed."

Jamie turned slowly to face her, the brandy bottle clutched tightly in his hand.

"That's right," Bliss said, responding cheerfully to his silence. "I mean to share your bed tonight. After all, Mr. McKenna, we are man and wife."

Before he could reply, Bliss swept past him, leading the way along the hallway and up the stairs. A backward glance revealed that Jamie's jaw was stubbornly set, but he was following.

117

Chapter 9 🌿

CARRA WAS PUTTING AN EXTRA QUILT ON THE BED, AND A BRIGHT
fire already blazed in the hearth, when Jamie and Bliss
walked into the room. The Maori girl's beautiful dark eyes
slashed from one to the other. Carra said nothing.

Bliss knew that if Carra was to be told of the marriage,
however unconventional it was, Jamie should be the one to
do the talking. With some difficulty, she pried the brandy
bottle out of his hand and left the room.

The kitchen was warm and lighted by lamps, and there
was a savory lamb stew simmering on the cookstove. The
delicious scent made Bliss's stomach grumble, and she
hastened to find a pan for heating Jamie's brandy. He could
have his nip of the sauce if he wanted; for herself, Bliss
wanted a bowlful of that stew.

She found a small kettle and poured half the brandy into
it, setting it on the stove. Then, after locating a bowl and
spoon, she served herself supper. Bliss hadn't realized, until
she began to eat, how ravenous she really was.

She'd taken only a few bites when the unexpected happened. The brandy must have gotten too hot, for there was a

sizzling sound, followed by a *whoosh-whoom* fit to freeze the blood, and then the entire stove seemed to be ablaze.

"Fire!" Bliss shrieked, jumping out of her chair and casting frantically about for something with which to fight the flames. She saw nothing that would do.

There was a clatter on the rear stairway and then Jamie arrived with a blanket in hand, beating out the fire. Carra and Bliss were both choking on the smoke by then, and Bliss's eyes felt as though they were awash in scalding water.

When Jamie was sure the fire was out, he opened the back door and one of the windows, coughing. The fresh but frigid air that poured into the room was no colder than the impatience in Jamie's eyes when he looked at Bliss.

"The brandy?" he asked, in tones too dulcet for Bliss's comfort.

She retreated a step, her heart in her throat, and nodded. Guilt washed over her; the blunder she'd made had been a serious one, the kind her father would have punished her for.

Jamie closed his eyes for a moment and then gave a long sigh. The smell of smoke was acrid in the air. "Thank God you weren't hurt," he said after an interval of silence.

Carra was already about the business of cleaning up the mess on and around the stove; if she was aware of the interchange between Jamie and Bliss, she showed no sign of it.

Bliss was still braced for an explosion. "Aren't you going to say that that was a stupid thing to do?" she asked, staring at her husband in dread and amazement.

"Do I have to say that, Bliss?" he countered, and his voice was gentle.

Her throat tightened and she shook her head, moved in a way that made it impossible to speak.

Jamie approached her and took her hands into his for a moment, giving them a light, reassuring squeeze. "Go to bed," he ordered quietly. "You're exhausted."

Bliss wanted to protest, but she couldn't. She nodded her acquiescence and climbed the rear stairway.

She was in bed and watching the flames dancing in Jamie's fireplace when he came into the room. It had been nearly an hour since the calamity in the kitchen.

"I've ruined the stew," Bliss said forlornly.

Jamie gave a lopsided grin and shook his head. "Aye, Duchess, you've probably done that, for a fact."

"The worst part is," she confided, the covers tucked beneath her chin, "that I'm still hungry."

Jamie's response to that was a throaty burst of amusement, which he quickly suppressed. Humor continued to dance in his blue-topaz eyes, however. "We can't 'ave that. I'll go back downstairs and see what I can find."

Bliss bolted upright, shaking her head. Being a little hungry seemed a proper penance, given the fact that she'd nearly caused a catastrophe of the most horrific porportions. "No. You need to rest—"

Ignoring her, Jamie opened the door and walked out. He returned minutes later carrying a tray, and Bliss again felt that strange, tender misery that had possessed her downstairs when he'd been so understanding about the fire.

"It's the stew!" she cried, astonished, when Jamie handed her the tray.

He chuckled as he moved nearer the hearth and began unbuttoning his shirt. "Aye. Carra managed to save some of it."

There was buttered bread, too, and a little bowl of cooked pears swimming in a bright red cinnamon sauce. In the true spirit of her name, Bliss enjoyed her meal. By the time she was finished, Jamie was stretched out beside her in bed. He took the tray and set it aside, then grinned at her.

"You're a lusty little scamp," he remarked, and even though his meaning might have been ambiguous, Bliss could find nothing to object to in his expression or his voice. "Everything you do, you do with spirit and flair—and fire."

Bliss felt almost as though she'd been flattered, but of

course with Jamie one couldn't always be sure. She reached over him to dip a finger into the luscious sauce left in her bowl, and the gesture put her in a position she hadn't anticipated. Her breast came within a whisper of Jamie's mouth, and of course he took immediate advantage.

Bliss groaned and allowed her eyes to close. The sensation was almost unbearably sweet; she wanted it to go on and on, forever.

Presently, however, Jamie shifted Bliss onto her back and poised himself above her. His voice was gruff, almost despairing, as he allowed her to feel the full, muscled length of him brush against her satiny flesh. "God 'elp me, Duchess," he whispered, "I don't think I can spend another night in the same bed with you and not 'ave you for me own."

Every inch of Bliss seemed to be tingling, humming like a string on some exotic instrument. Her breath was labored and she suffered a splendid ache as she felt her body expanding itself to accommodate her man. "You are—my husband," she managed to say.

"Aye, in a manner of speaking." Jamie spoke sleepily, and he slid downward a little way; he kissed her neck and then her collarbone and then, in a leisurely way, the rounded upper parts of her breasts.

Bliss was trembling, so great was her need for what this man offered her. She knew her heart would be broken whether he withheld the mysteries of lovemaking or bestowed them—either way, she could not win.

She whimpered softly as he eased her legs apart with a motion of one knee and, at the same time, took full suckle at her nipple.

"It'll 'urt a little," he said in husky apology when he'd had his fill of her special ambrosia.

Bliss had known that the first time she gave herself to a man there would be pain, and she was beyond caring. She entangled her fingers in Jamie's butternut hair and guided him back to her breast in silent relinquishment of her body.

Jamie took a long time pleasuring Bliss; the fire was burning low in the grate, the lamps had gone out, and the room was full of shifting moon shadows when he could no longer deny himself full satisfaction.

"Are you sure?" he asked raggedly, and Bliss, floating dazed in a state of exhausted contentment, nodded her head.

"Yes," she whispered. "Oh yes."

She felt the startling size and power of him at the portal of her womanhood and knew only the vaguest flash of fear.

Jamie trembled with restraint as he entered her, giving Bliss more and more of him as she urged him nearer, her hands moving fitfully from his buttocks to the small of his back. Her name fell from his lips over and over again, in a low, frantic whisper.

When he passed the barrier nature had set in place, Bliss gasped and tensed her body, and Jamie was instantly still. His mouth hovered over her own, then strayed to her jawline and the tender place underneath her ear. "There's no 'urry, then, is there?" he muttered, and Bliss didn't know whether he was reassuring her or himself.

As the discomfort subsided, Bliss began to feel the same fevered excitement as before, when Jamie had pleased her so relentlessly, so sweetly. By instinct, she began to move beneath her husband and he rose and fell in perfect rhythm with the pace she set.

She was caught unaware when the balance of power shifted to Jamie. Without warning, he was in command, and he guided Bliss skillfully, inexorably, toward a peak they had never scaled together before. They reached the summit at precisely the same instant, their moist bodies straining for the most complete union possible, ragged cries of triumph torn from their throats.

When the last joint tremor had subsided, Jamie rolled, gasping, onto his back and groaned aloud. Bliss knew without asking that the pain, from which he'd had a short surcease, had descended upon him again.

She was filled with tenderness and all the emotions of a young woman who has given not only her heart, but her body, to one very special man. Raising herself on one elbow, she stroked his fleecy chest with the palm of her hand and placed a gentle kiss on his forehead.

Jamie clasped her fingers with an abruptness that startled her. Holding her hand in his, he rasped, "I'm sorry, Duchess. God in heaven, I'm so sorry."

Bliss was crushed. He was apologizing for making love to her? She had so hoped that she'd pleased him, despite her inexperience, and thus dispensed with all his myriad doubts, but now reality was dawning. Merciless, glaring reality.

Her father had repeatedly warned her that men were utterly without honor when it came to such things. Jamie had assuaged his own needs because the opportunity had been so brashly presented, and taking was not the same thing as caring.

Not at all.

Realizing what she'd done, Bliss gave a wail of despair and grief.

Immediately, Jamie drew her into his arms, sheltering her against his hard chest, and his fingers moved gently in her fiery hair as she wept for what had been given—and lost.

It shouldn't have been such a brutal surprise, waking up and finding Bliss gone, but it was. It was.

Jamie's bruised ribs protested ferociously as he flung back the covers and bounded out of bed, his heart beating too rapidly for comfort and his breath tearing in and out of his lungs. It would have been a relief to delude himself for a few minutes, to let himself believe that Bliss was only downstairs, or outside somewhere, but he knew better.

The satchel was gone and that meant that Bliss had flown. The little fool—hadn't she learned anything when she'd run away before and found herself in the hands of men who'd just as soon use her to death as look at her?

Jamie swore under his breath as he wrenched on clean clothes, stockings, boots. He ran splayed fingers through his hair in lieu of combing it and dashed out the door, nearly colliding with Carra in the hallway.

"When?" he demanded of the girl, without even slowing his pace as he moved toward the main stairway. There was no point in mincing words, for he knew Carra understood what he was asking.

"Hours ago, I think," Carra called after him. "You'll never catch her now." There was just the slightest hint of exultation in the young woman's tone, and Jamie reminded himself that it would be imprudent to strangle her, that her father was a powerful chief with a gift for vengeance.

He stopped at the base of the stairs, gripping the newel post in one hand and breathing too fast. After a moment or two, Jamie knotted one hand into a fist and slammed it down hard on the banister. "Damn that little—"

"Better she's gone," Carra said in a songlike voice. "We don't need her."

Maybe you don't, Jamie reflected in miserable silence, but I do. And after I swore to God I'd never need anybody the way I need her.

Again he raked the fingers of one hand through his hair. "She's my wife," he said.

Carra was so quiet for so long that Jamie finally turned around to see if she was still there. She stood at the top of the stairs, biting down hard on her lower lip, her enormous brown eyes brimming with tears.

He felt like the worst kind of no-gooder, but Bliss's safety was paramount in his mind. "She'd be on her way to Auckland," he mused, climbing the stairs at a slow, thoughtful rate. Once Bliss reached the city, she would undoubtedly head for the docks; she'd made it clear enough that she wanted to work her way to America as someone's governess or companion.

Jamie shuddered as he considered just a few of the things that could happen to a young woman alone in the harbor district and stepped up his pace. Within half an hour, he had eaten, extracted a promise from Carra that the animals would be fed and watered in his absence, and saddled his horse.

Carra's great pride gave way when he was about to ride out, and she clutched at his leg with both hands, weeping softly. "Oh Jamie, don't go. Don't bring her back here—I know I can make you happy if you'll only give me a chance!"

Though he ached to be on his way, Jamie couldn't be unkind to Carra. In frustration, he swept his worn hat off his head and then put it on again. "Carra," he said, and the word was a gentle reprimand.

She released her grasp on his thigh and retreated a step, one hand over her mouth, tears still glistening in her eyes. "I'll stay until you send someone," she said, after several agonizing moments. "Only until you send someone."

Jamie understood that Carra's sensibilities would not allow her to remain in his house any longer than necessary. If it hadn't been for the stock, there would have been no real need for her to stay.

He promised to send one of the shepherds to tend the barn animals and rode away.

Finding the main flock and relaying the order took another precious hour, and the icy winter sun was high in the sky when Jamie finally set out for Auckland.

Bliss counted herself fortunate to have caught a ride with a farmer and his wife; she was more than happy to sit on the hard, splintery floorboards of their wagon, her feet dangling out over the rutted road, her satchel at her side.

In order to distract herself from an aching, hopeless desire to be back in that isolated farmhouse with Jamie McKenna and the rigors of a wagon trip that would take hours, Bliss planned for the future.

Upon reaching Auckland, she decided, she would go to her Aunt Calandra for guidance.

Bliss had never actually met her mother's older sister, but

there had been all those kind letters and the parcels, containing clothing and small gifts, that had arrived at Christmas and on birthdays. These things seemed to indicate a soft heart, and at this point in her life, Bliss Stafford McKenna was in sore need of a gentle-natured relative.

She drew a deep breath, let it out as a despairing little sigh. It would be better this way, she insisted to herself. She'd done the right thing to leave Jamie; her only regret was that she hadn't found a way to escape earlier, before he'd marked her, forever, as his own.

Maybe no man would want her now, even in faraway America, where her sins could not follow. Or could they?

It was too cold to cry—the tears would make ice on her cheeks, she was sure—so Bliss stood steadfast against the impulse. Inside, though, she was all broken and sore.

She sat up very straight on the floorboards of the wagon and forced her mind back to Auckland and Aunt Calandra. After a few days of visiting that lady, and recovering both her spirit and her energy, Bliss meant to find that position she'd been dreaming of for so many years. She'd leave New Zealand and all its unpleasant memories, Mr. McKenna included, far behind.

Bliss sighed. It wasn't going to be all that easy to forget Jamie, she had to confess. He kept coming to mind, summoned up by the smallest thing, and even when she was making a deliberate effort not to think of him, she was aware of the sweet elation he had stirred in her body. Much of that still lingered.

After many hours—Bliss was not only tired and cold, but excruciatingly hungry—the traffic became thicker on the road and she could see the first vague glow of the city lights. Excitement lifted her flagging spirits, and she was even able to smile. She'd find a place to spend the night, using money she'd borrowed from the top drawer of Jamie's desk to pay for her lodging. In the morning, she would buy two good dresses, in order to be decently turned out while seeking a position, and following that, she meant to present herself at her aunt's door.

The farmer and his wife let her off on the outskirts of the city, near a tram stop, and Bliss smoothed her hair and her rumpled coat and hoped that no one unsavory would notice her. Between the men who had kidnapped her the night she'd run away from the inn and the ordeal on the road with Jamie, Bliss had had enough such problems to last her for a lifetime.

A lamplighter came around before the tram, moving up and down the quiet streets, and Bliss watched him with interest. His task reminded her a little of the life she'd led at the lighthouse, though she'd had to keep the glass polished and clean as well as light the great lamp when darkness fell.

The lamplighter paused. "Lost, miss?" he asked kindly, peering at Bliss through spectacles as thick as the bottom of a teapot.

Bliss swallowed. The man was old, and he looked harmless. "I'm waiting for the tram," she admitted. "Do you know a good place to board for the night?"

The bespectacled eyes moved over Bliss's worn and somewhat dirty coat with polite dispatch. "You from the country?" he countered.

Bliss thought it must be perfectly obvious that she was, but she nodded all the same, and answered, "Yes. I've come to see my Aunt Calandra, and then I'm going to America."

"Isn't everybody?" complained the old man. "Going to America, I mean."

"I shouldn't think so," Bliss remarked. Plenty of people seemed to be perfectly happy living in New Zealand—Jamie McKenna, for instance.

"No more trams tonight," her companion boomed out, abruptly and belatedly. "As to passing the night, Miss Tilly's is as good a place as any, and it's right around that corner there." He paused and pointed. "And down a bit, across from the First Presbyterian Church."

Grateful not to be left waiting in the cold for transportation that wasn't going to arrive anytime soon, Bliss thanked the lamplighter for his help and set off determinedly for Miss Tilly's. Supper, a good hot bath, and a night of sound sleep would make everything look brighter, for sure and for certain.

Tilly Aurmont, a tall, angular woman of indeterminate age, was a bright-eyed spinster who gave the impression of being ever on the alert for evil in all its many forms. She took in Bliss's soiled, torn evening dress and leaped to the worst possible conclusion.

"Merciful heavens," the lady cried, laying one hand to her no-doubt hammering heart. "A harlot!"

The condition of her gown might have raised questions in anyone's mind, but Bliss took serious exception to the term *harlot.* Her eyes flashing and her cheeks hot, Bliss turned her back on Miss Aurmont and walked out. She would have spent the night in the cold had that good woman not come after her and prevailed upon her to have a warm meal in the kitchen.

Bliss was too hungry to turn down food, but she was eager to clear up any misunderstandings the tattered evening gown might have spawned in Tilly Aurmont's mind, too. She explained that she'd been wearing the dress, a hand-me-down from Alexander's sister, at her own engagement party, and realized that she simply couldn't enter into a loveless marriage even though her father had decreed it.

Leaving Jamie out of the tale entirely, Bliss went on to describe the rigors and horrors of being a woman alone on the road, especially in winter. Midway through a hearty supper of lamb chops, boiled potatoes, and creamed spinach, Bliss had won Miss Aurmont's complete and whole-hearted sympathy.

The spinster seemed to be assessing Bliss's size as she showed her new tenant a plain but very clean room at the front of the house on the second floor. "Yes, indeed," she speculated, "I think Mary's clothes would fit you." The woman sighed and made a tsk-tsk sound with her tongue. "Poor, poor Mary," she added as a charitable afterthought.

Bliss was feeling considerably more adventuresome now that she'd eaten and found a safe place to sleep, so she went ahead and asked, "What happened to her? Mary, I mean."

Miss Aurmont tsk-tsked again. "Died," she said. "Hadn't paid her rent in weeks, so, of course, I kept her trunks. Might be, you'd want to part with a few farthings in return for a dress or two."

Guilt, no stranger to Bliss since she'd encountered that cussed Jamie McKenna, washed over her as she thought of the money she'd taken from his desk.

She drew herself up, took herself in hand. She'd pay Jamie back as soon as she was earning a salary.

At her nod, Miss Aurmont called for her cook and the two women laboriously dragged a dusty trunk down the stairs from the third floor and into Bliss's room.

It never occurred to Bliss to be squeamish about touching or wearing a dead woman's clothes. She'd rarely owned a new garment; her coat, now so shabby and old, had once been her mother's.

She chose a practical black skirt from the trunk, along with two blouses and two complete sets of underthings. Bliss was no sophisticate, but she knew that she'd saved herself a considerable sum over buying such items in retail establishments, and she was pleased. Now she would be able to keep a small sum for emergencies.

Miss Aurmont was equally pleased by the bargain and left the room smiling, her cook following after, dragging the heavy trunk.

Bliss availed herself of the hot bath she had paid extra for—there was actually a room, at one end of the hallway, that had been set aside for the purpose—and then made a dash for her chamber, using her coat as a wrapper. Not for the first time, she regretted packing so hastily that first night.

Heaven knew, her wardrobe had never been anything to rave about, but she'd had nightclothes and more than two changes of underwear, at least.

She was settled in bed, the door locked and the electric light—what a marvel that was—turned off. Through the closed and curtained window, Bliss could hear the night sounds of the city, and for a moment she was filled with excitement.

Then she remembered a detail she had overlooked. In the eyes of God and man, she was Jamie McKenna's wife, and there could be no annulment now, because the union had been consummated.

Bliss blushed hotly in the chilly darkness, and once again held an onslaught of tears at bay. In the morning, she would find her Aunt Calandra and everything would be all right after that. Being older and wiser, the woman would surely be able to recommend some workable solution to the problem.

Still, Bliss's heart lay heavy in her chest, and it felt empty of all hope and all spirit. She wished she'd never met Jamie McKenna, for knowing him had taken all the glow off the glorious adventure that lay ahead.

"I hate you, Jamie," she whispered, immediately knowing that was a lie.

Early the next morning, Bliss packed her satchel, ate a hearty breakfast, and said farewell to Tilly Aurmont and Cook. She boarded the tram where Cook had said to and set out for Macomber Street, in the center of Auckland, where Miss Calandra Pennyhope resided.

Riding the tram was an experience worth ten times the ha'penny fare, as far as Bliss was concerned, although the constant clanging of the bell gave her a slight headache. She was already looking forward to her next ride, however, when she got off at the street Miss Aurmont had told her to watch for and began walking due south.

The houses along Macomber Street were tall and narrow and set so close together that they were almost touching each other. Bliss felt cramped for a moment, and she yearned for Jamie and the countryside and the sea. Then she found number 19 and climbed staunchly up the steps to ring the bell.

Only when she heard someone approaching from the other side of the door and grasping the knob did it occur to Bliss that Miss Calandra Pennyhope might not welcome her.

Chapter 10 ❧

JAMIE SLAPPED HIS HAT AGAINST ONE THIGH IN A GESTURE THAT revealed far more about his feelings than he knew. "I spent the night walkin' the streets near the 'arbor, and there was no sign of 'er!"

Peony Ryan gave a sigh and went right on filing her fingernails. How she could be so damn calm was a mystery to Jamie.

"Sounds like she can take care of herself, your Bliss," she said after an interval of reflection, blowing on one nail and then busily filing again, an expression of concentration turning her beautiful face solemn. Peony had changed little over the years: her golden hair was as bright as ever, and her eyes, green as the hills where Jamie's flocks grazed, could still draw a man's soul right out of his body. "For heaven's sake, have something to eat and get some rest. You're half-dead, in case you haven't noticed."

Jamie shoved a hand through his hair. Peony didn't understand, that was all. He wasn't going to be able to eat or sleep until he found Bliss. He ground his teeth together in a moment of pure fury. When he did find the Duchess, he promised himself, he'd see that she didn't sit down for a week.

The idea made him feel better, even though he knew he'd never carry it out.

"Whatever is going through your mind?" Peony demanded, unexpectedly attentive. "You've the most obnoxious grin on your face, Jamie McKenna!"

Jamie flung his hat onto one of the fancy settees that graced Peony's elegant parlor, still smiling, and then shrugged out of his sheepskin coat and tossed that aside, too. A maid immediately appeared out of nowhere and took them away.

"I've decided that you're right," he replied, going to stand before the blaze crackling in Peony's ivory fireplace. "It's not as if Bliss could 'ave found a post this soon, now is it?"

His oldest and dearest friend was still looking at him in bemusement, but she shook her head. "There aren't many ships sailing these days. The seas are too rough at this time of year." The emerald eyes studied him soberly. "What is it that you're not telling me, Jamie love?"

He hesitated. His involvement with Peony had never been a romantic one, but the news of his marriage was bound to set her back on her heels nonetheless. She would be hurt that he hadn't mentioned it first thing, and when Peony was hurt, there was hell to pay.

"Bliss and I—well, we're married."

Peony was agape. "What?" she asked after a few moments of uninterrupted astonishment. "Jamie McKenna, did you just say that you were—"

"Married," Jamie confirmed bleakly. Green blazes were flaring in Peony's eyes, and he held out his hands in a gesture meant to stay her notorious temper.

Peony shrieked an expletive and then snatched a priceless vase from the table beside her and flung it at Jamie. He dodged the thing at the last second, and it shattered musically against the fireplace.

"If you'll just listen," he pleaded as she looked wildly around for something else to throw. "It's only temporary, this marriage—'er father forced me into it at gunpoint!"

"Don't you lie to me!" Peony cried hotly. "I've never seen you forced into anything you didn't want to do!"

In the nick of time, it came back to Jamie—the secret of settling Peony's ire. "Then you've forgotten Queensland," he said with quiet valiance, "and the day Increase Pipher 'ad his vengeance."

Any mention of the whipping Jamie had endured that long-ago day could be counted on to reduce Peony to the most sentimental kind of sympathy. Like a doting elder sister, she wept a little at the memory.

"You're a no-gooder and a wastrel," she sniffled when she'd composed herself a little. "But I can't harden my heart against you and you know it, damn your eyes."

Jamie laughed and crossed the room to draw his friend into his arms. "Now, did I make a fuss like this when you married Ben Ryan all those years ago?"

Peony dried her eyes with a delicate handkerchief drawn out of one sleeve and sniffled again. Despite herself, she chuckled. "Yes, as a matter of fact, you did," she answered. "Oh Jamie, he was a good man, God rest his soul."

Jamie touched her forehead with his lips. "Aye," he said softly, "and you should be findin' a new one, love. It's time you 'ad someone to take care of you."

She reared back in his arms, looking up at him with tears shimmering in her eyes and a tremulous smile on her mouth. "Take care of me, is it? And who was it took care of you, lad, and brought you all the way to New Zealand in the bargain?"

The memory filled Jamie with gratitude. He'd have died, after that last encounter with Increase, if it hadn't been for Peony. Now, with Bliss making a sweet agony of his every waking moment, he was very glad he'd lived.

And, of course, Peony was right in declaring that she could look after herself. She'd been doing that for a long time, both as a wife and as a widow. The thriving shipping concern Ben had left her was proof of her competence, for it had not diminished, but grown.

"This girl you married," she mused when Jamie made no verbal response to her earlier questions. "What was her name again?"

The enormous irony of it made Jamie grin again, albeit

wearily. "Bliss," he answered, and before the sound of his voice faded away, he knew he'd die if he didn't find her.

Miss Pennyhope—if indeed it was the mistress of the house answering the door—was short and plump, with iron-gray hair and spectacles that perched on the end of her nose. "Yes?" she asked, and while there was no note of suspicion in her voice, there was no encouragement either.

Bliss battled an urge to bend one knee just slightly, in the bobbing curtsy she'd learned as a child. "I'm here to see Miss Calandra Pennyhope, please," she said, painfully aware of her tattered coat.

"I am Miss Pennyhope," came the cautious reply.

Bliss introduced herself, leaving out the surname she'd recently acquired, and then Miss Pennyhope was all smiles. "Heaven have mercy, you're Lilian's child!" she cried, stepping back and all but dragging Bliss after her, into a small, tidy entry hall that smelled pleasantly of beeswax and strong soap. "Come in, come in!"

Bliss tried not to look about her as she set her satchel out of the way near a brass umbrella stand etched with tiny rickshaws and Chinamen and pagodas, but her curiosity made it a hard bargain. "I know I should have written before I came—" she started to apologize.

"Nonsense," Calandra Pennyhope interrupted, in her chirping voice. "I was just having tea beside the fire. Of course you'll join me."

"Of course," Bliss echoed without certainty, unfastening the buttons of her coat as she followed her aunt into a tiny parlor so filled with furniture that it would be impossible to make a sudden move without overturning something.

"Do sit down," Miss Pennyhope said. She indicated a chair near the hearth and waited patiently while Bliss wended her way through settees and hassocks and plant tables to take her seat. On the mantelpiece, a little brass clock with roses painted upon its ivory face chimed nine times.

Bliss blushed at this reminder of how early it was to go calling and draped her shabby coat carefully across her lap.

"You so resemble dear Lilian," commented Miss Pennyhope when she'd settled herself in her rocking chair and poured tea for her guest. "I knew you instantly."

"Thank you," Bliss said moderately.

"You will address me as Aunt Calandra, I hope?" From her tone of voice, it sounded as though the woman did indeed hope to be spoken to in just that familiar fashion.

"Yes, certainly," Bliss agreed. She took a sip of her tea, wanting to add lemon and sugar but suddenly too shy to so presume.

"I was, of course, devastated by what Lilian did," Calandra confessed when the silence stretched. "I was some time recovering from the shock, I don't mind telling you."

She paused and sighed sadly. "Mama and Papa, God rest their souls, never wanted her to marry your father, you know. They said he had a contentious disposition."

That was an understatement to Bliss's way of thinking, but she saw no point in bringing up abuses she'd suffered at Nils Stafford's hands at this juncture. She had bigger and more serious concerns.

"If her letters are any indication, Lilian is still very stubborn and high-spirited," Calandra went on, her teacup poised near her mouth. "It only goes to prove that you can lead a horse to water, but you cannot make him wear his shoes."

Bliss blinked, certain that her aunt would correct herself, but the older woman only flushed with conviction and nodded her head.

"Yes, indeed," she added at length. "My sister is most stubborn."

Unsure of how to broach the subject of Jamie, Bliss sipped her tea in a mannerly fashion and kept her quandary to herself.

"What brings you to Auckland?" Calandra finally asked, a

note of cheerful interest in her voice. "Have you come to seek a post of some sort?"

Bliss nodded. "Yes, Aunt Calandra." She took a deep breath and then blurted out, "I want to join Mama in America, earning my passage by teaching children or keeping an elderly woman company, but there is a problem."

Calandra looked positively stunned. Clearly, she numbered among those who saw no reason to leave a fine country like New Zealand. "Problem?" she echoed, and her voice came out as a little squeak.

Again, Bliss nodded. Then, after drawing a deep breath, she rushed into her story, explaining as best she could why she'd left home in the first place and how she'd met Jamie. She hadn't even gotten to the shotgun wedding when tears sprang unexpectedly to her eyes and she couldn't go on for the lump in her throat.

Jamie. She would never, ever see Jamie again, and the knowledge was too much to bear.

"Oh, my goodness, what is it?" Calandra fussed, reaching out awkwardly with one plump hand to pat Bliss's slender, freckled one. "Why are you crying?"

"I'm married!" Bliss wailed. "And I've run away from my husband!"

Calandra withdrew her hand to fan herself with it. She truly did look as though she might suffer an attack of the vapors, and little sputters came from her lips.

Bliss forced herself to finish the shameful tale. "He didn't want to marry me, but Papa forced him."

Calandra had found her voice, and it showed remarkable control, given her near hysterics of moments before. "Do you love this man, Bliss?"

Wretchedly, Bliss nodded, using an embroidered tea napkin to dry her eyes. Hellfire and spit, she'd cried more tears since meeting Jamie McKenna than in all the rest of her life put together. "Yes, God help me!"

A stunned "My, my," was the response to that.

"He meant to get rid of me," Bliss said. At the look of alarm on her aunt's face, she hastened to clarify the statement. "Oh, I mean by an annulment. Jamie wanted to wash his hands of me, but—"

"But," prompted Calandra.

Bliss could feel the color of shame pounding in her cheeks. She might have lied, and saved herself a great deal of grief, but something inside her prevented that. "We were— intimate."

Calandra gave a little cry and fanned herself again, this time with an air of desperation, and then she reached out for a small silver hand bell and began to ring it frantically.

Bliss was certain that she would be sent packing, satchel, sad story, and all, and she prepared to leave on her own with dignity. Her pride demanded that much of her.

An elderly maid wearing a threadbare uniform and a mobcap appeared, looking put out. "Yes, ma'am?" she demanded of Miss Pennyhope. "What is it now?"

"I want a boy sent round for my solicitor, Mr. Wilson. He is to come here immediately."

The maid gave Bliss a skeptical assessment, at the same time addressing her employer. "He'll be thrilled to hear it, mistress. And what, pray tell, has this little redheaded urchin to do with the matter?"

Calandra gave a long-suffering sigh. "Really, Bertha, I do grow weary of explaining my every decision to you. Just send the boy round and go on about your business, please!"

Bertha's button-bright black eyes moved over Bliss once more, and then she said practically, "I'll just go over across the way and ring him up on the telephone." She shook one skinny finger at Calandra. "That's not to say he'll be pleased, mind you. Mr. Wilson is a busy man."

Bliss stared openmouthed as the intrepid Bertha ended her discourse and marched toward the front entrance.

"Mr. Wilson will see to everything, dear," Calandra assured her niece blithely, now engaged in the process of pouring herself another cup of tea. "Don't you fret one little bit."

"What—what will he do?" Bliss dared to ask. "Mr. Wilson, I mean?"

"Why, I would imagine he'll see that scalawag you married arrested," came the cheerful response. "More tea, dear? Your precious mother always liked lemon and sugar in hers, you know. It does seem that you share some of Lilian's— inclinations."

Bliss sank back into her chair. Her coat had long since fallen to the floor, but she made no effort to pick it up. Getting Jamie arrested was not at all the kind of solution she'd had in mind, but she hesitated to say so now, in the face of Calandra's enthusiasm.

"Can they do that? A-arrest a man for—for consummating his own marriage?"

Calandra smiled broadly. "I have no idea, dear," she replied.

Jamie hated the harbor, with its unremitting stench, its fishmongers and whores. It reminded him too well of Dublin and the privations he'd suffered there. . . .

"Lookin' for somebody, lad?" a male voice asked.

Jamie's revulsion deepened as he looked upon the twisted little man who'd spoken. It wasn't the blighter's disability that turned his stomach, but the yellow film that covered his half-rotted teeth and the filth that encrusted his skin. The smell fair made a man's eyes water.

"Maybe I am," Jamie answered after unbuttoning his coat, taking a cheroot and a match from the inside pocket, and lighting up. His blade, sheathed in its supple scabbard on his hip, was within easy reach again. He'd gotten careless of late; time was, he'd never have made a stupid mistake like that.

"Might be I could help." The sailor was sizing Jamie up, no doubt trying to decide if a warm coat and a few coins of the realm would be worth the scuffle.

Something in Jamie's bearing must have made him think twice. He smiled in an ingratiating way and said, "You be lookin' for a woman, mate?"

Jamie felt a shiver move up and down his spine at the thought of Bliss having to deal with this stinking bastard or one of the many like him. He made himself smile. "Not in the way you think," he said. "It's my wife I'm looking for. We had a little—run-in, you might say, and she's got it in her head to go running off to America."

The scrounger tried to look properly disapproving. "A bad business, mate. What's she look like?"

Jamie was reluctant to describe Bliss, but he didn't see where he really had a choice. If he wanted to find her, he was going to need help; driven as he was, he wouldn't be able to keep on searching day and night forever.

Once he'd given a brief verbal sketch of the woman he sought, Jamie offered a high price for news of her whereabouts. After taking his blade out to clean the fingernails of his left hand, he gave a casual warning: the man who touched Bliss Stafford McKenna would henceforth be able to relieve himself sitting down.

The cripple paled under the grime on his face, then backed away. "Yes, sir, Mr. McKenna," he said. "You can count on me. You can depend on old Wally Row, yes, indeed."

Jamie's knife flew end over end through the air, lodging itself with a whistling thump between two of Row's fingers in the wood of the piling he'd been grasping. "Remember what I told you," he said cordially.

Row's hand was trembling as he drew it close to his body. "I'll remember. I'd never lie to you, mate."

Jamie smiled. "I'm sure you wouldn't," he said. By the time he'd pulled the blade from the piling and slipped it back into its scabbard, Row had vanished.

To Bertha's obvious surprise, Mr. Wilson did indeed condescend to answer Miss Pennyhope's summons. He appeared in time for dinner, as it happened, and didn't even pretend to polite reluctance when he was invited to stay.

Calandra apparently saw no reason to beat about the bush. Once they'd all settled down to juicy slabs of some roasted meat, potatoes, and creamed peas, she plunged right into the subject at hand. "This is my niece, Bliss Stafford—er—what was that other name again, precious?"

"McKenna," Bliss supplied, almost in a whisper. If she hadn't been so hungry, she'd have gone back to the tiny room beneath the stairs, which had been allotted to her as her very own, and hidden.

Mr. Wilson, who had been attacking his food with relish, laid down his fork. His brown muttonchop whiskers, tinged with gray, bobbed up and down as he chewed. "McKenna," he repeated thoughtfully after some considerable time had passed.

The name reminded Calandra of the situation, which had apparently escaped her for a few minutes. "My niece married this fellow and came to rue the deed," she said, conveniently leaving out the part about Nils and his pistol. "Now she wants an annulment, but there is one rather serious—and quite embarrassing—tangle." Bliss should have known what was coming by her aunt's dramatic pause. "That beast forced himself upon her."

The piece of meat Bliss had been chewing caught in her throat, and she began to choke ingloriously. Calandra fanned herself and Mr. Wilson sputtered helplessly. It was Bertha who struck her a hard blow to the space between her shoulder blades.

The morsel was dislodged and Bliss was able to breathe again. After casting one grateful glance at the maid, she reached out for her water glass and took a steadying sip.

"Are you quite all right now, dear?" Calandra wanted to know.

"Fat lot of help it is to ask that," Bertha muttered, watching Bliss intently in case she should need another smack.

Red in the face, Bliss nodded and croaked, "Yes, Aunt Calandra, I'm just fine. But—"

Everyone was staring at her.

Bliss drew a deep breath, closed her eyes for a moment and blurted, "But Jamie didn't f-force himself on me. I was quite willing."

At this, Calandra swooned but did not faint dead away. Bertha stood ready to slap her mistress awake should the need arise.

Mr. Wilson tossed down his dinner napkin. "There you have it," he said abruptly. "Nothing can be done."

Bliss felt a crazy kind of relief, even though this could herald the end of all her wonderful plans. She wondered what Jamie would do if she went to him now and threw herself on his mercy.

Jamie lay stretched out on the bed in the room he always used when he visited Peony in Auckland, staring up at the ceiling. He was too exhausted to sleep, and too worried about Bliss.

Despite the fear he felt for her, he smiled in the darkness. God, what he wouldn't give to strip her naked and kiss every freckle on that delicious little body of hers.

The prospect made him harden uncomfortably. With a sigh, Jamie sat up and reached for the cheroots on the bedside stand. Peony didn't allow smoking in her house, but she probably wouldn't find out until after he was gone, anyway. He struck a match and held it to the tip of the small brown cigar.

As he smoked, he deliberately shifted his thoughts from Bliss and the thousand and one different predicaments she might have gotten herself into, to the skirmish on the road a few days before.

Dunnigan had worked for Increase in Queensland, when Jamie first knew him, and later he'd turned up in New Zealand. He'd wanted Eleanor, Dunnigan had, tried to force his attentions on her, in fact. Jamie had heard her screaming and permanently changed the shape of Dunnigan's nose.

He sighed, remembering. That had been before he'd learned, the hard way, how Eleanor liked to lead a man on and then watch Jamie take his vengeance on the poor bastard. He waited for the old pain to come over him, but when it did, it was little more than a twinge.

There was a rap at his door and then Peony let herself in, flipping on the electric light switch. The glare made Jamie flinch and close his eyes for a moment.

"Just as I thought," his friend complained good-naturedly. "You've been smoking in here."

Jamie smiled and shrugged. "Sorry."

Peony crossed the room and wrestled open a window. When she turned around, there was an expression of concern in her eyes. "No luck today?"

Jamie knew she was referring to the search for Bliss, and he shook his head. For some reason, he wasn't comfortable talking about the Duchess with Peony, and that was something new, for there had never been anything he couldn't talk to her about before. "I've been thinkin' about that tiff she and I 'ad with Dunnigan and 'is men—"

"Some tiff, that," Peony fussed. "You would have been killed if it hadn't been for Cutter—that old miscreant. I never thought I'd be grateful to him for anything."

"Will you let me finish, woman?" Jamie demanded, folding his arms across his chest.

Peony nodded grudging assent and sat down in a chair near the empty fireplace. "Go ahead, then," she grumbled, "and damn you for smoking."

He grinned. "Sorry. Anyway, as I was sayin', I've been givin' some thought to those blokes on the road." Jamie's expression turned sober. "Could be they were workin' for Increase."

Peony's beautiful complexion paled slightly. "Off with you," she protested after a moment with a weak wave of one

143

hand. "After all these years, that old devil's probably dead and gone—and good riddance to him, too."

"He hated me, Peony."

"He hated everybody."

Jamie sighed impatiently. "Maybe, but I've got a nasty feelin' that 'e's decided to call in 'is markers, love. And if that's the case, you're in a lot of trouble and so am I."

Peony gnawed at her lower lip, obviously remembering that vicious old man and the days when she'd been at his mercy, after her first husband, Will, had been killed in a fight. "It would be like him not to forget," she admitted in a very small voice. She turned frightened eyes to her friend. "What are we going to do?"

By then, Jamie wished that he hadn't mentioned Increase's name—at least, not that night. "We're goin' to be a little more careful than usual and go on about our business," he answered softly.

The lonely sound of a dog's howling floated in through the open window. Peony shivered, stormed across the room again, and slammed the window closed.

Jamie chuckled. "I'll protect you, love," he promised.

Peony only shook her head and walked out, closing the door behind her.

"The woman 'as no faith in me manly vigor," Jamie complained to the empty room. Then he got up, turned out the light, and opened the window again. He stood in the fresh air, smoking another cheroot and gazing out at the night, wondering where in blazes Bliss had gotten herself off to. He'd wager the little idiot hadn't even given a thought to all the dangers a city had to offer.

The dog was at it again; he let out a series of mournful yips, then began to bay once more, giving voice to his singular miseries.

"Me, too, mate," Jamie agreed in a raspy whisper as he closed the window. "Me, too."

Chapter 11 🌿

THE FIRST GRAY LIGHT OF A CRISPLY CHILLY DAWN WAS SHOWING at the windows as Bliss made ready to travel to the docks in search of work. Calandra, too, was up and about, brewing tea, toasting bread in the oven, poaching eggs.

All the same, the older woman had her doubts about the wisdom of Bliss's plans. "Perhaps it would be better, my dear," she ventured to say as the two sat together at a small table in the kitchen, having breakfast, "if you simply went back to your husband."

Bliss had been awake half the night, grappling with that same idea. The prospect of returning to Jamie was not without appeal, but she had to bear in mind that he hadn't wanted to marry her in the first place. Despite all his misgivings about her plans to travel to America, he was probably relieved that she was gone.

She shook her head in a wordless and belated reply to her aunt's suggestion. She'd brought nothing but trouble to Jamie, after all, and he couldn't be expected to welcome her.

The wooden clock on the kitchen mantelpiece made a whirring sound and then gave six ponderous bongs. "Well," Calandra chimed, "in any case, dear, you're certainly getting a timely start. One must remember that the early bird gathers no moss."

Bliss smiled into her teacup at this bit of convoluted wisdom, but made no comment.

Calandra's sweet expression changed to one of disquiet. "I did so hope that Mr. Wilson would be able to do something about your—predicament."

What little good cheer Bliss had been able to summon up deserted her. The fact that she was legally bound to Jamie was sure to cause problems at some later date. "I can't go back, Aunt Calandra," she said softly, "and there's no money for a divorce."

Calandra sighed. "The magistrate would want a reason, anyway."

That was another thing. Divorces were frowned upon by society and generally hard to come by. It seemed that Bliss was doomed to spend the rest of her life tied to a man who didn't want her. "I suppose he'll divorce me," she reflected after a few moments had passed, her voice small and sad. The knowledge should have comforted Bliss, but it didn't.

In the distance, she heard the clanging of the tram's bell. The distraction was a welcome one; Bliss bounded out of her chair, carried her empty plate to the sink, and put on her coat.

"Hurry, now," Calandra said, making a shooing motion with her hands when Bliss would have gone on clearing away the breakfast dishes. "Leave that to Bertha and me."

Bliss nodded. "Thank you," she said.

"Don't go near the docks, now," the older woman warned, following Bliss on her dash through the small house to the front door. "There's really no need. The people in the passage agencies will know who's looking for a governess or a companion—"

"I'll remember," Bliss promised, hurrying down the front steps as the clamor of the tram bell grew louder and more insistent. The air was cold enough that it turned her breath to fog.

She barely reached the tram in time, and she was breathing hard as she dropped her ha'penny fare into the metal coin box.

"Important business today, miss?" the driver asked. He was a young man who would have been handsome if it hadn't been for the deep pockmarks on his face.

Bliss nodded and found her way to a seat, and excitement filled her at the prospect of a bright new day. There might just be an adventure ahead.

People got on and off the tram at the dozens of stops it made along the way, and Bliss watched them, curious to know what business they were about, what their lives were like, what their hopes and dreams were.

In the heart of Auckland, where the tram made its turnabout to start on the return leg of its route, Bliss got off, admiring the tall buildings that rose along the sidewalks and taking care not to step in front of a buggy or coach as she crossed the road.

Heeding her aunt's advice, Bliss did not approach the docks as she'd originally planned, but sought out a shipping agency instead. The first one she came to had a wide front window with a title painted on the glass: RYAN FREIGHT AND PASSAGE COMPANY. Beneath this, in smaller script, were the words "P. Ryan, Prop."

After drawing a deep breath, Bliss opened the door and walked into the establishment. A clerk came forward from the rear, weaving between half a dozen desks crowded close together, and smiled. "May I help you, miss?"

Bliss felt shy, but she overcame that quickly enough. A person couldn't afford to hesitate, not if they wanted their dreams to come true. She introduced herself and related her desire to earn her passage to the United States.

The clerk seemed very understanding. "Well, we do get passengers in sometimes who are looking for help." He paused and assessed Bliss's hair, which was held back from her face with two small tortoiseshell combs and falling free down her back. "How old are you?"

Bliss was a bit shaken by that question, even though she was certainly of an age that permitted her to do as she wished. She did regret, however, not taking the trouble to put up her hair. That always made her look older.

"I'm nineteen," she answered.

The young man nodded and, taking up a pencil and a pad of paper, began to write. "What is your name and where can you be reached, please?" he asked, in tones that were carefully businesslike.

Bliss related the necessary information, then asked, "Do you think someone will want me?"

There was a look of kind indulgence in the clerk's eyes. "I don't believe there's any question of that, Miss Stafford," he said.

She smiled. "I suppose I should leave my name with the other shipping agents, too," she mused. "Are their offices nearby?"

Accommodatingly, the gentleman wrote out a list. "Stay away from this one," he said, putting a prominent check beside one company name. "There are rumors about some of the business they conduct in the Orient."

Bliss nodded, grateful for the warning, and took the list. After thanking the clerk for everything, she stepped out of the warm agency into the biting cold of a late-winter day.

The sidewalks were thick with people, and carriages, buggies, and saddle horses filled the cobbled street. Bliss felt uplifted by the hustle and bustle. In the very next instant, however, her heart was wedged into her throat.

An expensive carriage, drawn by four beautiful grays, drew to a stop directly in front of her. There would have been nothing remarkable about this if Jamie himself hadn't opened the door and stepped down from the rig, turning to lift a stunningly attractive woman after him.

Although Bliss couldn't hear what was said for the clatter of hooves and wheels on cobblestones and the thudding of her own heart, what she saw devastated her. Jamie laughed at something the woman said, his hands lingering on her tender waist, and then bent his head to give her a brief but tender kiss on the mouth.

The woman gently touched his face with a small gloved hand, and Bliss was abruptly and painfully reminded of her shabby coat, her scuffed shoes, her secondhand skirt and shirtwaist. Next to this vision, she was nothing but an unsophisticated bumpkin.

She retreated into the crowd praying that Jamie wouldn't see her, and God must have had sympathy for her situation. Her estranged husband said a few more words to his lady friend and turned to stride off in the direction of the harbor. Something drew the woman's attention, however, for after a few moments of utter paralysis, Bliss sensed a hard stare.

She forced herself to meet the bright green gaze of Jamie's mistress for a second or so and, then, horrified, she turned and began making her way, as rapidly as she could, toward the tram stop.

"Wait, please!" she heard a feminine voice call, and Bliss knew somehow that it was herself being summoned, but she didn't stop. Not many things had the power to frighten her into flight, but the prospect of an encounter with her husband's paramour did.

Mercifully, there was a tram to be boarded, and Bliss got on, not caring where the vehicle might take her. Only one desire pulsed in her mind: to get away.

The tram jerked and rattled into motion, and then it was making its way between the wagons and buggies that shared the street, its bell issuing a shrill warning for all and sundry to step aside.

"Damnation!" Peony fumed, slamming the door behind her and pulling at her bonnet as she approached the counter.

Her favorite clerk, Michael Potter, smiled at her. "Good morning, Mrs. Ryan," he said, used to her fiery moods.

Peony was still sputtering. "I don't know why I should

bother my head about that little redheaded snippet, anyway," she fussed. "She's Jamie's problem, not mine, and I don't care if she catches the first ship to Shanghai—"

"Actually," interceded Michael, "she's off to the States, if we're talking about the same 'redheaded snippet.' I just spoke to her."

Peony's mouth rounded into an *O,* and it was a moment before she could absorb the implications. "Of course," she said, on a long breath. "I presume the young lady left an address."

Michael held up a slip of paper. "Number nineteen Macomber Street," he replied. "Her name is Bliss Stafford."

"Her name is Bliss Stafford *McKenna,*" Peony corrected, perhaps a bit petulantly. She wanted more than anything to see Jamie happy—he deserved it, after all he'd been through—but she had her reservations, too. He'd been besotted with another woman—Eleanor Kilgore, her name was—and look where that had gotten him.

"Is something wrong, Mrs. Ryan?" Michael asked presently.

Peony shook her head and then pulled off her bonnet, hanging it on a coat tree behind the counter. "There is an errand I'd like you to run, though. You don't mind venturing down near the docks, do you?"

Michael swallowed visibly. "No, ma'am," he lied.

Peony gave him her most dazzling smile. "Wonderful," she replied. And then she told him who to find and what to say to them.

The end of the tram route was a dismal-looking place consisting of dim little shops, shoddy pubs, and old frame houses leaning against one another for support.

"You'll have to pay again if you ain't gettin' off, lady," the conductor said.

Bliss reached into her pocket for a ha'penny and paid the fare. It was very cold, and the tram was open to the frigid weather. "When will we be going back?" she asked.

"In an hour," was the desultory reply.

Bliss shivered. "An hour?"

The conductor sighed. "Yes, miss," he replied. "Must keep to the schedules, you know. There's a tearoom over there, if you want to warm up and get a bite to eat."

Mentally, Bliss counted what remained of the small amount of money she'd taken—borrowed—from Jamie. There wasn't much, but she was hungry and, if she was any judge, far from Macomber Street.

She stood up and left the trolley. Following the conductor's directions, Bliss found the tearoom and stepped gratefully in from the cold.

The small establishment was utterly plain in decor, but it looked clean. Bliss was relieved, having deduced from the condition of the neighborhood that this was not one of the better parts of the city.

Other customers crowded the place, and Bliss had to take an unladylike place at the end of the counter. A heavy woman huffed out of the kitchen and barked, "Name your poison, sweetie, I ain't got all day."

Bliss blinked. Apparently, she wasn't going to get a chance to look at a menu. "H-how much is the soup?" she asked, after risking a sidelong glance at the bowl steaming in front of the man beside her. If it wasn't too dear, she would have tea as well.

The woman named what Bliss thought was a reasonable price, and a bargain was struck. The soup, along with a cup of hot tea, appeared on the counter before her.

While Bliss ate, she listened in amazement to the good-natured abuse being exchanged by the cook and her customers. They called her Flossy, and beneath their barbs and her own was an undercurrent of coarse affection. Unprepossessing as that place was, Bliss felt strangely at home there.

The soup was good—spicy and brimming with fresh vegetables and bits of stewed chicken—and Bliss hardly noticed when the crowd began to thin out.

"That's some appetite you got there," Flossy commented,

startling Bliss, who had not seen the woman approach the counter. "Little down on your luck, are you, lamb?"

Bliss swallowed, thinking of Jamie and his elegant mistress. No doubt he'd told her about the wife he'd accidentally acquired and they'd laughed together over all her shortcomings. Color surged into her cheeks as she realized that Flossy had struck very close to the truth. "A little," she admitted.

Flossy smiled. "Well, you've come to the right place if it be work you need. I could sure use a girl to wash dishes and wait tables."

Bliss was about to decline by explaining that she meant to leave the country when she realized how handy it would be if she could earn a bit of money before the fact. It might be a long while, after all, before she found a position with a traveler or travelers, and her Aunt Calandra couldn't be expected to support her without some kind of compensation.

Besides, Bliss needed something to distract her from Jamie McKenna and the ruin he'd made of her life. She returned Flossy's smile, albeit somewhat sadly, and after only the briefest discussion, they reached an agreement.

Bliss was given an apron and set to peeling potatoes in preparation for the supper trade. For the next few hours, she forgot all about her problems, she was so busy.

"You'd best go, missy," Flossy said when full darkness had settled down around the tearoom. "The tram'll stop runnin' soon, and then where will you be?"

Realizing how far she had to travel and how worried her aunt would be over her late appearance, Bliss shed her apron and pulled on her coat. "The dishes—"

"They'll be here waiting for you in the mornin'," Flossy said easily. "Hear that bell? Hurry up now, or the tram will go without you."

Bliss ran to the corner, where the noisy conveyance was about to pull away, and scrambled aboard just in time.

"I was wondering where you got off to," the conductor

complained. He remembered that Bliss had already paid her return fare and didn't expect another ha'penny.

Bliss smiled and shrugged. A few customers had left coins on their tables, and Flossy had said she was welcome to them. Not only that, but at the end of the week she could count on wages—the first she'd ever earned in her life.

Satisfaction kept the cold winter wind at bay until Bliss reached the center of Auckland and found that she'd missed the connecting tram. It would be a long walk to Macomber Street, she knew, and a cold one, and she wasn't even sure of the way.

A family, a man and a woman and two little girls, passed Bliss as she stood helplessly at the tram stop. They were laughing and talking among themselves, and a lonely feeling washed over Bliss, making her feel homeless. Abandoned.

She squared her shoulders. She was tired, that was all, and waxing sentimental would do her no earthly good. She drew a deep breath and set out in the direction she hoped would eventually take her to the warmth and safety of her aunt's house.

He was a big man, Calandra Pennyhope thought. Yes, indeed, he was entirely too big for her cramped little parlor.

Watching Bliss's husband out of the corner of one eye, Calandra continued to rock in her chair, her hands busy with the bright blue scarf she was knitting. He stood in front of the fireplace, his arms braced against the mantelpiece, glaring at the clock as though willing the hands to stop turning.

It was late, and Calandra was heartily worried herself, but Mr. McKenna was no comfort to her and she was clearly no comfort to him.

"Perhaps Miss Stafford knows you're here and is avoiding you," the spinster suggested sweetly. He was handsome enough, this Jamie man, but in Calandra's limited experience, the good-looking ones were often shameless rogues.

"Perhaps," he agreed dryly. He showed no sign of leaving,

however—he didn't move or look away from the clock. He'd been standing where he was for nearly an hour, muttering the occasional oath under his breath.

Beast, Calandra thought, flushing angrily and setting her jaw. Why, for two pins she'd stab him with one of her knitting needles. She was just about to suggest that he vacate the premises, for the dozenth time since he'd arrived early in the afternoon, when the bell knob beside the front door was turned.

Calandra prayed fervently that Bliss had come home, and followed this with just as earnest an appeal that she had not. Mr. McKenna had strode into the entry hall and pulled open the door before either she or Bertha had had a chance to react.

"Oh, no," she heard Bliss say, in a weary voice.

"Oh, yes," responded that reprehensible husband of hers.

Calandra flinched as the door slammed with a reverberating crash. She and Bertha just weren't used to this kind of thing anymore. In fact, they never had been.

Jamie looked terrible. There were shadows under his eyes, his face was stubbly with a new beard, and Bliss would have been willing to bet that he hadn't had a decent meal or a good night's sleep in two days.

"Where have you been?" he rasped.

Bliss steeled herself against a tendency to sympathize with him. After all, if Jamie truly hadn't slept or eaten properly, it was only because he'd been too busy dancing attendance on that beautiful blond friend of his. Besides that, Bliss had just walked a long, long way in the cold, and she wasn't feeling too chipper herself. "That's a long story," she said, starting to go around him.

Jamie blocked her way, trapping her there in the entryway, against the door. "A story you're about to tell, Duchess. In minute detail."

Bliss sighed. She was too cold, too tired, and too hungry

for this. "It all started," she said caustically, "when I saw you help your mistress out of a carriage and kiss her, right there on the street!"

The expression on Jamie's face would have been amusing if it hadn't been for the circumstances. "My what?" he demanded.

"Your concubine, doxy, paramour—whatever you wish to call her," Bliss answered tightly, folding her arms.

Jamie rocked back on the heels of his boots. Though he spoke in low, carefully controlled tones, he lapsed into the brogue. "Am I missin' somethin' 'ere, Mrs. McKenna?" he wanted to know. "You're the one, lass, that sneaked out of me bed while I slept, robbed me blind—"

"Robbed you blind!" Bliss yelled. "I took three pounds from you—little enough, considering what you've put me through!"

"What I've put you through, is it? Why, you—"

Bliss could bear no more. She raised one hand and slapped Jamie across the face with all the strength and fury she possessed. He stared at her for a moment, crimson prints of her fingers glowing on his cheek, and then whispered, "Get your things together, Mrs. McKenna, for we'll be gone from 'ere as soon as me driver comes round again."

Setting her jaw, Bliss glared up at him, telling him with her eyes that she didn't plan on going anywhere.

"I won't leave without you, Duchess," he warned in a low voice, and that was when Bliss knew she'd lost the battle, if not the entire war. She could not subject her aging aunt to the kind of scene that would surely result if she continued in her rebellion.

Dropping her eyes, Bliss conceded temporary defeat. "All right," she whispered. "Just let me get my satchel."

Jamie stepped aside, allowing her to pass, and she went down the hall to her tiny room beneath the staircase. She had barely gone inside when her aunt joined her, looking very agitated.

"I knew I should have summoned the police," the old woman fussed and fretted. "When am I going to get it through my head that a stitch in time is only skin-deep?"

Bliss smiled as she packed her things carefully away in the satchel. "Everything will be all right, Aunt Calandra," she said. "I promise. Jamie can be very intimidating, but he's not cruel."

Calandra looked sad. "I often wish that I'd married, you know."

Bliss closed her satchel and then gave her aunt a gentle kiss on the cheek. Because the room was so small, she did both without taking a single step. "Good-bye, Auntie, and thank you for everything. I'll come to call if I get the chance."

Jamie was waiting near the front door, with his coat on and his leather hat pulled down over his forehead. Either the carriage had arrived, or he expected it at any moment.

"Scoundrel," Bliss muttered, and though she was very angry at his high-handed manner, she had to admit, at least to herself, that she was also glad to see him again.

Jamie glared at her, but before he could say anything, Calandra interjected yet another pearl of wisdom. "If the truth hurts," she told her niece's husband firmly, "wear it."

Jamie glanced at Calandra, looked away, then looked back as her words penetrated his quiet fury. Bliss wasn't sure, but she thought she saw a hint of a grin lift one corner of his mouth.

"Thank you," he said politely, tipping his hat to Calandra, and then he opened the door and all but thrust Bliss outside onto the steps.

A sleek carriage was waiting in the street, lamps glowing in the chilly darkness, matched gray horses nickering impatiently.

Jamie had taken Bliss's satchel from her, and he tossed it into the boot at the back of the carriage, then opened the door for her. "The Victoria Hotel," he said to the driver.

Bliss settled herself inside the carriage, wanting to stay as far from Jamie as possible, and he only chuckled at the maneuver, planted his feet on the cushioned seat opposite theirs and sighed contentedly.

"Again, Duchess," he said comfortably, "where have you been?"

"Working," Bliss answered, looking out at the night and despairing because somewhere in this big, confusing city, there was a woman who knew what it was to lie beneath Jamie McKenna, to run her hands down his naked back. A woman other than herself. "How did you find me?"

Jamie grinned beneath the slant of his disreputable hat, which he'd pulled down over his eyes in the way of a man about to doze off. "Workin' at what?" he asked, completely ignoring her question.

"Waiting tables in a tearoom."

He gave a hoarse burst of laughter. "Ah, Duchess, trust you to do the one damn thing I wouldn't have expected. Why the hell did you want to bring a lot of bleeders their tea?"

Bliss felt very virtuous all of the sudden. "To earn wages, of course," she said loftily. "So that I could repay you the money I borrowed."

Quick as that he'd reached out, caught hold of her, and wrenched her across his lap, so that she was looking up into his shadowed face. Heaven help her, she hadn't the spirit to fight.

"Borrowed, is it?" he drawled, his lips so close to hers that she could feel the heat of his breath. "Were you plannin' to come back then, Duchess?"

She trembled as he worked the buttons of her coat and then settled one proprietary hand over her breast. "You know I wasn't," she managed to say. "You'd made it clear enough that you didn't want a wife."

His thumb moved over her nipple, slowly, causing it to tighten and then rise beneath her shirtwaist and camisole. "You and I," he answered gruffly, "have a lot to talk about." A moment later, he was kissing her.

Chapter 12 🌱

THE VICTORIA HOTEL WAS THE GRANDEST PLACE BLISS HAD EVER seen, even more splendid than Alexander's house in Wellington. Furthermore, despite his rumpled clothes and that infernal leather hat, the staff deferred to Jamie as though he were Prince Albert himself.

Bliss was awed by the massive chandeliers that graced the ceilings, and the rugs beneath her feet were richly colored and so soft that she was certain her shoes must be leaving imprints.

Jamie strode confidently into the lift, but Bliss hung back. She'd read about these contraptions; sometimes they fell a story or two and somebody crawled out with broken ankles. Provided they'd been fortunate enough to survive, of course.

"I'll just take the stairs, thank you very much," she said.

Jamie's hand shot out, caught Bliss by the upper arm, and wrenched her inside the cubicle just before the operator closed the door with a disturbing clank. Bliss shut her eyes tightly as the conveyance began to lurch upward.

Jamie's chuckle was low and warm. "You're safe with me, Duchess," he said.

Bliss gave her husband a wry look. If ever anyone had misstated a case!

His fingers entangled themselves in her hair, which was now badly in need of brushing, and the mischief still danced in his blue eyes. Bliss thought he might actually kiss her in front of the lift operator and, even worse, that she might let him. She reminded herself that she was little more than an amusement to this man and twisted away.

Jamie shrugged and leaned back against the wall, his arms folded, while the metal box made its laborious way skyward. Finally, to Bliss's relief, it stopped and the operator grasped some kind of lever and opened the door.

Bliss leaped into the hallway, the way a climber might spring from a narrow mountain ledge to a wider one, and Jamie was grinning as he joined her, carrying her satchel. He and the lift operator exchanged a few words that she couldn't hear, and then Jamie led the way to a door at the end of the hall.

There was a number on it, in glistening brass: 29. Bliss swallowed nervously as Jamie took a key from his coat pocket and unlocked the door. At the twisting of a switch, the room was flooded with light, and it looked like a palace to Bliss, who had never been inside a hotel until then.

Before she could do more than peer past one of Jamie's shoulders, however, he turned and lifted her easily into his arms.

As he carried her over the threshold, Jamie kissed Bliss with a thoroughness that set her tingling in the most sensitive places, and she was breathless and flushed when he set her on her feet.

His lips brushed her forehead and one of his hands moved in her hair. Bliss knew that Jamie was in the grip of some powerful emotion; she could feel it pulsing around him like an aura, but what he said was commonplace enough.

"I suppose you're 'ungry, Duchess."

Bliss hadn't been aware of the fact until he mentioned it; now her stomach ground painfully. She nodded.

Jamie laughed and tossed aside his hat and coat, then proceeded to unbutton Bliss's. "I've sent word to the kitchen," he said, in the tone of one speaking to a weary child. "In the meantime, why don't you lie down for a while?"

Bliss immediately bristled. Recalling the intensity of Jamie's kiss, not to mention the games he'd wanted to play in the carriage, she blushed with temper. "You'd like that, wouldn't you?" she snapped.

He grinned. "Aye," he replied easily. "But there will be time for that later. Lots of time."

Bliss eyed him suspiciously. He sounded as though they would be together for the next fifty years, and that certainly wasn't the case. She waited, a stubborn set to her jaw.

"I've come up with a solution to our problem, Duchess," he said, turning away to approach a cabinet on the far side of what appeared to be a sitting room. Bliss had not seen a bed.

A feeling of weary tension coiled in her stomach, dispelling her hunger for a moment. Jamie was about to say that he was going to divorce her. She braced herself and whispered, "Yes?"

"We'll stay married," he went on, taking a bottle and one glass from the cabinet and blithely pouring himself a drink.

Bliss felt both stinging fury and sweet relief. "What?" she croaked, for that was all she dared say, all she could think of to say.

Jamie turned to face her, looking very pleased with himself, and leaned comfortably back against the cabinet. "We'll make the best of a bad bargain, you and I. I'll buy you a house and a carriage and some clothes and jewelry—"

Bliss saw a frightening picture forming, a portrait of herself as a kept woman. Knowing that her knees wouldn't support her any longer and that she'd turned pale, she sank into a plushly upholstered chair and clenched the arms so hard that her knuckles turned white. "And—and you would visit me whenever you had nothing better to do?" she interrupted, her voice small with shock.

Jamie was looking at her curiously. "I'm not a man who thrives in the city, Duchess," he said. "But you'd like it here. There are theaters and orchestras and shops—"

Bliss shot to her feet. "By God, Jamie McKenna," she screamed, "if I can't be a real wife to you, then I won't be a wife at all!"

By now, Jamie was staring at Bliss as though she'd just sprouted an extra head. He was saved from having to reply by a brisk knock at the door, which he was forced to answer because Bliss was rooted to the floor, her arms folded in defiance.

The food that Jamie had no doubt requested by way of the lift operator had arrived, and the scent weakened Bliss's resolve to give no ground. Deciding that she would be able to think more clearly on a full stomach, she marched over to the serving cart and began looking under lids.

Jamie watched with amusement, and a touch of smugness, as she filled a plate with venison, potatoes and gravy, and tender baby carrots swimming in butter. She was already chewing as she walked to a settee near the fireplace and sat down.

"You needn't think," she said, through a mouthful of the succulent meat, "that this means I'm agreeing to your outrageous proposal. I won't be a bird in a gilded cage."

Jamie rolled his eyes and began filling a plate of his own. "You haven't the table manners for it anyway," he replied.

Bliss swallowed, her cheeks burning. "I rarely talk with my mouth full," she argued. "It's just that I'm so hungry."

"You're always hungry."

She glared at him. "And you're always—like you were in the carriage."

Jamie laughed and sat down on a settee to eat. "Oh? And how was that?"

"Lecherous," Bliss said, before attacking her supper again. She hadn't eaten since the soup and tea at Flossy's, and she was famished.

"Tomorrow we'll buy you some decent clothes," Jamie

speculated, between bites. He looked as though he were imagining Bliss in fancy silks and velvets instead of seeing her as she was.

"I'm working tomorrow," Bliss said flatly. "Flossy is depending on me."

Jamie's voice was quiet in an unnerving way. "Flossy?"

"Of Flossy's Tearoom," Bliss answered, rising to carry her empty plate to the serving cart and dispose of it.

Jamie was shaking his head when she looked at him, his eyes on the bit of bread he was dragging through a pool of gravy. "Go to bed, Duchess," he said. "We can fight this out in the morning."

Bliss was tired, but if Jamie McKenna thought she was just going to fall into his arms, the way That Woman probably did—

"It's in there," Jamie said lightly, after setting his plate on the serving cart and reaching out for his coat and hat, pointing toward a separate room.

Bliss was staring at Jamie in surprise. "Where are you going?"

He smiled and gave her a brotherly kiss on the forehead. "Don't trouble yourself about it, Duchess—I've got some business to attend to, that's all."

Bliss glanced at the gaudy gilt clock on the mantelpiece. "At this hour of the night?"

Jamie had already reached the door, and he touched the brim of his hat in a blithe gesture of farewell. "Aye, love. Sleep tight, and all that."

An image of that blond woman greeting him at the door of some hideaway filled Bliss's mind, and she felt an almost incomprehensible rage. When Jamie actually had the nerve to walk out, she snatched one of the china plates from the serving cart and sent it spinning after him, to shatter against the wall.

The door opened again, and Jamie stuck his head inside to say, "Don't run the bill up too 'igh now, love, for you're already into me for three pounds."

Bliss gave a shriek and reached for the other plate, which he evaded by ducking outside. There was a tinkling crash as the dish disintegrated and little droplets of gravy decorated the door.

"Good night, sweetness," she heard Jamie call from the hallway. This was followed by the grating of a key in the lock.

Too exhausted to throw another thing, Bliss whirled and stomped off into the room Jamie had indicated earlier. There was nothing to do now but sleep; in the morning, she would decide how to deal with all the problems besetting her.

The bedchamber was graced with an enormous bed that had an intricately carved headboard, and in one corner of the room, there was a fancy teakwood screen. Curious, Bliss peered behind it and was astonished to see a stationary bathtub, with spigots and a faucet. She approached, full of wonder, almost unable to believe such luxury existed, even though she'd heard that Alexander had just such a tub in his house.

Water thundered into the tub, steaming hot, when Bliss turned a spigot, and she leaped back, startled. Then, realizing that she must put the plug in place before starting the water running, she crept back, turned off the spigot, and located the plug.

Minutes later, she was soaking happily in hot water, thinking that it would almost be worth being a bird in a gilded cage if she could have a bath every day. Almost, but not quite.

She bolted upright when she heard the door open in the distance. Somehow, Bliss had gotten the impression that Jamie meant to be gone all or most of the night, and she wasn't prepared for his return.

"Jamie?" she called, at the same time reaching out for a towel.

He came around the screen. "Aye, love, it's me," he said, and he looked as tired as Bliss felt. "Let's go to bed, shall we? I 'aven't slept since that last night we spent together."

Bliss was so glad that he wasn't spending the night with his mistress that she made no protest about sharing a bed. She rose from the tub once Jamie had rounded the screen again and modestly wrapped herself in the towel she'd been grasping in her hands.

Jamie had already stripped off his clothes and climbed into bed, and he watched Bliss with no expression at all in his eyes as she joined him, the towel around her like a sarong. She had no more than settled down when Jamie tossed the covers back and briskly divested her of the towel.

Bliss trembled, because the night was cold and Jamie's eyes were hot, and she knew she wasn't going to be able to refuse him if he wanted her.

He seemed captivated by the freckles that had always been Bliss's secret shame, and he bent his head to kiss her between her breasts and then on her belly. Despite her bone-deep weariness, Bliss was aroused, but Jamie only gave her a light kiss on the mouth, extinguished the elegant lamp that burned on the bedside table, and with an expansive yawn, stretched out to sleep.

Bliss was too worn out to fret and fume. She closed her eyes, and the moment she did so, sleep overtook her and carried her off to a safe, warm place where there were no thoughts and no images.

Feeling a warm brightness on her face, Bliss opened her eyes. Sunlight was pouring in through a huge window, and she sat bolt upright.

There was no sign of Jamie, and when she called his name, she got no answer. A horrible thought possessed her, and using the chenille bedspread as a cover, she dashed out of the bedroom and across the sitting room to grasp the doorknob.

After muttering a prayer, she flicked her wrist and the

knob turned. She sagged against the door, smiling with relief; Jamie hadn't locked her in.

A note had been propped against the ugly mantel clock, and Bliss unfolded it with more eagerness than she would ever have allowed Jamie to see. *Duchess,* he'd written, *I was afraid you'd climb out a window, so I took a chance and left the door unlocked. Mind you don't do anything stupid. I'll be back in a few hours. Love, Jamie.*

Bliss touched the word *love* with her fingertip, allowing it to warm her. Then, after another look at the clock, she realized that she was going to be late for work if she didn't hurry.

Hastily, she located her satchel, which had yet to be unpacked, and drew out clean underthings and her spare shirtwaist. She would wear the sateen skirt again, though it, like the blouse, was quite rumpled.

As Bliss wound her flowing hair into a coronet and pinned it in place, she despaired a little that her pride wouldn't allow her to let Jamie buy her new and beautiful clothes. It would have been lovely to have things to choose from—this dress for the tea, and that for the races. . . .

Shaking her head at her own foolishness, she washed her face, cleaned her teeth, and set out, spurning the lift for the stairs. She felt more than one pair of eyes upon her as she crossed the lobby, but she kept her chin high. If people were entertaining malicious thoughts, well, let them think what they liked.

Outside, the weather was crisply beautiful. The sun was shining brightly in the sky and there was the promise of spring in the air.

Bliss's step was light as she hurried toward the tram stop. She hadn't waited long before it came, crammed with people who worked in offices and shops and hotels.

During the ride to the end of the line, where Flossy's establishment was, Bliss thought of Jamie and the way he'd uncovered her the night before and kissed her so gently. Just the memory made her breasts swell with warmth and her nipples harden. She was glad of her heavy coat.

"Dammit all to 'ell!" Jamie roared as he came out of the bedroom, glaring at Peony as though everything were her fault. "To think I trusted that little—"

Peony smiled to realize how far gone her friend really was. The longer he knew Bliss, the more he spoke in the brogue, and that meant he was finally letting down his guard a little, allowing himself to be who he was: Jamie McKenna, of Dublin. "Calm down," she said, tugging at her gloves. "She told you she had a job."

"And I told 'er that she didn't need it!" Jamie yelled, gesturing wildly. "I offered to set her up in a 'ouse, for God's sake—"

"For God's sake, Jamie? Or for yours?"

He flung down his hat and then sank into a chair, burying his head in his hands. Ah yes, Peony reflected, with another small smile. He was the very picture of despair.

"I suppose," Peony ventured, some moments later, "that you generously offered to visit Bliss whenever the spirit moved you."

Jamie's bleak stare confirmed Peony's suspicions, though he didn't speak.

She took a chair, despite the fact that Jamie hadn't invited her to make herself at home, and loosened the strings on her bonnet. Lord, how she hated having ribbons under her chin. "How pompous you are, Jamie McKenna," she remarked, making no effort to hide her annoyance. "How infernally pompous."

He ignored her reference to his arrogant attitude and sighed. "At least I know where she is this time."

"Where?" asked Peony, with a tinge of impatience, for she could not have cared less. She hadn't felt like taking some bounding country woman shopping anyway.

"Flossy's Tearoom," Jamie answered.

A peal of laughter escaped her.

"It's not funny, Peony!"

Peony assumed some semblance of dignity, though her lips were still twitching. "Oh, but it is, darling," she said. "What in heaven's name does she do, read tea leaves?"

Jamie was obviously in no mood to be sporting. He glared at Peony.

She wasn't the least bit cowed. "Do you want me to tell your fortune, Jamie love?" she asked sweetly. "I can do it without tea leaves, a crystal ball, or even a glance at your palm."

He muttered something grossly impolite and thrust himself off the settee, putting on that seedy hat of his in almost the same motion. Of course, it did give him a rakish look, that hat. A look that was most attractive. "Come on," he grumbled.

Peony took her time. "Don't you want to hear what your future holds?" she chimed.

"I 'ave a damn good idea what me future 'olds, thank you very much!"

"Six or seven redheaded children, I should think," Peony mused, just to raise some steam from beneath Jamie's collar. "By the way, I'm getting hungry. Where are we lunching?"

Jamie took Peony's elbow in his hand and ushered her out of the suite. "Where else," he muttered, "but Flossy's Tearoom?"

When Bliss arrived at the tearoom, there was a "closed" sign in the window and she could see Flossy through the dusty glass, packing things into boxes. Boldly, she let herself in, expecting bad news.

Instead, Flossy blessed her with a broad and slightly rotted smile. "He's finally gone and struck lucky, that boy of mine." She beamed. "Got himself a little patch of land in Australia."

Bliss smiled, slipped out of her coat, and began helping her erstwhile employer pack plates. While they worked, Flossy regaled Bliss with plans for the future. She'd just be cooking for her son now—her days of working her fingers to the bone were past.

She gave Bliss a kindly, worried glance. "But I've gone and forgot about you, missy. What are you going to do, without work?"

Bliss smiled. She'd visit each of the shipping and passage agencies regularly, with the exception of the one with questionable dealings in the Orient, and one day things would come right for her. "I'll be fine," she said.

Flossy didn't look persuaded. "Sweet little dearie like you," she fussed. "Ought to have a husband to look after her."

Bliss had not mentioned Jamie to her friend, and she didn't plan to bring up his name now. After all, hers wasn't the kind of marriage one went around boasting about. "Someday," she said, and she thought of herself standing beside some nice man in America, before a preacher. He'd be a decent, trusting soul, and she'd be a bigamist, for even if Jamie divorced her, Bliss would always be his wife in her heart.

Flossy reached out and patted Bliss's hand, and then the two women fell to work, chatting as they packed up everything that could be wrapped in newspaper or crated. The time passed quickly, and Bliss was beginning to feel the first stirrings of real hunger—she hadn't had time for breakfast—when she looked up and saw the fancy carriage come to a stop in front of the tearoom.

"Oh no," she groaned as Jamie got out of the coach and came striding across the sidewalk. Of course, he paid no attention at all to the "closed" sign; he simply opened the door and walked in.

Worse than that, Bliss craned her neck to see, that awful woman was right behind him.

Jamie did not behave in the way Bliss would have

expected him to at all. He smiled, in fact, and swept off his hat, inclining his head to Flossy, who seemed charmed.

Bliss swallowed and then said, "Flossy, this is my—friend, Jamie McKenna."

Flossy was actually blushing under the dazzling warmth of Jamie's audacious smile. "Why, I believe I've heard your name before," she said.

Jamie's expression was one of ingenuous humility. Bliss had never wanted to kick him in the shin so badly as she did at that moment. "Looks like you're going out of business," he said cautiously, for, of course, he didn't know whether the circumstances of Flossy's retirement were favorable or not.

Flossy set that concern to rest by beaming and launching into a lengthy discourse on the attributes of her only son, who was going to take care of her for the rest of her natural days.

Since Bliss had heard the story before, she had time to sneak a curious look or two at the woman who had accompanied Jamie to the tearoom. She was just as enchanting up close as she had been from a distance. The fact that she seemed to be over forty was no consolation, for that gave her a sophistication that Bliss couldn't hope to match.

"You might as well just leave with your friends," Flossy told Bliss cheerfully, forcing money into her hand. "And I'm sorry the position didn't work out better than it did."

Bliss looked down at the wages Flossy had given her. "But this is a week's pay—"

"You keep it," Flossy said firmly. "It'll make me feel better about leavin' you high and dry the way I did."

Bliss thanked Flossy and put the money into the pocket of her sateen skirt, knowing that the woman's pride was at stake, and then impulsively gave her a quick hug. Following that, she took her coat down from its peg and put it on, fully intending to take a tram rather than ride with Jamie.

His lady love had gone to wait in the carriage, and when Flossy retreated to the kitchen in an effort to hide the fact that her eyes were moist, Bliss looked up at her husband and said flatly, "I will not sit in the same carriage with that hussy."

Instead of getting angry, as Bliss would have expected, or waxing sullen, Jamie threw back his head and laughed. "Careful," he said when he'd gotten control of himself again. "If Peony 'ears you call her that, she'll scratch out your eyes."

Bliss flushed with conviction. "Just let her try it," she warned.

Jamie opened the door of the tearoom for Bliss, a look of speculation on his face. "I think it would be a pretty fair fight, now that you mention it. And you *are* goin' to ride in the carriage with 'er—friend."

Bliss tried to move away, but Jamie's grasp on her elbow, while painless, was unyielding. "I couldn't very well refer to you as my husband," she pointed out.

Jamie's jawline was a little tight, even though he was smiling. "Are you ashamed of me, Duchess?"

Bliss whirled and glared up at him, her eyes smarting with tears only he could have caused her to shed. "I might ask that same thing of you," she spat. "How dare you bring that—that strumpet with you?"

"That what?"

"Pansy or Posie or whatever her name is!"

The carriage door flew open with a crash. "Now, just a minute here," the paramour cried, ascending none too gracefully and storming toward Bliss. "I'm willing to put up with a lot, but I draw the line at being called a strumpet!"

Bliss was about to push up her sleeves and wade into the fray when Jamie stepped between the two women and said, "Enough," with sufficient sternness to quiet both of them.

"My name is Peony," said that lady, after several seconds had passed. "Not Pansy, not Posie—Peony! And I swear I'd stalk off in a fit if that weren't my carriage!"

Jamie sighed. "That would be impractical, wouldn't it?" he asked.

Bliss was full of anger and pain, unable to believe his cruelty in flaunting this woman under her nose this way. She wondered what he hoped to accomplish. "I'll take the tram," she said, gazing toward the stop with longing.

Every inch the gentleman, Jamie squired Peony back to the carriage and helped her inside, while Bliss stood stiffly on the sidewalk, ready to die of the humiliation. He'd made his choice. He meant to leave her standing there. . . .

Bliss turned and started, with forlorn determination, toward the tram stop. Her throat was so thick she couldn't swallow, and tears were slipping down her cheeks, and she was damned if she'd ever let Jamie McKenna know how he'd hurt her.

Except that he fell into step beside her, settling his hat on his head with a practiced motion of one hand and grinning insufferably. Behind them, the coach containing his mistress rattled away from the curb, traveling in the opposite direction.

Chapter 13

BLISS SAT STIFFLY IN THE TRAM SEAT, REFUSING TO SO MUCH AS glance at the man beside her. If Jamie thought pretending that nothing was wrong could make up for the fact that he'd virtually taunted her with his mistress, he was sadly mistaken.

"I've done nothin' wrong, Duchess," Jamie said. "Therefore, I'll not be apologizin'."

A matron across the aisle listened intently for Bliss's response.

After tossing the woman a look meant to convey how she felt about snoops, Bliss folded her arms and said cynically, "Of course it's not wrong. You're a man, so everything you do is right."

Out of the corner of her eye, Bliss saw that Jamie's nostrils had flared slightly, and a thin white line edged his jaw. He muttered a string of curses and the woman across the aisle grew red in the face.

"You're impossible to reason with," Jamie accused.

Bliss sat up very straight and willed herself not to cry, wondering all the while what had happened to her. She'd always had a secret contempt for women who sniveled and mewled every time something displeased them, and now it seemed that she was battling back tears at every turn.

Aunt Calandra would probably say that there was no point in crying over a bird in the bush, she reflected, and that brought a tenuous smile to her lips.

"That's better," Jamie said softly, catching his hand under Bliss's chin and making her look at him. "I'm not your enemy, Duchess," he added.

Bliss was afraid to let her guard down. Whether or not Jamie McKenna was an enemy was certainly debatable; no one else on the face of the earth had the power to bring her this low. She blinked in an effort to clear her eyes and Jamie took one of her hands in his and examined it.

"One day in that place, and your 'and is red and sore—"

Bliss wrenched her fingers free of his and sat up very straight. "Don't make so much of a little chafing, Jamie," she warned. "I'm no stranger to hard work."

To her utter surprise, Jamie kissed her fingers, and there was a sad, faraway look in his eyes. Bliss sensed that he was thinking about someone in the distant past, perhaps in Ireland, but she dared not allow her heart to soften.

After an excruciatingly long time, and many stops, the tram finally reached the center of Auckland. There was something proprietary in the way Jamie took Bliss's elbow and helped her off the car. She suspected that he was really more concerned that she'd run away than lose her footing.

Instead of starting off for the hotel, he led her in the direction of a fancy retail establishment that towered four stories above the street. A man in an impressive uniform, with shimmering gold epaulets, stood outside, opening the door for those entering and departing, and Bliss thought he must surely be the proprietor, he looked so grand and important.

When she confided this to Jamie in an awed whisper, he laughed. "Whatever you say, Duchess," he conceded, and the warmth in his eyes enabled Bliss to believe that he cared for her, at least a little.

Jamie was treated with the same respect here that he had been accorded at the hotel, and Bliss's anger flared anew when a gentleman in a fancy suit came forward and asked, "Will we be dressing the lady today, Mr. McKenna?"

173

Bliss flushed with embarrassment at this and demanded, in a scathing undertone, as Jamie propelled her after the officious salesman, "Do you do this often?"

He grinned. "Do I do what often?" he countered.

"Dress a lady," Bliss whispered, wanting to stop and stomp her foot.

The grin broadened. "I prefer undressing them, actually."

Bliss sighed. There was simply no point in carrying on such a ridiculous conversation. If she did, she would only be beating her head against a brick wall.

The salesman led them into a private salon on the uppermost floor—to Bliss's relief, there was no lift—where a woman in flowing garb greeted them.

"My, my," she said, dragging her eyes over Bliss's second-hand clothing. "Some professional attention is definitely called for."

Bliss longed to turn and storm out, but she knew she'd never get past Jamie, and she wanted to spare herself any unnecessary humiliation. This woman's awed horror provided quite enough mortification as it was.

The saleswoman smiled obsequiously at Jamie. "What are your preferences, sir?"

Enough was enough. "What do you mean, what are his preferences?" Bliss demanded to know. *"He's* not going to be wearing these clothes, I am!"

Jamie swept off his hat and scratched his head, but he knew better than to open his mouth or even grin.

The clerk was not so prudent. She gave a tinkling laugh and trilled, "Well, of course he's not! What a ridiculous thing to say."

Bliss was advancing on the woman when Jamie caught hold of her upper arm and dragged her back, so that she collided with his chest. Familiar sensations were stirred by the contact, and she could not permit herself to meet his eyes.

"Can't I take you anywhere, Duchess?" he asked in a beleaguered tone that made Bliss want to stomp on his instep. "If it isn't too much to ask, could you mind your manners?"

Since his voice had begun to take on a lilt of the Irish, Bliss didn't respond. If Jamie wanted to buy her clothes, let him—some of them would come in handy in America, no doubt. The others she would simply leave behind, in the hotel room.

Even though Jamie's arms had been filled with boxes when he and Bliss had left the store, so much clothing had been purchased that deliveries arrived at the hotel all afternoon.

Bliss could barely hide her excitement, there were so many beautiful things—rich velvets, fine lawns and silks, bloomers, camisoles and petticoats, trimmed in lace. Oh, it was going to be most difficult indeed to leave such treasures behind when she struck out for America.

Jamie, who had been reading while Bliss examined her purchases, stood up and stretched. The pure animal grace of the gesture forced some unpleasant facts back into Bliss's mind.

"Do you love that woman?" she asked forthrightly, though she couldn't look directly at Jamie. She was standing behind one of the suite's matched settees, running her fingers over the soft shimmer of a petticoat.

"Who? Peony?" Jamie yawned, sounding surprised that such a topic could come up. Perhaps, Bliss reflected, he was one of those who believed it behooved a man to have a mistress as well as a wife. Lord knew, the idea was common enough.

Bliss was having trouble controlling her temper, not to mention the raging jealousy that was building within her. She swallowed and nodded her head, unable to speak.

"Yes," Jamie said, flatly and without hesitation.

Bliss felt as though she'd just been run through with a spear, but couldn't honestly say she'd been unprepared for that answer.

Telling herself that she had no real right to the feelings she was having, Bliss began folding and refolding the petticoat. Jamie had not become her husband by choice; she could not expect him to hold their marriage sacred.

She had been so busy searching her mind for something sophisticated and worldly to say in response that she was totally unprepared when Jamie gripped her shoulders in his hands and turned her to face him.

He laid an index finger to her lips, and his pale blue eyes danced with mischief and affection. "I don't think you understand about Peony," he said.

Bliss's throat ached. If things were as she suspected, she didn't want to understand. "I realize that our marriage is a—is a sham," she told him, in a miserable whisper. "I c-couldn't expect you to b-be faithful—"

Jamie's hands had returned to Bliss's shoulders, where they lay heavily upon her, making it difficult to stand. "A marriage is a marriage, Duchess," he said, in a voice that was, while gravelly, remarkably tender as well. "I'll 'ave no other woman in me bed." He paused to give her a playful swat. "Now, dress yourself in the finest gown you 'ave."

Bliss's indigo eyes widened. She had scarcely allowed herself to hope for a chance to wear the evening frocks Jamie had helped her to select. "Are we going somewhere?"

Jamie took his time in answering; first he smiled briefly and sadly, then he kissed her, his lips touching hers as lightly as the passing of a butterfly's wing. "To supper and, God 'elp us, the opera."

Heart hammering with excitement at the prospect of such an adventure, Bliss was already lost in a welter of momentous decisions. After all, there were at least five gowns that would be suitable for such an evening, and this was no time to be saving the best for last. There might never be another night like this.

Jamie kissed the top of her head, and there was amusement in his voice, if not in his eyes, as he crossed to the door and took his hat and coat from the brass tree beside it. "I'll be back in an hour or thereabouts, Duchess," he said in a curiously hoarse voice. "Do something with that wild tangle of 'air, will you?"

Bliss's hand rose to touch her hair as she watched the door close behind Jamie. For a change, she wasn't insulted by his remark, for she knew that he hadn't meant to hurt her.

Nonetheless, she dashed into the bedroom to peer into the full-length mirror that stood in a corner by the bureau. Sure enough, her thick, titian hair looked untamed and untended. Bliss found her brush and groomed the tresses with a thoroughness born of pride.

Following that, she started a bath running in the magnificent tub hidden behind the screen, then took her splendid new evening gowns from their tissue-lined boxes and spread them out on the bed. The choice was easier than she had expected: she selected the midnight-blue silk, with its beautifully smocked bodice. Tiny azure beads trimmed the full skirt, winking in the fading light.

Her mind spinning at all the evening might hold, Bliss braided her hair into a single plait and wound it into a coronet atop her head in order to keep it reasonably dry. Then, after gleefully stripping away her clothes, she plunged into a hot bath. Just for tonight, she decided, she would not think about the temporary nature of her marriage or Jamie's fondness for Peony Ryan. For this one evening, she would permit herself to enjoy playing Cinderella.

Heaven knew, she would be back to the pumpkins and mice of reality soon enough.

Bliss took great care with her appearance that night, and more than once she wished for rice powder, rouge for her lips and cheeks, and perfume. Despite the time she spent with her brush and comb, she still looked like a country girl with her hair up.

And it was thus that Jamie found her, wearing only her new pink satin drawers and camisole, both trimmed in the finest écru lace and fitted with tiny pearl buttons.

He was dressed for evening, and he looked so splendid

that Bliss's breath was fairly taken away. She gaped at his snow-white shirt, his crisp black trousers with their perfect crease, his dashing cutaway coat with tails.

"My stars and garters," she whispered. "You're God's own wonder, Jamie McKenna!"

Jamie was staring himself, and Bliss's compliment did nothing to jar him out of his stupor. Finally, he muttered something that sounded like, "Hollyberry, ruther be God," and shook his head as though dazed.

"I didn't put on my dress because I knew I wouldn't be able to do up all those buttons," Bliss announced with bright innocence.

Jamie's Adam's apple moved up and down his throat like a lift traveling between floors. "Aye," he managed to croak out. "That shouldn't be a problem." He stood rooted to the floor like a kauri tree, for all that, and Bliss had to walk over to him, once she'd wriggled into her dress, and turn her back so that he could fasten the buttons.

His fingers, usually so deft, were awkward and slow.

She finally turned, when he'd progressed about midway up her back, and demanded, "What on earth is troubling you, Mr. McKenna?"

A smile ignited blue fires in Jamie's eyes before progressing to his mouth. "What indeed?" he countered gruffly. "Tell me, Mrs. McKenna, just 'ow fond of opera are you?"

"I wouldn't know, never having been," Bliss replied, giving her husband a suspicious, determined look. "I'll have none of your smooth talk, either. You offered me supper and an opera, and you'll make good if you know what's best for you."

Jamie laughed and gave her a resounding kiss. "Supper and an opera it is," he said, with that curious gentleness that always excited Bliss. "After that—" He let his words fall away and shrugged.

Bliss was quick to turn her back again. "The buttons, if you will," she said formally. Damn and blast, if he set her now to thinking of his lovemaking, she'd be squirming uncomfortably all evening.

The lobby of the Victoria Hotel was all sparkling light and genteel chatter. Jamie left Bliss beside a potted palm while he went off on one of his mysterious errands, and she hoped he couldn't hear her stomach growling as he walked away.

"I don't know what I'm going to do," fretted a female—and foreign—voice, on the other side of the potted palm. "Oh, Henrietta, how will I ever face making such a journey without my Piedmont?"

Bliss was wondering what on earth a Piedmont was when another voice supplied the answer. "It was truly unfortunate, Minerva, that your husband passed away so far from home."

Dramatic snuffling sifted through the palm leaves. "You have no idea, Henrietta, what it did to me to see Piedmont buried on foreign soil. Of course, there was no possibility of taking him home to Sacramento—"

Sacramento. Bliss's heart pounded at her rib cage. Sacramento was in California. How far could that be from San Francisco, where her mother was living? She drew a deep breath, rounded the potted plant, and offered a half curtsy to the two women standing on the other side.

"Excuse me, ladies," she said sweetly, "but I couldn't help overhearing a part of your conversation. My name is Bliss Stafford, and I wonder if one of you isn't in need of a companion to—to share your journey back to America?"

The heavier of the two women stepped forward, squinting nearsightedly at Bliss. "You look unsuited for such a lowly station, Miss Stafford," she observed.

Reminded that she was wearing the expensive blue gown, Bliss cast about wildly for a sensible response, while keeping her smile firmly in place. "I am accompanying my current—employer—to supper and the opera tonight. Mr. McKenna and his—his wife wanted me to be suitably clothed."

"I see," said the elderly American lady. "Perhaps I should consider this young woman as a companion," she told her friend as an aside. Then she gave a long, sad sigh that turned Bliss's tender heart willy-nilly. "It will be desperately hard to leave poor Piedmont behind, of course."

"Of course," Bliss commiserated tenderly.

"Give her your calling card, Minerva," said Henrietta, elbowing the woman.

Over Minerva Wilmington's husky shoulder, Bliss saw Jamie striding toward her. She curtsied again and tucked the calling card into her blue beaded handbag. "I'll contact you tomorrow, Mrs. Wilmington," she said warmly.

The old woman harumphed. "There'll be a proper interview, you know," she warned, evidently feeling that Bliss was assuming too much.

"Yes, naturally," Bliss answered, and then she moved around the two women to offer her hands to Jamie and smile up at him with tender devotion.

Jamie looked at her quizzically for a moment, then said, "The carriage is 'ere, Duchess."

Bliss allowed herself to be ushered away, holding her royal-blue velvet cloak close around her as they stepped outside into the cold. Spring would arrive soon; the night air didn't have its usual wintry bite.

She balked at the sight of the carriage—it was the one she'd refused to ride in that very morning. The familiar driver tipped his hat and smiled. "Good evenin', mate," he said to Jamie. Another nod, formal and brisk, had to pass as a greeting to Bliss.

When Bliss would have resisted, Jamie grasped her elbow in steel-hard fingers and fairly thrust her over to the door and inside the richly outfitted rig. "You said we were going to supper!" she accused, ruffled.

"And so we are," Jamie told her, his nose not even an inch from hers. "It's time you got the straight of what's goin' on 'ere."

When his words sank in—they were having supper with

the elegant Peony Ryan—Bliss dived for the door on the opposite side of the carriage, but for all her haste she was too slow. Jamie caught her by the back of her blue silk skirts and pulled. Hard.

Bliss landed smartly on the seat. "You're just lucky you didn't tear my dress, you bloody idiot!" she cried, pushed beyond all semblance of decorum.

"What sweet memories you bring back, Duchess," Jamie said, confident in his strength and his sheer cussedness. "Didn't you say something similar to that"—he paused to raise one of her hands to his lips and kiss it elegantly—"on the morning we met?"

"I called you a bloody fool," Bliss said, wrenching her hand free and settling back in the seat, arms folded across her chest. "And I meant it, too."

The corner of Jamie's mouth quirked. "I 'ave no doubt that you were sincere, love," he replied as the carriage lurched out into the evening traffic.

Bliss sat up very straight and moved to one side so that there was a small distance between herself and Jamie. "I don't suppose it matters that I hate the idea of having supper with Peony Ryan."

"You're absolutely right," Jamie answered smoothly. "It doesn't matter."

Bliss folded her arms and bit down hard on her lower lip. Because having a tantrum would do no good at all, she focused her thoughts on tomorrow's interview with Mrs. Minerva Wilmington. She would wear something dignified, businesslike. . . .

A sensation of almost intolerable loneliness swept over her at the prospect of leaving New Zealand—and Jamie. This, when he didn't even want her, and insisted on rubbing her nose in the fact that he kept a mistress!

She glared out at the night, perilously close once again to the tears she despised. "I should have stayed in Wellington, with Alexander," she said.

Jamie's chuckle rumbled in the carriage like thunder in

the far distance. "You'd 'ave been most un'appy with that arrangement, Duchess, and so would Alexander."

Bliss whirled, forgetting the hurt she'd wanted so to hide, and spat, "Is that so, Jamie McKenna? Well, it just so happens that you've given me nothing that Alexander couldn't have—he's very well fixed, you know!"

Before Bliss was fully aware of what was happening, Jamie had shifted her so that she sat astraddle his lap. As though it were his right, he opened her cloak and kissed the curves of her breasts where they showed above the low neckline of her gown.

A groan that mingled defiance and surrender escaped Bliss as Jamie deftly began raising her skirts.

"Never challenge me that way, Duchess," he whispered against the fevered skin of her breast. "Me manly pride won't 'ave me let it pass."

Bliss could feel his hand moving along her inner thigh, teasing her through the soft fabric of her new bloomers. "Damn—your—manly pride!" she spat, but she bent her head back in absolute surrender as he managed to bare one of her nipples for suckling.

"It's times like this," he said, between sessions of greedy enjoyment, "when I think they named you right and proper after all. This, sweet Duchess, is bliss."

His fingers were dispensing with the tiny buttons that did up the front of her drawers. Soon enough, he stole beneath the fabric and Bliss moaned with glorious tension as he caressed her.

"We can't," she whimpered, in sweet desperation. "Oh—my—"

He possessed her in one smooth and searing motion while continuing to make free with her breast. "Ummm," he responded. "Tell me you want me, love."

The torment was exquisite; only Jamie could have torn her between the needs of her body and the dictates of her pride. "I—want you," she gasped, half-blinded by the sensations he was stirring.

"Tell me where," he said, then circled her distended nipple with the tip of his tongue.

Bliss hated him, momentarily, for the power he wielded, and she vowed that she would avenge herself somehow, someday. "Here!" she cried in delicious defeat.

But Jamie had not extracted the last concession yet. "When?" he asked, his voice throaty.

"Now," Bliss answered feverishly. "Oh, damn you, Jamie, now—now!"

It was a tricky bit of business, making love in a carriage, but Bliss should have known that Jamie could manage it. Without so much as a wasted motion, he turned her away from him and lowered her onto his lap, where all his glorious maleness waited to sheathe itself in her femininity.

Bliss saw dazzling light, and nothing more, as he slowly brought her down the length of him. When he was fully inside her, he lowered the bodice of her dress so that he might caress her bare breasts with his hands while his rod caressed the velvety depths of her.

For a few excruciatingly sweet moments, he let the natural motion of the carriage do his work for him. Then, ever so slowly, with low, desolate groans of his own, he grasped her narrow waist in his hands and began to raise and lower her in a steadily building rhythm as old as the stars.

There was an awesome trembling in Bliss's legs as she neared release; she truly feared that she would cry out in her ecstasy, and loudly enough for the carriage driver to hear. For all that, she could not contain what would be unchained by Jamie's pleasuring; she gave herself up to it completely and so did Jamie.

"Do you suppose he heard us?" Bliss fretted, once the last waves of elation had ebbed away and she'd laboriously put all her senses back in their proper places.

"Who?" Jamie asked, almost irritably. He was fully presentable again, within moments, while Bliss had to right her drawers, straighten her petticoats, and smooth her skirts.

She resented it heartily. "The carriage driver!" she snapped.

Jamie ran a hand through his hair. "'Ow should I know?" he muttered. "It isn't like I give a damn, Duchess!"

Bliss was livid. "You have so little concern for my reputation?"

Jamie was putting her bodice back in place. "What reputation? You're me wife—if I want to 'ave you on *top* of the carriage, I will."

Perhaps it was Jamie's audacity that made Bliss unbearably furious. Or maybe it was the fact that the law stood behind him in such matters. Whatever the case, she was outraged beyond all bearing and, for the second time since they'd met, she moved to slap Jamie, putting all her strength behind the blow.

He rendered the gesture impotent by grasping her wrist just as her palm would have struck his cheek. "Is that the thanks I get," he hissed, "for making you 'owl like the Banshee at an Irishman's deathbed?"

Before Bliss could think of a response to that, the carriage came to an unexpected stop. If it hadn't been for Jamie's grip on her wrist, in fact, she would have gone toppling into the opposite seat.

"I want you to divorce me," she said with chilly dignity. "Immediately."

With an insolent sort of tenderness, Jamie kissed her. "Me plans 'aven't changed, Duchess," he answered smoothly. "I'm settin' you up in a 'ouse first thing tomorrow. I rather like 'avin' a wife."

The driver opened the door just as Bliss would have told Jamie McKenna what she thought of him, his parentage, and his private parts.

"Here we are, sir," crowed the driver, pleased as punch.

The lights of a house that surely belonged to Peony Ryan glowed in the darkness.

Chapter 14 ❧

JAMIE PRACTICALLY HURLED BLISS UP THE STEPS LEADING TO Peony's elegant town house. Not even for food, she had decided, could she bring herself to endure this kind of humiliation. Just as she would have whirled on her troublesome husband and given him the kind of kick he'd long remember, the door opened and light spilled out of the house.

"Damn," Bliss muttered.

The young maid who had come to admit her mistress's guests took in Bliss's dress with undisguised admiration. "Ain't that some gown, now?" she trilled. "Did you buy that for 'er, Mr. Jamie?"

Bliss was getting damn good and sick of people acting as though she weren't even there. She slanted a look at Jamie, only to catch him winking at the maid.

"Aye, Molly," he freely admitted. "I did that for a fact."

The girl cooed as she closed the door. "Ooooooh, but it's some lovely!"

To Bliss's way of thinking, that dress might as well have been walking around on its own, with nobody inside it, for all the notice that was being taken of her presence. "Hello," she said firmly. "My name is Bliss Stafford McKenna and—"

The maid's giggles pealed in the entryway like shrill little bells, and she covered her mouth with one hand and disappeared, calling out, " 'E's back, missus. Mr. Jamie's back, and 'e's got a lady with 'im!"

"She noticed," Bliss marveled, half to herself, as Jamie smiled at her. He walked right into the drawing room, without so much as an invitation or a by-your-leave from anyone, and made himself at home.

Bliss hesitated, then followed. Jamie took off his cutaway coat, tossed it negligently over the back of a settee, and then sat down in a leather chair, putting his feet up on the hassock. A crystal jar full of cheroots rested on the small table beside him; he took one, along with a wooden match, and began to smoke.

"It's customary," Bliss pointed out stiffly, "to consult your hostess before smoking in her house."

"Not in this case," Jamie replied, unruffled, and then he gave a lusty sigh of contentment. "If I asked Peony, she would say no."

Bliss hated to agree with Peony about anything, but she despised cigar smoke herself. "If she doesn't allow smoking," Bliss reasoned, gesturing toward the crystal decanter, "why does she provide the materials?"

Jamie smiled. "This is Molly's work. She's the one sees that I 'ave what I need when I visit."

Bliss felt the color drain from her face. Of course. This house was home to Jamie. That explained why he'd sought out this room, this chair. Utter despair possessed her as various pieces of the puzzle began to fall into place.

There was a lump in Bliss's throat but, nonetheless, she tried to speak normally. Running one hand over the glistening white keys of a grand piano, which stood in a far corner of the room, she assessed Jamie's razor-sharp trouser crease and white linen shirt. "You came here to change into those clothes, didn't you?" she asked, and despite her efforts, her voice sounded small and weak. Jamie had only everyday trousers and shirts at the hotel, the kind of things he would have worn to shear sheep.

He was just opening his mouth to respond when Peony waltzed into the room, looking quite delicious in pink and white silk. When Jamie would have risen—he'd never once shown that kind of courtesy to Bliss—the stunning blonde pressed him back into his chair by laying one white, graceful hand to his shoulder.

"Relax, Jamie love. And do put out that nasty cheroot." With hardly a breath, Peony turned to face Bliss, giving her a charitable smile. "Why, Bliss," she said, "you look wonderful in that shade of blue!"

It did seem that Mrs. Ryan was sincere, but Bliss was on her guard all the same. The question that puzzled her most was whether Jamie was keeping Mrs. Ryan or Mrs. Ryan was keeping him. It was not the sort of dilemma she'd ever expected to face.

She frowned, perplexed. "Thank you," she answered belatedly.

"Well," Peony chimed, consulting a watch pinned to her bodice. The face was cleverly hidden behind a cameo. "If we're going to be at the opera by curtain time, we'd best eat."

Bliss was all for that. It had been a long time since lunch.

Tea was served in a formal dining room, and just getting there was an ordeal of the soul. Since there were two women and only one man, Jamie had to choose whom to escort to her chair first, and he chose Peony.

Bliss didn't wait to see if he'd come back for her; she walked in and seated herself.

Jamie's eyes were dancing as he drew back the chair beside hers, which conveniently put him between herself and Peony, and sat down. "In a rush, Duchess?" he teased, under his breath.

"I'm fair starving," Bliss replied. Unfortunately, the

words carried and elicited an indulgent smile from Mrs. Ryan.

The meal itself offered other agonies. Small roasted fowls were served by the giggling Molly—a whole one for each person at the table—and Bliss didn't know the proper way to eat them. At home, she would simply have torn the food apart with her fingers, but here, in a rich woman's house . . .

She watched Peony for a clue, not trusting Jamie's manners to be any better than her own. Finally, after dallying over her wine and discussing the prices of wool and gold with Jamie, Mrs. Ryan took up her knife and fork and began neatly dissecting her fowl.

Ravenous, Bliss nevertheless contented herself with tiny bites removed with surgical delicacy. Of course, long before she'd satisfied her appetite, Jamie and Peony had pushed away their plates. As if on cue, Molly swept in and took away everyone's dishes—Bliss having her fork halfway between her plate and her mouth—and returned with skimpy little bowls of tired-looking fruit.

Bliss's mood, never improved by hunger, went from bad to worse. If Jamie and Peony were going to talk about some stupid gold mine in Australia forever, they might at least make a halfhearted effort to include her in the discussion.

"I've never been to an opera," she announced bravely, wanting to remind them that she was present.

It was Peony who looked chagrined, oddly enough. Jamie only sighed and said, "You 'aven't missed much, Duchess," then went back to talking about sluicing ore and buying low and selling high.

"Any idiot knows that you buy low and sell high," Bliss put in, leaving that strange process called sluicing for greater minds than hers.

Peony gave a joyous squeal of laughter and clapped her hands together in what seemed to be genuine delight. If she lived to be a thousand, Bliss reflected, she was never going to understand this woman. Didn't it matter to Peony that she and Bliss both loved the same man?

"Enough talk about business," she said, consulting the watch behind her cameo broach again. "It's time we left for the opera house."

Jamie rolled his eyes and tossed his napkin onto the table. "If you were a true friend," he muttered to Peony, in an irascible tone, "you wouldn't put a man through this kind of grief."

Peony was smiling, unmoved by Jamie's lack of enthusiasm. "Quit fussing. I think Bliss will enjoy this evening very much."

Bliss had her doubts. She was still mourning her half-eaten roast chicken.

Twenty minutes later, the carriage pulled up in front of an enormous building with a glittering facade. Other rigs and people in fine garments were everywhere, and Bliss forgot her problems, temporarily, as she tried to take in everything.

The inside of the opera house reminded her of the lobby at the hotel, except that this place was even grander. The chandeliers were massive, made up of thousands of glittering bits of crystal, the carpets were plush, and the paintings on the walls were framed in gilt.

Her first close look at the paintings brought rich color to her face and a muttered exclamation to her lips. "They're naked!" she marveled.

Jamie grinned, looking up at a Rubenesque female lounging among stone pillars and various kinds of pottery. "She's a lot of woman, I'll say that for 'er."

Bliss's lesson in sophistication was just beginning. After a while, an orchestra began to play and huge double doors leading to the auditorium itself were opened.

Mrs. Ryan, Jamie, and Bliss were soon settled in a private box. The little swinging door bore a brass plate with Peony's late husband's name engraved on it.

Program in hand, Bliss committed herself to absorbing every nuance of this special evening. She tilted her head back and studied the beautifully ornate ceiling, with its intricate cherubs, birds, and flowers. She examined the heavy stage curtain, of scarlet velvet, with its golden fringe shimmering in the glow of the gas footlights. She scrutinized the occupants of the orchestra pit down front, thrilled by their music, and only as the lights were lowered for the performance to begin did she realize that Jamie was watching her with the most peculiar expression in his eyes.

The orchestra played with a new intensity as the curtain swept back to reveal a Viking scene. Bliss was on the edge of her seat when a man wearing nothing more than a metal band around his head and a loincloth began to sing in a foreign language.

Bliss's mouth fell open.

There was laughter in Jamie's voice as he bent close to whisper, "What's the matter, Duchess? 'Aven't you ever seen an Italian Viking?"

Bliss had never seen any kind of Viking, and she was boggled. "Glory be!" she whispered, and her eyes went so wide that they hurt. How she wished she could understand what that man was singing about with such fervor. And his voice! Why, it was fairly strong enough to bring all those angels and birds and flowers right down from the ceiling.

Bliss squirmed in her seat and looked uncomfortably up into the darkness.

Jamie chuckled, as if he knew what she was thinking, and then his hand reached out and closed over hers. A sweet thrill went through Bliss at his touch, and she didn't pull away, but she did bend forward and try to peer around him to see if he was holding Peony's hand as well.

On stage, the Vikings fought and died and sang fit to wear out a person's eyes and ears. Then there was an intermission, during which everyone went to the lobby and drank orange juice. Bliss meant to write everything down the second she had the chance; she didn't see how she could remember it all if she didn't put pen to paper, and she did so want to remember.

Jamie was watching her drink her orange juice with that same odd intensity in his eyes that she'd noticed earlier. He looked as though he wanted to spread jam and cream all over her, like a scone, and eat her up.

Bliss trembled at the sensations the thought produced, and then it was time to go back to the box and watch the rest of the opera.

It ended magnificently, Bliss thought, with an enormous woman singing at the top of her lungs and waving a sword. She had a horned helmet on her head and carried a shield in her free arm.

"I do have my misgivings," she confided to Jamie in a whisper, "about any country that expects its women to do the fighting."

Jamie laughed and shook his head and Bliss turned her attention back to the stage. The singer's thick, snow-white braids glimmered in the stage lights, and she wondered if they were real or attached to the horned helmet. Jamie was back to shifting uncomfortably in his seat, as he'd been doing intermittently all evening.

Before Bliss could see what the fat lady did with the sword, the audience rose to its feet, clapping. The tall man in front of Bliss blocked her view of the stage.

"Thank God that's over," Jamie muttered, and both Peony and Bliss glared at him.

Bliss felt expanded by the evening's experience. Now she was something more than a lighthouse keeper's daughter who had never been anywhere or seen anything. "You just don't have any appreciation for culture, that's all," she told Jamie in lofty tones.

"Amen," agreed Peony.

The first thing Jamie did when he and Bliss returned to the hotel was empty a packet of headache powders into a glass of water and drink the concoction right down.

"I didn't see what the fat lady did with her sword," Bliss complained, sitting down on the edge of the bed to kick off her blue satin slippers, which were beginning to pinch.

"If she asked," Jamie responded dryly, "I'd be 'appy to tell her what to do with that damn sword."

Bliss began to smile, but then she remembered Mrs. Minerva Wilmington's calling card, tucked away in her handbag, and a feeling of desolation swept over her. America seemed so very far away.

Jamie had noted the change in her expression, and he crossed the room to tuck one finger under her chin and lift it. Though his gaze was tender, that besotted look was no longer in evidence. "What is it, Duchess?" he asked. "Peony?"

Bliss had honestly forgotten about her husband's mistress, as incredible as that seemed, but she was quick to grasp an acceptable excuse for her mood. After all, she couldn't very well just blurt out that she was feeling sad at the idea of running away to the States.

She sniffed haughtily. "Perhaps," she conceded, unwilling to commit herself completely.

Jamie laughed and drew her to her feet, then held her close. Bliss felt herself flush with heat as now-familiar reactions to such intimate contact went through her body.

"You were a wonder in the carriage tonight," he whispered, his lips so close to hers that she could feel their softness, power, and warmth. "I thought I'd surely die of the pleasure, Duchess."

Bliss's cheeks were hot, no doubt making her freckles stand out on her face like dabs of brown paint, but she took a certain pride in knowing that she'd won such a confession from Jamie. He rarely spoke of his feelings.

The room seemed to dip and undulate and spin, all at once, as Jamie kissed her. His tongue explored the depths of her mouth and his hands cupped her bottom, pressing her close so that she could not help knowing the extent of his desire.

Bliss was ready to surrender fully when a sudden, insistent pounding began at the outer door of the suite. Muttering a string of curses, Jamie made sure his shirttails were still tucked into his trousers and went to answer. Weak in the knees, Bliss sank to the edge of the bed, struggling to breathe properly again, and listened with only half an ear to the exchange at the door.

She had gathered only that it concerned Peony when there was a slamming sound and Jamie came back to the bed-room, fairly tearing off his fancy linen shirt as he moved. Bliss was stunned to see that he'd been wearing his knife and scabbard, even with his evening clothes.

Jamie swore all the while he was changing into his customary rough trousers, cotton shirt, and boots.

"What . . . ?" Bliss finally managed as a beginning, having just then fully recovered from the kiss he'd given her earlier.

Jamie spat another colorful string of oaths, then stormed out in search of his hat and his sheepskin coat. "When I get me 'ands on that bleedin' coward—" he vowed through his teeth.

Bliss knew that Jamie was going to storm out without telling her anything if she didn't stop him. Barefoot, she ran after him, watching wide-eyed as he settled the familiar leather hat on his head.

"Jamie, what's happening?" she demanded. "Where are you going?"

Jamie's finger waggled before Bliss's nose; she had never seen him look quite so firm in his opinions. "You stay 'ere until I come back, Duchess," he ordered, not even bothering to answer her questions. "No matter 'ow long that takes, you don't go climbin' out any windows, you 'ear me?"

Bliss nodded and bit her lower lip. She felt terribly afraid, but not of Jamie. It was the mysterious something or someone he was going out to do battle with that terrified her.

His expression softened a little, and he gave her a hasty kiss on the forehead, but no explanations were forthcoming. Jamie left the hotel room and locked the door behind him.

Bliss began to pace, hugging herself against a chill that came not from the air around her, but from deep within.

Her every instinct screamed that Jamie was in worse trouble now than ever before.

"I'm all right," Peony insisted. "George should never have gone running to you that way—"

Jamie was prowling back and forth along the edge of Peony's drawing-room hearth, too furious to stand still. "All right, are you? You get a letter delivered by way of a brick through your parlor window, and you're 'all right'!"

Peony's lovely green eyes were shadowed by fear and weariness as she looked at the bit of paper lying crumpled on the table beside her chair. "Jamie," she said with quiet patience, "go back to the hotel and look after Bliss. I'm perfectly safe."

Jamie glanced at the note he knew by heart. *Tell your mick lover that I'm not through with him yet. The debt has come due and I'll be collecting soon—with interest.*

He swore, pulled his hat on, then whipped it off again and threw it across the room, bellowing, "Damn that bleeder!"

Peony sighed. "Cursing Increase will do no good. We both knew he'd catch up with us one day."

Jamie jammed splayed fingers through his hair. God, but the worst part was the waiting—for Increase to show himself, to make another move. Ah yes, the old man remembered how Jamie McKenna hated to stand by, helpless.

"Go and look after your wife, Jamie," Peony insisted softly. "Please. If Increase has learned how you feel—"

"She's locked in," Jamie said flatly, going to recover his hat from where he'd flung it. "All the same, I'd feel better keepin' an eye on 'er. Tell Molly to gather whatever you need for the night, Peony—you're going to the 'otel with me. And no arguments!"

Peony, who had opened her mouth while Jamie was speaking, closed it again, then reached out to pull a bell cord.

Molly, looking shaken and white, appeared within moments. "You goin' to call for the police now, missus?" she asked anxiously.

"Tomorrow will be soon enough for that," Peony said wearily. "Whoever threw that brick is long gone by now, I'm sure—"

Jamie broke in. "Pack up some things for Mrs. Ryan, Molly. She'll be away tonight."

Molly swallowed hard. "Yes, sir," she said, with a little curtsy, her eyes dodging to Peony. "May I go to me sister's, mum? I'd feel real scared, stayin' on 'ere alone."

"Certainly," Peony said gently, and Jamie ached with the special affection he bore her. She had a gift, Peony Ryan did, for giving tenderness when and where it was most needed. "We'll drive you there in the carriage."

Jamie, having collected his hat, took up the crumpled note, folding it carefully, and tucked it into his coat pocket. He hoped it wouldn't be long before Increase tipped his hand.

When Bliss dreamed, it was usually of Jamie's lovemaking or the color and scent of the blue, blue sea, chattering at the rocks and sand of the shore. Or of America as she imagined it to be, and the wonderful life her mother was living there. Occasionally, however, the dark dream came to call, to show her that it would not be forgotten.

That Colin would not be forgotten.

She saw him again, standing on the very edge of the cliff, and even though he was only a stone's throw from the lighthouse and carrying a lantern, the lashing of the wind and rain, coupled with the darkness, reduced him to a small, wavering shadow.

"Colin!" Bliss cried, knowing that she was dreaming, but unable to awaken herself. "Colin, I'm here—come to me!"

He was only seven, and he was a daredevil, loving above all things to show off. He balanced on the brink of the cliff, lifted his lantern high, and turned on one heel. "Look, sister!" he cried gleefully as Bliss crept toward him, her arms outstretched, the rain stinging her eyes and the wind stealing the breath from her lungs. "Look at me! I'm a lighthouse!"

"Colin," she whispered, in desperation.

And at her whisper, he fell. For long, agonizing moments, she fell with him, spinning round and round in the mist, too frightened to scream, knowing that the jagged rocks were coming ever closer.

With a shriek, she sat up, gasping for breath. She was soaked with sweat and her heart filled her throat, beating there like an enormous drum.

Jamie's hands were gentle on the sides of her face, his thumbs smoothing away her tears. "There now, Duchess," he whispered. "I'm 'ere, and what was that all about, anyway?"

With a hoarse sob of relief, Bliss flung her arms around his neck and held on tight. "Oh Jamie," was all she could manage to say. "Jamie, Jamie."

He held her close until she'd stopped trembling, then gently pressed her back onto her pillows. He fetched a cloth from somewhere and dried her face of tears and perspiration.

"Tell me," he urged.

Bliss squeezed her eyes shut, hating to entertain the memory even long enough to tell Jamie what had happened all those years ago. "There was a storm," she finally forced herself to say. "Papa sent my brother, Colin, out to fi-find me. He was playing—beside the c-cliff—"

She couldn't go on, but Jamie understood, she could see that. He closed his eyes and whispered, "Oh God, Duchess, I'm sorry."

Bliss wept miserably, for Colin, for her grief-stricken mother, who had run away soon after the tragedy, for her angry father, for herself. She was drenched in sweat from head to foot, and with light, deft hands, Jamie divested her of her satin bloomers and camisole to go on drying her with the bit of cloth. His touch and his presence were soothing.

"Don't leave me," she whispered just before sleep took her.

"No chance of that," Jamie answered without hesitation.

The dream did not come again, but it left a raw place inside Bliss, as it always did, a hollowed-out, hurting place. When she awoke in the morning, she felt depleted and weak, and she was alone in the bed, though she could hear Jamie's voice through the closed door of the bedroom.

She just couldn't make out what he was saying.

Feeling a sudden and strange tension, Bliss tossed back the covers and swung her bare legs over the side of the bed. She crossed her arms over her naked breasts, certain that she'd gone to bed in her satin underthings.

Then she remembered Jamie's arms holding her tightly after the dream, Jamie's hands taking off her camisole and drawers when it truly seemed the clothes would smother her for sure, Jamie's voice telling her that he was there with her. That she was safe.

Such a feeling of love came over Bliss in that moment that she knew she could never go to America, never leave Jamie. She might just as well drain the blood from her veins as try to live without him.

A woman's laughter sounded from the room beyond. Frowning, Bliss found one of her new wrappers, a favorite of lavender corduroy, and put it on. Then, after pushing her hair back from her face, she opened the door and went out.

Jamie and Peony were sitting at a small, round table, which they'd dragged over into the light of the largest window, eating breakfast and chatting like any happily married couple. For that matter, Mrs. Ryan had yet to dress; she was wearing what appeared to be a peignoir of embossed satin. Even though she was sitting down, Bliss could tell that the garment accented every luscious curve.

She felt sick as she thought of Jamie and that woman together, and she swayed a little as she closed her eyes and struggled for composure.

It was at that moment that Jamie saw her, and he had the gall to behave as though everything were normal and right. "'Ello, Duchess," he said happily. "Ready for some breakfast?"

Bliss couldn't bear it. He'd comforted her so tenderly, and then left her to go to this woman, either in a nearby suite or this very one . . . .

"Duchess?" Jamie prompted, sounding worried now.

Bliss looked around desperately. Since her blue satin slippers were handy, she picked them up and flung them, first one, then the other. They bounced, in turn, off Jamie's broad chest as he came closer and closer.

Chapter 15 🌿

THE EXPRESSION IN JAMIE'S EYES WAS ONE OF ANGRY BEWILDER-
ment, but Peony seemed to understand Bliss's fury. She rose
from her chair, fidgeting with the tie on her beautiful green
wrapper, and said, "It's not what you think."

Jamie looked back at Peony in annoyance. "And what is it
that she thinks?" he snapped.

"I can speak for myself, Jamie McKenna," Bliss flared.
"You needn't go asking somebody else how I feel about
things!"

He sighed, and a tiny muscle in his jawline twitched, then
went still. "All right, Duchess," he said evenly, "'ave it your
way. What the devil's goin' on in that erratic little brain of
yours that would make you throw your shoes at a man?
Answer me that!"

Bliss jutted out her chin. "You have your fair share of
brass demanding answers, Mr. McKenna!" she retorted.
"How dare you flaunt your mistress under my nose like
this!"

"I'm nothing of the sort," Peony interceded, fixing Bliss
with a cool glare, "and I'll thank you to remember that,
young lady." With these words, she swept into the suite's
small second bedroom and slammed the door behind her.

Bliss swallowed and made herself meet Jamie's gaze. She
waited for him to shout and rage at her, but he didn't. He
gave her a look that made her feel small and silly, and then
he turned around and walked out of the suite, pausing only
to collect his hat and coat.

It was all Bliss could do not to run after him and beg him not to be angry with her. How it galled her that she wanted to do that, when he was the one who'd transgressed!

She glanced toward the door of Peony's room. She felt so confused, and though she wanted to believe the woman's words, every jealous nerve in her body told her otherwise.

Bliss turned her attention to preparing for the day. She intended to seek out Mrs. Wilmington, the American widow, and be interviewed for the position of companion.

Never mind that she no longer wanted to live in America. It was obvious enough that Jamie was never going to be a real husband, and love him though she did, Bliss refused to overlook infidelity. Nor would she live in a house he provided, catering to his every whim like some besotted concubine, existing only for the crumbs of attention he deigned to toss her way.

She found Mrs. Wilmington in the dining room, having breakfast, and with that good lady's permission, Bliss joined her. It seemed that nothing could affect her appetite; she was famished. She ordered bacon and eggs with fried potatoes and toast and summarily charged the meal to Jamie's bill.

Not that he'd care, one way or the other.

Mrs. Wilmington, clad in a daunting amount of black sateen, broke into Bliss's fretful thoughts with an announcement. "I have decided to leave for Sacramento in precisely one week." She sighed, her sizable bosom jutting out over her platter of eggs, beef hash, and pancakes. "It's so difficult to think of sailing away without my dear Piedmont."

Bliss was sympathetic. After all, she had been bereaved herself. She nodded gently.

The elderly woman drew in a brave and quivering breath. "Nonetheless, one must go on, mustn't one? Tell me, my dear young woman, have you any references to show me?"

Bliss dropped her eyes for a moment, then brought them firmly back to Mrs. Wilmington's face. "No, ma'am," she said. "I've never worked, except for my father. He's a lighthouse keeper, near Wellington, and I used to help him."

Mrs. Wilmington permitted herself a stiff nod. "That would do little to fit you for a lady's companion, of course," she pointed out.

Bliss wasn't willing to be termed unfit for a job any half-wit could do. She favored the old woman with her most dazzling smile. "What would be required of me, please?" she asked sweetly.

A serving girl brought Bliss's breakfast and set it before her as Mrs. Wilmington answered, "Why, of course you'd be expected to accompany me about the ship and tend to my clothing." She paused. "And to read to me, of an evening. My eyes aren't what they used to be, you know."

Bliss said nothing. If she didn't swallow a few bites of her breakfast, her stomach would be grumbling in another minute.

Mrs. Wilmington watched her curiously for a moment, then asked, "Have you fallen upon difficult circumstances, my dear? I was certain you told me you were employed by a gentleman and his wife—"

Bliss nodded, barely able to keep from laughing out loud. She didn't know which was funnier: hearing Jamie called a gentleman or Mrs. Wilmington's obvious conviction that her prospective companion was a starvation case.

The lie sprang easily to her lips, as lies will when they've been told before. "Yes. I am Mrs. McKenna's maid."

The old woman's cold blue eyes swept over Bliss, taking in her neat coronet of cinnamon-colored hair and the simple blouse she'd ferreted out of her satchel to wear for the occasion, along with her tweed skirt. "Something about your story doesn't ring true, miss," she said briskly. "Nonetheless, I like you."

"Thank you." Bliss was ashamed to be telling such outrageous stories, and she longed to spill out the whole disgraceful truth about herself, but she didn't dare. If Mrs. Wilmington ever suspected that she was married, the position would be irrevocably lost.

"I'll expect a written reference, then, from your Mrs. McKenna. Just have it sent to Room Thirty-six, please."

Bliss's heart had stopped beating, and she nearly choked on the food she'd been chewing, not only because she was supposed to deliver a letter of recommendation but because Jamie had just entered the dining room with a group of gentlemen.

Even though his clothes provided a rough contrast to the suits and vests his companions wore, he wasn't the least bit self-conscious. In fact, Bliss noted irritably, the other men seemed to defer to him.

"Are you all right, Miss Stafford?" Minerva Wilmington demanded, looking stern. Evidently, she would not tolerate anything less.

Bliss nodded, reddening a little and ducking her head. If Jamie happened to see her, all would be lost. However, since Mrs. Wilmington was about to leave the table, Bliss had to rise to her feet. Good manners compelled her.

"I'll be looking for that letter of reference," the old woman said, and her black sateen dress crackled and rustled as she walked imperiously away.

Bliss sank back into her chair and then risked a glance in Jamie's direction. She instantly regretted the action, for her gaze locked with his. Without looking away, he spoke to his companions and rose from his chair.

In a few strides, he was standing beside Bliss's chair. "Hello there, Duchess," he said in a voice that gave no indication of what he might be thinking or feeling. "Climbing out windows again, are you?"

Bliss glared at him. "I am not a prisoner, Jamie McKenna, and I will not be treated as one. Mrs. Wilmington is a—a friend."

Jamie's eyes held a mischievous light as he bent toward her, one hand resting on the back of her chair, the other idly holding that scruffy hat against his thigh. "Aye," he agreed, in tones of mockery, "I'm sure you and that good woman 'ave a great many things in common."

Bliss folded her hands in her lap, her breakfast forgotten, and sat up very straight in her chair. Her chin was at a stubborn angle and she looked through Jamie rather than at him. "It just so happens that we do," she lied. "I believe I'll call on my Aunt Calandra this morning, if you don't mind."

"I do mind," Jamie said. He had not straightened up, and his breath ruffled Bliss's hair. "I 'ave important business to see to today, and I don't want to be worryin' about what mischief you might be stirrin' up."

Bliss simmered with resentment, but there was little she could do. "I suppose you're planning to shop for a suitable cage for me to live in," she hissed.

Jamie chuckled and shook his head in wry wonder. "You're a bristly bit o' baggage, Duchess, that you are. What you need is a good tumble in a warm bed—and I'll see to that when I get back from doin' me business."

Slowly, thoughtfully, Bliss refilled her teacup from the pot in the center of the table, and then she tossed the contents onto Jamie's midsection. "Oh!" she cried in pretended horror as he leaped backward in shock, "do excuse me for being so clumsy!"

Bliss wanted to laugh at the fury she saw snapping in his azure eyes, but she didn't quite dare do that, so she bit the inside of her lip and reached for a napkin. Jamie stepped out of reach when she would have dabbed at his wet shirt in reparation.

"You'd best be grateful," he rasped in an outraged whisper, "that I'm not a man to do a lass violence!"

Bliss slapped one hand over her mouth in an effort to stifle a burst of amusement. She couldn't think why she found Jamie's anger so funny, but she did. Perhaps, she reflected, this compulsion to laugh was a form of hysteria.

"I'm sorry," she squeaked.

Jamie smiled at her—actually smiled—as he took hold of her elbow and brought her to her feet, but his eyes were still glittering like bits of blue topaz. "Come along, dear," he said, forcing the polite words past his teeth. "You and I are going to 'ave a little talk."

Bliss was not afraid, for she couldn't imagine Jamie hurting her physically, but she was embarrassed. The dining room was utterly silent as everyone there watched her being marched away like a public drunk, and Bliss's cheeks flamed bright pink. "It isn't like the tea was hot or anything," she pointed out under her breath.

Bliss sniffled once, knotted one hand into a fist, and pounded at her pillow. The scathing lecture Jamie had delivered earlier was still ringing in her ears.

She thrust herself onto her back, suppressing an urge to kick both her feet in unrestrained rage. The worst part was that Peony had heard everything, and been there to see Jamie order Bliss off to their room like a naughty child.

Seething at the memory, Bliss got off the bed, stormed to the door, and peered out. There was no sign of either Peony or Jamie, to her relief.

She crept to the desk near the door and took out a good supply of hotel stationery and a pen and ink, then sneaked back to the bedroom again. Seated in the window seat, where she could look down on carriages and people passing by in the street, Bliss began composing a letter of recommendation. She would sign it "Mrs. James McKenna," which was both the truth and a lie.

Hours had passed by the time the letter suited Bliss. She could only hope that Mrs. Wilmington would not have occasion to compare the identical handwriting of the real Mrs. James McKenna and the mythical one until after their ship was far out to sea.

In the distance, Bliss heard a door open, and here were all those discarded, crumpled pieces of paper on the floor, evidence of forgery. She leaped out of the window seat, hid the letter of recommendation under a cushion, and frantically gathered up the wadded pages.

"Bliss?" The voice was Jamie's. She scurried behind the

screen that hid the facilities and heaped the papers in the commode. Then, with one of the matches Jamie used to light those infernal cheroots of his, she lit the pyramid of paper on fire.

It was going up with a *whoosh* when Jamie came around the screen. He swore and covered his eyes with one hand when the blaze licked at the wall behind the commode and then ebbed away to nothing, leaving bits of black ash everywhere.

"What were you tryin' to do, Duchess?" he asked, after regarding her in disbelieving silence for several long moments. "Burn down the place, or signal the rest of your tribe?"

Bliss wrinkled her nose in puzzlement. "Who?"

"All those other redheaded gremlins who 'elp you think up crazy ideas."

Bliss drew a deep breath and let it out again. "There is only me," she said seriously.

"Thank God for that," Jamie muttered, shoving a hand through his hair. "To think I came back 'ere to ask you to forgive me—"

Bliss's eyes went round. "You did?"

"Aye." He folded his arms stubbornly. "Of course, that's all changed now. What the 'ell were you doin'?"

Bliss bit down on her lower lip, running mental fingers along the shelves of her mind in search of a believable answer. "I was writing a novella," she said at last.

Jamie looked both wary and skeptical, and his arms were still folded. "About what?" he wanted to know.

Bliss dropped her eyes. "It's a love story," she confessed, with feigned shyness. "About you and me."

It was a mark of his male vanity, Bliss thought later, that he believed her.

During supper, when Jamie left their table temporarily to go and speak to some people on the far side of the dining room, Bliss flagged down a waiter and pressed her letter of recommendation into his hand. "Please see that this is delivered to Room Thirty-six," she whispered.

Peony, who was sitting across the table, looked every bit as bored and irritable as Bliss felt. "What are you up to now, Mrs. McKenna?" she asked dryly.

Bliss shrugged. She wasn't sure how she felt about Peony Ryan anymore. The woman seemed to have too much pride to ever stoop to being a man's mistress, and yet her relationship with Jamie was obviously intimate, emotionally if not physically.

Peony sighed and took a sip of her wine before trying again. "Jamie's not a man to trifle with," she said. "If I were you, Bliss, I wouldn't push him another inch."

Choosing to disregard the warning, Bliss watched Jamie as he shook hands with the man he'd been talking to and started back toward his own table. "What's happening, Peony?" she asked. "Why is he keeping us inside the hotel every moment of the day? I'm about to suffocate!"

"You're not alone there," Peony replied dryly. "But he has his reasons."

Bliss brought one fist down on the table for emphasis. "I want to know what they are!" she cried.

Peony's reaction was the last one Bliss would have expected. She began to laugh.

"What's so funny?" Jamie asked irritably as he rejoined them at the table.

Peony went right on laughing. Only when her mirth had subsided did she say, "I warned you to stay on the straight and narrow, didn't I? Now you'll have your comeuppance, Jamie McKenna!"

Jamie gave Bliss a wry, private look that said he'd have more than his comeuppance, and she felt her blood turn hot at the prospect of being alone with him.

As it happened, Bliss was asleep when Jamie joined her in bed, but she awakened to find him unfastening the buttons of her camisole with light, agile fingers. "Ummm," she whispered, stretching luxuriously as he slipped his hand between satin and alabaster to caress her bare breast. Her nipple went deliciously hard against his palm.

With a groan, Jamie slipped beneath the covers to take the tender confection between his lips and flick at it with the tip of his tongue.

Bliss whimpered, arching her neck and entangling her fingers in Jamie's hair as he teased her. Meanwhile, he smoothed away her drawers; it seemed that they'd dissolved into thin air, so easily did he remove them.

She wanted him to take her, then and there, she needed him so badly, but Bliss knew that Jamie would exact the last measure of response from her before giving her complete satisfaction. She wanted vengeance, and when Jamie was poised above her but still withholding himself, she began scooting downward.

She felt the beggar's badge touch her cheek, warm from its contact with Jamie's chest, and she kissed her way through coarse down to tease a masculine nipple with her tongue.

Jamie moaned as she repaid him for some of the sweet torment he'd put her through, stiffened as she slid lower and lower beneath him, kissing the taut expanse of his belly. His powerful arms, holding his torso up off the bed, trembled with the effort of remaining in that position.

A primitive groan of triumph and surrender escaped him as Bliss found what she sought. She teased him until he was wild with the need of her, until he was pleading in hoarse, senseless words, and then she progressed back up over his belly and his chest to kiss the underside of his chin.

With a surge of newfound strength, and of passion, Jamie entered Bliss in one powerful motion of his hips. Now, it was her turn to know that tender torment she had subjected him to earlier.

Her fingers grasped frantically at the muscular expanse of his back in an effort to hold him as he withdrew slowly, slowly, until he was barely inside her. "Please," she whispered.

Her reward was another deep and magnificent stroke,

followed by the inevitable, excruciating withdrawal. Again and again, he lunged and withdrew, hovering for long seconds on the brink of leaving Bliss, then delving far inside her again. She was near delirium when Jamie finally permitted her the ecstasy he had been taunting her with, and she was like a wild creature, flinging her head back and forth on the pillow, hurling her hips at him, crying out as glory exploded within and all around her. The light was white and dazzling, like fire sparked by the friction of angels' wings.

Now Jamie's pace grew more rapid as he too felt the sweet heat of angelfire. Bliss soothed him with whispers and with her hands, at the same time purposely driving him toward madness, sheathing him in rippling velvet.

In the shattering, seemingly endless moments of his release, Bliss once again found his nipple with her mouth and enjoyed him ruthlessly as he trembled upon her, her name like a war cry on his lips.

When he collapsed beside her, gasping so greedily for air that Bliss feared he would die, she whispered, "Jamie, I love you!"

His strong hands rose to clasp the sides of her head, fingers buried in her hair, but he was still breathing too raggedly for speech. Finally, he pressed Bliss's mouth to his and kissed her.

Through his chest she could feel the hard, steady beat of his heart. "And I love you, Duchess," he whispered, when he could speak.

Although they were both exhausted, their young bodies had been honed for sweeter battles; within minutes, they were needing again. Loving again.

And when that skirmish was over, they fell into sound sleep, their arms and legs intertwined as if they would cling together forever.

But forever is a thing sometimes denied to mortal man.

Chapter 16 🦋

IT WAS PURE LUCK, AND NOTHING MORE, THAT NEITHER JAMIE NOR Peony was in the suite when Mrs. Minerva Wilmington came to call. She was obviously disappointed at not being able to meet the woman who had written such a glowing letter of recommendation for Bliss.

Cheeks slightly warm, Bliss lowered her eyes and said, "Won't you please sit down, Mrs. Wilmington?"

"No time, no time," replied the woman. Jamie would have said that was typical of a Yank, being in a rush. "I have reached my decision."

Bliss held her breath, one hand clasping the other as she stood there facing Mrs. Wilmington, the door of the suite standing open. She longed to stay with Jamie, but he was even then out looking for a suitable place to tuck her away in, like a doll in a dollhouse.

He wanted a toy, not a wife and a partner.

"You'll do," Mrs. Wilmington said briskly. "We'll discuss your wages and the payment of your passage at another time. You will be prepared to depart in six days, won't you?"

Bliss nodded, so near tears that she didn't trust herself to speak. It was really going to happen; she was going to leave Jamie McKenna and her homeland behind—and never look back.

When she'd closed the door behind Mrs. Wilmington, Bliss leaned against it, bit her lower lip, and let the tears spill over. Suddenly America seemed big and strange and very far away.

The fact that her mother lived there didn't offer the comfort that it had in days gone by.

Resolutely, Bliss took herself in hand. The last few days had been a foretaste of the life Jamie meant for her; despite luxurious surroundings, Bliss was alone for the greater part of every day, and she was bored to distraction. Only when Jamie made love to her—which was always at his convenience—did she feel truly alive.

She had yearned for adventure all her life, and by heaven she was going to have it. Furthermore, she was bound to get over Jamie McKenna one day—though who knew how long that would take.

With a sigh, Bliss went into the bedroom and opened the huge armoire. It was time she decided which of the clothes Jamie had bought her were suitable for a widow's companion and which should be left behind—along with silly dreams and wishful thinking.

Increase Pipher settled back against the pillows on his bed, exhausted from his travels.

He smiled to himself. The exquisite irony of it all; after all these years of helpless fury, he was in a position to monitor virtually every move that arrogant young Irishman made.

The suite across the hall. Increase threw his head back and gave a raspy burst of laughter. Jamie McKenna would pay, in coin more precious than gold, for all the grief he'd caused. And as for that little bitch who'd helped him—

In the distance, there was a noise. Walter Davis, Increase's private secretary, had returned.

"Davis!" the old man shouted.

The clerk entered the master bedroom with trepidation. "How are you feeling, Mr. Pipher?" He spoke with respect, but Increase didn't miss the red flush climbing the lad's skinny neck.

"Never mind how I'm feeling. What did you learn?"

Davis kept his distance, probably because Increase had reached out for his cane and waved it for emphasis while speaking. The cowardly little whelp had learned to stay out of its range.

"He's got a wife, Mr. Pipher. Jamie McKenna's got himself a wife."

Increase digested this information with particular pleasure. "Have you gotten a look at her?"

Davis nodded. "Just briefly, in the dining room this morning. She's a saucy red-haired snippet with the bluest eyes I've ever seen. Got quite a temper, according to the staff."

Increase smiled. "She's the same woman, then. The one Dunnigan described. McKenna loves her, does he?"

"The staff uniformly agrees that he does, sir," said David, his tone obsequious and sugary now. He was always pandering, *the sniveling little worm,* and even though Increase liked to force people into doing both those things, he despised them for it, too.

"So it's a grand passion, is it?" Increase muttered thoughtfully. "Wonderful. I can't tell you how happy I am for the both of them."

Davis folded his arms across his skinny chest. "If you don't mind my saying so, sir, it seems—unprofitable to seek revenge after all this time."

Rage exploded within Increase. Unprofitable, was it? He'd lost everything the day Peony had rescued that miserable Irishman. He'd lost his mistress, his crop of sugarcane, his house. He looked down at his legs, clearly seeing the scars the fire had left even though they were covered by his trousers. He'd nearly lost two limbs as well.

The clerk read his expression accurately and held out both

hands in an effort to stay an outburst. "I'm sure you have your reasons, of course," he sputtered. "Is there anything else you'd like me to do?"

"Oh yes," Increase said, smiling. "I think a wedding gift is in order, don't you? And I know just what I want to send to the happy couple."

Davis's face went pale as Increase gave him his instructions. It was a sad commentary, the old man reflected later, that so few men had the stomach for seeing matters through to their just conclusions.

The package arrived by messenger just as they were about to go out for supper, and there was a card attached. Frowning, Jamie opened the envelope and read, *"For the newlyweds, with kindest regards for your future happiness. An old friend."*

Bliss appeared at his elbow, for she loved a surprise, but Jamie had a feeling this wasn't anything he wanted her to see. Nonetheless, he cut the twine away with his knife and laid back the plain wrapping paper.

The gift was a bullwhip, wound into a coil of lethal black leather. Jamie's knees weakened, and he closed his eyes for a moment, fighting against memories of another whip, in another time and place.

Bliss was stricken dumb, for once in her life, but Peony put one hand to her mouth and whispered, "Oh my God, Jamie—"

Jamie bolted out the door, bent on catching up with the messenger, but he was too late. The boy was gone.

"What does it mean?" Bliss asked, looking from Peony's face to Jamie's. "Somebody tell me what's happening!"

Jamie shoved a hand through his hair. "It's a long story, Duchess. Peony and I—well, we made an enemy when we left Australia."

Peony was pacing and wringing her hands. "I know this is all happening because I set the cane fields on fire," she muttered. "If I hadn't done that—"

"If you hadn't done that," Jamie broke in, anxious to reassure his friend, "I'd be a mess of bones underneath a tree. You saved my life, love."

Bliss's eyes were wide with the drama of it all, and she didn't speak. At any other time, under any other circumstances, Jamie would have laughed at her expression.

"What are we going to do now?" Peony whispered.

Jamie's hand moved, by habit, to the knife he was rarely without, his fingers resting lightly on the scabbard. "Just what he wants us to do," he answered. "Wait."

The day of her departure for America was drawing nearer and nearer, and with each passing moment, Bliss wanted less than ever to go. Even though Jamie would never have admitted it, he needed her.

As Bliss placed the few carefully folded items of clothing she meant to take with her into her satchel, she thought about the whip that had arrived several days before and shuddered. Something really horrible was happening, but neither Jamie nor Peony would tell her what it was.

It had to do with the scars on Jamie's back, though. Bliss had been able to deduce that much from the nightmares that set her husband to tossing wildly in his sleep every night.

She sighed. There was no use in worrying, for she could do nothing to help unless Jamie decided to share the problem with her. Not much chance of that, it appeared.

Bliss went back to the suite's main room, feeling bored and frustrated. If nothing else, Jamie had stopped locking her in; she would go out for a long walk. With the approach of September, spring was in the air.

She was just reaching for a lightweight cloak when someone knocked at the door. Forgetting Jamie's warnings—he could be such a fussbudget—she swung it open wide, pleased at the idea of company.

The young man standing nervously in the hallway was familiar to Bliss; she'd seen him in the lobby and the dining room of the hotel.

"Hello," he said, after clearing his throat. He was thin, with brown hair that stuck up rambunctiously, despite generous applications of pomade, and a poor complexion. "Please excuse me for troubling you, Mrs. McKenna. My name is Walter Davis and I'm here about—about my grandfather."

Bliss was puzzled. "How do you happen to know my name?" she asked.

Mr. Davis went ruddy. "I—I've inquired," he stammered. "The fact is, Mrs. McKenna, I need to find a chemist—so that I might purchase my grandfather's medicine—and—well—I do hesitate to leave the old fellow alone. I was wondering if you might stay with him, just for a few minutes?"

Bliss would have much preferred going on the errand, she so craved fresh air, but perhaps Mr. Davis had been shut up even longer than she had, looking after his sick grandfather and all. "All right," she agreed with a polite nod.

Mr. Davis turned and opened the door across the hallway. "Thank you so much, Mrs. McKenna. I know Grandfather will enjoy meeting you."

After only the briefest hesitation, Bliss preceded Mr. Davis into the other suite. Jamie would have said she was taking a foolish chance, but then, he had rather a suspicious mind. If it were up to him, she'd sit in the suite like a geranium on a windowsill, looking pretty and doing nothing.

A shriveled old man with white hair sat ensconced in the middle of the suite's front room, like a king holding court. Bliss felt a chilly finger touch her soul when he smiled at her, but she shook the reaction off. She'd been spending too much time inside the hotel, that was all. She was getting skittish.

"Hello there, my dear," the scratchy voice said, and one thin hand was extended. "It's grand to finally meet you."

Bliss worked up a smile as Mr. Davis began the introductions. "Grandfather, this is Mrs. James McKenna—"

214

The rheumy eyes seemed to flash beneath their heavy lids. "My name is Albert," he broke in. "Albert Davis."

The elder Mr. Davis's grip was strong, despite his advanced age and the fact that he sat in an invalid's chair. "Hello, Mr. Davis," Bliss said politely, wondering how long it would take for the grandson to visit the chemist's shop. The room was dark, since the drapes were pulled, and there was a musty smell in the air, along with an inexplicable sense of peril.

Bliss was relieved when the old man released his near-painful grasp on her hand.

"Do sit down," he said as his grandson left the suite.

Bliss had ever believed in making the best of any situation. "Are you visiting Auckland, Mr. Davis?"

He smiled, revealing huge yellow teeth. They gave him a cadaverous look. "I'm here on business, Mrs. McKenna. Tell me—might I call you by your first name?"

Bliss looked longingly toward the drapes. Oh, to open them and let in God's clean, bright sunshine. "I see no harm in that," she replied politely, folding her hands in her lap.

"Thank you, my dear. And that name is . . . ?"

"Bliss," she said.

Again, the leering yellow smile. "I daresay, it suits you. How long have you been married, Bliss?"

The question, innocent as it was, felt like a violation of some sort. Bliss blushed, growing more uncomfortable with each passing moment. "Only a few weeks," she answered.

Albert Davis raised his bushy white eyebrows and his smile remained fixed. "You're still honeymooning, then."

Bliss lowered her eyes. The only time her marriage seemed real was when she and Jamie were in bed together, but she couldn't very well confide as much to a virtual stranger. Especially not a male stranger.

"I've embarrassed you," the old man crowed delightedly. Then he composed himself. "I'm sorry, my dear. I truly am. Tell me about this husband of yours. What does he do with his time?"

Quick as that, Bliss felt her attitude changing. Jamie was, after all, her favorite topic of conversation. "He has sheep," she said happily. "Hundreds and hundreds of sheep. And I think he must be very important, for he's had meetings every single day."

"He's wealthy, then?"

Bliss hadn't really considered that, since Jamie wasn't a man to flaunt the fact that he had money. "I suppose he is," she agreed, with a note of surprise in her voice.

The sharp blue eyes were fixed on Bliss's bare left hand. "But you don't wear a wedding band," Davis muttered.

The reminder was wounding to Bliss. A man who had been forced to marry, at gunpoint, would naturally be disinclined to offer his bride a wedding ring. Still, Jamie McKenna availed himself of the advantages of marriage without any noticeable qualms. Full of conviction, Bliss silently vowed to turn away the very next time he touched her.

If she could.

"Forgive me," Albert Davis said smoothly. "It seems I've touched a nerve."

Bliss sighed. Mr. Davis was only trying to make polite conversation, she was sure, but there was something so watchful about him. Something shrewd.

"Does your husband love you, Bliss?"

The audacity of that question stunned Bliss. She was speechless for a moment, then her eyes shot indigo fire. "How could such a thing possibly matter to you?" she countered.

He sighed; the sound was long and thin and ragged—like a bit of tattered, dirty cloth. "Saucy," he said with a nod, as though confirming something.

Bliss was prepared to leap to her feet and make a dash for it if Mr. Davis started to rise out of his invalid's chair or wheel it closer. She wished now that she hadn't agreed to stay here until the other man returned. "I beg your pardon?"

Mr. Davis began to laugh. "I fear I've frightened you."

Bliss sat up very straight. "You flatter yourself if you think that," she said stiffly.

Again that laugh sounded; it was like the shrill caw of a crow. "Delightful!" he cried, slapping one blanket-covered knee. "Absolutely delightful!"

Bliss rose from her chair and moved to stand discreetly behind it. "I really don't understand—"

The old man was waving one hand in a shooing motion. "You may go, my dear," he said, dabbing away tears of laughter with his shirtsleeve. "I've learned all I need to know."

Bliss was eager to leave, but there was the small matter of a promise given. "I did tell your grandson I'd stay until he returned," she said.

But Mr. Davis waved his hand and wheeled himself around so that his back was to Bliss. He began to mutter, speaking as though he were already alone.

Bliss didn't need to hear more. She hurried out of the suite, across the hall, and into her own. Jamie was there, still wearing his hat and coat.

"And where 'ave you been?" he asked with a curious frown.

Bliss decided to evade the question. "I'm dying for some fresh air, Jamie McKenna, and if you won't go out walking with me, I'll go by myself."

Jamie grinned at her and spread his hands. "It just so 'appens that there's something I want to show you," he agreed. "So if you want to walk, Duchess, we'll walk."

Bliss kept her eyes on Jamie's profile as the lift carried them down to the lobby. It didn't seem possible that she would be gone in the morning, never to look upon that face again.

She wanted to cry.

"Why are you so sad, Duchess?" Jamie asked as they stepped out of the lift. His voice was very gentle, and tears welled in Bliss's eyes.

"I'm not sad," she lied.

217

He ushered her across the crowded lobby and outside. The sun was shining brightly, but the air was crisply cold. Although the brim of his hat mostly hid his features, Bliss could tell that Jamie was annoyed.

"All right, I'm sad!" she admitted. She'd taken Jamie's arm and they were walking steadily south.

"Why?"

Bliss could not answer that she was leaving for America in the morning and that she would miss her husband with all her heart and soul. She said the first thing that came to her mind. "Because you've never given me a wedding band."

She saw a muscle along his jawline tighten momentarily. "I see," he said in an expressionless voice. "Well, Duchess, as it 'appened, your father didn't give me much chance to go buyin' you a golden ring."

Bliss's throat felt tight and her eyes went all blurry with tears. How she wished Jamie's ardor extended beyond the edges of his mattress!

When her vision cleared, she realized that they were entering an elegant residential section, where town houses stood back from the brick-lined streets, behind stone walls and iron gates. She was just thinking that living there would be like being incarcerated in a sumptuous prison when Jamie stopped and extracted a key from his pocket.

While Bliss watched mutely, he opened the gate and drew her through. There was an unnerving clanging sound as it closed behind them.

The house they were approaching was a small mansion, with an empty stone fish pond and bare flower beds in front. Jamie pulled Bliss up the steps and used another key to open the towering double doors.

The inside was dark, but there was electricity, and Jamie turned a switch, revealing an elegant entry hall and curving stairway. "There's a fireplace in our room," he said, taking Bliss's hand and starting up the stairway.

She had no choice but to follow. This, of course, was the house Jamie meant to cage her up in, and by rights, she should have been angry. She supposed she wasn't because he'd said "our room," like they were going to be a real married couple.

Then Bliss remembered that she was never going to live in this house, with or without Jamie, and she couldn't help it. She started to cry.

Inside the spacious master bedroom, with its floor-to-ceiling windows and gracious ivory fireplace, Jamie pulled her close, his hands resting on the small of her back.

"What's the trouble, Duchess?" he asked.

Bliss rested her forehead against his chest, her shoulders trembling as silent sobs shook her. *Tell me you love me, Jamie,* she wanted to say. *Tell me that you're going to live here with me, and that I'm going to have your children.*

When Bliss didn't speak, Jamie reached inside his coat pocket with one hand and produced a small box, which he rubbed against the underside of her chin. "Maybe this will make you feel better," he said.

Bliss stepped back and he put the box in her palm. She sniffled inelegantly and lifted the satin-covered lid. "Oh Jamie," she marveled as an emerald ring, with a halo of diamonds, winked and shimmered at her.

He took the ring from the box and slipped it onto the very finger where a wedding band would go, and Bliss's heart nearly stopped at the significance of that. She lifted her eyes to Jamie's face, but his features looked watery.

He laughed and raised her hand to his lips. "What do you think of your gilded cage, Duchess?" he teased.

Bliss pulled her hand away, prepared to give back the ring if it came to that. She hoped, of course, that it wouldn't. "I won't live in a cage, Jamie McKenna," she warned. "No matter how splendid it is."

He caught hold of her again; his lips were brushing her palm and the inside of her wrist, where the skin was sensitive. Little heated shivers went through her. "Umm-hmm," he agreed.

Bliss trembled. "I'm serious," she insisted.

Jamie dropped her hand and drew her up hard against him, his head tilted to one side so that his lips were only a hair's breadth from hers. "Shut up," he said.

His kiss threatened to consume her. All thoughts of America and of the strange, scary old man she'd encountered fled her mind as Jamie's magic began. He filled her thoughts and her senses until there was no room for anything or anyone else.

She was never sure whether he lowered her to the cool marble floor or she simply sank there because her knees would not support her. Without breaking the kiss, he laid aside her cloak and opened the buttons at her bodice. She knew, when his hand slipped in to cup her breast, why he'd shown such partiality to that particular dress when she'd tried it on at the store.

Bliss pushed Jamie's battered leather hat away so that she could plunge the fingers of both hands into his rich, brown-sugar hair and moaned as he drew away from her lips to attend one swollen nipple. Meanwhile, with his other hand, he was lifting her skirts.

Jamie wanted to draw their lovemaking out to excruciating lengths, but Bliss would not permit that. Her need of him was too desperate and too great.

She opened his belt and then the buttons of his trousers, freeing him to her caress. He drew in a harsh breath as she stroked him, then whispered, "You win, Duchess. You win."

In one forceful thrust he had entered her, and Bliss did not allow him his usual lingering retreats; her hands clasped his buttocks, and each time he would have withdrawn from her, she drove him back to the very core of her. He seemed, in fact, to be touching her soul.

All the same, it was Bliss setting the pace, and she loved the joyous triumph of that. Her release came in a series of sweet, rippling waves, while Jamie's, occurring moments later, was almost brutal in its intensity, buckling his powerful body as though it were no more than a leaf in the wind.

He sank to cover Bliss's lips with his own, but he was breathing too hard to kiss her properly, and he finally raised his head in glorious defeat. She hadn't realized she was crying until she saw the fact reflected in his eyes.

"Duchess—"

She was shaking her head wildly from side to side. "Don't say anything, Jamie," she pleaded. "Please, don't."

He honored her request, giving her the distance she needed, turning away to adjust his clothing so that she could straighten hers in private.

Finally, she felt ready to speak. "I love you, Jamie," she said, to the broad expanse of his back. He turned, slowly, to face her. "But I won't share you with Peony Ryan or anyone else, and I won't sit in this house waiting for you to put your boots under my bed." She held up her left hand, and the beautiful emerald, with its circlet of diamonds, twinkled in the light. "If I'm going to wear this ring, I want to be a real wife, not a mistress."

Jamie looked baffled. He retrieved his hat and put it on, and Bliss knew that he was stalling. "I'm not sure I know what you mean by that, Duchess," he said quietly. "You've been me wife, in every sense of the word, for some time now. And I've explained about Peony again and again—"

Bliss shook her head, her throat so constricted that she could barely speak. Everything, *everything* depended on Jamie's understanding. "I've been your lover, not your wife. Once your needs were satisfied, you were willing to pat me on the head and put me back on the shelf until the next time."

She saw his jaw clamp down tight before he looked away from her and said, "There are places where a woman doesn't belong."

Bliss closed her eyes for a moment. Feeling faint. She'd forced this showdown, and she was losing it. "And Peony?"

"She's me friend, Duchess," Jamie said, looking exasperated. "If it weren't for 'er, I'd 'ave been dead a dozen times over. So if you're askin' me to turn me back on 'er, I'll 'ave to tell you no."

Bliss's pride was in shreds. "I see," she said. Before leaving the room she and Jamie would never share, she pressed the emerald ring into his hand.

Chapter 17 ❧

JAMIE TOSSED BACK THE LAST OF HIS WHISKEY AND SET THE GLASS down hard on the bar. "You an Australian, mate?" he asked the man next to him. "You talk funny."

The bloke looked wet behind the ears. He still had bad skin, and his hair stuck out every which way. Jamie's question made him smile, and he nodded as the barkeeper refilled both their glasses.

"I won't 'old it against you," Jamie said, feeling magnanimous. "I 'ave a brother that's an Aussie."

Having made this pronouncement, Jamie sighed and assessed his glass. He'd lost count of how many drinks he'd consumed since he and Bliss had parted company in the lobby; he'd headed straight for the pub while she'd gone back to the suite.

"Ever been to Australia?" the stranger asked.

That innocent question brought the place back to Jamie's mind so strongly that he could feel the bark of that tree against the insides of his wrists and smell the scent of his own blood. He shivered, as though a chill wind had caught him naked. "Aye," he said. He couldn't talk about that part

223

of his life, not when he'd been weakened by whiskey. "I 'ave a brother there, like I told you."

"So you did. What business is he in?"

Jamie looked at the stranger curiously. He was a nosy little bleeder, he'd say that for him. "Shippin', sugarcane—that kind of thing."

The small man nodded. "I don't believe I've introduced myself. I'm Walt Davis."

Jamie had already bought the bloke several drinks and considered him something of a mate. Still, it was good to know what handle a man went by. He nodded and concentrated on his whiskey.

Davis cleared his throat. "You in some kind of trouble, Mr. McKenna?" he asked.

It wouldn't occur to Jamie until much later to wonder how Davis had known his name when he hadn't offered it. He nodded and signaled to the barkeeper. "The worst kind, mate. The worst kind."

"Woman trouble," Davis said knowingly.

"Aye," Jamie agreed.

"Mistress?"

Jamie shook his head solemnly. "Wife."

"Oh," Davis replied with proper sympathy.

"Can't make 'er 'appy no matter what I do," Jamie complained. "If I say 'stay put,' she's got to go. If I say 'go,' she stays put." He paused and shook his head, marveling at the enormity of his dilemma. "I buy 'er a 'ouse, she won't live in it. I give 'er a ring, she won't wear it."

"Do you love her?"

Now that was a strange thing for a mate to ask, Jamie thought. But his brain was too whiskey-fogged to move beyond this observation. "Aye," he answered. "More than me life."

With that, he finished his drink, tossed a bit of money on the bar, and walked out.

* * * *

Bliss sat huddled in the middle of the bed, misery personified. Promptly at ten the next morning, Mrs. Wilmington would collect her and, probably with a great deal of fuss and ceremony, the two women would set out together for the harbor. Their ship was scheduled to sail at noon.

A feeling of dreadful homesickness washed over Bliss—and her not even gone yet—leaving her shaken and sick. She loved Jamie so much that it was all she could do not to go to him on bended knee and beg him for the privilege of living in his house and wearing his ring.

But Bliss's pride wouldn't let her do this. A marriage based on such cowardice would be no marriage at all.

The suite's door opened and closed and she waited, holding her breath. Instead of joining her in their room, however, Bliss heard Jamie knock softly at the door of the other bedchamber.

Jamie had gone to Peony for his comfort.

Despair made Bliss sway and cover her mouth with one hand. In agony, she rocked back and forth, back and forth, hugging herself as if to hold in the terrible pain of Jamie's betrayal.

He must have been with Peony for an hour or so, but that time was an eternity to Bliss, during which she suffered all the torments of hell. Then Jamie came to their bed, at last, and sat down heavily on the edge. He reeked of whiskey.

Bliss, pretending to be asleep, was all but choking on her rage; her throat was raw with the effort of holding back screams of fury, and her hands were knotted into fists. She wanted so desperately to batter that broad, impervious back with them.

Jamie was unbuttoning his shirt. After that, he kicked off his boots and then stood to unfasten his trousers. Bliss ached to think that this was the second bed he'd undressed beside that night, and not the first.

A tormented sob tore itself from her throat, betraying her. "Are you all right?" Jamie spoke hoarsely, as a guilty man

225

might. Then he drew back the covers and climbed into bed with Bliss.

She could bear no more. With a shriek, she flung herself at him in wrath, striking him in as many places as she could, as many times as she could. He finally grasped both her wrists in his hands to halt the siege, and when she continued to struggle against him, he hurled her onto her back.

The breath had been knocked out of her; Bliss could only stare up into Jamie's glittering eyes in anguished silence.

"Why, Duchess?" he rasped after a few moments. "Why?"

A strange hysteria possessed Bliss; she fought him still, her legs thumping against the mattress, her head tossing wildly from side to side. Jamie stunned her by wrenching her close and holding her as the ragged sobs began, rising from the depths of her spirit like the wails of an injured creature.

Bliss's hands moved up and down Jamie's bare back, the scars lying in smooth ridges beneath her palms. Her grief was fathomless; she had been forced to share the only man she would ever love, and tomorrow she would lose him forever.

His lips were gentle against her temple. "Duchess, listen to me," he pleaded in a broken whisper, still holding her fast. "Please, listen. I don't know what it is that's so terribly wrong, but I promise you this: if you'll just give me the chance, I'll make it right. Whatever it is, I'll make it right."

Bliss would have given anything short of her soul to believe Jamie, but she didn't. She couldn't, for he had just come to her from Peony's bed. No matter what happened, she must not let herself forget that.

She almost told him then that she would be leaving in the morning, but in the end, she couldn't. Jamie stretched out on the mattress, drawing her with him, holding her in an embrace that would leave her wondering, when she looked back on that night, whether he had been seeking to give comfort, or to obtain it.

226

Sometime before sunrise, Bliss lapsed into a fitful sleep. When she awakened, Jamie was gone.

Despondency twisted, spiky, in her throat.

There was to be no time for regrets, however, for a glance at the clock on the bedside stand sent her flying out of bed to have her bath and prepare for the momentous day that lay ahead.

By five minutes of ten, she had bathed, dressed, done up her hair, checked and rechecked the contents of her satchel, and composed a short note to Jamie. She propped that in front of the clock in the suite's sunny parlor and, after one last look around, crept out.

Mrs. Wilmington had commandeered a carriage, and she was supervising the carrying out of her trunks and valises when Bliss reached the lobby. To her moderate annoyance, Walter Davis was there, too, reading a newspaper. The group of potted palms and ferns behind his chair made him seem to be sitting in darkest Africa.

"There you are," Mrs. Wilmington thundered good-naturedly to her new companion. At the sight of Bliss's solitary valise, however, she frowned. "Is that all you're bringing?"

Bliss was nodding, about to explain that her needs were simple, when out of the corner of her eye she saw Walter approaching. Of course, if he should address her as Mrs. McKenna, he would spoil everything. Mrs. Wilmington would never be willing to engage a companion who was married.

Bliss muttered an excuse to her employer and hurried to intercept Walter, smiling warmly, if in a rather shaky fashion, as she greeted him. "Good morning, Mr. Davis. How are you today?"

He was looking at her valise. "Quite well, thank you," he said. "Are you taking a journey?"

Bliss nodded, hoping that he wouldn't press for too many details. "I—I'm sorry that our acquaintance was so brief—"

Walter had caught hold of her arm, and with a forcefulness she wouldn't have expected of him, he hauled her around to the rear of the crop of potted plants and said in a low voice, "I could have sworn you told me you had a husband!"

Bliss swallowed. "I do," she confessed.

A sympathetic expression crossed his face as he took in the smudges of fatigue beneath her eyes and the red puffiness of her lids—both evidences that she'd been unable to hide. "You've been crying. Did he hurt you? The brute—I shall box his ears!"

Bliss couldn't help but smile at the images that rose in her mind. There might well be some ear boxing should Jamie and Walter come to blows, but Walter would do the bleeding, not the boxing.

"Well?" Walter prompted. "Did he do you injury in any way?"

Bliss shook her head. "No—not in the way you mean." In the background, Mrs. Wilmington called her name. "I must go now. Good-bye, Walter."

"At least tell me where you're off to," Walter pleaded, sounding a touch desperate as he followed Bliss back to Mrs. Wilmington's side.

"America," Bliss said, so sadly that Mrs. Wilmington gave her an odd look.

"A-America!" Walter sputtered. "You can't do that! You really mustn't—"

"Good-bye, Walter," Bliss repeated, with less warmth than before. The last of Mrs. Wilmington's baggage had been taken out to the carriage; it was time to leave.

Bliss was silent during the long drive to the harbor, looking out at the storefronts and hotels of Auckland. Finally, they reached the waterfront.

It was an ugly place, where bawds lounged against the ramshackle walls of pubs and drunks lay sprawled in the road. Bliss watched in horror as the carriage wheels narrowly missed one reveler's outstretched fingers.

The stench of offal and rotted fish was almost enough to

set Bliss retching. Mrs. Wilmington must have agreed, for she raised a dainty handkerchief to her sizable nose in an effort to strain some of the foulness from the air.

The carriage lurched to a stop and the driver came around to peer in the window. His breath was almost as bad as the rest of it, and Bliss recoiled from him.

"Here we are, mum," he told Mrs. Wilmington. "It's this pier where the *Queen Charlotte* has her moorings."

"Thank you," Mrs. Wilmington said. "Please see that our baggage is carried aboard." She started to hand the man a pound note, but Bliss interceded by taking hold of the woman's wrist.

"Don't do that, Mrs. Wilmington," she said respectfully. "Not yet."

The carriage driver gave Bliss a look that would have spoiled cabbage, then went around to begin taking trunks and valises from the boot.

"Why on earth did you do that?" the American woman demanded.

"I don't like that fellow's looks," Bliss confided. "Maybe I haven't done much traveling, but I've got good instincts and I know a waster when I see one. Like as not, that bloke would have dumped us in the street and made off with your luggage and your pound note!"

Mrs. Wilmington looked impressed. "My goodness. I've always left such matters to Piedmont, and it didn't even occur to me that the man might be unworthy of our trust."

Bliss's smile must have appeared a little fixed; it took all the self-control she possessed not to go scrambling back to the hotel and hurl herself at Jamie's feet. "I don't look for him to help us out of the carriage, either," she went on. "So we'd just better see to ourselves."

With that, she opened the carriage door and lowered herself to the street. Knowing that Mrs. Wilmington would not be so nimble, with her greater age and bulk, she caught the driver's eye and glared at him until he brought a little step stool forward and set it with a thump on the road.

With Bliss's assistance, Mrs. Wilmington descended.

Bliss was looking all around her as she and her employer walked down the pier and up a long, slanting ramp to the ship.

The craft had three smokestacks towering above its decks, and a man in a blue uniform came forward, even as Mrs. Wilmington was speaking to the purser about Bliss's passage, to collect the younger woman's tattered valise.

"Hello there," he said, drawing out the first word in a jaunty fashion.

Bliss thought of Jamie, swallowed hard, and took back her valise with an eloquent jerk of her hand. Men. They were all alike—always trying to charm a lady. "Go away," she said.

"Yes, ma'am," said the young seaman with a crisp salute. His ears were red with embarrassment as he hurried off in another direction.

By that time, Bliss was feeling a little sorry for him. Since there was nothing for it, she sighed and turned her attention back to the arrangements at hand. Her passage to America was assured; she would share a stateroom with Mrs. Wilmington.

Between one instant and the next, some instinct made the small hairs on the back of Bliss's neck stand up in alarm. She turned at the sound of a slight fracas on the boarding ramp to see Jamie striding around the insolent carriage driver, who had been struggling with Mrs. Wilmington's baggage.

Bliss took a step backward, but even as she did so, she knew there was no place to run. A part of her rejoiced in that knowledge, but her pride demanded that she fight for her rights.

Jamie came to a stop directly in front of her, swept off his hat, and smiled winningly. "Well, 'ello, Duchess," he said. "Exactly where did you think you were goin'?"

"Now, just one moment," blustered Mrs. Wilmington, who looked uncertain. "Who are you, young man, and what do you mean by this affront?"

Bliss's face flamed as Jamie answered the woman in the politest tones. "Beggin' your pardon, mum, but me name is James Marcus McKenna and I'm this lady's 'usband."

"Is this true?" Mrs. Wilmington demanded of her companion, in a withering voice.

"No," Bliss lied firmly. "I've never seen this dreadful person before in my life."

At this, Jamie threw back his head and laughed. "Allow me to introduce myself, Duchess," he said, catching her by the waist and flinging her over one shoulder as though she were a bag of barley. "I'm the bloke that's goin' to show you the error of your ways."

Bliss gave a shriek and kicked, but it did little good, so she began striking Jamie with her valise. That didn't help, either.

"Young man," protested Mrs. Wilmington, with what seemed to Bliss a serious lack of conviction. "I'll call for assistance if I must!"

"You do that, m'lady," Jamie responded, and a motion of his right shoulder told Bliss that he'd doffed his hat to the woman. "Keep in mind, though, that you're goin' to need an army."

The blood was beginning to rush to Bliss's head. Again, she slammed her satchel into Jamie's back. "Damn you," she spat, "let me down!"

"I'd love to," Jamie replied smoothly, venturing dangerously close to the side of the ramp. "Trouble is, Duchess, that the water's some filthy 'ere. God knows what diseases you'd get if I threw you in."

Frustration made Bliss emit another shriek, and Jamie responded by landing a hard swat on her upended bottom. Neither Mrs. Wilmington nor anyone else came forward to help.

"Help!" Bliss screamed at the top of her lungs, clasping her satchel's grip in one hand and holding her bonnet on with the other.

231

Jamie laughed. "Don't waste your breath, love. None of these louts'll 'elp you. It's the neighbor'ood, you know—it's gone down'ill these past fifty years."

"I hate you," Bliss whispered furiously, and at that moment, she meant it.

Again, Jamie's hand rose to her bottom. Only this time, he gave her an arrogant squeeze instead of another smack. "I feel the same way about you, me precious darlin'," he responded warmly, and there was no break in his stride.

Bliss was seething. "Put—me—*down!*"

"If I do," Jamie replied, "it'll be to turn you over me knee. Is that what you want, Duchess—with all these people lookin' on and all?"

"No!" Bliss cried in a strangled voice. Trust Jamie to threaten her with the one thing more humiliating than being carried down a ramp and along a pier over a man's shoulder!

"I didn't think so," he agreed reasonably.

Bliss was seriously considering throwing up when Jamie came to a jarring stop. She heard the creak of a carriage door, and then she was set, none too gently, on the floor of that vehicle, which put her at eye level with a very irate Jamie.

His nose was nearly touching hers. "If you ever do anything like that again, Bliss," he warned, "I swear by all that's 'oly that I'll blister you."

There was no doubt in Bliss's mind that Jamie meant what he said, at the moment at least. She scooted backward until she was inside the carriage, then hauled herself up onto one of the seats. Not once in all that time did her eyes stray from Jamie's face; if he made any sudden moves, she wanted to be ready.

He rapped at the outside of the carriage with his knuckles and the rig bolted forward.

"How did you find me?" Bliss asked in a small voice, still watching Jamie.

He settled back in the seat, as though hauling women off ships over one shoulder were a normal morning's work, sighing and tugging his hat down over his eyes. "I 'ave me sources," he said.

Bliss ached to kick him, but there was such a thing as pressing one's luck. Besides, even though she didn't plan to admit it anytime in the next hundred years, she was relieved not to be going to America, even if it did mean that she might never see her mother again.

"What are you going to do now?" she asked, to distract herself.

Beneath the brim of his hat, Jamie grinned. "I don't know—maybe I'll 'ang you by your thumbs in one of the shearin' sheds. Two or three days of that ought to teach you your place."

"My what!" Bliss cried, scooting forward on the seat and forgetting all caution. She snatched the hat from his head to force him to look at her, but the advantage, as usual, was his.

More quickly than Bliss would have believed he could move, Jamie had pulled her out of her seat and onto his lap. She defended herself with both feet and both hands, but he subdued her by forcing her into a kiss. She squirmed for a moment, then went limp with a soft moan.

One kiss followed another, and Bliss was in a daze when the carriage came to a stop. It took her several seconds to recall what had gone on that morning, but when she did, she was furious.

She drew back one hand to slap Jamie, but the look in his eyes stopped her—it was an odd mingling of challenge and tenderness, that look.

Jamie set her off his lap and got down from the carriage, taking Bliss's satchel with him. She waited for him to offer her a hand, but he didn't, nor did the carriage driver.

Finally, red-faced, Bliss got out of the rig on her own and followed her husband inside the lobby of the Victoria Hotel. Since he took the lift, Bliss climbed the stairs.

It was a pitiful rebellion, and she knew it, but under the circumstances it was the best she could do.

When she let herself into the suite, Jamie was seated

comfortably on one of the settees, reading a newspaper and looking for all the world as though he'd never gone to the wharf and carried his wife off the *Queen Charlotte* like a pair of saddlebags.

Chin high, Bliss retreated to the bedroom, but there was no solace to be found there, either.

Peony and her maid were packing the clothes Jamie had bought for Bliss into sturdy-looking trunks.

"What's going on here?" Bliss demanded, folding her arms.

Peony excused the maid before squaring off with her adversary. She pointed to a chair with such authority that Bliss felt called upon to sit down.

"Now," the older woman began in a low but not-to-be-ignored voice, "you listen to me, you little hoyden, and you listen well!"

Bliss glared at her. "I don't have to take this," she said, even though she knew she did.

Peony was pacing back and forth, her beautiful complexion tinted with pink, her green eyes flashing like the stone in the ring Jamie had offered Bliss. "Oh yes, you do," the woman sputtered. "If you think differently, you just try getting past that man out there!"

Bliss swallowed. She'd run enough risks for one day.

"What, pray tell," Peony went on, "were you trying to do?"

"Escape," Bliss answered. The word squeaked out of her throat, and she felt her face growing hot at the memory of her grandest failure.

With a sigh, Peony sat down on the edge of the bed, looking directly into Bliss's eyes. "Why?" she asked bluntly. "I may not know much, Mrs. McKenna, but I have grasped the fact that you love your husband."

Bliss bit her lower lip. She'd rather die than let Jamie's mistress see her cry. "I love him, but he loves you," she said with quiet dignity. "He was with you last night. In—in your room."

Incredibly, Peony smiled. "Yes, you little twit, Jamie did come to my room. He was so drunk he wouldn't have been able to touch the floor with his hat without help."

Bliss felt her eyes go round. For the life of her, she couldn't say a word, but she remembered that Jamie had smelled of whiskey when he'd joined her in bed.

"I don't know what you did to him," Peony said evenly. "I haven't seen him hurting that way since—well, in a long time." She paused, then went on. "Bliss, Jamie and I don't sleep together. We never have."

Bliss sank her teeth into her lower lip and ducked her head. She wanted so desperately to believe Peony, but she didn't. "He loves you. He's told me so himself," she said.

Peony's voice was remarkably gentle, given her earlier ire. "There are many kinds of love," she reminded Bliss. When there was no response, she stood up and began packing clothes again.

"Am I going somewhere?" Bliss wanted to know.

"Yes. If you want to know any more than that, you'll have to ask your husband. Frankly, I'm tired of wasting my breath talking to someone who refuses to listen."

Feeling chagrined, Bliss rose out of her chair with dignity and went back to the front room. Jamie was sharpening that lethal-looking blade of his against a bit of round stone, and he didn't look up at her approach.

"Peony says I'm going away," she ventured, standing a little distance away.

"Aye," Jamie answered hoarsely. "And so am I. We're going 'ome, Duchess, to the farm."

So he'd given up the gilded cage idea. At least she'd succeeded there. Bliss lowered her head for a moment. "What about Peony? Is she going, too?"

Jamie still didn't look up. "She refuses to leave her business," he said.

"But you asked her?"

At last, Jamie met Bliss's gaze, and she saw a weary

235

challenge in his eyes. "Yes, Duchess, I asked her," he answered.

Bliss felt utterly defeated. "I see."

Jamie shook his head. "No, I don't think you do," he replied, and once again, he was sharpening his knife.

Bliss took a single, tentative step nearer. "Explain it to me, then," she said. "I do want to understand."

The blade made a rhythmic, scraping sound against the stone. "Aye," Jamie responded skeptically. "That was evident this mornin'."

"I love you, Jamie. Believe it or not, that's why I left you."

His jawline tightened and he was stubbornly silent. The friction between blade and stone grew fiercer.

Bliss would almost have preferred the high-handed, jocular Jamie who had carried her so unceremoniously off the *Queen Charlotte*. At least that one had been willing to speak to her.

Just then, Peony and her maid came out of the bedroom. Jamie shoved his knife back into its scabbard and, without a word or a look for Bliss, donned his hat and coat and left with the two women.

Jamie's only farewell to his wife was the grating of his key in the lock.

Bliss went to the desk and began a letter to her mother, weeping as she explained that she wouldn't be coming to America.

Chapter 18 ❧

AFTER GIVING THE DOORKNOB A FEW FRUITLESS JIGGLES, BLISS moved to the suite's window and looked out.

It was a long way to the ground.

On an impulse, she progressed to the bedroom and pulled back the draperies. A metal staircase, no doubt for the purpose of escaping fires, met her widening eyes.

"Eureka!" she breathed. Having read the word once in a book, Bliss had been waiting for a chance to try it out.

The window catch was high up, so she dragged a chair over, climbed up to stand in its velvet-upholstered seat, and began working at the lock with her fingers. After almost a minute of unrewarded efforts, she sighed and looked around for something to pry the thing open with.

Just then, someone knocked at the door of the suite. Bliss got down from the chair and dashed into the front room.

"Hello? Who's there?" she called, pressing her ear to the door.

"It's Walter—Walter Davis."

Bliss, hoping for a maid or a waiter—someone with a key—was disappointed. Too, she had her suspicions as to who had told Jamie where she'd gone that morning. "Traitor!" she called back.

Even through the heavy door, Bliss heard Walter's sigh. "I had to tell him, Bliss. The man was frantic."

Bliss tried to imagine Jamie in such a state and failed roundly. "I don't believe you!"

"If you'll only open the door, I'll explain everything," Walter called plaintively.

"I can't open the door!" Bliss responded, arms folded in annoyance. "My devoted husband locked it when he left."

"The blackguard!" Walter shouted. "That's inhuman!"

"At least," Bliss called back, "he can be trusted with a confidence! That's more than I can say for you, Walter Davis!"

Walter said something, but it was plain enough from his tone that he wasn't talking to Bliss. A possibility struck her, and remembering Jamie's vow to "blister" her if she ever tried to run away again, she raced for the bedroom. She drew the drapes back into place and had just put the chair where it belonged when Jamie came in and tossed his hat onto the bed. He was shrugging out of his coat when he said, "Meetin' men be'ind me back, are you, Duchess?"

Bliss knew he was teasing, but she was in no mood for one of Jamie's mercurial mood changes. "If I was going to take up with another man," she said in a stilted voice, "I wouldn't pick Walter."

"You'd be right not to," Jamie agreed, sitting down on the edge of the bed and pulling off his boots. "Got no social graces, that one. Called me a name in the 'all just now—and me just mindin' me own business."

Bliss did a slow, simmering burn as Jamie stretched out on the bed, cupped his hands behind his head, and uttered a long sigh. "Did you strike poor Walter?" she demanded.

Jamie grinned but didn't open his eyes. "Aye, Duchess. I did at that."

Bliss decided to change the subject. Since Walter had

betrayed her, she wasn't quite so sympathetic as she might have been. She sat down in the same chair she had stood in only minutes before and said coolly, "I was certain you'd spend the whole day with Peony. And possibly the night, too."

"Were you now?" Jamie responded with sleepy disinterest, settling deeper into the mattress.

Twiddling her thumbs and biting her lower lip, Bliss struggled to contain her impatience. It was during this inner tussle that something occurred to her: the key to the suite was probably in the pocket of Jamie's coat. If she were to let herself out when he was sleeping, and lock the door behind her, then Mr. McKenna would have a generous dose of his own medicine. He would learn, with no harm done, how it felt to be held captive.

"Jamie?" she ventured softly when the meter of his breathing had fallen into a regular rhythm.

"Hmmmm?" he responded, in the way of the barely conscious.

Smiling to herself, Bliss took an extra blanket from the chest at the foot of the bed, shook it out, and gently covered her husband with it.

He muttered a few inaudible words and Bliss couldn't resist placing a light kiss on his forehead, even though he was a scoundrel of the first water. Then, making every effort to behave normally—for if she'd learned one thing about Jamie it was that he was often most alert just when he appeared not to be paying attention at all—she collected his coat and hat from where he'd thrown them and strolled idly out of the bedroom.

She waited several long minutes before thrusting a hand into one of Jamie's coat pockets. On the first try, she brought out the key, along with the note she'd left for him that morning on the mantelpiece. Even though she remembered precisely what she'd written, Bliss unfolded the paper anyway, and scanned it with her eyes.

I will always love you, Jamie, she read. *I've got to say good-bye and we both know why, so I won't belabor the point. I do hope you'll be happy. Forever, Bliss.*

Her throat thick, Bliss refolded the note and put it back into Jamie's pocket. After collecting her cloak, she slipped out of the suite and locked the door behind her.

"Hello," said a ragged, familiar voice as she withdrew the key.

Walter's grandfather, the senior Mr. Davis, was standing behind her, his skeletal hand on the knob of the door leading into his own suite. He showed his piano-key teeth in a smile that made Bliss want to dash back inside her own rooms.

"You're—standing," she observed stupidly. Until that moment, she'd thought Mr. Davis was permanently confined to his invalid's chair.

"Yes," the old man conceded with a nod. "I can, for short periods of time." His misted eyes went over her with a disconcerting thoroughness. "Going out?"

Bliss forced herself to smile pleasantly. After all, it wasn't Mr. Davis's fault if he wasn't very personable. "I thought I'd take a walk."

Mr. Davis seemed to be looking at—no, *through*—the door, and seeing something there that he hated abjectly. "It seems to me," he said presently, "that your husband takes a great many chances with your safety."

Bliss was about to answer lightly, but then she remembered the whip, sent as a wedding present, and shivered a little.

Mr. Davis had not missed her reaction. "Something wrong, my dear?"

Bliss wanted to get away from the sight of this old man, and the mood he created. "Certainly not," she said with a bright smile.

Her neighbor seemed a bit wobbly; his hand began to tremble on the knob, and his legs looked unsteady as well. He was about to speak when the knob of Bliss's door rattled ominously and Jamie called out, "Duchess!"

Bliss smiled and dropped the key into the pocket of her cloak, standing back from the door. "Yes, dear?" she sang sweetly, forgetting all about Mr. Davis and his peculiar remarks.

"Open this damn door!" Jamie bellowed.

"Oh, but I couldn't do that," Bliss replied. "I must consider your—your safety."

She heard Jamie's sigh, could envision him resting his forehead against the door in frustration. "All right, Duchess," he said. "You've made your point. Now let me out of 'ere."

"I will, of course. At suppertime, or thereabouts." With that, Bliss turned and strolled down the hallway to the stairs. When the door of the suite began rattling on its hinges, she quickened her pace.

By the time Bliss had reached the lobby, she was beginning to regret the rashness of her actions. Alas, there was no going back, so she hurried out into the fresh air and walked rapidly away from the hotel without any particular destination in mind.

She passed a series of noisy pubs and began to feel uneasy when she noted that there were loose women beneath every lamppost. They looked at her fine dress and cloak with kohl-blackened, disdainful eyes.

Bliss had just turned to start back toward the hotel when she collided hard with a burly man who smelled of rank sweat, beer, and strong tobacco. The automatic "Excuse me," froze on her lips when she looked up into that face.

Bert Dunnigan looked alarmed, until he'd ascertained that Bliss was alone. Then he smiled. "Well, if it isn't McKenna's pretty little bird. What're you doin' way down here, lass?"

Bliss took a step backward. Her throat felt as though she'd just swallowed a whole potato and her heart was hammering. Her mind was filled with fear and the knowledge that this man and his confederates had meant to kill Jamie that

241

day on the road, and would have succeeded if it hadn't been for Cutter and Dog.

Dunnigan reached out with a grimy hand to caress Bliss's cheek. "What's the matter, darlin'? Cat got your tongue?"

Bliss gathered enough presence of mind to slap the offending hand away. How she wished she hadn't been so bent on teaching Jamie what it meant to be locked away in a hotel room!

She took another step backward and came up against a steely structure of muscle and bone that could belong to only one man. Relief swept over her.

At the same moment, Bert Dunnigan lost his expression of superiority and began retreating himself. Clearly, facing Jamie without his compatriots to back him up was not a prospect he favored.

Jamie took Bliss's shoulders in his hands and moved her aside. There was an easy, companionable smile on his face as he looked Dunnigan over and said, "I've been 'opin' to see you again, mate."

Bliss swallowed and clasped a lamppost in both hands for support. Her eyes were wide as she watched Jamie back Dunnigan slowly into the street.

Dunnigan held his hands out. "No hard feelin's now, McKenna," he said quickly. "We was only doin' what Pipher paid us to do."

Jamie's knife sprouted in his hand like a plant from fertile ground. "So it was me old friend that set you bleeders on me like a pack of dogs?"

Dunnigan nodded, sweat beading on his forehead, his eyes never leaving the glistening steel blade. "It was him, all right." He came up hard against the back of a wagon just then, and the point of Jamie's knife rested against his jugular vein.

"Tell me more," Jamie said evenly.

"He wants you—you and the Ryan woman—"

"He's 'ere, isn't he?" Jamie broke in, his patience clearly waning. "In Auckland?"

242

Dunnigan swallowed and nodded again. "Yes, but I don't know where, McKenna. I swear to God I don't know where!"

Bliss had crept forward without realizing it, and a chill swept over her as she looked at Jamie's taut profile. For an instant, at least, he had wanted to kill Dunnigan, then and there, and let his blood drain out in the street.

"Tell Increase I got the weddin' present 'e sent," he said moderately.

Dunnigan went pale. Obviously, he'd known about the whip that had been delivered as a gift.

A smile spread across Jamie's face, and it was terrifying to see. Bliss began, in fact, to have a sense of the trouble she'd brought upon herself. The blade made a slight nick in Dunnigan's flesh; blood appeared in a crimson *V*.

"And give 'im this warnin', Dunnigan," Jamie went on when he'd given the man a few moments to reflect. "If I see the old bastard, I'll kill 'im—but only after I've fed 'im that whip of 'is, inch by inch."

Dunnigan was nodding frantically. "I'll see he gets the message, McKenna," he vowed.

"Good," Jamie said. He lowered the knife, and Dunnigan turned and ran, as hard as he could.

Bliss thought that idea was a feasible one, given the mood Jamie was in, and she fled in the other direction, skirts held high, cloak flying behind her, heart pounding. She'd traveled some distance before she dared to look back and see whether or not Jamie was gaining.

He was nowhere in sight.

Confused, concerned, and relieved, all at once, Bliss slowed to a walk. She was gasping for breath and casting the occasional glance backward when she walked directly into the arms of the man she was trying to avoid.

"How did you do that?" she demanded. Such was her consternation that she set aside all thought of the peril she might be in.

243

Jamie grinned. "Cut through the alleyways is all. Surprised, love?"

"Not in the least," Bliss said stubbornly. "How did you get out of the suite?"

"I've picked a lock or two in my time, Duchess." The fact that the brogue hadn't come into evidence was encouraging. "You almost caused us to miss our train, you know."

"Our—our train?"

Jamie's hand rested easily on the small of her back, and he propelled her along as he walked. "You didn't think I was going to take a chance on the open road again after what happened last time? Unlike some people I could name, Duchess, I don't go around making the same mistakes over and over."

Bliss swallowed, unsure whether this was a reference to her latest exploit or not. She was taking no chances. "I wasn't going to run away, you know. I just wanted you to realize what it's like to be held prisoner."

Despite the smile on his lips, there was a fathomless grief in Jamie's eyes, for just the merest flicker of a moment. "Did you think I didn't know?"

Bliss thought of the scars on his back and dropped her eyes. "I would have come back and let you out. Honestly, I would have."

"Aye," Jamie responded. His voice sounded taut, and he was gazing straight ahead.

"You don't believe me!" Bliss accused.

Jamie's gaze sliced toward her, sharp as that knife he carried. "Should I? This morning, you were off to the States with nary a look back."

Bliss sighed. "Only because my husband is in love with another woman," she said patiently.

Unexpectedly, Jamie stopped, and one of his hands rose to grasp her chin. His blue eyes glittered as he rasped, "I've 'ad all I can take of that nonsense, Bliss. I'll not 'ear another word about Peony, is that clear?"

"I'll tell you what that is, Jamie McKenna!" Bliss cried,

244

boiling over. She tried, and failed, to twist free of his hold on her chin. "It's mighty damn convenient for you!"

"So it is," Jamie agreed insolently. "So it is, Duchess." With that, he caught Bliss's elbow in his hand and started thrusting her down the street again.

There was something in his manner that warned Bliss not to press him. She bit back all the angry things she wanted to say and, as best she could, matched her strides to his long, angry ones.

She was exhausted by the time they reached the hotel.

Jamie was not inclined toward mercy, however. He dragged her into the lift, knowing she hated it, and tipped his hat to the operator.

When they had reached their floor and the metal door clanged open, Walter was waiting to step inside the lift. His right eye was blue and purple, and swollen shut, and he backed away at the sight of Jamie.

"You really did hit him!" Bliss marveled, outraged.

Jamie's smile was lethal. "And I'd do it again," he assured her.

Walter slid along the wall as Jamie and Bliss passed him in the hallway, then he dived into the lift. Jamie chuckled to himself, pausing in front of the door of the suite. Jagged wood and a hanging knob indicated that he had not picked the lock at all, but forced it, probably with the heel of one boot. Bliss's mouth rounded into an *O*.

"Some locks are easier to 'andle than others," Jamie observed dryly. Then he pushed the door inward and executed a sweeping bow. "After you, Duchess," he said.

Bliss had serious misgivings about proceeding into that suite, but she didn't have any viable alternatives. After drawing a deep, shaky breath, she entered the rooms where she had spent so many hours as a virtual captive.

She lowered her head. If she were to be entirely honest, those had been some of the happiest hours of her life.

"I suppose now you're going to make good on your promise and—and blister me."

Jamie had gone to pour himself a drink at the liquor cabinet along the far wall, and Bliss couldn't read his face because his back was turned to her. He took a thoughtful sip of his whiskey before replying, "I suppose I should. A man's got to keep 'is word."

"Not necessarily," Bliss pointed out hopefully.

At that, Jamie gave a hoarse chuckle and turned to look at her. There was no sign of amusement in his eyes, only a haunted, mystified expression. "God 'elp me, Duchess, I couldn't lay a 'and on you even if I caught you tryin' to cut me throat." He pushed his hat to the back of his head and looked away. "I'll thank you not to put me through another day like this one," he added presently. "I'm not as young as I used to be."

Bliss started toward Jamie, meaning to embrace him, but he sidestepped her. Oddly, that hurt more than any "blistering" could have.

Before anything more could be said, two stewards appeared to carry away the trunks Peony and her maid had packed for Bliss earlier.

Barely ten minutes later, she and Jamie were in a carriage, riding toward the railway station. After Jamie had bought their tickets, they boarded the train.

It was the first time in Bliss's life that she had ever set foot inside such a conveyance, let alone been a passenger. In a way, she supposed, it would make up for the missed experience of sailing over the seas in one of Her Majesty's steamships.

She looked at Jamie from under lowered eyelashes as he ushered her into the dining car and seated her at a table before removing his hat and joining her. He seemed so tired and beleaguered that Bliss longed to comfort him.

"I didn't get a chance to thank you for rescuing me from that dreadful man," she said.

Jamie glared at Bliss over the top of his menu, and she was too intimidated to press the point. A waiter appeared, wearing a suit every bit as grand as the one worn by the president of that retail establishment in Auckland, and Bliss studied his shiny buttons and velvet-smooth coat with wide eyes as Jamie gave their orders.

"Thank you for consulting me as to what I might like to have for supper," Bliss said with a sniff. "Maybe I don't want broiled fish. Did you ever think of that?"

"And maybe," Jamie replied evenly, "I could take you back to our sleepin' car and raise welts on your backside after all. Did you ever think of that?"

Bliss subsided, and when the fish arrived, she ate it without complaint, even though it did taste like a blend of kelp and driftwood.

When Jamie had had all the dinner he wanted, which wasn't much, judging by the food he left on his plate, he stood to leave without so much as a word of explanation to Bliss.

"You're just going to leave me here?" she asked, feeling a bit panic-stricken. She'd never been on board a train before, and she had no idea where to go when it was time to leave the dining car.

Jamie paused, his expression absolutely unreadable, and said, "I'm off to the club car, Duchess, where a man can smoke and 'ave a drink in peace."

Resentment flared within Bliss. It wasn't as though she hadn't had a hard day herself. "I'll just come with you, then," she said, about to rise from her chair.

But Jamie held her firmly in place by laying one hand to her shoulder. "Sorry, Duchess," he said with the slightest hint of a smile in his eyes. "No women allowed."

Bliss knew all her freckles were standing out on a field of bright pink. "No women—that's preposterous!"

Jamie shrugged. "Maybe so, dear 'eart, but such is the way of it. If you try to go in there, they'll throw you out on your pretty little—ear."

"At least show me to the sleeping car, then," Bliss whispered desperately. It seemed to her that the other diners were looking on, and listening, and she felt self-conscious.

"It's too early to sleep," Jamie scolded, and Bliss thought she saw one corner of his mouth quirk, although she might have imagined it.

"Not after the day I've had, it isn't," she replied ruefully, and Jamie condescended to draw back Bliss's chair and lead the way to the tiny chamber where they would spend the night.

He unlocked the door for her and waited until she was inside. Soft gaslights gave the cubicle a romantic glow.

"Good night, Bliss," Jamie said with stiff formality.

Bliss ached for a little understanding and a lot of forgiveness, but she was too proud to ask Jamie to stay. She had a suspicion he would have refused, because of his own pride. "Good night," she said softly, lowering her eyes.

Jamie closed the door and walked away, and Bliss stood there, fighting tears, for a minute or so. Then, with a rueful sigh, she let herself into a washroom roughly the size of a hatbox and performed her evening ablutions, taking special care in case Jamie should return in a generous mood.

Her satchel had been brought to the car, but Bliss did not put on a nightgown. She stood at the window, peeping out through the blinds, watching as the darkened landscape slipped by. Jamie had told her they would reach their destination before dawn; perhaps that was why he didn't plan to sleep.

She sighed. The truth was that Jamie wanted to hide out in the club car; that was the one place his troublesome wife couldn't get at him. This being a moving train, he had the added benefit of knowing that she wouldn't be able to work any real mischief while he was avoiding her.

Bliss looked at the two narrow berths the cubicle offered, one above the other, and shook her head. Even if she and Jamie had been on the best of terms, they would have been hard put to do anything about it.

Resigned, she climbed into the lower berth and closed her eyes. She hadn't expected to sleep so readily, but within moments a sweet, heavy lethargy came over her, dragging her downward into the safe darkness. Later, she was awakened by a piercing sort of joy that seemed to spiral magically from the very center of her womanhood.

With a gasp of pleasure, she opened her eyes. Jamie was kneeling beside the berth, caressing her, and she moaned and moved her legs further apart to accommodate his gentle exploration. In the meanwhile, he lowered his lips to her bare breasts, covering them with soft, moist kisses that made their points strain toward him.

Bliss entangled her hands in his rich, rumpled hair and purred with pleasure. "Oh Jamie," she confessed breathlessly, "I didn't think you were ever coming back—"

He chuckled hoarsely as he singled out one pulsing nipple to enjoy. "Where—did you think—I would go, Duchess?"

Bliss arched her back as a shaft of joy knifed through her, and Jamie didn't relax his efforts. "I didn't—oooooh—know—" She dragged air into her lungs, starved for it, unable to get enough. "Oh, Jamie, I'm so—sorry I t-troubled you—I love you—I love you—"

"Shhh," he said, and he began kissing the undersides of her breasts, and then her rib cage, and then her belly, progressing ever closer to where his fingers wreaked such delicious havoc.

But Bliss maneuvered him back, until his lips covered hers in a kiss every bit as desperate as the one she returned to him. Long moments later, when the contact was broken, his breathing was ragged.

Bliss unbuttoned his shirt, as far as she could, and slid her hands inside, urging him toward her with light caresses that seemed to leave a fever in his flesh wherever they touched.

Now, Bliss wasn't too proud to plead. "Come to me, Jamie," she whispered. "Love me. I need you so much—"

He laughed softly, and the sound was a mingling of joy and torment. "On that thing? I've seen bookshelves wider than that bed."

"Jamie," Bliss insisted, drawing him back into her kiss. There were no more protests after that; his tongue sparred fiercely with hers and then, in a wink, he'd shed his clothes and poised himself above her.

"It's only fair to say," he whispered hoarsely, "that every day I've known you 'as been sheer 'ell. And for all that, Duchess, I wouldn't change a minute of it."

Bliss felt tears of happiness and humor burn in her eyes. She tilted her head back and raised her hips in proud surrender, for that was the only way she could answer, and Jamie entered her with a fiery stroke and broken, incoherent words of need and love.

Chapter 19 🌺

Yawning, her mind happily befuddled from the delightful rituals Jamie had put her through in the sleeping car, Bliss strained to make out the train depot in the predawn darkness.

There was nothing to be seen, except for the outline of a tiny shack with a crooked chimney and the team and wagon waiting nearby. The horses nickered and pranced as the train whistle shrilled in the gloom.

Jamie leaped to the ground and then lifted Bliss after him. Her trunks were unloaded with unceremonious dispatch and left in a heap beside the tracks.

A dog began barking in protest as the whistle blew again and the train huffed away into the night, wheels making a raucous squeak against the metal rails.

As they approached the wagon, Bliss recognized the bushy figure of Cutter O'Riley. "Hello, Jamie boy," he said. He tipped his hat as Jamie hoisted his wife up into the seat. "And hello to you, too, missus," he added.

Bliss yawned, politely covering her mouth with one hand and settling herself, as best she could, on the hard seat.

"Hello, Cutter," she responded. Behind her, in the wagon bed, Dog whined and nudged her shoulder until he'd had a greeting, too.

Jamie's acknowledgment of his friend was without sentimental adornment. "Cutter," he said with a brisk nod of his head.

Cutter got down and together the two men put Bliss's baggage into the back of the wagon, then Jamie climbed deftly up beside her, released the brake lever with one foot, and took the reins in his hands.

Dawn was just beginning to extend tendrils of light over the hills and Cutter's chuckle gave Bliss a feeling of camaraderie that pushed back the chill and the shadows a little way. She rested her head against Jamie's shoulder and closed her eyes.

"What's so funny, old man?" Jamie asked with a companionable sort of insolence.

Cutter's amusement came out as a chortle this time. "You are, Jamie-me-boy. You are."

Jamie didn't pursue the point, for reasons of his own. "Any trouble since I've been gone?"

"Nothing the rest of us couldn't deal with," Cutter said. "That Maori girl up and left right after you did, so Dog and I have been doin' the cookin' and cleanin'."

Bliss dreaded to see the state of Jamie's house, but at the same time, she was relieved that Carra would not be there to assist with the work. That kind of help she could do without.

She sighed contentedly to think how romantic it would be, just her and Jamie in that isolated house. Surely, they would be able to resolve all their differences under such ideal circumstances. And he'd brought her along, at least, instead of leaving her in that fancy cage he'd bought in Auckland.

By the time they'd reached home and come to a noisy stop in front of the barn, the sun was up. Feeling very domestic indeed, Bliss set out for the house as soon as Jamie had lifted her down from the wagon seat, Dog prancing happily at her heels.

She gave the animal a cheerful pat on the head before opening the back door and stepping into the kitchen. The smile faded from her face when she saw the stacks of dirty pots, pans, and plates.

With wifely resolve, Bliss took the apron that had been Carra's from a peg beside the door and slipped it on. She was hard put to find a clean kettle to heat water in so that she could wash the other things, but it was steaming away on the stove when Jamie came in.

Bliss had taken the enamel coffeepot outside to wash and fill it at the pump, and her hands were numb and awkward with cold as she measured fresh grounds into its basket and set it on to perk.

Jamie stopped her and lifted one of her reddened hands to his lips. There was a weary smile in his eyes when he said, "To bed with you, Duchess. You must be dead tired."

"I'm not going to bed unless you do," Bliss asserted, then she blushed hotly. Cutter, who had come in with Jamie, made a great business of not having heard what she'd said, while Jamie grinned.

"'Tis a silver tongue you 'ave, lass," he teased, his eyes twinkling. "Now that you mention it, I could use a wink of sleep." Following that, he yawned with such emphasis that Cutter laughed out loud.

Bliss was furiously embarrassed, and she might have kicked Jamie McKenna square in the shin if she hadn't been so bent on being the best wife any man ever had. "You'll have a decent breakfast if I have to cram it down your throat, Mr. McKenna," she said firmly.

Jamie arched his eyebrows as he took off his hat. "You cook, do you?" he asked, sounding damnably skeptical.

Bliss glared at him as he shrugged out of his coat and hung it on a peg with his hat. Cutter followed suit, taking care not to notice anything that might be going on around him.

"I do," she said with a lift of her chin. "Who did you think prepared the meals at the lighthouse after Mama went away? My father?"

"To tell you the truth, Duchess," Jamie answered, kissing the tip of her nose, "I never gave that much thought."

"Well," Bliss went on, after taking an audible breath, "I did all the work of that nature." *Never mind,* she added to herself, *that Papa always said a man could starve to death on cooking like mine. Papa was impossible to please anyway.*

Without so much as a by-your-leave, Cutter went to the stove and helped himself to the hot water Bliss had been reserving to wash up the mountain of dirty dishes and kettles. He proceeded to pour that water into a basin and lather his face and hands with pungent yellow soap.

Jamie must have read Bliss's expression, for he touched her cheek with gentle, wind-chilled fingers, running the pad of his thumb over her lips, stirring a sweet shiver in the depths of her. "No worries, Duchess," he said. And then he took up two buckets and went outside, returning only a short time later with a generous supply of water.

Cutter was so pleased to have a woman in the house that Bliss could not sustain her annoyance. She made up a meal of what was on hand—a few eggs and some salt pork—and both men ate heartily even though the meat was black around the edges and the egg yolks were hard clear through.

At least the coffee was perfect, Bliss thought, looking down into her cup and listening with half an ear to the conversation going on between Jamie and Cutter. They'd talked of nothing but sheep throughout the meal.

With a yawning sigh, Bliss got out of her chair and went back to the heap of soiled dishes. Now that breakfast was out of the way, she'd just tidy up the kitchen.

When Cutter took the scraps out to Dog, Jamie came to stand close behind Bliss, his hands coming around to gently caress her breasts. "Go upstairs and rest," he said, his voice moving warm and low past her ear. "All this work will still be 'ere when you wake up, Duchess."

254

Bliss let the back of her head rest against his granite shoulder, surrendering to the sleepy delight he was causing her. "Come with me," she whispered, trembling as a wave of anticipation washed over her.

But Jamie stepped back and gave her a mischievous swat. "For once, woman," he said with mock sternness, "just do as I tell you."

Bliss turned, purposely letting him feel the softness of her breasts against his chest. She traced the outline of his jaw with the tip of one index finger, then caressed his lips. "Do you still want me, Jamie?" she asked.

He caught her hand and held it tightly in his. "Birds still fly, rivers still flow into the sea, and what goes up still has to come down. Aye, Duchess, I want you." He turned her and pointed her toward the rear stairway, giving her a slight push. "Now go, before I 'ave you right 'ere, dammit."

Bliss laughed and went upstairs. By memory, she found Jamie's room; it was frigidly cold.

Since there were shavings, kindling and firewood on the hearth, and matches on the mantel, Bliss got a nice blaze going before exchanging her clothes for one of Jamie's flannel shirts. Her trunks had not been brought into the house yet.

The sheets were like thin layers of ice when Bliss crawled between them, and she shivered, wishing that Jamie were there to hold her close. She yawned, and her eyes drifted shut, and the next thing she knew someone was washing her face with what felt like a slice of raw liver.

Bliss gave a little squeal when she lifted her lids and found herself eye to eye with Dog. She heard a male chuckle as she bolted upright, ran one hand through her hair, and squinted into the deep shadows that filled the room. "Jamie?"

He was a tall, broad-shouldered outline, stirring the dying fire with a poker. "Aye, Duchess. It's me. Are you 'ungry?"

Bliss yawned. "Yes," she said, with conviction. "What time is it, anyway?"

"It's night, love."

"You mean, I slept the whole day away?" Bliss was filled with chagrin. She'd meant to do so many constructive things with her time.

Jamie raised a mug to his lips, then set it on the mantel. "There'll be another along tomorrow, like as not," he observed dryly before striding over to the bed. "Cutter and I will go to town for supplies in the morning. For now, this is all I could come up with."

Neat slices of bread and cold mutton and dried fruit tempted Bliss's appetite. She accepted the plate with thanks and ate hungrily. "There's a town around here?" she asked between bites.

"Not much of one," Jamie answered, with a kind of remote amusement in his voice. He was sitting on the edge of the bed now, idly stroking Dog's furry head. "Most of the necessities can be 'ad there, anyway."

Even though Bliss had slept the day away, like some slattern given to drink, she was far from rested. The rigors of past days, it seemed, were catching up with her. "I'm sorry," she said when she'd finished eating and set the plate aside.

"For what?" Jamie immediately asked.

Bliss sighed and settled back against the pillows. "I'd planned to show you what a fine wife I'm going to be," she lamented.

Jamie muttered a command to Dog, and the animal slunk away to settle itself by the hearth with a whimper. Bliss smiled. "I thought he was Cutter's pet," she said.

"No sheepdog is a pet," Jamie answered, and he spoke with a seriousness that gave Bliss pause. "They earn their keep."

"And if they don't?" Bliss asked, supposing that wives were expected to earn their keep as well.

"We shoot them," Jamie replied.

Bliss felt cold, even though the room was warm. "As easily as that? You just dispense with the poor beasts because they've displeased you?"

Jamie sighed and began undressing. "Cutter and I are off

the 'igh country for a time, Bliss, startin' day after tomorrow. Do you think we could manage to get along in the meantime?"

Bliss was near tears again. Lord, she hated how she'd become so weepy these past few weeks. It was all she could do not to grasp Jamie's arm and beg him not to leave her behind, and her throat was so constricted that she could barely speak. "I want to go along," she said hopelessly.

"Not this time." Jamie tossed back the covers to lie down beside her, and the fading firelight flickered over his bare flesh with a pagan rhythm. "It's too cold in the 'ills, Bliss."

Bliss knew by Jamie's tone that there was no point in arguing; he'd made up his mind, and for now at least, she wouldn't oppose him. "What if those dreadful men come here and try to hurt me?" she demanded.

Jamie's hand rested lightly on her naked thigh, causing little sparks of splendor to crackle through her veins. "They won't," he said with a quiet assurance that was all very well for him to espouse when he wasn't going to be in any danger.

Bliss trembled as his fingers moved along her upper leg, laying claim to the satin flesh they passed over, and Jamie laughed, his voice at once soft and gruff.

"If you were any kind of husband, Mr. McKenna," Bliss whispered as a lovely ache began deep in her middle, "you wouldn't go off and leave me to fend for myself!"

He rolled over to give her a lingering kiss that set her languid senses throbbing. "If I thought you wouldn't be safe 'ere," he retorted, nibbling at her lower lip, "I'd take you with me. And as for that remark about the kind of 'usband I am, love—"

Bliss groaned as he slid down to take leisurely suckle at her breast. In the coming minutes, she was forced to concede that Jamie McKenna was the grandest of husbands.

The look of concentration on Bliss's face was so intense that Jamie had to stop and watch her. Holding an upended broom with both hands, she advanced toward the rooster guarding the henhouse door. At the last second, the bird flew at her in a flurry of squawking rage, and Bliss shrieked, dropped the broom, and whirled to run away, colliding hard with Jamie.

He loved it when she did that.

"Is there a problem, Duchess?" he asked smoothly, watching with delight as her indigo eyes flashed and her freckles stood out prominently.

"Yes!" she cried, full of fury. "That stupid, vainglorious chicken won't let me gather the eggs! I've been trying all day!"

Jamie held back a smile. "No wonder he doesn't like you," he observed solemnly, his hands resting on her trembling shoulders. "You've insulted 'im by callin' 'im a mere chicken. Caesar's a rooster, love."

That fabulous blue fire was still burning in her eyes. "Caesar's going to be a *shepherd's pie* if he keeps this up!" she shouted.

Unable to hold back his amusement any longer, Jamie laughed and kissed Bliss on the forehead. "There now, Duchess, is that any way to greet your own dear 'usband when 'e's been gone all the day long?"

Bliss sighed and a smile sneaked across her mouth. She let her forehead rest against Jamie's chest and he thought the seawind-and-wildflower scent of her hair would be his undoing. "I wanted those eggs for a cake," she said. "I was going to surprise you."

Jamie was unaccountably touched. He held Bliss close for a moment, not caring that Cutter and the rest of them would see and give him hell all the while they were away in the sheep camp. "No need for that, Duchess," he said hoarsely. "As it 'appens, I brought you a few surprises from town."

"Surprises?" Her wonderful eyes were dancing when she drew back her head to look up at him in mischievous curiosity, her white teeth sunk into her lower lip.

Thinking of the lonely, miserable week that lay ahead, Jamie ached. He couldn't take Bliss along to camp—she had too great a gift for getting into trouble. It was spring, the ewes would be lambing, and there would be no time for keeping track of what the Duchess was up to at any given moment.

Too, the weather was still cold, at least at night, and camp was a crude place, hardly fit for a man, let alone a lady.

"Jamie?" Bliss prompted, prodding him a little with that infernal broom of hers. Little wonder she'd gotten off on the wrong foot with the rooster. "What surprises? Show me!"

He put aside his despair at the prospect of leaving her, even for such a short time, and grabbed her hand, dragging her toward the house.

Much of Bliss's frustration over being thwarted by the rooster was assuaged when she saw the things Jamie had brought her. For one, there was a ring—this time just a plain gold band. It was to her liking, though, and she allowed him to place it gently on her finger.

"Just so nobody gets any ideas," he said, with such seriousness that Bliss wanted to laugh.

"What kind of ideas?" she asked, but Jamie only shrugged and averted his eyes.

After that, he presented her with a cookbook, a box of chocolates, and a beautiful set of combs for her hair.

Tears filled her eyes, fairly blinding her. "Damn that rooster!" she cried, and then she turned on one heel, clutching Jamie's gifts to her bosom, and ran up the rear stairway, sobbing.

"What did I do?" Jamie asked Cutter, who had just stepped through the kitchen door.

The old man grinned. "All the right things, I reckon."

Jamie glared at his friend, all the time wondering if he'd insulted the Duchess by giving her a cookbook. He hadn't meant to imply that her concoctions were bad—exactly.

"What things?" he snapped.

"That'd be your business, mate," Cutter replied, taking a mug from a shelf and shuffling over to the stove to fill it with day-old coffee. "Could be, though, that them ewes out there in the hills ain't the only ones what got a baby started."

Jamie felt the color drain from his face and the starch go out of his knees. He groped for a chair and collapsed into it, shoving one hand through his hair. He muttered a curse.

"Would it be so bad as that?" Cutter asked quietly, sitting down across from Jamie at the table.

Jamie closed his eyes, remembering Eleanor. She'd borne him a child, too, and he hadn't known until it was too late. "Maybe," he said.

Elisabeth believed that his brother, Reeve, was her father. That was probably for the best, yet there wasn't a day when Jamie didn't think of his daughter and grieve.

"Jamie boy," Cutter insisted gruffly, "Bliss ain't the same kind of woman as Eleanor was. You know that."

Jamie sighed. "Maybe not, but they've got one thing in common, me friend—a knack for disappearin' when they 'ave a mind for it."

"This calls for a drink," commiserated Cutter. If the truth be known, Cutter thought just about everything called for a drink. He disappeared into the study, returning moments later with a bottle of whiskey. This he added in generous measures to his mug of coffee and the one he poured for Jamie.

"Maybe I ought to go up there and find out why she's cryin'," Jamie speculated. The whiskey made that damnable coffee palatable, at least.

Cutter shrugged. "Like as not, she won't tell you."

Jamie nodded philosophically. "Seems like when you ask a woman what's the matter, she always says 'nothin'.'"

Cutter laughed. "Aye. Real primlike, she says it, whilst snifflin' like a lamb with the slobbers."

By the time Bliss came stomping down the rear stairway, her eyes all puffy and her nose red, Jamie had consumed enough whiskey to make him forget what it was that was troubling him so much.

He gave Bliss a perfectly harmless pinch as she passed him

and she whirled around and fairly broke his knuckles with a wooden spoon. Cutter, who'd downed his share of the whiskey, howled with amusement, while old Dog crouched in the corner by the stove and whimpered.

It turned out that Dog had the best handle on the situation.

"Jamie McKenna," Bliss said through her teeth while Jamie was still rubbing his sore fingers, "you march right out to that henhouse and gather those eggs. If you insist on keeping that wretched rooster, then you can deal with him yourself!" With that, she shoved a basket into his hands and set to putting away the supplies he and Cutter had bought in town.

Cutter ran for the door like a man with hot grease in his mouth, but even when he was outside, his guffaws of laughter sounded clearly in the kitchen.

Jamie muttered every oath he knew as he stormed outside, egg basket in hand. He was never going to hear the last of this. He'd be the laughingstock of every sheep camp in New Zealand.

Jamie sat at his desk in the study, head bent over a pile of ledger books, hand moving swiftly as he figured. Bliss was in the rocking chair near the fire with a book in her lap.

She'd been over the beginning four times and still hadn't made sense of it. "Jamie," she ventured.

He didn't look up. "What?" he asked shortly.

"I only cried because you brought me all those lovely things and I couldn't even surprise you with a yellow cake."

Jamie's pencil stopped its rapid motion, but he was far too stubborn to meet her eyes. "No worries," he said remotely.

Bliss set her book aside, got out of the chair, and approached her husband, standing behind him to massage his taut shoulders. "I don't believe you, Mr. McKenna," she said softly. "I think you're very worried."

"Shows what you know," he muttered, but his muscles

were relaxing beneath Bliss's hands and, probably without even knowing it, he let the pencil fall to his ledger book.

Bliss bent and kissed his temple. "I know more than you think I do," she persisted.

Jamie sighed. "Is that so, then?"

"Yes," she said firmly. "I know that I embarrassed you in front of Cutter, and I'm sorry. It's just that I'm about to—I get very cranky when—" Her voice fell away, in utter embarrassment.

Jamie turned in his chair to look up at her and what she saw in his face hurt her terribly. He understood what she was trying to say, that she'd have the curse any day, and he was relieved.

Relieved that his irksome wife wasn't about to burden him with a child he didn't want.

She backed away from him, fighting back the tears that were always so close to the surface. "Oh Jamie," she whispered brokenly. "Jamie."

He stood and reached out for her, but she shrank back, shaking her head.

"Don't touch me," she said.

"Bliss—"

Again, she shook her head. "I—I think it's best that you'll be going away for a while," she managed to say.

She'd forgotten how quickly he could move; he'd caught her chin in his hand and forced her to meet his eyes before she had an inkling of what he intended. "Does that mean you're plannin' to leave again?" he demanded in a furious undertone. "If it does, Duchess, tell me now."

A soft, ragged sob escaped Bliss. "I won't go, Jamie McKenna, till you send me away!"

He searched her face, as though desperate to believe her, and then released her. "Go to bed," he said harshly, and went back to his damnable ledger books and his figures.

"I will go to bed when and if I choose," Bliss said with dignity, "and it won't be with you, Mr. McKenna."

"Fine," Jamie snapped, concentrating on his books.

Bliss picked up the volume she'd closed earlier and, after a moment's thought, slammed it down on the desk as hard as she could. The report was as loud as a gunshot and, she noted with satisfaction, she had Jamie's full attention.

"What the 'ell are you tryin' to do?" he demanded, glaring at her.

"I want to know why you don't want me to have your child," Bliss informed him bluntly, and even though everything she valued, everything she loved, was riding on his answer, her look was level. Fearless.

"It's a big responsibility, a child," he hedged, averting his eyes.

"Not good enough, Jamie," Bliss persisted, folding her arms. "You seem happy to make love to me. Hasn't it ever occurred to you that a baby could be conceived?"

He didn't answer, and Bliss could only conclude that he didn't want her to be the mother of his children. Perhaps he found her wanting, or he had someone else in mind.

She took her book and left the study without looking back, Dog slinking along after her, and when she'd reached the top of the stairs and entered the room she and Jamie shared, she locked the door.

It would have been easier, she supposed, if she'd been able to go right to sleep, but she didn't. She couldn't. She tossed and turned, her heart aching.

Sometime later, she heard Jamie in the hallway. When he tried the doorknob, Bliss held her breath, but he only said, "Good night, Duchess," in a low, despairing voice, and went away.

It was all Bliss could do not to run after him and beg him to lie beside her, where he belonged, and to hold her in his arms. She resisted, though, and somewhere in the blackest, bleakest part of the night, she fell asleep.

When she awakened the next morning, Bliss knew that the house was empty, except for Dog, who was whining in the hallway. Feeling unbearably lonely, she pushed back the covers and moved to sit up.

The cramps grabbed at her like a powerful, squeezing fist, and she lay back down with a groan of pain. Not only was the house barren; so, for the time being anyway, was her body.

Tears seeped through her eyelashes. Maybe Jamie didn't want her to bear his child, but she would. If it was the last thing Bliss ever did, she vowed to herself, twisting the golden band on her finger and biting down on her lower lip, she would bear that stubborn blue-eyed Irishman's baby.

Chapter 20 🦋

Bliss was in no mood for an extended tussle with that hell-born rooster. After a careful search of the premises, she found a dirty, rusted old washtub in the barn and hauled it to the doorway of the chicken coop. Dog stood nearby, looking on, his head tilted to one side.

"Oh Caesar!" Bliss called sweetly, turning the wooden latch on the wire gate and opening it wide. "I'm here to gather the eggs!"

He appeared from out of nowhere, flapping his wings and carrying on fit to scare the devil himself, but Bliss was ready for him. Swiftly, she lowered the upended washtub, trapping the nasty rooster beneath it.

Dog yipped in delight, running round and round in circles, and Bliss hummed as she gathered the eggs, leaving Caesar as he was when she went inside the house. The bird needed time to consider the error of his ways.

She was aproned and squinting at the words in the cookbook Jamie had given her when she heard a wagon coming up the road. Dog dashed toward the front of the house, barking uproariously.

Bliss was certain that Jamie was back from the sheep camp. She dropped the cookbook and ran her hands over her flyaway, tumbledown hair, wishing that she'd taken the time to put it up. . . .

She ran out of the kitchen and along the hallway to pull aside a curtain in the front parlor and look out. If Jamie turned toward the barn instead of coming directly to the house, she would have time to dash upstairs, exchange her flour-dusted dress for a clean one, and wind her hair into a ladylike coronet.

The wagon lumbered toward the house, but the driver was not Jamie; Bliss had never seen the man before. The woman sitting rigidly upright beside him, however, was all too familiar.

It seemed that Peony Ryan had come to call.

Tight-lipped, but determined to be mannerly, Bliss opened the front door and went out. Dog stood just behind her, growling uncertainly.

Peony was pale as death. "Is Jamie here?" she asked in a faint voice as the driver pushed the rig's brake lever into place and wrapped the reins around it.

Bliss shook her head and, after a sharp word to Dog, started down the stone walk. She was no longer self-conscious about her wild hair and floury dress, as she had been a moment before.

Something was terribly wrong.

"Peony, what is it?" she asked as the strange man leaped down from the wagon to walk around the other side and extend his arms to his passenger.

Peony closed her eyes and went a shade whiter. "I must see Jamie," she said, clinging to her escort's arm for support as he guided her toward the house. "Where is he, Bliss? Will he be back soon?"

Bliss hurried ahead, racing up the steps and across the porch to hold the front door open. "He's in the sheep camp, with Cutter and the others," she answered breathlessly. In her anxiety over Peony's obvious state of ill health, she'd forgotten all the reasons why she disliked the woman.

The man led Peony into the parlor, helped her into a chair, and then went back outside, without a word, probably to fetch her baggage.

Bliss gazed at her visitor in puzzled concern. "Please," she said, "what's happened to you?"

Peony's skin was chalky, and she began to weep, something Bliss wouldn't even have been able to imagine her doing before. "I can't speak of it—just send someone to find Jamie—"

Bliss had no idea where to begin looking for her husband, and there was no one to send. She cast a desperate look toward the stranger when he brought in two matching leather valises and set them on the parlor floor.

"My name's Sam Winters," he said politely, with a tip of his weather-beaten hat. He was a sturdily built man, of medium height, with craterlike pockmarks visible above the lines of his dark brown beard and eyes that were nearly black.

Bliss nodded and glanced anxiously at Peony before introducing herself. "I'm Mrs. McKenna," she said.

Peony was sitting on the edge of a chair, her eyes tightly closed again, her color slightly better. "I do need some tea, and poor Sam is probably starving. He's traveled all this way with little or nothing to eat."

Wishing that Jamie were there, Bliss went into the kitchen and put water on to boil. Like Dog, Sam had followed her, and since he looked like a kindly sort, she ventured to ask, "What happened, Mr. Winters?"

Sam took off his hat and, when Bliss nodded that it was all right, his heavy coat, too. "She was hurt, Mrs. McKenna. She was hurt bad."

Bliss felt weak. "How?" she asked, measuring tea leaves into a blue crockery pot.

It was clear that Sam hated to answer. "She was—

267

assaulted, missus. Two men broke into her house, they did, and—and one of them, well, he burned her with a hot poker."

Horror washed over Bliss; she could no longer think about the tea or what she might give Sam to remedy his hunger. She went back to the parlor, where Peony sat, her breath slow and shallow.

"Come with me," Bliss said, helping the woman carefully to her feet. "You need to lie down."

Peony flinched and rested on Bliss's strength for a moment. Tears had left streaks through the layer of dust on the older woman's cheeks. "I know how this must appear to you—"

Bliss shook her head and interrupted. "Why did you travel all this way when you're in such obvious pain? Why didn't you summon a doctor?"

She led Peony toward the downstairs bedroom Cutter had used. Bliss had aired the place out and changed the sheets that morning, thank goodness.

Peony didn't answer until Bliss had closed the door and begun helping her out of her clothes. "I did see a doctor, Bliss," she answered with grim impatience. "And I was afraid to stay in Auckland." Her lovely green eyes were glistening with tears again. "I should have listened to Jamie."

Bliss felt a chill as she had her first look at the burn in the middle of Peony's back. It was angry and seeping, and it seemed to form initials, or a sign of some sort. "In the name of God, who would do such a thing?"

Peony sighed, holding her arms crossed in front of her bosom in an effort to be modest. "Friends of the man who wanted me to bear his mark," she answered. "His name is Increase Pipher."

Bliss mulled the name over while she went back to the parlor for Peony's satchels, but she couldn't place it. If she'd heard of the man before, it had escaped her memory.

Peony put on a cotton nightdress, with Bliss's help, and

crawled into bed on her stomach. She must have been exhausted, for by the time Bliss had returned with her tea, she was sound asleep.

Bliss entered the kitchen, where Sam was sitting patiently at the table, and went on out through the rear door. Behind the chicken coop, where Caesar was still trapped underneath the washtub, she threw up until there was nothing left in her stomach.

She paused at the well to splash cold water on her face afterward and rinse out her mouth, then walked resolutely into the house again.

"Sit down, Mrs. McKenna," Sam pleaded. "You look near as peaky as Mrs. Ryan."

Bliss thought of the brutality that had been inflicted on Peony and did as Sam asked. Her hand shook visibly as she poured tea for herself and took a cautious sip. "Sam, are you a friend of Mrs. Ryan's?"

Sam shook his head, looking hungrily at the bowl of fresh fruit sitting in the middle of the table. "My brother-in-law drives her carriage," he answered. "I be a seafarin' man, myself, between voyages. After this awful thing had happened, Mrs. Ryan wanted someone to bring her to your husband. We came as far as we could on the train, then hired a wagon."

Bliss slid the fruit bowl toward Sam. "Help yourself," she said. "I've got bread, too, and cold meat—"

Sam looked so grateful that Bliss got up from her chair to find the bread and meat right away. While he ate, the sailor related all that he knew about Peony's attackers, which wasn't much. The maid and cook had been out the night it happened, and the ordeal was long over before Mrs. Ryan was found.

"You got a rifle here?" he asked as he finished both his story and his food. "Won't be safe, two women alone."

"No rifle," Bliss said, then bit her lip. Jamie hadn't said good-bye, let alone given her instructions about what to do in an emergency. He'd only said that Dog would take care of her. She patted the animal's massive head and frowned distractedly.

"Well, I'd stay and look after you ladies," Sam said apologetically, "but I've got a ship to catch." A bright smile lit his face. "She's a trade ship now, is the *Elisabeth Lee,* but once she was a whaler. Aussie she is—out of Sydney Town—and I've got myself a berth."

Sam's enthusiasm was such that Bliss allowed herself to be distracted from her dilemma for a few minutes. "And where will you be going?" she asked, truly interested.

"To San Francisco, in the States, missus, by way of Fiji and the Hawaiian Islands."

Bliss sighed. San Francisco, the city she had dreamed of so often. "That's wonderful. You'll see such grand sights."

"I will at that," Sam agreed. Then, with great ceremony, he took a watch from his pocket and opened the case. "Got to go, now, missus. When the train comes through from Wellington, I'd best be at the station with my ticket in hand."

Bliss gave him a letter she'd written to her mother, along with a few coins, and he promised to mail it as soon as he stepped off the ship.

When Sam had rumbled away in his hired wagon, the house seemed bigger and much emptier. Bliss looked in on Peony, who was sleeping fitfully, and then went outside to free Caesar from his washtub prison.

He ruffled his feathers, squawked once, and strutted away, a changed rooster.

That task tended to, Bliss put her hands on her hips and looked out at the surrounding green hills, trying to guess where the flock might be, hoping to see a curl of smoke twisting against the sky.

At sunset, she fed the chickens and the barn animals before coming inside to light lamps and make sure the doors and windows were soundly locked. She was frying potatoes and onions at the stove when Peony came in, looking worse than she had earlier.

"Have you heard from Jamie yet?" she asked pitiably.

Bliss shook her head, thinking to herself that life certainly had its odd twists and turns. Here she was, cooking supper for a woman who might well have been her husband's mistress. "Sit down," she said.

Peony obeyed, keeping to the edge of her chair. She smiled wanly when Bliss set a pot of fresh tea in front of her, along with a clean cup and saucer and a bowl of sugar.

"I'm afraid we haven't any milk," Bliss apologized. "I'd have sworn there was a cow in that barn when I got here."

Peony poured herself a cup of tea and added sugar, still smiling. Bliss thought it was remarkable that she could do so, after what she'd suffered. "Jamie told me that he found you sleeping in the hay, but I thought he was just spinning one of his yarns."

Bliss added eggs and a tin of hash to the concoction she was frying, stirring them in vigorously. Now that it was dark outside, she missed Jamie even more keenly. "Tell me," she ventured, without meeting Peony's eyes, "how you met him."

Peony was silent for a long moment. "If Jamie didn't tell you," she answered finally, "I'm not sure I should."

Bliss got two plates from the shelf and set them on the table with resounding thumps. "That's just the trouble around here," she fussed. "Nobody wants to tell me anything."

"You do deserve to know, I guess," Peony conceded, albeit reluctantly. "Jamie and I were friends in Australia, before we ran away from the man who had made us his slaves—Increase Pipher."

The forks, knives, and spoons Bliss had taken up clattered back into their drawer. After taking the potato, egg, hash, and onion mixture off the heat, she sat down at the table, all her attention fixed on Peony.

The story was long and grisly. Increase Pipher was the same man who had scarred Jamie's back with his whip all those years ago. By setting fire to Pipher's cane fields, Peony had managed to divert the plantation owner's attention long enough to free Jamie from the tree he'd been bound to, lead him away, and tend his wounds.

Together, with Jamie only half-conscious much of the time, the two of them had made their way to Brisbane, riding in farmers' wagons when they could, traveling on foot when there was no other choice. In the city, Peony had sold the jewelry Pipher had given her—she freely admitted that she'd been the man's mistress, despising him all the while— and bought passage for herself and Jamie on a ship bound for New Zealand.

In Auckland, though, they'd come to a parting of the ways. Jamie had taken up with a sheep thief of considerable renown—Cutter—and gone back to his larcenous ways, while Peony had sought out a married cousin and asked for help.

Eventually, Peony had married a shipping agency owner named Ben Ryan—her eyes misted over with tears when she talked about him—and they'd been blissfully happy together. Alas, he'd died of an illness after only a few years.

Bliss got up when Peony fell silent, and busied herself brewing another pot of tea. She was just about to ask Peony more questions when Dog began to fidget. A moment later, she heard a noise in the distance.

"A rider and a horse," Peony said, but she didn't sound pleased.

Although Bliss hoped the rider would be Jamie, she was struck by caution. Suppose, she thought to herself, the visitor were Increase Pipher, or one of his henchmen, come to find out whether the house was unguarded?

Putting a finger to her lips to bid Peony to be silent, Bliss took a cast-iron skillet from the pan cupboard and started toward the front of the house, Dog traipsing along at her heels. She could barely see the stranger in the gloom, through the parlor window, but she knew this was not Jamie, nor was it anyone else she was acquainted with.

The man was very tall and broad in the shoulders, and he

dismounted with an easy grace that said he was accustomed to riding. As he strode toward the house, Bliss saw the moonlight catch in hair as black as a politician's heart.

She held her breath as the man came up onto the porch and knocked resolutely at the door.

Dog barked hysterically, but Bliss bit her lower lip and glared Peony into silence when she would have called out.

"I know you're in there," the man shouted, knocking harder. "In the name of all that's holy, open the door! I didn't come all this way to stand in the cold, dammit!"

Bliss drew a deep breath and let it out again. Obviously, the night visitor wasn't going to go away just because she was ignoring him. "Who is it you want to see?" she asked in a clear, if tremulous, voice.

The man swore. Roundly. "Jamie McKenna, that's who," he answered angrily. "And when I do, I'll teach him to treat a guest this way—"

A light went on in Peony's eyes. She grasped Dog by the scruff of the neck, and before Bliss could stop her, she'd unlocked the door and swung it open.

Dog, that traitor, welcomed the man with a benevolent yap and then dashed out through the open doorway to chase something. It was clear that Bliss could depend on no one but herself to defend hearth and home.

She swallowed hard as she lifted the skillet high in the air. Peony had probably made the same rash mistake in Auckland, inviting those terrible men right inside her house.

"Bliss, no!" Peony cried, but it was too late.

The skillet crashed into the back of the man's head—he was so big that Bliss had had to rise up on her toes to strike him—and he crumpled to the floor, unconscious.

"Oh lord," Peony wailed, disappearing into the kitchen and returning almost immediately with a lamp. She knelt awkwardly beside the man and opened his coat and the collar of his shirt, revealing a medallion exactly like Jamie's except that it hung from a golden chain instead of a string of rawhide.

273

"Don't stand there like a ninny," Peony hissed when it became apparent that Bliss had been rendered speechless. "Get a cold cloth. You've just beaned your own brother-in-law!"

Bliss dropped her skillet and scrambled into the kitchen, where she ladled water into a bowl. Then, after grabbing a clean tea towel, she hurried back to the parlor, where Jamie's brother was stirring on the floor and murmuring ominous things in a brogue.

"Would you be sister to a Yank with a penchant for playactin'?" he asked cryptically, looking up at Bliss with bewilderment in his aquamarine eyes.

Baffled, Bliss simply shook her head and spread her hands.

"The lady who clouted you is your brother's wife," Peony said as he got to his feet, one hand lifted to his head. "Bliss, this—unless I've missed my guess—is Reeve McKenna."

"Aye," said Reeve, extending a hand toward Bliss with comical caution. "Named you Bliss, did they?" he muttered, as an aside. "Fancy that."

Peony was still smiling. Either she thought it was funny that Bliss had brained her own kin by marriage, or she saw him as protection against the evils that might be lurking in the night. "I'm Peony Ryan," she said, taking Mr. McKenna's arm. "Your brother and I are great friends."

"Your brother and I are great friends," Bliss mimicked under her breath as she followed the two into her kitchen. Even with a brand in the middle of her back, that Peony had a way of taking over a situation.

In the kitchen, she made fresh coffee and offered Reeve a meal. He accepted the former and declined the latter, saying that he'd eaten at the hotel in town.

"I'm sorry," Bliss said once she'd completed her duties as hostess and joined Peony and Reeve at the table. "Jamie's in the hills somewhere, with his sheep, and I don't know when he'll be back."

Reeve grinned, showing teeth as white and straight as

Jamie's. "And 'imself leavin' a new bride all alone," he said, his brogue growing more intense by the moment. "It appears 'e needs a talkin' to, that little brother of mine."

"He usually does," replied Bliss, with a smile, and Reeve laughed.

"So that's the way of it, then," he said.

"You must forgive Bliss," Peony said with a pointed look at the mistress of the house. "She thought you were a hooligan."

Reeve rubbed the back of his head and winced. "Seems like she'd be equal to any no-gooder that might 'appen along," he observed.

Bliss glared at Peony, but abstained from commenting on the fact that it was better to be safe than sorry. She was smiling warmly again when she turned her attention back to her brother-in-law. "Jamie tells me that you have a wife and two children."

Reeve looked baffled for a moment, as though he'd misplaced his family and couldn't think where. "Oh yes," he finally said. "There's Maggie—that's me wife—and Elisabeth and J.J."

Just then, there was a scratching sound and a plaintive whine at the door. Bliss recognized Dog's plea for admission instantly and crossed the room to let him back inside the house. "You're no watchdog," she said, patting the animal's head, "but I love you."

Dog wasn't supposed to eat in the house, but Bliss was in the mood to flaunt Jamie's rules. She gave him a generous helping of the potato hash.

"He wanted to make sure Peony and I were all right," Bliss explained, giving Dog the benefit of the doubt, when she turned and found Reeve and Peony looking at her.

"Aye?" Reeve countered. "And what was 'e to do if you weren't?"

Bliss remembered the day Dog had saved Jamie—and probably her as well—from Bert Dunnigan and his men, along that isolated road leading away from the inn. "You'd

275

be surprised what Dog can do, if there's real danger to contend with," she said, watching fondly as the creature ate.

At least there was someone in that house who liked her cooking.

Dog wandered into camp, exhausted, just after sunrise the next morning. Someone had made a makeshift collar of braided rags and tied a rolled piece of paper to it with a bit of string.

"He looks terrible, don't he?" Cutter asked, frowning, as Dog nuzzled him and then went to Jamie.

Jamie drew the paper free, a mingling of alarm and amusement spinning in the pit of his stomach. "Bliss probably forced 'er cookin' on the poor bastard," he said, to hide his fear.

"Thought I smelt onions on his breath," Cutter observed, scratching his head.

Jamie got to his feet and flung the note into the campfire. "That dirty bastard—" he spat.

"What is it?" Cutter wanted to know. He was content to remain where he was, sitting on the cold ground in front of the campfire. All around, sheep *baah*ed ceaselessly.

Jamie was striding toward the tree where the horses were tethered. "Increase put 'is name on me friend," he replied, over one shoulder. "Now, I'm going to put mine on 'is ass!"

Cutter rose from the ground and trotted toward Jamie. "Now, don't go doin' anything hotheaded and stupid, Jamie boy."

Jamie's horse was ready to ride before he replied through his teeth, "I'm done waitin', old man. I should 'ave gone after that bleeder long before now."

Cutter's voice was a raspy plea. "Jamie boy, you've got a wife to think about now—"

Looking down at his friend from the saddle, Jamie countered, "And I'd best be thinkin' about 'er, 'adn't I, mate?"

* * *

The ride home took a bit over an hour, and Jamie was in the barn, rubbing down his lathered horse, when Reeve appeared.

"Nice little wife you've got in there," he said, folding his arms and leaning against one of the stall gates.

Jamie didn't know his brother well—they'd been apart for too many years—but he was glad to see him. And surprised, since Bliss's note hadn't mentioned his presence. "Thanks. Your Maggie is proof you 'ave good taste, so I trust your judgment."

Reeve laughed and then raised one hand to the back of his head, flinching as though his amusement had hurt. "Damn," he muttered.

Jamie put away the grooming brush, gave the gelding a pat on the neck, and slipped out of the stall. "What's the matter with you?" he asked, frowning at his brother.

"Maybe me judgment is good," Reeve confided, "but me manners must not be. When I walked into your 'ouse last night, little brother, your lovely wife brought me to me knees with a fryin' pan."

Despite everything, Jamie grinned at the image that rose in his mind and slapped his elder brother on the shoulder. "Man's got to 'ave a care when 'e deals with Bliss," he said.

Reeve looked worried. "Can you imagine the mischief she and Maggie could do, if they put their 'eads together?"

Jamie executed a mock shudder, but he knew the expression in his eyes was serious when he asked, "How's Elisabeth?"

His brother spoke gently. "Your daughter is fine," he said. "You might come and see 'er now and again, you know."

Jamie sighed. "That would only complicate things."

Reeve shook his head as the two men left the barn and started toward the house. "Maggie and me, we decided it was best that she know the truth, Jamie. We told 'er about you and Eleanor."

Jamie stopped cold, staring at his brother, uncertain whether to be angry or relieved. "Dammit, Reeve," he muttered, "you might 'ave asked me what I thought, at least. 'Ow can a little one like that be expected to understand, and 'er barely five?"

"She understood," Reeve assured him quietly. "Elisabeth needs to stay with Maggie and me, for now," he went on, when Jamie had had a few moments to absorb his words. "Later on, when she's older, I imagine she'll want to know 'er father better."

Jamie looked toward the house, where Bliss waited, and his feelings must have been in his eyes.

"You 'aven't told Bliss about your past, then?" Reeve asked.

Jamie sighed, lifting his hat with one hand and running the other through his hair. "The right moment never seems to come along," he said. "God in 'eaven, Reeve, if I ever lost 'er—"

"I know," Reeve said. "I know." Then he lightened the moment with a grin and, "It's not so easy to lose these women after all. I've tried it with Maggie, and damned if she doesn't find me every time!"

Jamie laughed and, for a few minutes at least, he forgot that there was a monster lurking just out of sight, bent on destroying everyone and everything he cared about.

Chapter 21 ❧

Jamie's only greeting to Bliss, when she met him halfway between the house and the barn, was a polite nod of his head. She blushed at the rebuff, which was all the more humiliating because Reeve was there to see it.

"Where's Peony?" Jamie demanded the moment they'd entered the house.

Bliss was determined to be reasonable about the whole matter. "I've put her to bed," she answered, "in Cutter's room. She's—she's not doing very well, Jamie."

His jawline was tight as he took off his coat and hat and hung them up. "Aye," he said grimly, and then he started toward the downstairs bedroom.

Bliss followed, at an eloquent nod from Reeve. If Jamie was aware of her presence, he gave no indication.

He knocked lightly on the door of Peony's room and entered at her feeble, "Come in."

"Jamie!" she cried at the sight of him, holding her arms out.

Jamie sat down on the edge of Peony's bed and embraced her gingerly, but with a tenderness that twisted Bliss's heart and brought stinging tears to her eyes.

279

Peony was sobbing and clinging to him, her face buried in his shoulder. "Oh Jamie, it was terrible—I was so frightened—"

"I know," he said gently, still holding her in that careful way. "Everything's going to be all right, love. I promise it will."

Peony wept wholeheartedly for long minutes, during which Bliss felt like an intruder but could not turn away. Finally, Jamie said hoarsely, "Let's 'ave a look at this burn."

After casting an anxious look in Bliss's direction, Peony shook her head. "No. I've never undressed for you before, Jamie McKenna, and I won't start now."

Bliss, hovering in the doorway, spoke for the first time since she'd told Jamie where to find Peony. "I saw the wound this morning," she said woodenly, "and I didn't like the looks of it."

Jamie didn't so much as glance in his wife's direction. His orders were simple and to the point. "Turn over," he said to Peony.

Peony again looked to Bliss, her eyes appealing for understanding. "Look away, then, Jamie," she murmured. When he did, Peony removed her bed jacket and lay down on her stomach.

Jamie cursed when he saw the gruesome initials burned into the flesh between Peony's shoulder blades. "Bring some whiskey and a clean cloth, Bliss," he said in the next moment, and he might have been a stranger for all the warmth his voice held.

Bliss hurried to fetch a linen sheet from a cabinet in the upstairs hallway, then found the liquor supply in Jamie's study and grasped a bottle. When she returned to the downstairs bedroom, Peony was paler than ever and biting her lip, while Jamie stood at the window, every muscle in his body rigid with outrage.

He turned when he heard Bliss enter the room and gave her a despondent smile. So briefly did it touch his lips that Bliss wasn't sure she'd really seen it.

"Not whiskey, Jamie," Peony whispered. "Please—"

Jamie didn't even seem to see Bliss as he took the bottle and sheet from her and approached the bed again. "I'm sorry, love," he said quietly. "If I could suffer this for you, I would. You know that, don't you?"

His words broke Bliss's heart, as did Peony's trusting reply. "Yes, Jamie love. I know."

Bliss bit her lower lip as she watched Jamie tear away part of the sheet she'd given him and soak it in whiskey. He spoke in a gentle murmur to Peony—Bliss could not make out the words—as he began to clean the infected wound.

Peony stiffened and screamed into her pillow, but there was never a break in Jamie's quiet reassurances. Bliss turned and stumbled back along the hallway, into the kitchen, and out the rear door.

There, in the windswept winter grass, she covered her face with both hands and sobbed out her anguish.

"'Ere now," said a low masculine voice behind her, as strong hands turned her so that she could rest her forehead against a chest as broad and steely as Jamie's. "It can't be so bleak as all that, now can it, Red?"

Bliss looked up at Reeve and trembled with grief. He was a man, and Jamie's brother in the bargain, and he would never understand. She sniffled bravely and dashed at her tears with the back of one hand.

"It's time I gathered the eggs," she said with resolve.

Reeve bent to place a brotherly kiss on the top of her head. "You're the best thing that ever 'appened to Jamie, little one. Don't forget that, no matter what."

Bliss nodded and made herself smile, and when she reached the chicken coop, Caesar was up to his old tricks. Apparently, he hadn't learned his lesson after all.

Again, Bliss imprisoned him beneath the old washtub, again he railed and squawked and flapped his wings. With a sigh, she found a good-sized rock and gave the metal tub a hard, resounding thump with it.

Caesar promptly fell silent. In fact, he was so quiet that

Bliss lifted the washtub and freed him. He staggered away and minded his own business all the while that Bliss was gathering eggs.

When she returned to the kitchen, Jamie was there, quite alone, sipping coffee from a mug with a chip in the rim. Bliss's straight little shoulders stooped a little, under the weight of her discouragement. "Hello," she said, thinking how stupid and inane that word could sound as she set the egg basket on the counter and reached back to fiddle with her apron ties.

She felt Jamie's gaze on her breasts when they were thrust forward by the motion.

"How are you, Duchess?" he asked softly.

"As if you cared," Bliss muttered, and she was immediately remorseful because Peony's injury was real and it was serious and she hadn't meant to make light of it by indulging her own jealous feelings.

She felt his hands on her shoulders. "I do care, Duchess," he said.

Bliss turned in his grasp to look up at him, searching his handsome face for any sign of deception. Her throat was thick with emotion; just standing so close to Jamie made her yearn for him.

"Hold me, Jamie," she implored him in a despairing whisper.

He drew her to him, and she took comfort from the strength of his embrace. After a few moments, though, he drew back, allowing his hands to rest on her waist. "I want you to do something for me, Duchess—with no arguments."

Bliss didn't like the sound of this, but she kept her peace, determined to listen if not obey.

"When Reeve leaves for Australia at the end of the week, I want you and Peony to go with him."

Bliss's mouth dropped open. Of all the things Jamie might have said, she had never expected that. "Wh-what about you?" she asked finally. "Aren't you going, too?"

"Aye," Jamie answered after a short silence, and there was

an angry distance in his eyes that frightened Bliss. "I 'ave business there. But I've got some things to tend to before I leave, so I won't be travelin' with you."

Bliss fought an urge to cling to him; she couldn't have Jamie thinking that she was weak, and no wife for a man like him. "I'll wait for you, then," she said, with a proud lift of her chin.

Jamie shook his head. "No, Duchess. I want you kept safe, and this is the only way."

Bliss lowered her eyes for a moment, struggling to retain her composure. "I'm never safer than when I'm with you," she said softly.

"Aye," Jamie said with a skeptical chuckle that was utterly devoid of amusement. "Were you 'safe' that day when Dunnigan and 'is men jumped us along the road? If it 'adn't been for Cutter and Dog, we'd both be dead by now."

Boldly, Bliss lifted her hands to the sides of Jamie's face. "But we aren't dead, Jamie—that's the important thing. And I don't want to be separated from you."

Jamie bent his head and gave her a brief, nibbling kiss. "I've got to go back to camp for a few days, Duchess," he said. "When I get 'ome again, will you be ready to give me a proper welcome?"

Bliss knew that welcome would also be a good-bye, but she nodded and smiled, tears shining in her eyes. "Aye," she teased, mimicking his brogue. "'Twill be a proper welcome indeed, me love!"

He laughed and wrenched her close, and this time his kiss was thorough, sending heat surging into every part of her body. Heat that burned away Bliss's doubts and fears like dry grass in the path of a fire.

As it happened, Jamie changed his plans and returned to the sheep camp only long enough to explain the situation to Cutter. When he got back, he divided most of his time between Peony and Reeve, but Bliss was determined not to mind.

Five days had passed, during which Peony had largely

recovered and Reeve had grown homesick for his wife and family. Bliss had slept beside Jamie every night for the best part of the previous week, aware of every sinewy, rock-hard muscle in his body, desire tightening within her, like a fiery coil. Now, her system had completed its mysterious cycle, and she could wait no longer.

She found her husband in the barn, in virtually the same spot where he'd nearly run Bliss through with a pitchfork, pitching hay for the horses. Since the day was warm, he'd left his coat in the house and unfastened his shirt to his midriff.

Bliss had bathed, put on perfume and her favorite spring dress, one that Jamie had shown a special preference for. Her curly cinnamon hair had been washed, then brushed and toweled until it was nearly dry, and fastened with combs that Jamie had given her.

He paused in his work, gave a low whistle, and shoved his decrepit hat to the back of his head when he saw her. The muscles in his bare forearms corded as he shifted the pitchfork handle so that it rested between his hands.

Bliss was filled with love and the knowledge that she would soon be parted from Jamie. There was a bittersweet ache in her throat when she said, "I need you, Jamie McKenna, and I won't be put off until you've finished your blasted work."

Jamie gaped at her for a moment, then laughed and tossed the pitchfork aside. "So it's that way, is it?" he asked, putting his powerful hands on his hips.

Bliss drew nearer, sliding her fingers inside his open shirt and delighting in his groan of welcome. "Are my hands cold?" she teased.

"No," Jamie answered, his lips moving closer and closer to hers, "but your feet are, as a general rule."

Bliss giggled, but her amusement caught in her throat when Jamie's mouth claimed hers in a kiss that stole her breath away and electrified all her senses. Her hands were trapped inside his shirt, while his molded her neatly to him.

For all that he could so easily dominate Bliss, Jamie was breathless when he broke that kiss to grind out, "God in 'eaven, Duchess, show a man some mercy. It's the bright light of day and we aren't alone—"

Bliss rested one index finger lightly on his lips. "We are, though. Peony is asleep and Reeve is in the study with his feet up on your desk, reading a book." She swept Jamie's hat from his head and flung it away, then buried her fingers in his hair. "Resist if you can," she added in a saucy whisper, with a little wriggle that made him moan like a man in agony and then kiss her as if that were the only antidote for his pain.

"Up there," he rasped, long, delicious minutes later, pointing toward the loft. When Bliss hesitated mischievously, he added a hoarse, "Please?"

She laughed and started up the ladder, and when she reached the top, Jamie gave her a pinch that sent her rolling in the sweet-scented, scratchy hay. He was poised over her in a move so quick that the battle was lost before it had even begun, catching her wrists together in one hand and holding them high over her head.

It was Bliss who moaned now as she felt the power of Jamie's manhood pressing against her thigh. He kissed her with a fierce, primitive hunger, and his light, deft fingers were unfastening the buttons of her dress all the while. He made short work of the camisole beneath and then, still stretching her arms as far above her head as he could without hurting her, he eased downward to enjoy the warm, plump breasts that awaited him so eagerly.

Bliss closed her eyes and bit down on her lower lip in sheer ecstasy as he drank his fill at her throbbing nipples. By the time he lifted her skirts and drew down her drawers, she was aching to be filled with him.

But Jamie had other ideas. He placed her legs over his shoulders and, supporting the small of her back in his strong, callused hands, burrowed past the silken barrier to satisfy another craving.

Bliss was blinded by the dazzling sensations that were overwhelming her. A soft, whimpering cry came from her throat as Jamie took his pleasure, now with a pirate's gluttony, now with delicate nibbles that made her clutch at the straw with frantic hands. He was caressing her ever so gently with his tongue when a grinding release caught her small body and shook it, like a great beast shaking its captured prey.

She lay dazed in the straw when it was over, the back of one hand resting against her mouth as she struggled to breathe normally. Jamie stretched out beside her, his hand making gentle circles beneath the folds of her skirt and petticoat on the quivering flesh of her stomach. Her breasts were still bared to the spring air, and their peaks contracted as Jamie assessed them with new appetite.

"Ummmm," he said, and his breath was warm against the nipple he'd chosen.

Arching her back, Bliss closed her eyes and rested her fingers lightly in Jamie's hair. As he suckled, she purred in tranquil rapture.

After a delectable interval, Bliss began to feel a new heat in her loins, and she could only imagine what Jamie was feeling. She wanted to raise him to the same fierce level of need and response that she had reached.

She unfastened his belt buckle and the buttons of his trousers, and freed him to caresses that set him to trembling. He drew in a harsh, rasping breath when she tested him in a tentative way, groaned when she became greedy. Jamie submitted as long as he could bear before taking Bliss by the waist and setting her astride him. His eyes, full of passion and challenge, never broke contact with hers as she slowly, proudly admitted him to her body.

Never before had Jamie allowed Bliss to set the pace and tone of their lovemaking for so long, but that day he did. She saw the muscles in his throat move convulsively as she subjected him to sweet torment by rising and falling, rising and falling upon his manhood. She rode his magnificence as though it were a mythical winged steed.

Somewhere high in the clouds, however, Bliss lost her way and was blinded by the mists that surrounded her. Resting her hands on Jamie's shoulders, she flung back her head and cried out as elation found her and sent her spiraling into an exploding sun. Jamie followed close behind, feasting feverishly on her breast even as his powerful hips were stilled in a final, savage spasm of release.

Bliss rested her head against Jamie's shoulder, long minutes later, while he set her camisole and dress to rights with slow, soothing motions of his hands. Only when she had been taken care of did he attend to his own clothes.

She wasn't sure whether he'd said it aloud, or whether his gentleness had told her, but Bliss knew that Jamie loved her. In that time, and that place, at least, he belonged exclusively to her.

She smoothed his rumpled hair with her fingers, smiling through a mist of tears. "It was the smartest thing I ever did, Jamie McKenna, falling asleep in your barn that night."

"I'd 'ave gladly shared me bed," he teased, and his eyes danced as he watched her picking straw from her hair.

He stood when Bliss did, and preceded her down the ladder, retrieving his hat and his pitchfork and then standing there grinning at her while she plucked at the straw that seemed to cover her from head to foot.

"How do I look?" she asked, craning her neck to try and peer over her own shoulder.

"Like you've just been tumbled in a hayloft," Jamie answered, without hesitation, and then he went back to his work, whistling in a carefree fashion as he wielded the pitchfork.

As Bliss stood there watching Jamie, it came home to her that she would be forced to leave him soon, and that whatever he meant to do in her absence was dangerous. A shiver touched her spine, and made her tremble.

She might never see him again after she and Peony and Reeve sailed away from Auckland.

"Do you love me, Jamie McKenna?" she demanded, her eyes burning suspiciously.

He stopped pitching hay to look at her squarely. "No worries there, Duchess. Didn't I just surrender me virtue, without so much as a fight?"

Bliss took a step nearer, her hands clasped together. "Don't tease me, Jamie," she said. "I'm serious."

He dispensed with the pitchfork and walked toward her, cupping her face in his hands. "And so am I," he said gruffly. He gave her a little shake. "Are you listenin' now, Duchess? I love you!"

Bliss put her arms around his neck and held on. "Let me stay with you, Jamie—please!"

He shook his head and set her away, just as she'd feared. "No. And that's the end of it, Duchess. I've done all the explainin' I'm goin' to do."

Bliss drew a deep breath, let it out again. It was true that Jamie had made his position clear over the past few days. He intended to look for Increase Pipher, his old enemy, after she'd sailed for Australia with Reeve and Peony. When he'd resolved the matter once and for all, he would come for her. "There's no reasoning with you, Jamie McKenna," she complained.

"You're right," he replied stubbornly, and when Bliss left the barn, he was pitching hay again.

Peony was in the kitchen brewing tea when Bliss reached the house. She smiled and said, "Hello, Mrs. McKenna."

"Hello," Bliss sighed, sinking into a chair.

"My goodness," commented Peony. "Don't we just look like desolation itself?" She reached out and, with a frown, picked a bit of straw from Bliss's hair.

Bliss blushed and averted her eyes, and Peony laughed.

"Don't be so hard on yourself, love," she said good-naturedly. "The man's your husband, after all."

Bliss's gaze was level as she looked at Peony. "I don't want to share him. Ever."

Peony shrugged and poured tea for both herself and Bliss before answering. "I don't imagine you'll have to, if you look after his needs. Jamie's not a man to wander from bed to bed."

"You seem to know him awfully well," Bliss dared to say.

"I do," Peony replied blithely. "Perhaps better than anyone else in the world does." She paused, probably for effect, then went on to say, "Jamie loves you, Bliss, with his whole heart and soul, and he'd never betray you. Not unless you betrayed him first, that is.

"Let me just give you a little warning, though. If you ever hurt that man, I'll see you pay for it if it's the last thing I ever do."

Bliss's eyes widened and, for once, she had no ready answer.

The next morning, early, Jamie left the warmth of their bed and began getting into his clothes.

"It can't be time already," Bliss said with despair, longing to slide down under the covers and hide there until Jamie forgot that he'd ever wanted to send her to Australia.

"Sorry, Duchess. Today's the day." Jamie's voice was hoarse.

"I don't want to go!" Bliss wailed. "Why won't you listen to me?"

Jamie sighed. "I've listened to you until me ears are ringin'. Get out of bed, Duchess. The train leaves in a couple of hours."

Bliss nestled into the linen sheets for a few more precious seconds, letting memories of the night just past glide over her. When Jamie had gone downstairs, she dragged herself out of bed.

Reeve, Jamie, and Peony were all in the kitchen when she reached it, sipping coffee and talking among themselves.

"I'll fix breakfast," Bliss said brightly.

"No!" chorused the three people seated at the table.

At Bliss's expression, Jamie was quick to smile and get to his feet. He gave her a kiss on the forehead and said, "What we meant was, there's no need to worry about food now. You can eat on the train."

Bliss glanced suspiciously at Reeve and Peony, but they were looking away and she could tell nothing from their expressions. "Well," she finally began uncertainly, "if none of you are hungry—"

Too soon, Jamie and Reeve were loading Bliss's trunks, which she'd never bothered to unpack after her return from Auckland, into the wagon. She and Peony would travel with Jamie, while Reeve would ride the horse he'd hired in town.

In daylight, Bliss could see that the railroad station was flanked by one hotel and a few houses and shops, by means of which the place generously dubbed itself a town. This, then, was where Jamie had bought the cookbook, and the chocolates, and the golden band for her finger.

Bliss looked down at that wedding band through a blur of tears. There was no point in pleading with Jamie not to make her go, for he'd already made up his mind, but he couldn't stop her heart from breaking.

Reeve lifted Peony down from the wagon seat, and the two of them wandered discreetly into the ramshackle station house. In the distance, the train whistle howled plaintively, as though it shared Bliss's grief.

Jamie's hand cupped her chin and raised it, so that her eyes met his. "Don't make it 'arder than it is, Duchess," he said. "It's nearly more than I can bear now."

Bliss didn't trust herself to speak. She bit down on her lower lip and nodded, and a tear tickled her cheek.

Jamie brushed it away with his thumb. "You'll like Australia," he promised.

Bliss let her forehead rest against his shoulder, drawing in the scent of him, memorizing his substance and his strength. The train whistle grew louder and louder, and she had to fight against more tears and a rising sense of panic. "Don't let it be a long time, Jamie," she finally managed to say. "Please, don't let it be a long time until you come and get me."

He put his arms around her and held her close, and she knew that he didn't trust himself to speak.

When the train pulled in, Jamie was still holding her, and she was praying that he would change his mind and let her stay. Instead, he gave her a lingering kiss, jumped to the ground, and extended his arms to her.

It was all a blur, the last good-bye. Peony was emotional and Bliss felt frozen inside. She allowed Reeve to help her onto the train, along an aisle, into a seat beside a window.

"It's all for the best, lass," her brother-in-law assured her, but his voice sounded sad, as though he might be inclined to shed a few tears himself if he'd had the privacy for it.

Peony sat down in the seat across the aisle, her handkerchief pressed to her eyes, and one or two other passengers found their places as the whistle shrieked a farewell to the little town huddled beside the railroad tracks.

Reeve took Bliss's hand awkwardly into his and patted it. "You'll like Maggie," he said, in a touching effort to console her. "For all that she's a Yank, she's not 'ard to put up with."

Bliss nodded, unable to respond, and looked out through the sooty glass window. Steam billowed past and, through it, she saw Jamie climb back into the seat of his wagon and take the reins into his hands.

Bliss laid her fingers to her lips and pressed them to the glass, whispering a soundless, "Good-bye."

Jamie touched the brim of his hat in a farewell of his own, and then the train was moving steadily away from the station. Soon, Bliss couldn't see him anymore.

Chapter 22

THE FARM HAD NEVER SEEMED SO EMPTY OR SO ISOLATED AS IT DID when Jamie returned to it that day. If he'd had anywhere else to go, he might have driven right on past.

As it was, Dog came bounding out to the road to meet the wagon, and there was smoke curling from a couple of the chimneys. Jamie reined in the team and pushed the brake lever down with an automatic motion of his left leg, grinning as the sheepdog gave a yip of delight and bounded up into the bed of the wagon.

"'Ello, you worthless old 'ound," Jamie said, as Dog gave a short, joyous bark. When they reached the barn, Cutter was waiting to help unhitch the team, a pipe between his teeth.

"Dog and me," he began gruffly, "we thought you might be needin' a mate or two right about now."

Jamie nodded and got down from the wagon. He felt all raw and broken inside, as though something vital had been dragged out of him, thoroughly crushed, and then stuffed back into place.

The two men worked in silence for the next few minutes, taking care of the team. Cutter hung up the harness and

Jamie led the two horses to their stalls and gave them food and water.

Just walking into his own house was an ordeal for Jamie; if he'd been alone, it might have proven impossible. As it was, Cutter plopped down in a kitchen chair and sighed. "I was just gettin' used to the way she made coffee."

Jamie ached. "Aye," he said as Dog wandered into the next room and began whimpering when he didn't find Bliss. His despair was an uncomfortable reflection of Jamie's own feelings. "Is 'e goin' to keep that up?" he demanded shortly as Dog continued his mournful search.

Cutter shrugged. "Been through the house once already, Dog has. I should be grudged over that, I reckon. Raised that scapegrace from a pup, I did, and here he is whinin' over a red-haired woman."

Jamie shoved a hand through his hair, took the coffeepot from the stove, and then set it down again with a crash. He didn't have the heart to drink that brew, knowing that Bliss had made it and wondering how long it would be before he had any that bad again. "I'd like to do a bit of whinin' meself," he confessed quietly.

Cutter crossed the room to give his friend a slap on the back and collect the coffeepot. While he was outside getting water, Jamie whistled for Dog, unable to stand the animal's grief any longer.

Dog came and laid his head on Jamie's knee, making a melancholy sound in his throat.

"She'll be back," Jamie promised, hoping to God it was true.

For two nights before boarding the steamer bound for Brisbane, Reeve, Peony, and Bliss stayed at the Victoria Hotel, and there Bliss had seen Walter Davis again. Once she'd told him about her impending trip to Australia, Walter said that he and his grandfather planned to return soon themselves.

It was nice, she thought to herself as she stood at the

railing for a long look at Auckland, to encounter friends unexpectedly. A surprise like that had a way of cheering a person, distracting them from their miseries.

And Bliss, missing Jamie as she did, was awash in misery.

"There now," Reeve said proudly, pointing to a majestic boat swaying at anchor in the distance. "That ship belongs to me. Bound for the States, she is."

Bliss's interest was piqued. She thought of Sam, the man who'd brought Peony out from Auckland, and peered toward the ship, squinting as she tried to make out the name painted on the bow.

"She's the *Elisabeth Lee,*" Reeve said, looking at Bliss with mingled concern and amusement. "Do you need spectacles?"

"No," Bliss said, offended, even as Peony nodded in the affirmative.

Reeve chuckled and shook his head.

"The *Elisabeth Lee* is the name of the ship Sam was so worried about catching!" Bliss cried, delighted by the small coincidence. "He said she used to be a whaler."

It seemed to Bliss that a shadow moved in Reeve's blue-green eyes, but like Jamie, he was quick to hide his emotions. "Aye," he said remotely. "She was a whaler. Now she carries trade goods."

"Who's Sam?" Peony asked, frowning.

Bliss gave her traveling companion an impatient look. "He's the man who brought you to the country—your carriage driver's brother-in-law, or some such."

Peony sighed. She'd been recovering steadily from her ordeal, but there was still a wan look about her and she tended to weaken easily. "I can't be expected to remember everything," she muttered. One of her hands tightened on the railing, Bliss noted, and the other rose to her forehead.

"You're tired," Bliss said quickly, taking Peony's arm. "Come along—we'll go to our cabin and you can lie down and rest."

After a few words with Reeve, Bliss led Peony away. Their quarters were easy to find, being on that same deck, and Peony was soon settled into her bed for a nap. Bliss immediately went back out to explore—to keep her mind off Jamie for a little while.

When the ship set sail, Bliss was standing at the starboard railing, impervious to the brisk wind, watching New Zealand recede into the distance. Her eyes burned and her throat was thick; leaving home wasn't nearly so grand as she'd once dreamed it would be.

A gentleman's handkerchief was extended, and Bliss looked up through a mist of tears to see Walter Davis standing beside her. She accepted the neatly folded cloth and dabbed at her eyes. It seemed a remarkable thing that Mr. Davis should be on board the very same ship, but Bliss's surprise faded quickly.

After all, he'd said that he and his grandfather wanted to return to Australia.

"I used to long to travel far and wide," she confessed in a sniffle, after several minutes of sheer misery had passed. "When I lived at the lighthouse, I'd see the ships passing in the distance and cry because I wanted so badly to be aboard one. Now here I am blubbering away because I've gotten my wish."

Walter's smile was gentle. He looked as though he might have patted Bliss's hand, had he dared to be so familiar. He nodded in response to her words and then ventured to change the subject. "That man you're traveling with—he's a Queenslander, isn't he?"

Bliss had gone a long way toward composing herself. "Of sorts, I guess. That's my husband's brother, Reeve, and he does own a plantation near Brisbane. It's my understanding, though, that he and his wife spend just as much time in Sydney as they do in the country."

"Now that I think of it," Walter reflected, his expression faraway, on the roofs of Auckland, "I recall your husband telling me that he had a brother there. It's strange that Mr.—that Grandfather hasn't spoken of Mr. McKenna, having considerable holdings in the Brisbane area himself."

Secretly, Bliss was relieved that the elder Davis wasn't a confederate of Reeve and Maggie's; she thought him odious, though she'd never have been so rude as to say so, and would have found it a trial to have to be polite to him on a regular basis. She managed a smile and a shrug, turning her attention back to the sea.

She sensed that Walter was working up his courage long before he spoke again.

"Bliss, what happened? Why are you aboard this ship without your husband?"

Bliss looked down at the handkerchief wadded between her hands. Walter had a gift for asking questions that were entirely too personal, but he did it in such a way that one felt it would be mean-spirited not to answer. "There's a man Jamie hates," she said miserably. "A terribly cruel, vindictive man."

Walter looked distinctly uncomfortable, and he didn't speak, but his knuckles were white, so tight was his grip on the railing. There was still a faint bruise around his eye, a reminder of his own encounter with Jamie.

Bliss drew in a deep breath and let it out again. She'd begun, she might as well finish. "I'm so frightened, Walter. This man laid Jamie's back open with a whip, years ago, and he had the most horrid thing done to our—our friend, Mrs. Ryan. Now Jamie's determined to find him."

"And do what?"

Bliss closed her eyes for a moment. She knew that Jamie would kill Increase Pipher if he came face-to-face with him, and she was terrified that her husband would either be hanged for the crime or die in the process of taking vengeance. "I don't even want to think about it," she said.

"I believe I'd better look in on Grandfather," Walter replied, and as abruptly as that, he was gone.

Bliss kept her vigil at the railing until she could no longer see New Zealand. Then, because she needed so much to feel close to Jamie, she hurried back to the cabin to record the day's experiences in the letter she'd begun aboard the train.

Jamie spent three days and nights in the worst part of Auckland, the welter of pubs, opium dens, and whorehouses encircling the harbor, before he was approached by one of the men he'd been waiting for.

"Is it about Mrs. Ryan, mate?" the man asked, dropping into a chair across the table from Jamie's. He was a little bleeder, wearing a layer of filth that probably dated back to his childhood, and he looked familiar.

Jamie's right hand rested idly on the hilt of his blade, still in its scabbard on his hip. With his left, he raised a glass of whiskey to his mouth, took an unhurried sip while he studied the man with a thoughtfulness he knew was unnerving. "What's your name?" he finally asked.

"Johnson," replied the emissary from the city's underbelly. "Nate Johnson, Mr. McKenna."

Jamie smiled, slowly and viciously, and took another draft of his whiskey. He remembered Johnson now; he'd been with Dunnigan on the road that day. He'd been brave enough then, the bastard, with Jamie sprawled on the ground, half-conscious. Aye, Johnson had been pleased to put a boot to him.

But he was sweating now. Copiously. "I weren't in on burnin' the lady," he sputtered, shaken by Jamie's silence. "I swear to God I didn't have nothin' to do with that, Mr. McKenna."

Jamie sat back in his chair, at the same time reaching for the whiskey bottle and refilling his glass. The stale stench of Johnson's sweat throbbed in his nostrils and turned his stomach. God, but it would be good to get out of this place and have a bath and a shave.

"Who sent you 'ere?" he asked when the little man across from him was squirming.

"I ain't s'posed to tell you that."

Jamie's fingers flexed over the handle of the blade. "If I 'ave to, mate," he muttered, his shark's smile never wavering, "I'll *cut* the name out of you."

Johnson paled beneath his coating of grime; clearly, Jamie's reputation had preceded him. "Now, you just keep that blade right where it's at. I don't need no trouble. 'Twas Bert Dunnigan what made me do it. Said he'd tangled with you once too often."

"Aye," Jamie reflected. "He did that, for a fact. Tell me, was it Bert that put Pipher's mark on Peony Ryan?"

Johnson shook his head wildly. "No! That were just some scum off a ship from the States, lookin' for easy money."

Easy money. Jamie felt sick, and he marveled that he'd ever been a part of this man's world, lifting wallets and watches and eventually learning less subtle thievery from Cutter. "They're gone again, I suppose," he prompted, setting aside his own shame to deal with Johnson.

The little man shrugged. "Dunno, mate. They might be, and they might not." There were crescents of sweat under Johnson's arms. The stuff stood out in beads on his upper lip, and he was having trouble meeting Jamie's gaze.

Jamie sighed and sipped languidly at his whiskey, lulling Johnson into a false state of security. In the next instant, however, he'd not only drawn his blade, but planted it firmly in the tabletop between two of his companion's grubby fingers. "Names," he breathed.

His meaning was obviously clear to Johnson. "Mig Wilbertson and H. P. Cook!" he spat. "They're holed up down at Shallie's place—probably drunk as lords in the bargain!"

Jamie knew Shallie's—it was a pub at the end of the street, close on the water. Idly, he worked the knife free, but his lack of hurry was deceptive. He ached to find Wilbertson and Cook. "If you warn them," he said quietly to Johnson, "I'll break all ten of your toes, one at a time. And when I've finished that, mate, I'll start on your fingers. Now, did you get all that, or do I 'ave to repeat meself?"

Johnson shook his head. "No, sir, I heard you clearlike."

"Fine," Jamie said with a smile that was at once affable and quietly lethal, and he kept his knife in his hand as he rose to his feet. "There's just one more thing I want to know. Where do I find Increase Pipher?"

The thug swallowed visibly. He couldn't have guessed, from Jamie's manner, how important the answer was to him. "Pipher had a room at the Victoria Hotel, uptown, but he's gone now. Dunnigan said the old man went back to Brisbane."

Jamie's face was still impassive, giving no indication that his mind was reeling. Pipher had probably been in the Victoria Hotel all the time that he and Bliss were there. He'd been watching, and waiting, and when he'd seen how much Bliss mattered to Jamie, he'd sent the whip as a grisly wedding present.

Now he was on his way to Australia, like Bliss, and the width of the Tasman Sea separated the both of them from Jamie.

He strode out of the tavern where he'd encountered Johnson without so much as a look back, and started toward Shallie's. He'd think things through while he took care of his business there.

Johnson had been right about the Yanks. They were both at Shallie's, grogged to their eyeballs and sharing a whore when Jamie kicked in the door of their room.

The whore squealed in alarm and scrambled out from between her clients, her painted face contorted with fear. "I ain't done nothin', love," she wailed to Jamie. "I swear I ain't!"

Jamie had no quarrel with the woman. He gestured toward the door and muttered, "Get out."

The whore didn't need to be told twice.

Wilbertson and Cook, meanwhile, were just sitting up on that flea-ridden, sloping mattress, gazing blearily in Jamie's direction.

"Who the hell are you?" one of them asked.

Jamie's blade materialized in his right hand, as it had a way of doing when he was furious. Images of the ugly burns on Peony's back filled his mind and soured the back of his throat, like vomit. "Me name's not important, mate," he said evenly, with an acid smile. "And I'm straight out of the worst dream you ever 'ad."

A few screams never meant much of anything at Shallie's, especially when they came in the night, and nary a man so much as looked up from his mug when Jamie McKenna came back down the same set of stairs he'd climbed earlier and strode outside. There were some people it was just better not to see.

Bliss liked Maggie McKenna the instant she saw her. She was a beautiful blonde, with wide gray eyes and a ready smile, and she flung herself into Reeve's arms without a care for the disapproving looks she got from the other people on the wharf.

"Hello, Yank," Reeve said tenderly, and then he kissed her before turning to introduce his traveling companions. He presented Peony first, and then, with a sparkle in his eyes, he said, "And this is Bliss. She's Jamie's wife."

Maggie's wonderful charcoal eyes rounded in delight and her face glowed. "Jamie's married!" she crowed in her strange accent. "I don't believe it!"

Bliss was about to offer the golden ring as proof when Maggie hugged her and then planted a kiss on her cheek.

"Welcome to the family, Bliss," she said, putting one arm around Reeve's waist and one around her sister-in-law's, Peony walking a little ahead and to the side as they started up the wharf. "These McKenna men are stubborn, but there are ways to keep them in line," Maggie went on to say.

"Jamie will appreciate this," Reeve commented dryly. His brogue had relaxed now to a mere lilt in his voice. "Your telling his wife how to keep him in line, I mean."

"I'm assuming," Maggie proceeded in bright tones, "that the same things that work with you, Reeve McKenna, will work with Jamie."

Listening to the banter between Maggie and Reeve, Bliss was more homesick than ever for Jamie. She averted her eyes, in the hope that no one would see the tears gathering there.

Maggie gave her a slight squeeze, as if she'd sensed that her sister-in-law needed reassurance, and Bliss felt a little better just for having a friend. She'd grown up entirely without them, after all.

It was at the base of the wharf, when Reeve was off seeing about the baggage, that Peony had her fainting spell. Walter Davis and his grandfather had just paused to bid Bliss farewell and every good fortune, and when the old man extended a clawlike hand to Peony and smiled, she simply crumpled to the ground.

When Bliss couldn't revive her immediately, Maggie had hurried away to find Reeve.

"Imagine that," said the elder Mr. Davis, leaning on Walter for support, and that strange, grimacelike smile was still on his face.

Moments later, Reeve arrived and lifted a conscious but dazed Peony into his arms. In the shuffle of getting her into the hotel, where a messenger was dispatched to find a doctor, Bliss forgot all about Walter and his grandfather.

Peony was pale as death when she opened her eyes from a second swoon. She was lying on a sofa in the hotel lobby, with Maggie waving smelling salts under her nose, and the first thing she said was, "Increase. Dear God in heaven, that was Increase."

Bliss was uneasy at the mention of that name. She frowned. "Where?"

Peony trembled. "That old man who stopped to speak to you. Bliss, that was Increase Pipher."

There was a wicker chair behind her and Bliss backed into

it, the muscles in her knees having melted to nothing. "It's impossible," she breathed, looking wildly from Peony to Reeve to Maggie. "That was only Walter's grandfather."

Peony was shaking her head very slowly from side to side, and her eyes were vacant of all expression.

Quickly, Maggie took Peony's hand in hers and began patting it. "There now," she said in her odd, flat voice. "No one's going to hurt you, not with all of us around."

Presently, the doctor arrived and Peony was led away to a room, examined, and put to bed under light sedation. Reeve had already told Bliss that they would all be staying in the hotel that first night, since it was a fair distance to Seven Sisters, his plantation, and she was glad to retire to her own room. There, she tried to put her thoughts in order.

A single one filled her mind. While she and Jamie had been making love and war in that suite at the Victoria Hotel, Pipher had been across the hall, plotting demon's tricks. And how very amused he must have been by Jamie's naive little wife. Increase had enjoyed her blithe chatter, no doubt, and taken her confidences into consideration as he prepared to destroy the man she loved.

Bliss brought her notebook from her baggage and continued her letter to Jamie, her pen racing across the paper as she told him about the man she'd thought was Walter Davis's grandfather. Shadows had fallen on the sea by the time a knock sounded at her door. With a weary sigh, Bliss laid down her pen and walked across the room to admit her caller.

It was a flushed, bright-eyed Maggie. Bliss was still a new bride, but she knew well enough what had made her sister-in-law glow like that, and her yearning for Jamie was as sharp as broken glass.

"It's just occurred to Reeve and me," Maggie confided with some embarrassment, "that you might be waiting on us—to go to supper, I mean. Here it is, so late—you must be starving."

Bliss was hungry, but she hadn't suffered for it because

she'd just realized that her stomach was empty. "I'll be all right, provided the dining room is still open," she said.

Maggie laughed. "I wouldn't have had the nerve to come here if I hadn't checked first and found out that it was," she admitted. "How is your friend, Mrs. Ryan? Have you looked in on her?"

Bliss felt a degree of shame. She'd been so involved in her letter to Jamie that for hours she hadn't even thought of Peony, except to record an account of her swoon at the foot of the wharf. "I'll go and see how she is right now," she muttered, starting through the doorway.

Maggie stopped her with a gentle hold on her arm. "Bliss, who is that woman and what does she have to do with Jamie?" she asked. "Reeve wouldn't tell me a thing, so I'm counting on you."

Bliss wasn't sure how to answer, and her face must have reflected this, for Maggie quickly spoke again.

"We'll talk about it at supper," she promised. "Reeve's sound asleep, so he won't be there to order me to mind my own business. And something tells me that your friend will want to eat in her room."

Bliss smiled, even though she was exhausted and so lonesome for Jamie that she was likely to die of it. She closed her door and went across the hall to knock at Peony's.

"Yes?" a voice called sleepily.

Bliss tried the door and found it unlocked. She went inside, approaching Peony's bed. "How are you?" she asked softly.

"I just want to sleep," Peony replied in rummy tones.

Bliss nodded and left the room to join Maggie in the hall, and then the two of them went downstairs to enter the dining room and place their orders. Both asked for venison pie, which was delivered promptly, and they ate with hearty appetites.

"Reeve tells me that you have two children," Bliss ventured, wanting to put off talking about Peony's relationship with Jamie for as long as she could.

Maggie nodded. "Elisabeth—but of course you know that she's not really ours—and James. We named him for your husband, of course, but we call him J.J. to avoid confusion."

Bliss's tired mind had snagged on Maggie's odd remark about the little girl. "What did you mean when you said that Elisabeth isn't really yours? Is she adopted?"

Maggie's lovely skin blanched a little beneath her light suntan and the glow that a man's loving leaves behind it. "Adopted?" she echoed.

Bliss felt uneasy, as though she were expected to play a game without knowing all the rules. "I guess if Jamie were here," she said, "he'd tell me that I'm sticking my nose in where it doesn't belong."

"If Jamie were here," Maggie muttered, "I'd wring his neck!"

"What?" Bliss asked, still uneasy and puzzled as well.

"Never mind," Maggie answered with grim resolution. "Tell me about Mrs. Peony Ryan."

Bliss dropped her eyes. "Both of them deny it—and I've got to admit that they're pretty convincing," she confided in a small voice, "but I can't help thinking she's Jamie's mistress."

"Thunderation!" cried Maggie, with such spirit that several of the other diners turned to stare. "You can't be serious! Does Reeve know this?"

Bliss swallowed, a little awed by Maggie's fury. Of course, one looked for brashness and a temper in a Yank. "I would imagine he knows," she said. "He and Jamie spent hours talking—mostly in private."

Maggie shoved back her chair and shot to her feet. "Great Zeus!" she exclaimed. "I'll murder that Irishman with my own hands if he's been a party to something like that!"

Heat climbed Bliss's face and her eyes went so wide that they hurt. She couldn't speak for the life of her.

"And wait until I see Jamie McKenna again!" Maggie fumed on. Then, without warning, she stormed out of the dining room, leaving Bliss to endure the resultant attention alone.

She smiled at the men and women who were staring at her in stupefaction. "It's just that she's an American," she said bravely, and everyone went back to eating their dinner.

It took more than an embarrassing scene to ruin Bliss's appetite. She finished her venison pie, and when Maggie didn't return after a reasonable time, she ate her sister-in-law's portion as well. It seemed probable that she'd need to keep her strength up if she was going to be a part of this McKenna mob.

Chapter 23

THE CHILD WAS BEAUTIFUL, WITH LONG, DARK HAIR AND AQUAMA-
rine eyes that should have marked her as Reeve's. As Bliss
watched the little girl scamper happily after a dog in the
garden at Seven Sisters, she felt an odd uneasiness that had
been plaguing her intermittently since her arrival two weeks
before.

"She's lovely, isn't she?" she asked as Reeve sat down
beside her on the stone bench facing the place where
Elisabeth played.

Her dark-haired, handsome brother-in-law nodded. His
coloring was very different from Jamie's, and yet there was a
distinct resemblance between the two men, something of the
soul rather than the body. "I think so," he said, and his
voice sounded hoarse.

"I'd swear she was really a McKenna, with that
coloring."

Reeve gave a sigh that seemed weary to Bliss. "Aye," he
said. "The lass is the image of Callie McKenna, God rest her
soul."

Bliss turned to look at her brother-in-law, trying to read
his expression. A sensation of leaping anxiety played in the

pit of her stomach when she realized that he regretted what he'd just said.

"Your mother?" she pressed.

Reeve would not look at her, and it was then that the awful truth dawned on Bliss.

"Elisabeth is Jamie's," she whispered, and it was not the fact of Elisabeth's birth that caused her nearly unbearable pain. It was Jamie's failure to tell her.

"Bliss—"

She shot to her feet, unable to endure all that she was feeling. Tears scalded in her eyes, blinding her. "Who was she? Who was Elisabeth's mother?"

Reeve was silent for a moment. Then, reaching out to take one of Bliss's hands in his, he answered, "'Tis not my place to be explaining, little one. The words have to come from Jamie."

Bliss whirled and cried out, in her sudden and fiery anguish, "You've got to tell me, Reeve, because I can't stand not knowing! I can't bear to wait until I see Jamie again!" Through her tears, she could see that he believed her.

He rose slowly to his feet, resting his big hands on her shoulders in an awkward effort to lend comfort. "Do you see the position you're putting me in, Bliss? To talk of that is to betray a promise I made to my only brother—"

"*I* didn't make any promises to your dratted brother," an angry female voice put in, and both Reeve and Bliss turned to see Maggie standing nearby with her arms folded.

Reeve approached his wife in a way that would have daunted most women, waggling one index finger. "You stay out of this, Yank," he warned in a tone made all the more dire by its low, even pitch.

Maggie stood firm, her chin out. "Bliss has a right to know about Jamie's past," she said.

"Well, she doesn't 'ave to 'ear it from you!" Reeve roared, slipping ominously into the brogue. Bliss had already discerned that he spoke in the Irish only in Jamie's company or when his control over his emotions was threatened.

Maggie retreated a step in the face of his anger, but her gray eyes were still snapping with furious conviction. "Stop trying to intimidate me, Reeve McKenna! It isn't going to work!"

"Isn't it?" Reeve breathed, backing Maggie so far into a rosebush that thorns caught on her skirts.

"Absolutely not!" she cried intrepidly, trying to free herself from the bush. "You tell her about Eleanor, or I will!"

There was a thundering silence, and then another voice startled them all.

"That won't be necessary," said Jamie. "I can speak for meself."

Bliss spun around, unable to believe her ears, but Jamie was standing there, looking weary and reluctant. A day, a week, an hour before, she would have hurled herself into his arms; now, she stood gazing at him, crushed that he hadn't trusted her enough to share something so important as the existence of his child.

"Aye," Reeve agreed as his wife tore her skirts from the rosebush and glared at Jamie.

"Welcome back!" Maggie snapped, and her words were so utterly at variance with her tone that Jamie chuckled.

Reeve was not amused, however. He grasped Maggie by one elbow and propelled her toward the house. Elisabeth and her dog continued to play in the near distance, undisturbed, and Jamie watched the child with such an injured expression in his eyes that Bliss nearly forgave him his deception.

Nearly, but not quite.

"I planned to tell you, Duchess," he said after long moments had passed.

"When?" Bliss demanded, dashing at her tears with the back of one hand. "After our children were born?"

His jawline tightened at the challenge in her tone. "I never intended for us to 'ave children, Bliss," he countered coldly.

"I married you to keep from bein' shot, in case you've forgotten."

The words affected Bliss like a slap across the face. Oh, she'd never forgotten the circumstances of their wedding, not for a moment, but she had believed that Jamie had grown to love her just as she loved him.

He'd told her so.

The starch went out of her knees and she sank to the bench in horror as the realization struck her. Each time Jamie had said "I love you," he'd been in the throes of passion. Had he ever truly meant the words?

He took a step nearer, and the edge was gone from his voice. "Bliss, listen to me," he began, sitting down beside her on the bench and reaching for her hand.

She promptly wrenched it away.

Before Jamie could say anything more, Elisabeth caught sight of him and came running over to fling her arms around his neck. "Hello, Uncle Papa!" she crowed.

Jamie said something to the little girl that Bliss couldn't make out, for she was suddenly overcome with pain. It was like a haze within and around her, pervading her very spirit, inescapable, torturous.

She bounded to her feet and ran toward the house, fleeing from her anguish, fleeing from her confusion.

Fleeing from Jamie.

After a short and innocuous conversation with Elisabeth, Jamie gave the child the trinkets he'd brought for her and entered Reeve's house through the French doors opening onto the garden.

His brother was alone in the parlor, standing beside a teakwood liquor cabinet and pouring a drink for himself. Maggie's touch was everywhere, giving the room a fragrant, bright spaciousness.

"I could use one of those," Jamie said, nodding toward the drink in his brother's hand.

309

Reeve glared at him. "Fix your own," he replied.

Fine welcome he was getting around here, Jamie thought, but he suppressed his annoyance. After all, he wasn't entirely without fault in this situation. He should have told Bliss about Eleanor and the child she'd borne him long before now, he wasn't denying that. He poured a generous portion of brandy into a glass. "If you've got somethin' you want to say, brother," he began quietly, "say it."

"She's a fine lass," Reeve reflected, and Jamie knew his brother was speaking of Bliss. "The kind of wife any man would be glad to 'ave, Jamie."

"Aye," Jamie agreed wearily, after a sip of his brandy. It should have steadied him, but it didn't. "The Duchess is the best thing that's ever 'appened to me, Reeve. You must know that."

Reeve turned, his blue-green eyes fierce as an Irish sea in winter. "Why do you treat 'er the way you do, then—like there were a dozen more where she came from, to be 'ad for a ha'penny?"

Jamie tossed back the rest of his drink and set the glass down hard on a highly polished table. "So you know, do you, 'ow I treat me wife?" he demanded in a scathing undertone, all the old anger he felt toward Reeve welling up within him.

"Damn your eyes, Jamie," Reeve growled, gesturing toward the French doors, "she came through 'ere not ten minutes ago, lookin' as though the soul 'ad been torn out of 'er! What the devil did you say—or do?"

It was all Jamie could do to retain his composure. He retrieved his glass and went back to the liquor cabinet, keeping his back to Reeve as he poured another double shot of brandy. "You know," he said evenly, "if I 'ad any sense at all, I'd just ride out of 'ere and forget I ever 'ad a wife—or a brother."

Reeve was light on his feet for a big man. Jamie hadn't heard him approach, and he was stung to fury when a fist caught him by the shoulder and wrenched him around. He knocked Reeve's hand away and whiskey flew, leaving a plume-shaped amber stain on Maggie's white settee.

"I'll throw your own words back at you, little brother," Reeve breathed, taking a hold on the front of Jamie's shirt. "If you 'ave somethin' to say, say it!"

Adrenaline surged through Jamie's body. The last time he'd fought Reeve, nearly three years before, in Brisbane, he'd lost. That wouldn't happen again. "Take your 'ands off me, Reeve," he said.

Reeve's grasp on his shirt relaxed, was relinquished. "You can say anything you want to me, lad," he warned, looking as ferocious as ever, "but you won't mistreat that little bride of yours. Not under this roof."

Jamie felt a muscle twitch in his cheek; he stilled it by sheer force of will. "You'll not be tellin' me 'ow to do anything," he spat. One part of him craved to make peace with Reeve; another, a terrified boy with his hands tied to an acacia tree and his back bared to a madman's whip, wanted to rage at the brother who hadn't been there when he needed him. "Did I ever tell you 'ow Bliss and I came to be married?" he went on when Reeve was silent.

"Aye," Reeve answered with weary irony in his tone. "You were forced into it, if I remember correctly. Well, I'm tired of 'earin' it, Jamie boy. You 'ad your blade, didn't you? Since when is one old man, with or without a gun, enough to force the likes of you into anything?"

Jamie hadn't been prepared for that question; he couldn't think of a response.

Reeve arched one dark eyebrow in affable triumph. "That's what I thought," he said, as though Jamie had answered him. "You didn't fight because you wanted to bed the lass, and despite your sticky fingers, mate, you were too honorable to do that without marryin' 'er first!"

Jamie felt as though scalding hot water had been flung all over him, so keen was his rage at being taunted with his past. He stepped back and unfastened the scabbard from his belt, setting that and the blade aside. "Per'aps," he said through

311

his teeth, "Maggie's parlor wouldn't be the best place for this to be settled."

Reeve nodded, unbuttoned his shirtsleeves, and rolled them up, one after the other, as he led the way out through the garden doors. Since Elisabeth was no longer playing in the side yard, he stopped there, turning to face his brother squarely.

And God in heaven, Jamie reflected, the bastard was bigger than he'd ever realized.

Reeve smiled, as though reading Jamie's thoughts. "Aye, lad, I'm still your big brother," he said smugly. "Like I was in Brisbane three years ago, and in Dublin before that."

Jamie seethed at the reminder. No man, besides Reeve, had ever bested him in a one-on-one fight. "Aye, in Dublin. That would be when I was a pickpocket," he responded, putting an emphasis on the last word.

Reeve spread his hands, damnably confident of his ability to defend himself. "That would be the time I meant, all right," he answered. "I guess I shouldn't 'ave expected a petty thief to treat 'is wife properly."

Jamie swallowed a bellow of rage. Reeve would be pleased if he lost his head; it would give him an advantage. He clenched his jaw tight and stood his ground.

Reeve gestured with both hands. "Come on, lad," he taunted. "You're the man every bleeder in New Zealand is afraid of. Show me why." He paused, drawing a deep breath and letting it out again. "Just remember, though, that this is Australia. 'Ere, you're just Reeve McKenna's baby brother."

A shimmering red fog moved in front of Jamie's eyes. "You bastard," he breathed, and with those words the fury he'd held inside him escaped in a torrent. He lunged at Reeve, with all the power that love turned to hatred can unleash.

Reeve hardly responded to the blow Jamie landed in his stomach. He gave a breathless, chortling laugh and returned the punch.

Jamie's rage was fathomless. "Where—were you?" he

demanded as they struggled, too equally matched for the fight to fall easily to one or the other. "Where the—hell were you—when that bastard was laying open me back!"

Reeve was caught off guard, but only for a moment. In a move as swift and unpredictable as a bolt of lightning, he caught Jamie in a neck hold that cut off his breath. "What the devil are you talkin' about?" he wanted to know.

Jamie broke the hold and whirled to face his dumbfounded brother, breathing so hard that he couldn't speak.

Reeve was a bit winded himself. "All that anger inside you—good God—you've got your dander up because you needed me—and I wasn't there!"

Never, never could Jamie have acknowledged the moisture in his eyes, though it burned like hell and made it next to impossible to see for a moment. "Needed you?" he rasped. "I screamed your name in me sleep, big brother!"

Now Reeve's voice was quiet and gentle. Hoarse. "Jamie, I looked for you for twenty years—here, and in New Zealand—"

Reeve had said all this before, but not until now had Jamie really heard what his brother was telling him. He had to have time, to think, to pull himself back together.

He turned and walked away and Reeve made no effort to stop him.

Jamie had stood for some time alone in a copse of gum trees, trying to come to terms with all the things he was feeling, when he heard light footsteps approaching. Hoping for Bliss, he was disappointed to see Peony.

"Go and talk to Bliss," his friend pleaded softly. "She's in pieces, Jamie. I don't need to tell you how impetuous she is—God only knows what she might do."

Jamie felt as though he'd taken his own blade through his middle, and his eyes got damp again, so he looked away. "Run away to America, probably," he said hoarsely.

Peony stood close to him, laying one light, gentle hand on his arm. "Could you live with that?"

He shook his head, keeping his eyes averted.

His friend let her head rest against the rounding of his shoulder. "I thought not. That leaves you with only one choice. You know that, don't you?"

"Aye," Jamie managed to answer. "I know."

Peony stood on tiptoe to kiss his cheek. "I'm going back to Auckland, Jamie," she announced quietly. "I've got a shipping agency to run."

"But Increase—"

She silenced him by laying her fingers to his lips. "Increase is here in Australia, and I'll be in New Zealand. Just look after your wife, Jamie—the only way that old viper could bring you to your knees would be through Bliss, and he knows that."

Jamie nodded. He never forgot, waking or sleeping, that Bliss was in the worst kind of danger. "It's not far from 'ere," he said in a haunted voice, "that place of 'is—"

"Don't torture yourself, Jamie," Peony interrupted. "That time is over."

He shook his head. "No. It won't be over, for me or for Bliss, until Increase Pipher is dead."

Peony closed her emerald eyes for a moment, and when she opened them again, they were glistening with tears. "Be very careful, Jamie. You're still regarded as a criminal here in Australia, while Increase is a rich planter. If you search him out and kill him, chances are you'll hang for it."

There had been times in Jamie's life when he'd expected to hang, when he'd have welcomed it, but things were different now. Life, once so cheap to him, had become precious because of Bliss. "I'll be careful."

She walked away, and Jamie followed her with his eyes. He'd make sure she was escorted safely on board a ship in Brisbane, of course.

Against his will, he lifted his gaze to Reeve's impressive house. He could feel the brass medallion beneath his shirt, burning into his flesh.

They'd come a long way, he and Reeve, since that day in Dublin when their mother lay dying. Jamie sighed. He'd been a thief, but he'd never begged. By God, he'd never held out that beggar's badge and asked another man for food to fill his belly.

And neither had Reeve.

Jamie drew a deep breath and started back toward the house. He'd apologize to Bliss first, and explain about Eleanor and Elisabeth as best he could, and then he would set things right with his brother.

Bliss stood staring out her bedroom window, watching Jamie stride toward the house from the stand of gum trees at the far end of the lawn. Only a few minutes before, she'd seen Peony making her way back from that same place.

She turned on her heel, one thumbnail caught between her teeth. She didn't understand why she was so surprised, and so wounded, when she'd known what kind of man Jamie was almost from the first.

She dragged one of her trunks out of a closet and was taking folded garments from the bureau and dropping them inside when the door opened and Maggie stepped in.

With a sigh, Bliss's sister-in-law sat down on the edge of the bed and said, "Planning to run away again, are you?"

Bliss turned to glare at her. "There are times when it's sensible to—to chart a new course for your life."

Maggie nodded. "Yes, but you're not doing that. At least listen to what Jamie has to say—"

"So now you're on his side?" Bliss demanded. "Not an hour ago, Maggie McKenna, you were furious with him!"

Maggie lowered her eyes. "Reeve was right. I should have minded my own business. I got upset because I like you so much, Bliss, and I knew you were hurt, and how I would feel if Reeve kept something like that from me—"

Bliss sniffled. She'd done all the crying she was going to do over Jamie McKenna, and all the forgiving as well. And that was that. She should have followed her first instinct and gone to America.

Her mother had found a new life there. She could have done that, too. Resolutely, she went back to her packing.

Maggie crossed the room and took drawers and camisoles and petticoats out of the trunk as fast as Bliss could put them in. In total frustration, Bliss put her hands on her hips and cried, "Hellfire and spit, Maggie, will you stop that!"

Maggie laughed. "No," she answered just as there was a rap at the door. "Come in, Jamie," she called, with a smug little smile.

Bliss dived into the armoire and closed the doors. She wasn't going to deal with one more cussed McKenna even if she had to hide there all night.

After a moment or so, she heard the outer door close and dared to hope that both Maggie and Jamie had given up and gone away. Cautiously, Bliss peered out of the armoire, only to see Jamie sitting on the bed, watching her.

"If you're goin' to act like a child, Duchess," he said, "I'll 'ave to treat you like one."

Bliss was admitting nothing, but she did climb down and go back to her packing.

"Eleanor and I used to steal together," Jamie said, just as if Bliss had invited him to unburden his soul. "I thought I loved her, though I realize now that I didn't even know what love was then. You taught me that, Duchess."

Bliss was unable to keep herself from turning and looking at Jamie, but if he thought she was going to forgive him, he could think again. She was through. She was leaving. . . .

"What happened?" she couldn't resist asking.

There were sad memories in Jamie's eyes. "Eleanor liked fights, especially if they were over 'er favors. It gave 'er a sense of power, I guess, to convince me that some poor bastard 'ad forced 'imself on 'er and then watch me kick in 'is rib cage. One night, I came 'ome early and caught the wrong part of the show—Eleanor and one of 'er beaus were 'avin a grand time in our bed."

Bliss lowered her eyes, hurting for Jamie but unwilling to

let him see that. "You were married to her, then?" she dared to ask.

"No," Jamie answered. "Eleanor never demanded that of me, and I never offered."

Bliss swallowed. "She didn't have a father to force you?" she asked, hoping that the words sounded flippant.

Jamie gave a raspy chuckle. "No, Duchess, she didn't." His face was solemn again in an instant. "What she did 'ave was me child, growin' within 'er, though I didn't know that until after Reeve and I met up again."

Wearily, Bliss went and sat down beside her husband on the bed. "Why didn't you tell me, Jamie? I would have understood."

He ran a hand through his hair. "I was afraid," he admitted.

Bliss knew the cost of those three simple words to Jamie's pride, and she felt an aching warmth in her heart. She couldn't speak, she was so moved.

Jamie got up and crossed the room, and for a moment Bliss thought he was going to leave her. Instead, he opened the door and the two little black girls who helped the housekeeper tumbled through the opening, giggling.

Bliss, familiar with the children by now, smiled and shook her head. "You know Goodness and Mercy, I assume?"

Jamie grinned, but he looked so tired that Bliss's heart twisted. "Aye. Like you, Duchess, they've been grossly misnamed." He frowned at the girls and added, "Tell Kala I want hot water and a bathtub!"

They scampered off in a gale of childish laughter to do as they were bidden.

"What do you suppose they hoped to hear?" Bliss speculated.

Jamie only gave her a wry look in response, then he sat down on the side of the bed and pulled off one of his boots with such a show of effort that Bliss volunteered to remove the other.

317

"Does this mean I'm forgiven?" he asked with an exaggerated yawn.

Bliss nodded, but her thoughts had already taken one of their quicksilver turns, and her expression was serious. "Jamie, did Peony tell you that—that Increase Pipher was on our ship when we came over from New Zealand?"

He looked at her incredulously. "What?"

Bliss nodded. "Do you remember Walter Davis? From—from the hotel in Auckland?"

"Aye," he replied in an ominously low voice. "I remember, Duchess."

Bliss dropped her eyes again. "Mr. Pipher was pretending to be his grandfather. They were staying in the suite across the hall from ours."

Jamie was so still that Bliss had to relent and look at him. "I knew Pipher was at the Victoria when we were—it makes sense, lookin' back. 'E'd enjoy that kind of irony."

"You're going to k-kill him, aren't you?" The question had been tormenting Bliss ever since Jamie had sent her away on the train that day.

"Yes," he answered without hesitation. "Now, come 'ere, wife. You 'aven't given me so much as a kiss yet."

Bliss stumbled toward him, let him pull her down on the bed, and trembled with anticipation and fear as he stretched out beside her—anticipation because she wanted him, needed him, so desperately, fear because she was beginning to have a glimmer of the risks Jamie would be running.

He left her long enough to lock the door and unbuttoned his shirt as he approached the bed again. When he was lying beside her once more, he drew her into a kiss that set her soul to spinning within her, one hand unfastening the buttons of her blouse at the same time.

Bliss gave a little crooning moan as he bared one of her breasts and took hungry suckle at the nipple; she'd ached for Jamie during their weeks apart, and to give herself to him was the purest joy.

Still, as the sweet, heated ritual began, Bliss could no

more contain her questions than her responses to Jamie's lovemaking.

"Are—are you a free man here in Australia?" she whispered in delicious misery as he moved from one breast to the other.

"No," he answered, before teasing the nipple thoroughly with his tongue. "I'm wanted."

Bliss whimpered, her hands entangled in Jamie's hair. She wanted to push him away, but she couldn't. "Oh God, Jamie—they could—arrest you?"

He seemed completely unconcerned by the possibility as he bared her stomach and began kissing his way down over it. "Aye, Duchess, I suppose they could—"

Bliss was writhing on the bed in an anguish of desire and despair. By the time Jamie had smoothed away the last of her clothes and attended to all the sensitive places that he alone had charted, there was no room in her mind for the past or the future.

All her thoughts were on the tender and tempestuous now.

Chapter 24 🦋

THERE WAS STILL ONE THING LEFT UNSETTLED, FOR ALL THE FOR-
giveness and the lovemaking, and Bliss flung the sponge into
Jamie's bathwater in fury when she remembered it. The
splash was horrific.

Jamie groaned. "What now?" he asked.

Bliss's color was high. "There's still that little matter of
what you said down in the garden, Jamie McKenna! 'I never
meant for us to have children, Bliss,' you told me. 'I married
you to keep from being shot, in case you've forgotten'!"

"God," Jamie breathed, "what a memory you 'ave, Duchess, and for all the wrong things, too. I didn't mean anything
by that and you know it."

"I know no such thing," Bliss retorted, kneeling there
beside the bathtub. "And don't start thinking you can just
make whatever nasty remark comes into your brain and
then smooth it all over by taking me to bed, Mr. McKenna!"

He was watching her lips as she talked with a half grin on
his face. "Oh, I won't think that, Duchess," he breathed,
and then, without giving Bliss any warning at all, he grabbed
her and hauled her into the tub with him, clothes and all.

She shrieked with rage and struggled hopelessly, subsiding only when he kissed her so soundly, so thoroughly, that her entire body went limp.

Jamie laughed, his voice low and husky, when he drew back from her and looked into her wide, bewildered eyes. "Ah, Duchess," he said, "I do love you. I do indeed."

The words were precious to Bliss, but so was her pride. Her dress was wet clear through, and there was such a thing as maintaining personal dignity, after all. "Let me go!" she ordered breathlessly.

"Never," Jamie answered, catching her lower lip gently, tantalizingly between his teeth. "Seems to me that it might be time to start that first red'eaded baby growin' inside you."

A tremor went through Bliss. "Jamie—"

He started kissing the sensitive hollow at the base of her neck and his hand moved beneath the water. "Ummm?"

"Damn you," Bliss gasped as he began causing her an exquisite pleasure. "Baby or no baby, I won't be had in a bathtub!"

Jamie laughed again and lightly bit her earlobe. "Won't you, Duchess?"

Increase Pipher traveled to Brisbane and appeared before the magistrate in person. "James McKenna is an escaped felon, Your Grace," he said, pushing an old handbill under the man's nose. "And he's being harbored illegally at Seven Sisters, his brother's plantation near—"

"I know where Seven Sisters is," the magistrate broke in, sounding impatient. He was studying the tattered paper with a frown puckering his brow. "This bloke is Reeve McKenna's brother, is he?" Without waiting for an answer, he sighed and added, "Old bit of business, this. Best forgotten, don't you think?"

Increase trembled, putting most of his weight on his walking stick, and young Walter Davis hurried forward to support him. "It was thanks to that young hellion that I lost the strength in my legs, Your Grace," Pipher bit out, barely able to keep his tone civil, "as well as a year's crop of sugarcane, my house—"

And the only woman I ever really wanted, he added in his mind. Something far down in the dark, twisted depths of his soul began to expand. The sensation was at once heady and painful.

"Very well." The magistrate sighed. "I'll order McKenna taken into custody for questioning." He shook a finger at Increase in warning. "Anything beyond that will require that you file formal charges, Mr. Pipher, and you will need witnesses for that. Proof."

Increase smiled broadly. "Thank you, Your Grace," he said with a cordial nod, and then he nudged young Davis in the ribs, a signal that he wished to vacate the magistrate's chambers with all haste.

In the street outside, he laughed outright and rubbed his hands together in anticipation. "At last," he said. "At last!"

Walter was frowning at him. "It's been so long, sir. Do you really think—"

Increase glared at the lad. He'd suffer no cowardice in his ranks, not when revenge was so close at hand. "Worried about that red-haired snippet, are you, Davis?" he demanded. "You shall have her for a plaything, once her wounds heal."

Davis blanched. "God in heaven, Mr. Pipher," he whispered. "Bliss has done nothing to hurt you or anyone else!"

Increase smiled. "She is a means to an end," he exulted, relishing the thought of what lay ahead, his right hand flexing and unflexing. "We'll see Jamie McKenna on his knees—on his belly, begging like the dockside whore's whelp he is—and all because of sweet Bliss!"

Davis was silent. He was a smart young man, was Walter, Increase reflected. Smart enough to know when he'd said enough.

* * *

Jamie was awake when Reeve's soft rap sounded at the door. He sat up carefully, not wanting to awaken Bliss, and got out of bed.

"Aye, Reeve," he called in a loud whisper, "I 'ear you." Swiftly, he pulled on his clothes and strapped the scabbard into place, then joined his brother in the hallway. "So they're comin', are they?"

Reeve's eyes were suspiciously bright in the light of the kerosene lamp he carried. "Does it 'ave to be this way, Jamie?" he asked, and the lilt of the distant land neither of them would ever see again was in his voice. "I'm a powerful man, if I do say so meself. I can get you out of this—"

Jamie shook his head, putting on his hat, and looked back through the open doorway toward the tangle of shadows where Bliss lay sleeping. "That would take too long, Reeve. I can't risk bein' be'ind bars when Increase makes 'is move."

Reeve nodded and gave his brother an affectionate slap on the shoulder. "I'd feel the same in your place."

"You'll look after the Duchess, then?"

"You know I will," Reeve replied as the sound of horses' hooves became audible in the distance. "Now, get out of 'ere, damn you!"

Jamie's throat had shut. He went back into the bedroom, to touch Bliss's tousled hair once more, and then he strode down the hall to the rear stairway.

At the top of the steps, he turned and, with a sad grin and a gesture of his hand, said good-bye to his brother.

Reeve's eyes glistened as he raised his own hand in response.

Someone was shaking Bliss hard. Mumbling, half in a dream and half out, she raised herself on one elbow and peered into the darkness.

"It's me, Maggie," whispered her sister-in-law, her outline just visible in the gloom.

Bliss yawned. "What—what is it?"

"There are soldiers here," Maggie said, "looking for Jamie."

Bliss was wide-awake. She reached toward his side of the bed and found him gone, and her heart twisted painfully within her. "Dear God, Maggie," she mourned. "If they catch him—"

"They won't," Maggie assured her readily.

Bliss wasn't comforted. Everybody knew that Yanks sometimes tended to be overly optimistic. "I want you to tell me that he's gone back to New Zealand—but you're not going to do that, are you?"

Maggie shook her head. "He told Reeve that he's got business here in Australia."

Bliss shuddered, knowing all too well what that business was. The guilt she felt was almost beyond bearing; if it hadn't been for her, things wouldn't have come to this. Jamie had to run and hide and live like a bushranger because of her.

She was a liability to him. A hindrance.

"The soldiers want to question you," Maggie went on, keeping her voice low. "Reeve will be with you, and so will I, so don't be afraid."

Bliss wasn't afraid for herself, but she was terrified for Jamie. He was rushing headlong into a situation that could so easily destroy him. "What am I supposed to say?" she asked, wriggling out of her bed and hurrying to the armoire for a dress.

Maggie was right on her heels. "Reeve wants you to tell the soldiers that you and Jamie had a dreadful row and you're sure he's not coming back. If you can shed a few tears, that will probably help."

Bliss sighed as she scrambled into a cambric dress. Crying would be no trick at all, not with Jamie out there in the darkness somewhere. "Maggie, this is all my fault!" she fretted.

"Nonsense!" Maggie responded with typical spirit. "Jamie's own thievery is the cause of this, far behind him though it is, and don't forget that, Bliss McKenna."

Downstairs in the parlor, Reeve was chatting amicably with half a dozen men in uniforms. At Bliss's appearance, he gave her a smile sympathetic to the point of pity and held out one hand. "Here she is now, gentlemen," he said smoothly. "My poor sister-in-law."

Bliss felt color surge into her face. She was not used to having people feel sorry for her; it nettled her pride. Only Maggie's subtle nudge from behind kept her from protesting. Biting her lip, she lowered her head to hide her expression.

Maggie slid an arm around her shou..ders and smiled at a tall man with an officer's insignia on his coat. "Our Bliss," she said with a fond sigh, "has had a most devastating week, Captain. And of course, it is the middle of the night—"

"I'm aware of that, Mrs. McKenna," the fellow responded. "I wonder if I could speak to your sister-in-law alone?"

Out of the corner of her eye, Bliss saw Reeve shake his head, and she was infinitely grateful. She gave a loud, wailing sob that wasn't entirely feigned and clasped one hand over her face. "Oh, Jamie," she called, "why did you leave me?"

"Don't overact," Maggie warned in a sharp undertone as she hustled Bliss toward a distant settee. She seated her solicitously and even patted her on the head. "There, there, dear," she said.

Bliss sobbed again, but more moderately this time, and the captain, she saw through her splayed fingers, looked chagrined as he strode over and sat down beside her.

"I'll try to make this as painless as possible, Mrs. McKenna," he said gently. "Tell me, when did you last see your husband?"

Bliss took a wild guess as to what she was supposed to say. "Today," she began. Then, at Reeve's glower, she retracted that with, "No, it was yesterday."

Reeve's nod was nearly imperceptible.

Bliss sniffled and accepted the handkerchief Maggie thrust at her, using it to hide behind. "He told me that our marriage had been a mistake," she squalled. "There's no room in his life for me or for our baby!"

Reeve's lips twitched slightly, and there was a light in his blue-green eyes.

"Then he is most definitely a fool and a rounder," sympathized the captain, going so far as to touch Bliss's hand. "You're better off without him, my dear lady."

Bliss gave a cry that would have done a banshee proud and buried her face in Maggie's hanky.

"You can see how upset my sister-in-law is," protested Reeve's wife, patting Bliss's shoulder with tender industry. "I do think you could let us all return to our beds, Captain."

The officer sighed and then spread his hands. "We shouldn't have disturbed you," he apologized. "It was our hope that we might be able to have a talk with Mr. McKenna—we only wanted to question him, you understand."

"After you'd shackled him, of course," Reeve put in dryly, lifting a glass of whiskey to his mouth.

The captain looked annoyed. "Good night," he said in clipped tones, striding toward the doors opening onto the entry hall, his troops following wearily behind him.

When Bliss was upstairs again, she did not undress and crawl back into bed, but sat in the window seat, staring out at the night. She examined the situation from every angle, and there was no escaping it. There was one person in all the world who could save Jamie, and she was that person.

She went to the door of her room and looked in one direction and then the other, squinting. There was no one up and about.

Cautiously, she began creeping toward the stairs. She went down one, down another. And came nose to chest with a human wall.

Looking up, Bliss made out Reeve's square jaw and caught a glint of moonlight in ebony hair.

"And to think I didn't believe Jamie when he warned me you might try this," he said, striking a match and lighting the lantern he carried in one hand.

Bliss swallowed hard. "I was only planning to get something to eat," she said.

Reeve shook his head in mock amazement. "He said you'd lie as well," he marveled. Then his eyes narrowed and he leaned a little closer to Bliss. "Listen to me, love. Jamie probably wouldn't lay a hand on you, being your husband and all, but I regard myself as your brother, and I've got no qualms at all about turning you across my knee and paddling you just as I would Elisabeth, should the situation warrant it. Is that clear?"

Bliss climbed a step higher on the stairs, trying to decide whether or not Reeve was bluffing. She was certain that he was, but taking the chance seemed highly inadvisable, and anyway, he was as impassable as a mountain.

For the moment.

Meekly, Bliss turned and went back to her room, where she lay tossing and turning all the rest of the night.

If only Jamie hadn't left without her. She almost hated him for doing that, she thought, drying her eyes on a corner of the sheet. Almost.

In the morning, Peony prepared to depart for Brisbane with Reeve and Maggie's neighbor, Duncan Kirk, and a half dozen of his men for an escort.

She called Bliss to her in the parlor, and said, "I can't leave with you thinking that Jamie and I have ever been anything more than friends."

Bliss lowered her eyes. She'd been giving the matter a lot of thought of late. "I'm sorry for the way I acted, Peony. I guess I just love Jamie so much that I can't imagine another woman not wanting him, too."

Peony smiled. "Take care of him, Bliss. There's never been another man like Jamie, and there never will be."

327

Bliss nodded, her throat thick, and the two women embraced.

Everyone watched Bliss when she came forward to say another good-bye an hour later, as though they expected her to bolt and run. Of course, it wouldn't have taken any genius to guess that she was waiting and watching for her chance.

The rest of the morning passed before the opportunity arose. For once, there was no one watching her except Elisabeth, who was sitting quietly on the floor of the parlor, sketching.

"That's a 'roo," she said proudly, holding up a drawing Bliss would have been glad to claim as her own.

Bliss gave the kangaroo only a cursory glance, since she was occupied in checking names off a mental list. Reeve, in the stables, where a valuable mare was foaling. Maggie, that turncoat, upstairs feeding the baby. Kala, the housekeeper, down the path, in the cookhouse. . . .

Bliss rose cautiously to her feet. Elisabeth's aquamarine gaze shifted to her face in an instant, suspicious and accusing.

"You'd better not go anywhere," the child warned with the authority of one who had had disciplinary dealings with Reeve McKenna before. "It's bad to run away. There are snakes in the 'cane and bushrangers on the roads."

Bliss smiled and patted Elisabeth's head. "Thank you for those reassuring words," she said, knowing that such a chance wouldn't come again. "Sweetheart, you love your Uncle Papa, don't you?"

Elisabeth nodded, a smile lighting her beautiful little face.

Bliss crouched, lowering her voice to a conspiratorial, child-to-child tone. "I love him, too. And I think he's in terrible trouble. Elisabeth, I've got to go and help him, before it's too late."

Elisabeth McKenna might still be young, but she was nobody's fool. She shook her head. "You're supposed to stay here," she said flatly. "No matter what."

Bliss sighed. To think that she had come to such a pass as

to be held prisoner by a child. "I'll just go upstairs and get a book to read, then," she ventured when Elisabeth was thoroughly absorbed in her sketching again.

"All right," the little girl replied, so sweetly that Bliss felt guilty for planning what she did.

Moving at a sedate pace, she proceeded out of the parlor and into the entryway. When Elisabeth didn't sound the alarm, she crept to the front door and turned the knob. It made no sound, but the hinges creaked when Bliss flung herself headlong into freedom.

Holding her skirts high, she dashed down the long road leading between two rows of banana trees, her heart hammering against her rib cage. Behind her, she could hear Elisabeth shouting for her papa.

Bliss ran blindly on. Only as she was nearing the main road did it occur to her that she might be better off hiding from whoever was in pursuit. Hurtling down the driveway in her sunshine-yellow dress, she was easy prey.

She leaped into the tall grass, praying none of the snakes Elisabeth had mentioned would greet her, and ducked, gathering her skirts around her as closely as she could. She hardly dared breathe, hearing Reeve's footsteps on the road as she did, along with his curses.

Finally, he paused, so close that Bliss might have reached out and touched the toe of his boot. "All right, Bliss," he said, "I'll give you your way. Come out, and we'll go looking for Jamie together."

Bliss buried her face in her knees. She wanted to trust Reeve, but she didn't. She hadn't known him long enough, or well enough.

It was a rustling sound in the grass that betrayed her. A milk snake passed by her right hip, going on its merry way, and she uttered a shriek of complete terror.

Reeve reached down and caught her by the upper arm, causing her no pain but not exactly holding her gently, and hauled her up onto the road. "Do I 'ave to lock you up in the attic?" he demanded furiously.

329

Bliss stared at him. Now she was going to find out whether he'd been bluffing that night on the stairs or not, and she had an awful feeling that she'd pegged Reeve McKenna wrong. Tears of fear and frustration sprouted in her eyes. "You promised that we'd go and find Jamie together!" she cried.

Reeve surprised her by drawing her into his arms and holding her. "It's all right, Bliss. I'm scared, too. Scared as hell."

Bliss rested her forehead against his strong shoulder and sobbed, and Reeve let her cry until the worst had passed, then led her back toward the house, his arm around her shoulders.

"When are we leaving?" she demanded when they reached the porch steps.

"Don't press your luck," Reeve countered, but there was something distracted about his manner. He was watching the horizon, listening for something, and Bliss watched and listened, too.

Almost a minute had passed before she caught the sound of horses' hooves on hard ground. She braced herself for more official questions from the captain who had come to call once before.

Instead, Mr. Kirk and three of his men came down the driveway at breakneck speed. Reeve went to meet them, grasping the reins of his neighbor's mount and biting out, "Good God, Duncan, what happened?"

Duncan Kirk, a handsome man with a noticeable fondness for Maggie, was doubled over in the saddle. "They took her," he said, and then he slumped to one side, Reeve barely managing to catch him before he fell. The whole front of his shirt, Bliss saw now, was covered with blood.

"There were at least twenty of them!" one of the three men shouted.

Duncan managed to stay on his feet as Reeve helped him up the steps and into the house, but just barely.

"Maggie!" Reeve shouted.

Bliss's mind was reeling. "Who—what happened?"

Duncan ignored Bliss; his words were directed to Reeve. "I'm sorry—God, I'm sorry—they jumped us from out of nowhere—they took Mrs. Ryan." Kirk passed out just as Maggie dashed into the room. She and Reeve stretched him out on the floor and Reeve opened his shirt. He regained consciousness while they were examining the bullet wound that had torn his side. "Just—like old times—right, Maggie?" he choked out.

"Don't try to talk," Maggie said, concentrating on his wound. "I'll need alcohol, Reeve, and some sheets or something for bandages."

Reeve hurried away to fetch the requested items.

Bliss's eyes went wider, and her knees felt weak. She drew deep breaths in an effort not to faint, but the smell and the scent of blood seemed to be everywhere.

"God knows, I'm—no friend—of Jamie McKenna's," Duncan went on, despite Maggie's earlier words. "But— Reeve should know—"

Bliss drew nearer, holding her breath. There was no chance of her swooning now; the mention of Jamie's name had brought her around as effectively as smelling salts could have.

"The old man—said this would—explain." Duncan opened his hand, and what rested inside it made Bliss bound forward with an anguished cry. She snatched the blood-covered beggar's badge on its rawhide strip from his fingers.

With a scream of grief, she whirled and ran blindly outside, ignoring Maggie's cry of, "Bliss, come back!"

Duncan's terrified gelding nickered and danced in the road, its reins dangling along the ground. Forgetting that she knew little or nothing about riding a horse, Bliss managed to drag herself into the saddle and gather the reins into her hands.

Some instinct told her that she need only follow the road

to Brisbane. She wouldn't have to find Jamie's captors; they would find her.

Tears were streaming down Maggie's face as she knelt beside a half-delirious Duncan on the floor and stared up at her husband, who had just returned with the supplies she'd asked for. "They've got Jamie," she sobbed. "Oh dear God, Reeve, they've got Jamie! And Bliss has gone after him!"

Reeve swore, torn between Maggie and the brother he'd failed once before, however inadvertently. "Yank," he whispered brokenly, "can you 'andle things 'ere, if I go?"

Maggie nodded, after only the briefest hesitation. "God be with you, Reeve McKenna," she whispered. "And no matter what happens, don't you forget that I love you!"

Reeve bent to kiss her briefly, then, after collecting a rifle and scabbard from a locked cabinet in his study, ran out of the house and around toward the stables. He'd have given nearly anything he had for one of the racehorses he kept at Parramatta, but there was little point in making wishes. He saddled a buckskin gelding and set out after Bliss.

It was no real surprise that she'd vanished, even though she'd been only minutes ahead of him. That was the kind of day it was turning out to be.

Walter Davis came forward, wearing rough, bushman's clothes rather than those of a gentleman, when Bliss was brought into camp. "You little fool," he rasped, gazing up at her with misery in his eyes.

Bliss was weary and dirty and afraid, and she looked around the strange little compound with rounded eyes. There was no sign of Jamie, although she could see Peony lying on the ground, a stone's throw away, motionless.

Bliss dismounted, shunning Walter's offer of help, and raced toward Peony. It took only one look to realize that she was dead.

Her head spinning, Bliss battled back the sickness burning in her throat. It was then that she heard the cry, like the keening of a furious, tortured animal. Lifting her eyes, she saw Jamie, bound to a tree, with his hands behind him, his face so bloody that his features were barely recognizable.

"Oh God, Bliss," he choked out, "not you, not 'ere—"

She ran to Jamie before any of them could stop her, and put her arms around him, resting her head against his shoulder. His medallion was still clutched tight in her fingers. "I love you," she said softly.

Jamie's whisper was a grating sob. An anguished prayer. "Sweet Jesus, no—no—"

Bliss lifted her hands to his bloody face, her heart breaking within her. Hard, thin fingers curled around her arm and tore her away from Jamie. She was stunned that Increase, that tremulous old man, had such strength.

She soon saw that it was the hatred within him that gave him power, and the terrible, fathomless evil. He laughed with delight at Jamie's agony.

"I told you, didn't I, you filthy little mick? I warned you that you'd pay, and pay dearly, for what you and that whore did to me!"

Jamie strained at his bonds, almost insane in his rage and his frustration. Bliss knew that however Peony had died, he had been forced to look on, helpless, and with a shiver she realized that this was what was planned for her as well. A terrible death, with Jamie as a witness. For him, there could be no greater torture.

She lifted her chin, determined not to let either Increase or her husband know how frightened she really was.

"Let 'er go," Jamie bit out, twisting against the rawhide that held him. "It's me you want—not 'er!"

Increase smiled with pleasure. "Ah. And now the pleading begins," he said.

Chapter 25 🌿

BLISS WRENCHED HER ARM FREE OF INCREASE PIPHER'S GRASP AND hurried back to Jamie. She planted a gentle kiss on his lips and then carefully slipped the rawhide chain over his head, so that he once again wore the beggar's badge. The torment she saw in his eyes as he watched her made her regret every sharp, angry word she'd ever said to him.

It was as though Bliss were looking deep into Jamie McKenna's soul, seeing for the first time who and what he really was—the most honorable, the bravest of men. She swallowed a hard lump of shame to know that she'd brought him here, to this time and this place, and hot tears of regret burned in her eyes.

She was quick to force them back, to raise her chin. For Jamie's sake, and her own, she must be stronger and more courageous than she'd ever been before.

"I love you, Duchess," Jamie said brokenly. The bloody medallion resting against his torn, stained shirt was dull even in the late-afternoon sunshine.

Increase stepped between them, smiling that cadaverous smile of his, one thin hand resting against his chest. "Such sentiment," he taunted, his sunken eyes glowing as he looked at Jamie. "It's worthy of a sonnet, my boy. What exquisite agony it will be for you to watch your Juliet suffer."

Jamie didn't speak, and his gaze was level. His contempt for Increase was almost palpable.

His calm manner infuriated the old man. He hobbled over to Walter Davis, who was looking on with an unreadable expression on his face, and snatched the riding quirt the man held from his hand.

Bliss glanced at Jamie and saw a flicker of fear in his eyes as Increase stormed toward them. The expression changed to one of relief when the old man struck him with the whip instead of Bliss. The lash, striking Jamie's right cheek, turned his head but did nothing to dislodge the pride that held him upright as surely as the bonds held him to the tree.

For her part, Bliss would have preferred taking the blow herself. She cried out as though she had, and attacked Increase in hatred and fury, her fists and feet flying.

"Bliss, stop it!" Jamie bit out the order, and it was not one she dared defy. She stepped back, breathing hard, her hands clenched at her sides.

There was a terrible silence, and then Increase touched the tip of the quirt beneath Bliss's chin and hissed, "For that, little kitten, you will shed many tears of remorse."

Bliss thought of poor Peony, only now being carried away by a silent Walter, and of all Jamie had suffered. She spat in Increase's face.

He gave a strangled cry of rage that attracted the attention of the other men in the camp. Their expressions reflected a desultory sort of interest, along with a measure of amusement, but nothing else.

Bliss knew that none of them would come forward to defend her. These, after all, were the same men who had stood by and watched Peony die as a sacrifice to Increase Pipher's hatred.

She stood her ground as Increase advanced toward her with the quirt unraised.

"Don't," Jamie whispered.

Increase halted, turning his devil's smile on Jamie. "Do my ears deceive me, or did Jamie McKenna just ask for mercy?"

Jamie closed his eyes for a moment, opened them again. "Don't 'urt 'er," he said clearly. "Please."

Increase laughed, slapping the quirt against one scrawny leg. "Not good enough, Irishman. Not nearly good enough."

As far as Bliss was concerned, the most savage beating could not equal the torment of seeing Jamie, proud, strong Jamie, reduced to hopeless pleas. "Stop it," she screamed, flying at Increase once more and snatching the quirt from his hand. She went on with her senseless raging as she lashed Pipher, again and again, and it took Walter and another man to subdue her.

Increase was trembling visibly, long red welts rising across his face and neck where Bliss had struck him with the quirt. "Tie her to the wheel of that wagon," he grated out, gesturing behind him.

"No." The word left Jamie's throat with a scraping sound, husky and painful to hear.

Walter and the other man hesitated only an instant before obeying Increase's orders. They forced Bliss to her knees, wrenching her hands high and wide of her body before binding her wrists tightly to the rim of the wagon wheel. She looked back over one shoulder, her eyes shooting blue fire as she called out to her husband, "Don't you dare give in and crawl for these jellyfishes, Jamie McKenna! Don't you dare!"

"My God, Bliss," Walter whispered desperately near her ear. "Shut up! Can't you see that you're making things worse?"

Bliss's throat was parched, but she would not ask for water—or clemency. The other man had walked away, but Walter lingered, and Bliss knew then that he wanted to help but was far too frightened to try. Despair cooled her fiery temper.

"How could you, Walter?" she asked in a despondent whisper, her eyes closed, her cheek resting against a hard, splintery spoke of the wagon wheel. "How could you just stand there and watch Peony Ryan die, without lifting a finger to help?"

She heard Walter swallow. "Have you looked around you?" he countered after a moment's hesitation. "There are twenty men here!"

She bit her lower lip, gathering the courage to hear the answer to the question she was about to ask. "Was it—bad?"

"Yes," Walter answered, and Bliss heard all the brokenness and pain of mortal man echoing in that one word. "Yes, it was bad."

"And J-Jamie?"

"He didn't break, Bliss," Walter marveled. "He was like a man made of stone. But you could feel the hatred coming out of him like heat from a fire." He paused, tensing, and then whispered an oath.

Bliss turned her head to see for herself what was coming and then wished she hadn't. Increase was approaching, carrying a blade as formidable as Jamie's in one hand.

Muttering to himself all the while, he crouched and rent the back of Bliss's bright yellow dress, as well as the camisole beneath, with the point of the knife. She trembled slightly as she felt a warm spring breeze touch her bare skin.

Visions loomed in her mind; she saw the ugly whip, wrapped as a wedding present and delivered to the suite she and Jamie had shared at the Victoria Hotel, and then the terrible, ridgelike scars on her husband's back. Bliss closed her eyes and prayed silently for the courage to bear whatever she must.

Jamie saw a mist rising out of the ground, like smoke. He knew it would grow denser and denser, until it finally enshrouded his mind and extinguished his sanity.

337

A few yards away, Bliss was kneeling in the dirt, her yellow dress torn open to the waist, her arms outstretched on the wagon wheel, tightly bound at the wrists. Jamie did not feel his own injuries, he felt Bliss's.

The sun was still fairly high. He ran a dry tongue over even drier lips and waited, as his enemy wished him to do. That was Increase's favorite form of torture, after all; he wanted Jamie to sweat, and sweat he would. It might be hours before the old man used that whip on Bliss, and it might be minutes.

For now, Increase was inside that tent of his, in the center of camp.

The things Pipher had done to Peony rose in his mind, but Jamie forced them back. When he thought of them, the smoky mist grew thicker, more deadly. . . .

One hour passed, and then another. At intervals, Bliss looked back at Jamie over one naked, freckle-spattered shoulder, willing him to be strong. Jamie didn't know which would kill him first, the fear of seeing her suffer or the awesome, aching love he felt for her.

Increase's men began to move restlessly around the camp, no doubt hankering for the sport of watching another woman die. Bile rose in the back of Jamie's throat, and his numb hands craved the sweet labor of vengeance. The men brought out bottles and cards and began amusing themselves as they waited.

By the time Increase made his appearance, strutting out of the tent with the coiled bullwhip in one hand, his cohorts were drunk to a man, but Jamie had no interest in them now. All his attention was fixed on Bliss; he saw her look at Increase and then lift that insolent little chin of hers, and in that moment his love for her bit into his middle like the teeth of an animal.

Like a ringmaster in a circus, Increase took his time, relishing the moment. To Jamie, he was as repulsive as a coffin worm.

The old man came over to him, shoving the whip under his nose. "Do you smell your own blood on this, McKenna?" he asked, sawing each word off with a rusty rasp. "You should."

Jamie spoke evenly, quietly, and without betraying any emotion at all. "If you want to whip somebody to death, make it me. You've no quarrel with Bliss."

Increase smiled and touched a welt that lay across his face in a red streak, thanks to Bliss's temper. "Don't I?"

"Mother of God, man," Jamie breathed. "Tell me what you want to hear, and I'll say it!"

Pipher laughed and strutted away toward Bliss. With a practiced flip of his wrist, he unfurled the lash, and the snapping sound made vomit rush into Jamie's throat.

His knees weakened when he heard the sound of a snapped twig behind him and felt the rawhide binding him beginning to loosen. "This will make up, I'm thinkin'," Reeve said in a whisper, "for that other time when you needed me and I wasn't around."

In an instant, Jamie's hands were free; he felt the familiar handle of his own blade pressed into his palm. He didn't look back, lest he reveal Reeve, and even as he stepped away from the tree he feared he might be hallucinating.

A man rushed toward him with a drunken shout, and the blade penetrated that man's chest with a resounding *thunk*. His compatriots stood back, their eyes nervously scanning the trees.

Increase's throat worked as he saw Jamie walking toward him; terror widened his eyes until they seemed to fill his head. His ceaseless hatred made him draw back the whip to strike Bliss, but Jamie stepped into the lash before it reached her. He felt it tear through his shirt, but there was no pain. That would come much later.

Wildly, Increase struck another blow, but Jamie didn't feel that, either. He just kept advancing until he was face-to-face with the old man. He wrenched the whip out of

339

Increase's hands and flung it aside. The old man screamed as Jamie grasped him by the front of his collar and lifted him off the ground.

He watched, with satisfaction, as the viper began to die, his own collar a hangman's noose.

Jamie heard Reeve shout at him, but the sound seemed to come from far away. He dismissed it, caring about nothing except this vengeance that he craved from the very core of his being.

Bliss gave a hoarse shriek and struggled violently against the bonds that she had tolerated until that moment. Jamie was killing Increase Pipher by inches, and in her mind she saw her husband dangling at the end of a rope as punishment for the murder.

"Jamie, no!" she screamed. "No!"

He was deaf to her words, but Walter Davis wasn't. Shamefaced, he used Jamie's bloody knife, wrenched from a dead man's chest, to free her hands.

Bliss's legs would not support her at first; she stumbled and fell twice in her desperate scramble to reach Jamie. To stop him.

Reeve got to him before she did, dropping his rifle to the ground in an effort to break Jamie's hold on Pipher, but it was useless. In his all-consuming fury, Jamie was impervious.

Increase's eyes had rolled back into his head and his face was a crimson purple.

"In the name of God, Jamie," Reeve bellowed, "stop before one of these troopers shoots you!"

Bliss looked around her in a frantic twist of her neck and saw the captain and some of his men. Increase's people were already under control and now, sure enough, the soldiers' rifles were fixed on Jamie's back.

Sliding under the outstretched arm that held Increase suspended in the air, grasping the front of her dress in place with one hand, Bliss positioned herself directly in front of

Jamie and raised gentle fingers to her husband's filthy, beard-stubbled face.

"Jamie," she cried. "Jamie, listen to me—if they don't shoot you, they'll hang you—and—and there won't be any redheaded babies!"

A strange expression crossed Jamie's face; he looked as though he'd just been wrenched back inside himself from somewhere far away. He released his hold on Increase and the man toppled, unconscious, to the ground.

Jamie's eyes glistened and his hands trembled as he reached for Bliss and drew her close, so blessedly close, to him. "Thank God you're safe," he said thickly, his breath ruffling her hair. "Thank God."

Even when he turned to look at Reeve, Jamie didn't release Bliss, and that was fine with her, because she didn't ever want to be separated from him again. His eyes were bright with questions that had apparently been cut off at his throat.

Reeve laid a hand on his brother's shoulder. "I found your blade along the road—catchin' the sunlight, it was—and right after that, the captain and 'is lads caught up to me. I don't mind tellin' you, little brother, that it was glad I was to see them."

Jamie's voice was almost gone. "These soldiers—will they be takin' me away, then?"

Bliss tensed for the answer to that question; her breath stopped and she would have sworn that her heart did, too.

But Reeve shook his head. "No, Jamie. You're a free man now."

"I'll never be able to repay the debt I owe you," Jamie told his brother as the soldiers gathered Increase's men into custody. Pipher, just recovering consciousness, had been left on the ground.

It was assumed that the battle was over, and no one, including Increase himself, who was now sitting up, was prepared for what happened next.

Walter Davis produced a small handgun from his coat

pocket and, seeing this, Jamie thrust Bliss roughly behind him, acting as a barrier. Everyone was stricken to silence, except for the captain, who said calmly, "Give me the gun, lad."

Walter didn't seem to hear—or to see anyone but Increase, who was whimpering now, as he'd hoped to make Jamie do. "Hateful—vicious—" Walter seemed to be reciting the words or reading them from a book. "You made her scream. I can still hear her screaming—I will always hear her—screaming, screaming—"

The gun went off, a wispy puff of white smoke billowing from the barrel, and a bright red bead of blood appeared in the middle of Increase's forehead. He fell over, a look of bafflement marking his face for eternity.

Bliss had had enough. She clasped one hand over her mouth and fled, and she didn't get far before she was violently ill. The sound of a scuffle and a second shot brought on a fresh spate of retching.

"There now," Jamie told her, in that dear, musical brogue of his, "and everything will be all right now, Duchess." He had found water somewhere, cool, clean water, and lifted the canteen to her lips so that she could rinse her mouth and then drink. When she'd had her fill, he helped her into a man's shirt, fastening the buttons with slow, awkward fingers.

"That second shot," she managed to get out, after long, difficult moments of struggle.

Jamie shook his head and drew her close. "Not now, love," he said. "Not now."

But Bliss guessed what had happened—Walter, in his despair and his horrible remorse, had shot himself after killing Pipher. "He wanted to help us," she said sadly, her head resting against Jamie's shoulder, "but he was too afraid."

"It's over now, Duchess," Jamie said, and she felt his lips brush her temple.

She was weary clear through to her soul, was Bliss

McKenna, but she felt a surge of gratitude that she and Jamie were safe, with the rest of their lives before them. That knowledge sustained her until they were back at Seven Sisters again, many hours later.

Bliss helped Jamie with his bath, being careful of his many wounds. She was quiet, still seeing that haunted look in his eyes. She feared that it would never fade away.

That night, he made love to her with a violence of need, as though certain that if his passion were consuming enough, all the terrors of the day would be overshadowed. He lay exhausted and gasping, his head resting on Bliss's breast, when it was over, and fell into a troubled sleep. She felt the warmth of his tears against her flesh as he dreamed.

Her own deep, tender satisfaction made the motion of her hand languid as she lifted it to caress Jamie's rumpled hair. At the same time, she stroked his shoulder, feeling the flesh and muscle quake beneath her palm as Jamie awakened and struggled to contain his grief.

Bliss said nothing, for there were no words that could, or should, spare him the mourning that he had to do. Peony had been his closest friend. He had loved her, he had seen her die, and now he had to face his own feelings.

Bliss loved Jamie enough to allow him that process, painful as it was for her, and she was sensible enough to know that it could take a very long time.

Three weeks later, Jamie and Bliss said good-bye to Maggie and Reeve in Brisbane and set sail for Auckland. Peony had been buried at Seven Sisters, but there was business to attend to concerning her estate, and Jamie threw himself into the task with ferocity. Bliss, wandering like a lost urchin through the elegant rooms of the grand house he'd bought for her, barely saw him for days at a time.

At night, he loved her hungrily, fiercely, but there was a distance between them for all that, that broke Bliss's heart. She began to wonder if Jamie had lost the true love of his life in that hellish camp in Queensland—perhaps she herself was only a substitute for Peony Ryan.

Bliss found this possibility so unbearable that she couldn't voice it—not to Jamie, anyway. But she did seek him out, in Peony's offices in downtown Auckland, to say good-bye.

He looked up from the papers he'd been going over with a frown. "What the 'ell do you mean, 'good-bye'?" he snapped.

Bliss's heart splintered. She couldn't remember the last time he'd called her Duchess, or laughed with her, or really made love to her, instead of just using her to vent the powerful emotions he was grappling with.

She lifted her chin. "What does *good-bye* usually mean, Mr. McKenna?" she countered. "I'm leaving you."

Jamie muttered an oath, shoved back his chair, and shot out of it. "And goin' where?" he demanded.

Bliss didn't retreat, cower, or avert her eyes. "Maybe I'll fall asleep in some other man's barn and see what comes of it," she said.

Jamie's eyes went as wide as she'd ever seen them, and his Adam's apple moved the length of his throat. "By God, Duchess, you'll never do that as long as I'm still breathin'!" he roared. "You'll lie in no other barn—or bed—than mine!"

So he did care. That hard shell he'd surrounded himself with was beginning to thaw and fall away. Bliss could not have been more pleased, though she was careful to hide her feeling behind a saintly expression and a sigh. "In that case, I'll have to content myself with going back to the country. I want to take up cooking again, and see Cutter and Dog, and find out if that old rooster is still on the straight and narrow path." She paused, rising on tiptoes to kiss Jamie's cheek. "Good-bye."

He caught her shoulders in his hands, his blue eyes searching her face. "Don't you dare go," he bit out. "I need you."

"What for?" Bliss asked sweetly, batting her eyelashes.

Jamie stared at her for a moment, and then he laughed,

and the sound was wonderful to hear. He shoved a hand through his hair. "You're right," he marveled, as though that were a very unusual thing. Then he pulled Bliss close to him, subjecting her to a most intimate, and delicious, contact. "You didn't need to go quite so far as to threaten me with your cookin', though," he added, sounding hurt.

Bliss's eyes brimmed with happy tears. "My Jamie," she whispered. "I missed you terribly."

He kissed her much too lightly and much too briefly, then pushed her toward the door, reaching for the tailored suitcoat he'd been wearing of late, and the smart gentleman's hat.

To Bliss's enormous relief, he had second thoughts and left both items behind. When they boarded the train, just over an hour later, he was wearing the familiar leather hat that had seen better days. He watched her with a mischievous blue heat in his eyes, and Bliss was squirming in her seat before they'd even gotten past the outer perimeters of Auckland.

"Are you going to hire a wagon?" she asked, hours later, when they left the train in the little town of Halifras. Jamie had his own name for the place, Bliss remembered: Half-assed.

Jamie chuckled and resettled his hat. "Right now, I'm more interested in 'irin' a room, Duchess."

Bliss blushed, even though she knew he couldn't possibly be any more interested than she was, and kept her eyes averted all the while Jamie was signing for their room and chatting with the hotel's proprietor. She felt as shy as a bride.

In the privacy of the little room tucked away in the right rear corner of the second floor, Jamie made a slow, tender ritual of removing Bliss's clothes, garment by garment, kissing selected places as he bared them.

Bliss trembled in the foreshadow of ecstasy when he finally knelt before her. He'd aroused her so skillfully that release was upon her with the first teasing flicks of his

345

tongue. He kissed her smooth stomach as she clung to his shoulders with her hands, unable to stand alone.

After a few moments, however, he drew back, looked up at her curiously, and laid one tentative hand to the curve of her abdomen. It was new, that gentle rounding, and Bliss smiled as Jamie came awkwardly to his feet, his eyes puzzled.

"Yes," Bliss said softly, laying her hand over his. "You'll be a father in June, Jamie. It'll be a boy and we'll call him Reeve."

He looked down at her stomach, as though he expected to be able to see his child through skin and muscle, and the expression of wonder on his face was more precious to Bliss than anything she possessed. "Aye," he finally replied, and then he swallowed.

Bliss stood on her toes to kiss him, catching the musky scent of herself on his skin. His hand rose, with a clumsy caution that further endeared him to her, to caress her breast as they kissed.

That night, their lovemaking was a celebration.

Bliss stirred the contents of the kettle industriously, Dog at her heels. "Have a taste," she offered, plopping some of the mixture into a bowl and setting it on the kitchen floor.

Dog whimpered and skulked away, to lie under the table.

"Fine friend you are," Bliss said, laying one hand to her protruding stomach. "This is perfectly good lamb stew, you know."

Just then, Jamie came in, grinning. Some of the chill of the winter day followed along. After giving Bliss a lingering kiss, he stood behind her and splayed his fingers over her stomach, something he loved to do. "I've got a surprise for you, Duchess. Cutter's gone to town to fetch 'er—I mean, it."

Bliss turned awkwardly in his arms, her jealousy flaring. "You said 'her,' Jamie McKenna!" she accused.

He gave her a kiss, which she found anything but soothing, and shrugged. "So I did, love. 'Er name's Ella, and she's a cook."

Bliss was infuriated. She'd been trying so hard to learn, studying her cookbooks hour after hour and testing new recipes on Dog. "You could have a little patience!" she cried.

Jamie's hands moved tenderly up and down her back. "That kind of patience involves starvin' to death," he reasoned. He went to kiss her again, but she pushed him away and, after grabbing her heavy cloak, stormed out the door.

Jamie followed her, keeping pace easily as she hurried down the rear path.

"I don't want a cook!" she yelled, wrenching open the door to one of the sheds.

"I know," Jamie answered, beginning to look insulted now because Bliss was having the temerity to throw his gift back in his face—figuratively speaking, that is. "But then, nothin' spoils your appetite, does it, Duchess?"

Bliss came out of the shed carrying a washtub and looked about for a rock. When she had one in her hand, she advanced on Jamie, who prudently backtracked toward the house.

"What the devil are you doin'?" he demanded.

Bliss smiled, still closing in, and answered, "It worked with the chicken!"

AUTHOR'S NOTE

In both *MOONFIRE* and *ANGELFIRE*, I have tampered with history by extending the transportation of criminals from the British Isles to Australia by some twenty years, this being necessary to the stories.

Reeve, Maggie, Jamie, Bliss, and I all beg your kind indulgence.

Linda Lael Miller
P.O. Box 2166
Bremerton, WA 98310